A TASTE OF PASSION ✦

Sarah took a cautious step away from her dinner companion and surveyed the room. A fire crackled on the hearth. There was a table for dining, but by far the most prominent piece of furniture in the room was a long couch. Pillows were everywhere.

"Just why have you brought me here, Mr. Bennet?" she asked warily.

"Why, to enjoy your company, of course," he drawled. "And you agreed to call me Tyler."

She retreated another step. "That was before I knew you well enough to realize you might be more rogue than gentleman."

He closed the distance between them. "I thought you came to California looking for adventure."

"Isn't it time for dinner?" she gasped as he leaned over her.

"There are other kinds of hunger that need satisfying, my dear Sarah." His warm lips met hers in a slow, lingering kiss, sending waves of heat through her. . . .

Contemporary Fiction From Robin St. Thomas

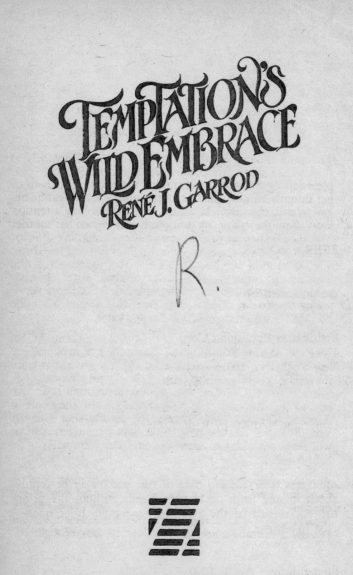

TEMPTATION'S WILD EMBRACE

René J. Garrod

R.

ZEBRA BOOKS
KENSINGTON PUBLISHING CORP.

To my grandmother,
Mary Rathwick

Chapter 1

Henry was dead.

A cold March wind whipped Sarah Williams's black cloak about her slim ankles as she stood over the grave of her husband. He had died as he had lived — quietly, without fanfare. She smiled wanly. Henry would have been proud he had managed to depart this life so neatly.

She had been a widow six months now and had adjusted to her loss. Their marriage had not been a love match. Henry had no time for such frivolous notions as love. At sixty-seven he was forty-five years her senior, and if Henry had ever been smitten by that tenderest of emotions, the years had erased all trace of the memory.

Sarah sighed as she brushed a wisp of nut brown hair from her eyes. She had always known Henry Williams had married her for convenience sake. Her mother had convinced him in his declining years he needed someone to run his household, a pretty hostess

7

to oversee his social obligations, and most important, a wife to bear him an heir. Amanda Jenkins had made it sound so comfortable, Henry had found it expedient to accept her eighteen-year-old daughter as a wife.

Her mother lived free from want on the generous stipend provided by her wealthy son-in-law as part of the marriage contract.

Sarah expelled another long sigh.

She had done her best to do her duty, and Henry was not displeased with his decision. The only circumstance marring his satisfaction was her inability to produce an heir. Initially he had been angry with her, but after the first two years of their marriage, he rarely berated her for her barrenness and confined his censure to looks of disgust each month when her woman's time arrived.

She blinked back tears of pain. How cruel of fate to deny the one thing she and Henry mutually desired. A child would have given her someone to love. A child would have made the marriage more bearable.

Marriage. The word left a bad taste in her mouth. She had lobbied earnestly against the match with Henry, protesting she was being sold to the richest bidder like a slave on the auction block. But somehow, as always, her mother had turned her into the villain, and in the end she had meekly acquiesced. Henry had been well aware of her reluctance but steadfastly discounted her feelings as insignificant. He had been ever so fond of telling her that she was too young to know her own mind.

Pulling her cloak more snugly about her shoulders, Sarah continued to muse upon her past. She and Henry had married in a simple ceremony, and for four long years he had told her how to dress, whom to see, when to speak, and what to think. She had become the submissive wife he wanted but at onerous cost to herself. A blithe soul could only bear so much repression before it began to wither.

Though her face in the mirror remained unlined, her brown hair untouched by gray, and the green eyes staring back at her still held the sparkle of youth, she had begun to feel as old as the frumpish matrons Henry had chosen for her friends. A few more years of marriage to Henry and she would have been just like them — faded before their time, with nothing better to discuss than their various bodily complaints and what the cook would be serving for dinner that night.

Sarah suppressed a shudder, sending up a silent prayer of thanks she had escaped such a fate. Many she knew would chastise her for such a prayer, but long ago she had concluded there was little point in trying to deceive God about her indelicate thoughts. In truth, her husband's death had evoked sorrow and relief in equal amounts. Gently placing the flower she held in her hand on the well-tended grave, she turned her steps toward her mother's home.

Today was Tuesday, and she was expected to spend every Tuesday and Thursday afternoon with her mother. As she strolled past block after block of stately brick residences, she drew in deep breaths of the crisp air. Walking was an act of rebellion, as both her mother and Henry felt it undignified to traverse the streets in anything meaner than a barouche, but she was willing to risk a scolding. She had been feeling restless of late. Bold thoughts flitted in and out of her head like hummingbirds in a flower garden.

Upon reaching her mother's doorstep, Sarah took a moment to check her appearance before lifting the door knocker.

"Mrs. Williams, do come in. I'll tell your mother you have come for your visit," the housekeeper greeted her.

"Thank you, Judith. I'll show myself to the sitting room."

A few minutes later Amanda Jenkins crossed the threshold of the sitting room with a rustle of black silk. She was a tall woman, with only a salting of gray through her jet black hair — a woman who might have been judged handsome by some if her face did not perpetually wear the look of one who had just swallowed something extremely unpleasant.

"Good afternoon, Mother."

"Good afternoon, Sarah."

The two women seated themselves in straight-backed chairs. Painful silence followed. Sarah focused her eyes on the floor

No matter how she intellectualized her strained relationship with her mother, in her presence she always reverted to the role of the errant little girl. She hated the feeling.

"Well, as usual, you are making a muck of it, Sarah. If this is your idea of how to conduct yourself during a social call, I can do naught but shudder. Don't look at the floor, girl, chin up and straighten your spine. Don't think because you are in mourning you are excused from correct deportment."

"I'm sorry, Mother." Sarah instinctively stiffened to a more upright posture.

"You should be." Amanda wagged her finger at her

daughter, her expression one of long suffering. "It is such a disappointment to know all my years of drilling have come to naught, such a disappointment. But enough said on that subject. We have important matters to discuss today."

"We do?" Sarah asked warily.

"Yes indeed. I have been in contact with a Mr. Walters. As he already has several children from his previous marriage, he has indicated a willingness to overlook your barrenness. You have mourned Henry long enough. It is time you remarried."

Sarah stared at her mother in disbelief.

"His wealth exceeds Henry's by a considerable sum." Her mother cheerily offered what she thought should be a more than adequate explanation.

Closing her eyes, Sarah could see her life stretching out before her—a succession of loveless marriages to wealthy gentlemen of advanced years, all of her mother's choosing, all for her mother's financial benefit. Something in her snapped.

"I don't want Mr. Walters or his money. I will never marry for the wrong reasons again," Sarah announced vehemently, suddenly realizing the twenty-two years she had spent subjugating herself to her mother's wishes had not earned her one whit of the maternal affection she so desperately sought. It would never be hers.

Henry's death had left her a woman of independent means. It was past time she learned to act like the adult she was and took control of her own fate. Rising to her feet, she faced her mother squarely. "In fact, I have no intention of marrying again for any reason. I don't know what I will do with my life, but whatever I do will be of my own choosing."

"What an unbecoming thing to say."

"I'm sorry you feel that way, because I speak from the heart. My marriage to Henry provided you with more money than you can possibly spend. You don't need me to get you more."

"One can never have too much money," Amanda countered. "You will do as I say."

Since finding herself a wealthy widow, Sarah had had much time to muse upon her favorite childhood dream. Maybe she was grasping at straws. Maybe she was just looking for an excuse to escape her present life. Until this moment she had not been decided on any course, but the thought of being coerced into another passionless marriage made her reckless and resolute. "No. I am leaving Baltimore."

"Leaving?" Her mother's eyes narrowed. "I can't believe I heard you right. No. Of course I didn't. You'll have to repeat yourself, and this time pronounce your syllables more distinctly."

Sarah cleared her throat, enunciating each word slowly so there could be no mistaking them. "I am leaving Baltimore within the week. I am not sure how long I will be gone, but I am sure it will be for quite some time."

"Why?" Amanda demanded.

"Because I want to."

"What kind of answer is that? 'Because I want to.' I don't know what kind of foolishness this is, but you will put it out of your head this moment."

Sarah remained firm. "No."

"Abandoning me just like your father, aren't you?" Her mother dabbed at mock tears with an ornately embroidered handkerchief, her voice becoming harsher with each word. "I should have known all the training in the world couldn't conquer bad blood."

"I am not abandoning you," Sarah assured her. She paused, giving herself a moment to regain control over her trembling limbs. Was it fear or excitement that made her quake? It didn't matter. She had the means, the opportunity; she was going. Her voice was strangely calm when she continued, "I'll have my lawyer draw up papers in the morning to see you are given a sum in addition to what Henry was in the habit of providing you. You won't want for anything while I'm gone."

"I'll need double what I'm getting now."

"Fine," Sarah agreed without argument.

Amanda Jenkins's lips curled upward into a facsimile of a smile but was quickly replaced by her usual dour look. "Well, where is it you're going?"

"To San Francisco."

"Why there?"

Sarah hesitated before she replied. She knew her next words would provoke her mother's full-blown wrath, but she felt she owed her mother the truth. "Because I would like to try to find my father, and his last known address was there."

Amanda Jenkins paled. "I absolutely forbid it!"

"I did not ask your permission," Sarah replied softly.

Amanda's cold blue eyes bore into her daughter. "Obviously. That would require a modicum of affection for the woman who has sacrificed her *all* for your happiness. After what your father did to me, that you would even think of striking up an acquaintance with him . . . why, it is too cruel to countenance."

13

"I know how painful it was for you raising me alone. I'm sure it was made worse since my many faults seem constantly to remind you of him. I don't want to hurt you, really I don't." Though her resolve did not waver, Sarah could not compel herself to meet her mother's intimidating gaze. Marshaling her flagging courage, she forced herself to continue, "I just want a chance to meet my father. To satisfy my curiosity. To see if I am really as much like him as you say."

"It should be abundantly clear *he* doesn't want to see you," her mother countered.

"In all likelihood, he probably never will. The chances of me finding him after twenty-two years are not great."

Sarah was too busy making plans for her imminent departure to notice the expression of relief that flooded her mother's face.

Chapter 2

San Francisco

Tyler Bennet's ears pricked at the sound of the door chimes tinkling below stairs, and he tugged on the chain of his gold pocket watch. It was still a half hour before his afternoon appointment was due to arrive, and he returned his attention to the papers stacked neatly on the large oak desk before him. Agnes would take care of whoever it was.

A moment later there was a timid knock on his office door. "Tyler, I mean Mr. Bennet, there's a Mrs. Williams come to see you. Would you like to speak with her now, or shall I tell her you're busy and she must make an appointment and come back later?" Agnes Johnson asked in tremulant tones.

Glancing up, Tyler smiled. "Did she say why she was here?"

"No, only that she has a letter of introduction from Mr. Filmore of Baltimore."

Rising to his feet, he retrieved his jacket from the back of his chair, speaking as he slipped his arms into the sleeves. "My uncle must be steering another client my way. Remind me to send him a note of thanks. . . . I have a few minutes before Mr. Kruger is scheduled to arrive. Why don't you show her up."

"Yes, sir."

"And Agnes, there's no need to be so formal just because we're in the office. If you promise not to put frogs in my pockets and I promise not to dip your pigtails in the inkwell, I think the conventions of business will be served."

Agnes colored scarlet at the reminder of their schoolday high jinks. "But Papa said if I was to come work for the two of you, I had to remember my p's and q's at all times. I don't want to disappoint him . . . or you," she added shyly.

He sighed. He didn't understand why Agnes was acting so flustered around him of late. They had known each other since they were small children. Perhaps she found her new responsibilities as receptionist of the law offices of Johnson & Bennet intimidating. As he tended the buttons of his jacket, he decided he would discuss the matter with her father. Abandoning his musing, he focused on the matter at hand. "In the presence of clients, I agree formality is desirable, but it seems silly when we are out of earshot. Regardless, it isn't right for me to encourage you to go against your father's wishes, especially since he is the one who hired you — though I still don't know why a man of his affluence thinks his daughter needs to work at all. But enough of that. We have a prospective client cooling her heels downstairs."

Agnes nodded. "I'll send her right up."

16

Tyler Bennet's gray-blue eyes widened in surprise as Sarah Williams stepped over the threshold and into his office. He had been expecting a matronly woman, someone close to his uncle's age, but the rosy-cheeked woman standing before him barely looked old enough to wear the title of "Mrs."

Bedecked in a skirt of white muslin with row upon row of flounces and a trellis of violet ribbon, she wore an overdress that matched the color of the ribbon. Beneath its cropped sleeves extended undersleeves of puffed muslin lavishly decorated with more violet ribbon. In her hand she held a silk parasol.

However, it was not the fine cut of her gown that attracted him, but the trim figure beneath the yards of fabric and the pretty head perched upon her gently sloping shoulders. He was shocked by his lusty and very unbusinesslike reaction to the woman standing before him. He enjoyed the company of women as well as the next man, but it had been quite some time since he had been thus affected.

"Mrs. Williams?" he asked tentatively as he bowed over her extended hand.

"Yes. And you must be Mr. Bennet," Sarah smiled sunnily, oblivious to his discomfort. She was too busy enjoying her own surprise. Mr. Bennet was neither portly nor balding; in fact, he looked nothing like the unflattering portrait of him she had painted in her mind. The man before her wore his sandy blond hair a tad shorter than was fashionable, but the style went well with the square planes of his face and was softened by an elegant mustache. He was tall and well muscled, though a little on the lean side. Looking at him made her heart flutter. Without conscious intent she found herself speaking her thoughts out loud. "I must say, you're much younger than I anticipated."

"I was thinking much the same thing." Tyler bit his tongue, the heat in his cheeks rising to match that in his loins. He cursed himself under his breath. "What I meant to say was: How may I be of assistance?"

Sarah laughed at his pained expression. "Please, I'm not the least bit offended. I am rather young for a widow, so the misconception is quite understandable."

"A widow?" Tyler queried, struggling to mask his delight. The seed of an idea took root and began to flourish.

"Didn't my lawyer, Mr. Filmore, state that in his wire? I thought sure he would."

His expression became perplexed; then he remembered receiving a telegram from his uncle announcing the pending arrival of a widow of one of his longtime clients. If memory served, the names matched, and if the widow Williams was a venerated client of his uncle, he had best put more effort into cultivating a decorous image before he completely discredited himself. Squaring his shoulders, he assumed a more detached mien.

"Forgive me. I did receive the wire . . . but it came over a month ago, and it completely slipped my mind. Miss Johnson mentioned you have a letter of introduction."

"Yes." Sarah handed him an envelope as she accepted the chair he offered her. Tyler rounded the desk and took his own seat.

Opening the letter, he glanced at the date and then back to her. "This was written shortly after the wire

18

was sent. I hope some mishap on your journey was not the cause of the long delay."

"Oh, no. I've been staying at the Grand Hotel for quite some time. There are just so many things to see and do in San Francisco . . . and it has been twenty-two years." She paused; then her eyes began to twinkle merrily, despite the guilty blush staining her cheeks. "I've been having myself a bit of a holiday."

Sarah did not add that she was so thoroughly enjoying her anonymity in the city, she was loath to end it. She was free — free from the burden of being Amanda Jenkins's daughter and Henry Williams's widow — and the unaccustomed license left her giddy.

Since taking up residence in a suite in the Grand Hotel, she had spent each day doing naught but pleasing herself. Her wedding ring had been banished from her finger to her jewelry case. She ate in the finest restaurants, shopped in the most fashionable shops, and attended the theater nearly every evening, and she had walked holes in the soles of her high-top, buttoned shoes, stopping to chat whenever and with whomever she wished.

As Tyler watched a medley of winsome expressions dance across her fair face, he found himself enchanted and confused in equal measure and deemed it best he read his uncle's letter before their conversation continued any further.

March 14, 1873

Dear Tyler,

This letter is being written to introduce you to Mrs. Sarah Williams, the widow of my late client Mr. Henry Williams. She has informed me she intends to stay in

19

your part of the country for an extended visit, and I have advised her to seek your legal counsel should she have any questions regarding the management of her fortune, which is extensive. See enclosed summary of assets and stipulations as set forth in her husband's will.

I will remain her primary legal adviser, but would appreciate your assistance. I would also ask that you keep a vigilant eye on Mrs. Williams. She has never been on her own in the world, and I fear some would take advantage of her naiveté.

Sincerely,
Your loving uncle,
Wesley Filmore

After briefly perusing the remaining papers in his hand, Tyler set them on the corner of the desk. They told him little that he didn't already know, except that Sarah Williams was a very wealthy woman and his uncle's request that he watch over her confirmed his relative held her in high regard. Tyler's lips stretched into a broad, contented grin. His uncle's petition suited perfectly the course he had wanted to follow from the moment he had laid eyes on her. He could think of nothing that would give him greater pleasure than to keep an eye on Sarah Williams. A pretty lady alone in a strange city needed a gentleman to watch over her, and he had always regarded himself as a gentleman.

"We best get down to business," he stated, trying in vain to suppress the enthusiasm in his voice. "What can I do for you today?"

Sarah returned his broad, friendly grin. "I thought you might know the best way to begin my search."

"The letter mentions nothing of a search."

The lights in her eyes dimmed as her expression became more somber. "I didn't tell Mr. Filmore because I was afraid he might not approve, and I didn't want him to worry needlessly. I have come to California in search of my father, Elijah Jenkins."

Tyler matched his mood to hers. "I take it you don't know his present whereabouts."

"No."

"Do you have his last known address?"

"Yes." Sarah handed him a faded envelope.

He had to strain to read the return address. "This place was torn down years ago. When was the last time you saw him?"

"I never met my father. He left before I was born," she admitted reluctantly. "I found that envelope on the floor in the corner of the attic under some boxes when I was ten years old. There was nothing in it, but I kept it just the same."

"I don't wish to open old wounds, Mrs. Williams, but perhaps you better start at the beginning."

"There is really very little to tell. My father left Baltimore in '51 in hopes of making his fortune in the California goldfields. My mother was carrying me at the time, and her health would not allow her to accompany him. He was suppose to send money for us to join him when I was old enough to travel, but he never did."

Tyler smiled sympathetically, but when he spoke, logic ruled his tongue. "I don't know all the circumstances of this situation, but even so, a man who would desert his wife and child cannot hold my high opinion. Forgive me for being blunt, but if you do

21

manage to track him down, you may not like what you find."

She lowered her eyes. "I know. I think I have been avoiding beginning my quest for that very reason."

"Then why put yourself through an unpleasant experience that isn't necessary?"

"Because it is necessary. At least to me. All my life I have wondered what he is really like, wondered if I was like him."

He stared at her a long moment, and Sarah met his compassionate gaze with one of steadfast determination.

"Did your mother tell you nothing?"

"She speaks often of my father," she hesitated, trying to find a delicate way to explain her mother's bitterness. After a moment's silent contemplation, she concluded there was none. "It is just . . . that I need to know him for myself. . . . I am so unlike my mother in nature."

Tyler stroked his mustache thoughtfully. "I suppose I can understand your feelings. If you are determined, I can arrange a meeting with a reputable detective."

"I plan to be my own detective."

He made no attempt to mask his astonishment or his disapproval. "I don't think that would be suitable. You have no idea where your search might lead."

Sarah groaned inwardly. This was just the sort of reaction she had been expecting, and she was resolved not to be swayed from her original course. The long train ride from the east coast had given her more than enough time to contemplate her situation. She welcomed the prospect of adventure as much as she did that of finding her long absent father. "May I speak

22

plainly?"

He nodded. "Please do."

"I am twenty-two years old, Mr. Bennet, and for all of those twenty-two years I have done what others have told me was suitable. Until these last few weeks, I had no idea how much of life I was missing. I wish to conduct the search for my father myself, and I will do so whether or not it is deemed *suitable* by you or anyone else. If you try to thwart me, I will find another lawyer."

"I don't think you realize what you're facing. It is true we are quite cosmopolitan here in the city, but much of the outlying areas are still frontier, and even within the city there are neighborhoods where a lone lady would be seen as easy prey."

"Then I will disguise myself as a man."

Gazing into her earnest green eyes, Tyler began to chuckle. "I don't wish to appear argumentative, especially since you have threatened to fire me before you have even hired me, but have you looked in the mirror lately? You could no more disguise yourself as a man than I could disguise myself as a woman. You're too —" he caught himself before some romantic phrase slipped past his lips "— feminine."

"Then I shall learn to use a gun or whatever else it takes. I am through sitting on the shelf while life passes me by. All I require from you is that you tell me whether or not you will help me."

"Yes."

Sarah was startled to her feet by his rapid agreement. "Really?"

"I'm a man of my word," Tyler assured her without elaborating. What Sarah Williams needed was a gentle scare. He would take her to a few select places to show her what she would be up against; then, she would be more than eager to let him help her hire an experienced detective. In the meantime, he could indulge his ardent fancy for her. He watched with satisfaction as the gregarious sparkle slowly returned to her eyes.

"Thank you for seeing things my way."

He did not respond to her statement of gratitude, knowing full well his agreement to help her had nothing to do with his "seeing things her way." He just didn't want her to walk out his door and into the arms of some other less scrupulous lawyer who might take unfair advantage of her charms. If she was going to fill anyone's arms, he intended they be his. He grinned.

"Is something funny?" she asked, still marginally suspicious of his swift acquiescence to her wishes.

"No. Nothing at all." He sobered his expression, but he could not suppress the fire dancing in his eyes. "Would you do me the honor of allowing me to escort you to dinner tonight?"

She bit back the "yes" on the tip of her tongue. Her heart had been beating at an accelerated rate since the moment she had stepped over this man's threshold. It was an undeniably pleasant yet odd reaction to a stranger. She would be wise to proceed with caution. "Do you take all of your clients to dinner?"

"No, but most of my clients aren't female or possessed of a winsome face."

Sarah blushed at the unexpected compliment. "Then this is not a business invitation?"

"No."

"I have heard mixing business with pleasure is a

dangerous thing, Mr. Bennet," she warned, thoroughly fascinated and slightly daunted by his intense regard.

"Life is dangerous, Mrs. Williams," he drawled. "If dinner with me frightens you, you had best climb back on your shelf where it is safe and leave the detective work to the professionals."

A trill of excitement ran down Sarah's spine, and she met his challenge head-on. "Shall I expect you at seven?"

"Seven it is."

Chapter 3

Sarah grinned at her reflection as she artfully arranged the cascade of curls she had just tied over her left shoulder. Climb back on her shelf, indeed. She had looked far too prim and proper this afternoon. Tonight, Mr. Bennet would see that Sarah Williams was a woman of the world, not some child in need of coddling.

After leaving Mr. Bennet's office, she had not been able to shake the feeling tonight's invitation had a purpose behind it. His goading statement had followed too close upon his agreement to do things her way. She could not help but be suspicious.

Sarah fastened a dark red fabric rose over her ear, completing her toilet. Burgundy silk and black lace should change his image of her. She had purchased the gown on a whim shortly after arriving in San Francisco and had yet to muster the nerve to wear it on the street, but this evening it would serve her well. The bodice hugged her firmly, pushing the swell of her modest bosom above the lace-trimmed deep vee neckline. The belted waistline and generous skirts were equally complimentary to her figure. She hardly looked herself, and Sarah was enormously pleased.

She had never dressed herself with a man in mind, but there was something about Tyler Bennet that was different from other men. Her intent was not to please him but to get his attention, and intuition told her the burgundy gown would achieve her aim. She was looking forward to spending the evening with him, whatever his motives. He was a very handsome man, and she was growing bored with her own company. She was in the mood for a little adventure.

A knock at her door brought Sarah's perusal of her person to a halt. Upon answering the door she was presented with Mr Bennet's calling card.

"Tell Mr. Bennet I shall be down in a twinkling," she instructed the bellboy.

"Yes, ma'am."

Sarah reached for her reticule, then paused. Returning to her dressing table, she dabbed a drop of rose perfume behind her ears, adding another touch in the valley formed by her compressed bosom. She ran a critical eye over her reflection, lowered the draped shoulders of her gown another inch, then straightened.

"Now, I'm ready," she spoke to herself. "Mr. Bennet shall see I am no coward."

Tyler Bennet rose to his feet and swallowed hard as Sarah swept into the lobby. His reaction to her this afternoon had been extreme, but tonight it was even more intense. Seeing her charms so freely displayed, he found himself having difficulty breathing. Who was this Sarah Williams who looked like an angel one minute and a temptress the next and managed to set his loins on fire in either role?

When Sarah spotted Tyler Bennet, she was a little disgruntled to see him looking every bit as handsome as she remembered him from the afternoon. His elegantly cut coat of black superfine with velvet collar and a silk top hat accentuated his masculine assets. She repressed a frown. If her heart was going to insist on pounding like a bass drum, how was she to keep her wits about her? There was nothing to do but brazen ahead.

"Good evening, Mr. Bennet." She extended her hand. "You didn't say where we were to dine, so I just took a chance and pulled a gown from my wardrobe. I hope my attire is suitable." Though she managed an urbane tone, she could not prevent the color from rising in her cheeks as his gaze riveted on the bare region below her collarbone.

He tore his eyes away from the display of her creamy white breasts in hopes of formulating an articulate reply but ended up settling for an unadorned "Yes."

"Is something wrong, Mr. Bennet?" Sarah asked innocently as she gazed up at his fixed expression.

"Ah, no." He took a firm grip on himself, regaining his composure. "I was just admiring your gown. The color becomes you."

"Why thank you, Mr. Bennet."

As they spoke the high color in her cheeks slowly spread down her neck and shoulders. Tyler was intrigued by the incongruity of her cool replies and warm coloring. His lawyer's mind took over.

"Why is it I get the feeling you are toying with me?"

"Because I am," she replied without hesitation. "You issued a challenge this afternoon. I want to show you I am neither easily intimidated nor devoid of resourcefulness. There is nothing I can't handle, including you."

"I see."

"You sound doubtful."

"Do I?"

"Yes." Her gaze held his, but she could not read his mood.

Tyler smiled and changed the subject. "I thought you might enjoy a brief tour of the city before we dine at Delmonico's. I've hired a chaise."

Sarah accepted the offer of his arm and allowed him to lead her out into the night. As the cool air assaulted her bare flesh, she immediately regretted having left behind her shawl. She had been so intent on making a grand entrance she had completely forgotten that in San Francisco, no matter how warm the day, a wrap was a necessity each night at the moment the sun began to fade and the fog rolled in. She contemplated returning to her room, but decided to bear the discomfort.

Tyler handed her up into the chaise, then settled himself beside her, nodding to the driver, and they started off down the street.

Without asking her permission, Tyler laced his fingers with hers and brought their hands to rest on his thigh.

A surge of warmth shot from her captured hand upward, but she ignored it, refusing to be so easily undone.

"Where are we going?" she asked casually.

"Portsmouth Square, the factory district, the Barbary Coast," he listed their destinations. "Unless you'd rather not."

Sarah had been in the city long enough to know full well what he was about, and she smiled sweetly. "The Grand Tour. I can hardly wait."

Tyler masked an expression of bemusement and settled back on the seat. Either Sarah Williams was more naive than he had previously surmised, or she didn't scare easily. Then again, she could be bluffing, assuming he would call a halt to their tour before they reached the truly unsavory sections of the city. Only time and careful observation would tell the tale. She exhibited such a strange combination of innocence and sophistication, he would be a fool to attempt to read her mind.

The festivities that went on nightly were in full swing as their carriage turned onto Clay Street. Portsmouth Square had become more respectable since its infant years — boasting a few professional offices of doctors, lawyers, and the like — but the predominant enterprise of the square was still the sale of pleasure. Elegant gambling halls and saloons snuggled next to fancy parlor houses. The voice of an opera singer floated through an open door joining the general medley provided by pianos and melodeons.

They passed respectable-looking businessmen with doxies clinging to their arms, two staggering drunks, a bevy of giggling soiled doves, and a street gambler all in the space of a block.

Sarah shivered as they rounded the corner to continue their way around the square.

"Had enough?" Tyler queried solicitously.

"Heavens, no." She gifted him with a charming smile. "I've been here before, you know. Only it was during the day. It is ever so much more interesting at night."

"But you're trembling," he countered, a scowl creasing his brow.

"From the chill air," she explained, patting his hand. "I foolishly left my wrap at the hotel. I am sorry to disappoint you, but my tender sensibilities are not offended."

"Portsmouth Square is but a taste of what is to come. The pleasure seekers who frequent its establishment come from the more elevated strata of San Francisco society." He paused, waiting for her to respond. When she did not, he hid his disappointment and continued, "Driver, the factory district."

As they headed toward their next destination, he removed his coat and settled it about her shoulders.

Sarah smiled gratefully but attempted to hand the coat back to him. "There is no reason you should suffer on account of my oversight," she protested.

"I am perfectly comfortable in my shirt and waistcoat. As you can see, I am well covered." He pulled at the fabric covering his chest. "You, on the other hand," his eyes drifted to her bosom as he settled his coat back around her bare shoulders, "are in need of more substantial clothing. If not for your comfort, then for mine." Deliberately crossing the bounds of propriety, he added, "The beauty of your breasts is nigh unto irresistible."

His look was so voracious, Sarah pulled the coat snugly up to her chin without further argument.

She lowered her gaze to her lap, not sure how she should respond. Her breath was coming in erratic gasps, but she was filled with exciting sensations. It rather gave her a feeling of power to inspire such a look of desire. The emotion was short lived, and she began to fan herself with her hand. She reminded herself her experience with men was next to nonexistent. No doubt Mr. Bennet was not responding to her any differently than he would any other woman of his acquaintance. As handsome as he was, she was sure he had more than ample opportunity to practice his seductive skills upon the female of the species.

Chiding herself for letting the intensity of his gaze intimidate her, especially when her aim was to promote her own competence and confidence, she stilled her hand, raised her head, and looked him directly in the eye.

He met her gaze. "Yes, Mrs. Williams . . . is there something you would like to say?"

"Since you have gifted me with the loan of your coat, I feel it only right I offer you something in return. I would be most pleased if you would call me by my given name: Sarah." There — I sounded quite cool and collected, she congratulated herself.

Tyler brought one of her hands to his lips and kissed the palm. "I am honored by your generous offer of intimacy, Sarah."

"I didn't offer intimacy. I offered my Christian name," she quickly corrected, afraid she might have given the wrong impression. "I just meant I was willing to be friends."

"That is exactly what I assumed you meant," he assured her, grinning as she squirmed beneath

32

his gaze.

"Oh. I was afraid . . ." She let the rest of what she was going to say trail off. At the moment, silence seemed a more prudent course than further explanation.

When she did not continue, Tyler gallantly came to her rescue (though he still refused to release her hand). "You are afraid it will sound odd if I call you Sarah and you call me Mr. Bennet. Quite so. My Christian name is Tyler. You have my permission to use it or Ty, whichever you prefer."

"Thank you." Sarah sighed and they both knew her thanks was meant more for his turning her ill-spoken words aside than for permission to use the less formal address.

Sarah remained slightly flustered, and her reaction gratified Tyler. He had engineered the previous exchange in hopes of determining if she was more blushing beauty or seductive siren. He liked the answer.

The factory district, though quieter, was far more foreboding than the square. Ringed by the shanties of the workers, the many warehouses and factories loomed dark. Here the pedestrians wore not smiles but tired, desperate expressions as they shuffled to their various destinations. The sounds of industry rent the night air.

Sarah made no attempt to hide her surprise or concern. "How late must they work?" she asked.

"Some of the factories run twenty-four hours a day. The shifts are long and the pay meager," Tyler explained.

"Why are you showing me this?"

"Because I want you to understand danger is not

only present in the pursuit of vice, but in the sufferance of poverty. When a man is hungry, he is willing to do almost anything to put food in his belly."

"I see." Sarah accepted his warning, but the thoughts occupying her mind were not of the threat of danger to herself should she ever have need to venture to this neighborhood, but of how she might alleviate the grinding need she saw here. She decided that first thing in the morning she would seek out a listing of the local relief organizations and make a generous contribution. She snuggled deeper into Tyler's coat. "The Barbary Coast is next, if I am not mistaken," she said, her voice more subdued than before.

Tyler nodded, pulling a gun from the small holster he wore strapped beneath his waistcoat.

Sarah's eyes widened. "What's that for?"

"Just a precaution. Only a greenhorn ventures to the Barbary Coast at night without a gun. The thugs and thieves prey mainly on sailors, but they're not averse to bludgeoning a head wherever they feel there's a profit to be made."

She instinctively moved a little closer. He accommodated her by laying his arm along the back of the seat.

The "Coast," though it had no official boundaries, encompassed roughly the area from the East Street waterfront to Chinatown and from Clay and Commercial Streets up to Broadway. It was largely a collection of slop shops, gambling dens, booze parlors, and bawdy houses, with the occasional pawnshop or cut-rate clothing store sandwiched between. Lewd entertainment was a mainstay, and much of it was going on out in the streets.

Sarah blushed at the sight of a young woman, clad

in nothing but garters, silk stockings, and a transparent chemisette, dancing provocatively near the doorway of one establishment. She started at the sound of gunplay, her expression becoming worried.

Tyler gave her shoulders a comforting squeeze; however, he was betrayed by a victorious mien.

Determined not to be bested, Sarah straightened her spine, casting her gaze with studied indifference about the neighborhood.

"I know full well you are trying to frighten me into hiring a detective as you suggested, and it won't work. I do not pale at the sight of a whiskey bottle or swoon at the sound of cursing."

"I was told you'd lived a sheltered life."

"I have, which is the very reason I am so determined to conduct the search for my father myself. Adventure of any kind will be a relief. You have no idea how deadly dull my life has been."

"How so?" he asked, truly interested in learning all he could about the woman sharing his chaise.

"Imagine, if you will, a stately home with servants to do your slightest bidding. A lady mustn't soil her hands, so gardeners tend the garden and cooks provide the meals. We even had a separate maid to tend the linens. To stroll the city streets was considered vulgar, as was the theater, a picnic in the park, and any other activity that might give hope of pleasure." As she spoke, she slowly began to relax back against the seat. "I was given a small allowance so I might donate to the local charities but never allowed to engage in any actual labor for the less fortunate, whom Henry deemed intellectually and socially beneath our collective dignity. I don't wish to appear ungrateful to

35

my late husband. He was a good man; he provided well for both me and my mother. But the sole purpose of my existence was to ornament his house, which I could not leave without first soliciting his permission."

"You must have made a very lovely ornament," he complimented.

Sarah scowled at him.

Tyler realized he had said the wrong thing the moment the words had slipped past his lips. If he wanted her confidence, he had best be more sympathetic. "So your marriage was not a happy one," he encouraged her to continue.

"Happiness is something Henry did not understand. At least not the kind I needed. I made him content," she assured him as she folded her hands in her lap. "I know I am saying this all wrong, and you will think less of him because of it. He allowed me my books, for which I am appreciative," she added in her late husband's defense. "The mood of our marriage was as much my fault as his. We just had nothing in common."

"Then why did you marry him?"

"My mother arranged it, and I had not the strength to fight her will. I tried to tell them it was wrong, but neither she nor Henry would listen. Mother never listens. To be honest, I came out west as much to escape another such marriage as I did to find my father."

"I'm glad you did. Come out west, I mean." He smiled at her.

"Why?"

His smile broadened. "Because if you hadn't, I would never have met you, and I find you a most fetching woman."

"Then you aren't offended by my weaknesses as a wife, or that I am not taken aback by this display of wanton vice." She gestured to the boisterous streets with a sweep of her hand.

"Surprised, yes. Offended, no," he replied honestly, his expression sobering. "I'm showing you all this for your own protection. I can understand your desire to enjoy your newfound freedom, but I cannot condone you putting yourself at risk unnecessarily."

"Rest assured, I have no intention of throwing caution to the wind. You needn't worry on my account."

"But I do worry."

"You shouldn't." Sarah willed him to understand. "I'm only looking for a little fun."

"If it's fun you're seeking, I'm just the man you're looking for." He was suddenly cheerful again. "Are you ready for Delmonico's?"

"Yes, now that you mention it, I'm quite famished."

Tyler signaled the driver, and they were instantly on their way. He kept the conversation light, and Sarah was more than happy to follow his lead. She basked in his charm, which to her mind was richly abundant.

The uncommon physical reactions he evoked, though they had never ceased throughout the entire carriage ride, once again captured her full attention. She wasn't sure what he was about, but she was sure she wanted to find out.

They arrived at their destination, and Sarah handed Tyler his jacket before alighting from the chaise.

Delmonico's was every bit as elegant as its reputation claimed. As they stood among the crowd waiting to be seated, Sarah's gaze moved over the sparkling crystal chandeliers, festooned windows, and gleaming table services. She couldn't imagine why she had neglected to come here on her own. Her gaze came to rest once again on her companion.

"It's lovely," she commented.

Tyler agreed, adding, "But the true test of a restaurant is the quality of its cuisine, and Delmonico's chef is one of the best."

Their conversation came to a temporary halt when the maitre d' came to escort them to their table. Despite the crowd, they were seated in a quiet corner. Sarah watched with interest as Tyler discreetly passed several bills across the maitre d's palm.

"Do you dine here often?" she queried.

"Fairly frequently. Why do you ask?"

"The thought has occurred to me that you might be a womanizer."

He laughed. "Womanizing requires a heavy investment of time and energy. I'm afraid I've been too busy arguing legal cases to pay proper attention to my social life. But if you think I have a chance, I'll do what I can about remedying the situation."

"You're teasing me," Sarah protested.

"I suppose I am." His look told her he felt his response perfectly justified, considering her comment.

"Perhaps it was forward of me to speak my thoughts out loud, but you asked me to join you for dinner on such brief acquaintance, and you are very free with your compliments. It does make one wonder."

"I assure you, I am a gentleman of the first degree." He flourished an exaggerated bow from his seat. "My only motivation is the pleasure of your company. If you'd like, I can have a list of character references sent over to your hotel tomorrow morning."

It was Sarah's turn to laugh. "I don't believe that will be necessary." She picked up her menu in hopes of turning the conversation. "What do you recommend?"

"The lobster," Tyler advised. "It's the house specialty."

The waiter came to take their order, and they both decided on the lobster. Appetizers, soup, and side dishes were added to compliment the main dish, as was a bottle of French Chablis.

Each dish was a delight to the palate. At first Sarah sampled the fare with ladylike reserve, but when she realized what she was doing, she cast off the fetters one was told a lady must impose upon her appetite and applied herself to the meal enthusiastically.

She judged Tyler an excellent conversationalist as they discussed a variety of topics—the theater, the import of the railroads connecting the country, popular novels, world affairs. He formed his opinions intelligently, and the more she listened to him, the more she wanted to know about him.

"I have told you quite a bit about me," she said between sips of *potage de poisson*. "What is there to tell about Tyler Bennet?"

"I was born in Philadelphia," he began at the beginning. "My mother died when I was four. Came out west with my father during the gold rush days. He quickly learned there was more money to be made settling claim disputes than panning gold, so he set up a law practice. When the time came, I was sent back east to be educated, then I joined the law firm."

"So you were given no choice but to follow your father into his profession," Sarah commiserated. "It appears we share a common burden."

"A career in law was my choice, not my father's," Tyler corrected. "Dad would never presume to tell me how to live my life."

"You're a lucky man to have such a parent," she remarked.

"Yes, a very lucky man."

When he showed no sign of resuming the narrative of his life, Sarah encouraged him with a question. "The shingle over your door says Johnson & Bennet. Who is Johnson?"

"Thaddeus Johnson became my father's partner in '52, and he is mine now. Thaddeus has always been like a second father to me, and I have immeasurable respect for the man." Tyler paused, laying his spoon aside. "My father passed away three years ago."

"I'm sorry."

"So am I."

Sarah's green eyes darkened with sympathy.

"Now, don't go melancholy on me," Tyler protested. "Dad would rise from his grave and beat my backside with a switch if he knew I made you sad. He was a practical man and one who believed it was a mortal sin to abuse an opportunity. I can still hear his words." He lowered his voice an octave and pulled at his chin, "Women look their best when they're smiling, so keep them happy, son."

His antics elicited a blithe smile from Sarah.

Tyler grinned. "That's better."

"What else did your father say?" she queried, hoping her own father, if she found him, would be a little like Tyler's.

"Be honest; don't cut corners; and eat your peas," he

again imitated his elder's voice.

Sarah laughed. "Anything else?"

His eyes took on a roguish gleam, and he reached across the table for her hand. "Good women are hard to come by, so if you find one, kiss her quick, and don't let her go."

Her color heightened. She quickly averted her gaze and pulled her hand from his. "Look. Here come our lobsters. Don't they look delicious?"

He leaned back in his chair. "Blushing becomes you."

"It's an annoying affliction," Sarah demurred, silently cursing the heat in her cheeks. How on earth was she supposed to cultivate the aura of a worldly woman if her cheeks flamed at his every compliment?

The arrival of their main course brought a halt to the conversation.

Sarah resisted the urge to thank their waiter for his timely interruption. Tyler Bennet might disclaim the appellation of womanizer, but he was flirting outrageously, and she had no experience dealing with a man such as he. She wasn't offended; quite the contrary. She liked the way he looked at her with his smoky blue eyes and the way the corners of his mouth twitched upward when he spoke his words of flattery. She just felt off-balance.

As their waiter set the steaming platters of lobster before them, a second man supplied each with a finger bowl and a stack of cloth napkins. They withdrew, leaving Sarah staring at the red-orange crustacean in consternation.

How to tackle the lobster lying on her plate without disclosing her ineptitude would be a formidable task, but she was determined to triumph. She told herself all she need do was watch carefully and follow her dinner companion's lead.

Tyler picked up his lobster in his hands and twisted off its claws.

Sarah did likewise.

Using the mallet provided, Tyler cracked one claw, extracted a piece of flesh with the tiny fork, and dipped it in his dish of herb-flavored melted butter. Her gaze followed the bite on its journey to his lips.

The heat she had been battling in her cheeks moved to her veins, filling her with a delicious sensation she was coming to recognize as the brand of her friendship with Tyler Bennet. As his wide, smiling lips moved rhythmically against each other, she felt an unexpected yearning to reach out and touch them. She sat mesmerized as he took another bite.

Never in her life had she dreamed the simple act of consuming a meal could be so intoxicating. The energy she had discerned arcing between them in the carriage was nothing compared to this. She could almost feel his mouth caressing the lobster. She imagined it caressing her.

His gaze met hers, and she quickly averted her eyes. Picking up her mallet, she gave one of her lobster claws a hearty thwack.

As she picked the meat from the shell, she could feel Tyler watching her intently, and she was afraid to raise her eyes to meet his. What if he had read her thoughts? What would he think of her? What did she think of herself?

The golden butter dripping slowly off the white meat of the lobster was somehow sensuous, and she popped the meat in her mouth before she was further undone by the sight. The butter-coated lobster tasted sweet and salty, its texture firm upon her tongue.

Against her will, she let her gaze seek out Tyler's. His eyes were warm and dark and compelling.

Sarah sighed her pleasure.

He took another bite under her ardent regard, glancing away only long enough to skewer a morsel of sweet meat. Her eyes riveted to his lips, lowering when his Adam's apple rode up then down in the manly column of his throat as he swallowed.

Each one ate in turn, the other beholding the act in silent relish until the claws were picked clean.

"You like the lobster?" Tyler's words were more statement than question — a low, contented murmur rising from his chest.

"Yes," she whispered.

His eyes never left hers as he twisted the tail from the lobster body. She followed suit. They were forced to spare the lobsters an occasional glance as each worked the chunks of thick, white meat through the wide end of the tail. Disposing of the task with feverish determination, they were once again at liberty to feast their eyes upon each other with glorious abandon.

The other patrons of the restaurant were reduced to an insignificant blur — the sensations of taste, touch, and the fervid passions evoked by the sight of each other all that existed.

A challenging gleam sparked the fire in Tyler's eyes, and he tore off a leg from her lobster, holding it to her lips as she sucked out the juice and meat. She smiled, reached for his lobster, and offered him one in return.

With every bite, every look, Sarah could feel her heartbeat increase. Her thoughts floated, dégagé, in a heady haze.

She ran her tongue across her bottom lip to capture a droplet of butter. Tyler could not resist the urge to let a finger follow its path. He moaned as Sarah sucked the salt from his fingertip.

Prudence demanded he do something to break the spell, or he risked disgracing himself and dishonoring his dinner companion by pulling her under the tablecloth and having his way with her on the dining room floor. Lust was a compelling emotion, but he wasn't given to casual affairs, and he liked Sarah too much to allow carnal indulgence to preclude friendship.

Reluctantly pulling his hand away, he picked up his fork and concentrated on consuming the tomalley, while he tried to think of some neutral topic to promote.

"What would you like for dessert?" he asked in a strained voice.

Sarah was startled back to reality by the question. Blushing profusely, she picked up a napkin and began dabbing her throat. "My, it's hot in here."

"I expect it's the crowd," Tyler offered her an easy excuse.

"Yes, I expect it is." She reached for her glass of wine and took a large gulp. Choking and sputtering, Sarah groaned miserably into her napkin as she struggled to catch her breath.

Tyler smiled to himself. He liked the effect he had on her. He liked the effect she had on him. He had the distinct feeling he was falling head-over-heels in love with the widow Williams, and rather than being alarmed by the notion, he felt pleasantly giddy. In the courtroom he often depended on his instincts; he trusted them. They told him Sarah Williams was a woman with whom he could share his life. He had celebrated his birthday not a month before. Thirty-two was an excellent age for a man to start thinking of settling down.

Sarah watched the unrestrained display of emotions play across his face. He looked too pleased with himself for her peace of mind. This evening was not going at all as she had planned. She had lost control of it somewhere between the soup and the lobster. She probably didn't *want* to know, but she *needed* to know what was going on in that handsome head of his.

"Penny for your thoughts," she offered, interrupting his musings.

"What?"

"You're smiling," she explained as calmly as she was able. "I was wondering what you were thinking about."

"Oh," he shifted uncomfortably. "Sorry to drift off like that." It was too early to commit himself. He needed to buy himself time to think, and he judiciously changed the subject to one of business. "Now, about the matter of finding your father . . . why don't you stop by my office first thing in the morning? We can start mapping out a strategy."

Suspecting a change of topic was probably a more prudent course, Sarah let her question drop. But her tour of the city was still fresh in her mind, and she had no intention of being maneuvered into agreeing to anything she might later regret. "No more talk of hiring detectives?"

"I've decided to handle the investigation myself. Under your direction," he quickly amended when a scowl lined her fair face. "What I'm proposing is a partnership: Williams and Bennet."

Her eyes twinkling as she warmed to the notion of spending her days and nights in Tyler Bennet's company, Sarah added, "Detectives-at-large."

He offered his hand and she accepted it, giving it a hearty shake.

Chapter 4

"I wish you had consulted me first." Tyler paced back and forth before his desk.

"I placed the ads before I met you. Beside, I don't see what harm there is," Sarah countered.

"First of all, your reward is far too generous. You could have offered half the amount, and the sincere would still have come forward. Second, to use your hotel address is to invite disaster. Third, you should never have identified yourself as his daughter. Fourth . . ."

"Enough. You've made your point," she interrupted. Last night Tyler Bennet had been so . . . nice. Today he was all business. Ever since she had walked through his door, he had behaved as if nothing had happened between them. It disgruntled her he could so completely dismiss it from his mind when she had lain awake half the night trying to sort out what it all meant. Obviously it meant nothing. She pursed her lips, determined she would show like indifference to matters personal.

"It is too late to do anything about this," he indicated the copy of the *Morning Chronicle* he held in his hand, "but we can kill the ad in future editions."

"No."

"What?"

"I said you had made your point, not that I agreed with it," she informed him. "First, I purposely made the reward generous to overcome anyone's reluctance to step forward with information that could lead to my father. Second, I am surrounded by people at the hotel, and it's patently impossible for anyone with nefarious designs to do me harm. Third, by stating I'm his daughter, I will show his friends my motives are pure." Sarah smiled triumphantly, proud of the efficient manner in which she had disposed of all his objections.

Tyler met her smile with a frown. "All I am trying to say is, it could have been handled better. The informants could have been screened through this office, saving you much time and trouble. Placing the ads was not a bad idea, just a little misguided."

Even if he was acting obtuse, she believed him to be genuinely concerned. *Just a little misguided,* she mentally echoed his opinion of her acumen, struggling to veil her amusement at the private joke. "If it will quiet your fears, I promise I shall use the utmost caution. We really have no idea if anyone will actually answer my ads."

"You've put it in all the local papers." He tossed the *Chronicle* on his desk with the others. "There are going to be plenty of respondents. Fifty dollars to fabricate a convincing lie is pretty tempting wages."

"I think you have a rather a jaundiced view of mankind and overstate the possibility of fraud," she argued.

His pacing came to a halt, and he stood legs spread, arms folded across his chest, so close Sarah was forced to tilt her head back to see his face. "And I think I'm a sight more experienced than you in such matters."

His nearness was unnerving and caused a telltale blush to stain her cheeks, but she stood her ground, tinging her tone with anger in hopes he would misinterpret the flush in her cheeks as a sign of ire. "I will not argue the point. Unfortunately, as a lawyer, your experience has been colored by your dealings with the criminal element."

"The bulk of my clients are corporations, not criminals, my dear lady."

Sarah lifted her eyebrows. "No wonder you have developed so suspicious a nature."

"A rich radical?"

"I do read the papers. It seems California politics are not all they should be."

Damn, she was good at engaging in a battle of tongues. He admired intelligence even more than he admired beauty in a woman, and he had been secretly admiring Sarah's beauty since the moment she had walked through his door. Still, it would never do to let her know how much power she held over him. He masked his high regard as he gave reply. "Quite so, but that has nothing to do with this. We are talking about you, not politics. You came to me for guidance, yet you balk every time I try to give it."

Her blood was beginning to boil, and she saw no advantage in concealing her displeasure. "I *do* want guidance. What I *don't* want is mollycoddling! Why do you seek to thwart my efforts to manage my own affairs?" Her eyes flashed. "If it was another of your clients standing in this office . . ."

"I am giving you exactly the same advice I would give any client."

"Are you sure?" Her tone remained terse.

"Yes," Tyler calmly informed her.

He sounded honest, but she wasn't certain she should concede on any point. In the past she had been too vulnerable to manipulation, and if she erred, she preferred the sin of obstinance to that of her lifelong sin of chronic capitulation. Sarah studied him carefully. He looked inoffensive, hopeful. . . . He did come highly recommended by Mr. Filmore, and she had asked his advice. "Maybe I could have the ad changed just a little before it is printed in future editions," she spoke her thoughts out loud, her tone becoming less tentative as she continued. "In any case, as long as you understand the final decision is mine to make, I'll think about what you've said."

"And in the meantime, should someone respond to these ads," he lifted the stack of newspapers from his desk, "you'll contact me at once?"

She hesitated, choosing her words carefully. "If I feel the slightest twinge of trepidation, I'll not proceed without you," she assured him.

Tyler opened his mouth to thank her for her sensible surrender, then thought better of it. He was fast learning that any comment, however innocent, perceived as an attempt to stifle her freedom or impeach her competence set her off like a Fourth of July firework.

His eyes began to twinkle. He'd rather like to see just how hot she could get—but not with anger. He wanted to set her aflame with passion for him. He licked the inside of his lips and gifted her with his most charming smile.

"Now, on to more pleasant matters. Where would you like me to take you tonight?"

His sudden change in manner startled Sarah. "Excuse me?"

"We have disposed of our business, now we can pursue our mutual pleasure," he explained.

She swallowed the knot forming in her throat. She was dealing with a chameleon. The man changed character as easily as other men changed hats. How did he do it? More important, why did he? Her senses pricked, causing a fiery rush of expectation, and she took a step backward. "I thought I came here to discuss strategy," Sarah countered, grasping for some way to keep the conversation under her control.

"As I said before, placing want ads in the local papers was an excellent idea — the very one I had planned to suggest this morning, had you given me a chance. At this point I think it best we wait to see if we get any leads before we plan our next move."

What he said made sense; it was how he said it that bothered her. Her "good" idea had been elevated to "excellent," and his casual use of the pronoun "we" was more than a little disconcerting.

What did he want of her? No, she amended her thoughts, the question she should be asking was what did *she* want of *him*. She was a free woman, the mistress of her own destiny. She ran her gaze up and down his lean frame, appraising what she saw. He was still grinning at her, and a thousand conflicting and confusing opinions filled her head; however, one voice spoke louder than all the rest: she enjoyed the company of Mr. Tyler Bennet immensely. Why, she wasn't sure . . . but she did.

Since enjoying life was now her principal goal, she should not hesitate to accept his invitation. God knew she needed to make up for the many years she had merely gone through the motions of living.

"Well?" Tyler prodded.

"The opera." Sarah settled on the first idea that popped into her mind. "There is one now being presented at Maguire's Opera House the papers say is very good."

"The opera it is," he announced. "And a light supper afterward?"

Sarah wavered, then mentally chided herself for her lack of nerve. "That would be lovely."

She rose to leave, and Tyler escorted her to the door. As she stepped into the hall, a thin man with a balding pate and gray goatee stepped out of the door across the hall.

"Thaddeus," Tyler greeted him by his first name. "I would like you to meet my newest client, Mrs. Sarah Williams. She is the one I was telling you about this morning. Sarah, I would like you to meet my partner, Mr. Thaddeus Johnson."

"Pleased to meet you." Sarah blessed him with a winsome smile as she offered her hand.

"Likewise," he responded politely, though from his expression one would judge him anything but pleased to make her acquaintance.

"Arthritis bother you again this morning, Thaddeus?" Tyler asked solicitously.

"No more than usual," Johnson responded. "When

you're finished with your client, I'd like a word with you." Nodding curtly, he stepped back into his office.

Sarah knew she had not had time to do anything to pique the man in the brief seconds of their acquaintance, and that left only one logical explanation. She glanced up at Tyler.

He shrugged, indicating his innocence to her unspoken accusation. "I swear, I didn't say a word that wasn't complimentary when I talked to him this morning. In fact, I was positively profuse with my praise. But then, what man wouldn't be?"

"Mr. Johnson," Sarah offered, still dubious.

Tyler could not deny Thaddeus was not his customary self, and he sought to cover for his partner's deficient congeniality. "Perhaps he didn't sleep well, or a case is going poorly. I'm sure the next time you meet he will be less brusque."

"Well, be that as it may, I have obviously made a poor first impression, but I suppose it is of no import." She offered her hand. "Until this evening."

Tyler touched her hand lightly, smiling as he brought it to his lips. "Until this evening."

As usual, his touch evoked a surge of exhilaration. Their eyes met, but Sarah quickly looked away.

Releasing her hand, Tyler walked her down the stairs. She bid a friendly farewell to Agnes Johnson, whose company she had enjoyed while waiting for Tyler to finish with another client, and stepped out into the fog-filtered sunlight.

Before leaving the Grand Hotel, Sarah had procured the addresses of several charitable organizations, and she spent the remainder of the morning visiting their directors and making contributions where she thought they would do the most good. She treated herself to lunch at Mayes Oyster House, then strolled back to the hotel.

There were several messages waiting for her when she arrived. She took them from the desk clerk and retired to a chair in the lobby to read them.

In all there were five, each a response to her advertisement. She had just been given the perfect opportunity to prove to Tyler she wasn't as inept as he assumed, and she felt not a twinge of trepidation. Sarah smiled to herself. Mr. Bennet might think she had bowed to his demands, but if he had listened more carefully, he would have realized she had done no such thing. Rising to her feet, she approached the front desk.

"Excuse me, but could you tell me where I might purchase a map of the city?"

The clerk gave her instructions to a nearby dry goods store, and after thanking him, Sarah was on her way.

The morning fog had finally burned off, and the day promised to be warm and sunny. She drew in deep breaths of the salt-scented air. As she strolled briskly to her first destination, she mentally plotted her course of action.

Until she was sure the information she was given was honest, the reward money would remain safely in the bank. Her most formidable obstacle was how to determine the truthfulness of the informants. The only solid pieces of information she had about her father were his name and an address that no longer existed. The few clues to his physical appearance she had gleaned from her mother's tirades were ofttimes contradictory. She could safely assume his eyes green like her own, his hair red—those descriptions had remained constant; but his features were alternately portrayed as "possessing a wicked handsomeness used to beguile the innocent" and "intolerably coarse and vulgar." She had not a clue if he was tall or short, thin or stout. Too, even if her mother had given her an exactingly accurate description, twenty-two years were bound to make more than a few changes in a man's appearance. Her only course it seemed was to inject information she knew to be blatantly false in hopes of tripping up the less than honest.

After a brief stop to purchase the map, she continued on her way. The first address led her to a modest boardinghouse, and she knocked firmly on the door.

"May I help you?" A pleasantly plump woman in her mid thirties answered the door.

"I am here to see a Mr. Amos Boggs."

"He's off to work hours ago and won't be back till evening."

"Could I see him where he works?"

"Not likely. He works over at the soap factory. They aren't too keen on their people visiting during business hours. Probably give him his walking papers."

"I wouldn't want that. Perhaps I should just leave a message."

"That might be best, young lady."

Sarah drew pen and paper from her reticule and scribbled a brief note, which she handed to the landlady.

The next address sent her further north. The buildings lining the streets gradually deteriorated in appearance, but the neighborhood did not generate a sinister air and Sarah remained unconcerned. There were plenty of perfectly pleasant-looking people on the streets going about their business.

There was no answer at the second address on her list. She sighed in disappointment. At this rate, she would have nothing to show for her efforts.

The third street number on her list was only a few doors down, but one glance gave Sarah cause to hesitate. The establishment was obviously a parlor house.

"Well, Miss Caroline Poulet," Sarah spoke her thoughts out loud as she rechecked the name and address on the slip of paper, "need I wonder what you do for a living?"

The temptation not to continue on was strong. After all, she argued with herself, any information Miss Poulet gave her was likely to be as tainted as her virtue. Still, if her father was the scoundrel her mother painted him to be, a prostitute might be the very one to have knowledge of his whereabouts. Besides, she told herself, I am being judgmental . . . for all I know, the poor woman was forced into the trade by some unfortunate circumstance and was in truth possessed of a heart of gold.

Having settled the matter in Miss Poulet's favor, Sarah climbed the three steps leading to the door. It took less than a minute for someone to answer her knock.

"What do you want?" a woman with heavily kohled eyes and red-painted lips asked tersely. Before Sarah could reply, she continued, "If it's work you're looking for, the madam ain't in. If it's trouble, we already got enough."

"I'm looking for neither," Sarah responded. "I'm

56

looking for Caroline Poulet."

"Why?" the whore demanded suspiciously.

The woman's voice was strident, her stare threatening, causing Sarah to consider a strategic retreat, but she stood her ground. This was a test of her mettle, a chance to prove herself. She would lose all respect for herself if she didn't see this to the end. She answered the woman in cool tones. "She came to see me at my hotel, but I was out. We have business to discuss."

"What's your name?"

"Sarah Williams."

"You wait out here. I'll ask her if you're telling the truth."

As the door slammed in her face, Sarah stepped back, catching her heel in the hem of her gown. She tumbled down the steps, landing on her bustle with a dust-raising thud.

She scrambled to her feet. This interview would not go well if she couldn't maintain more dignity than this, she cautioned herself. A few furtive glances over her shoulder left her feeling a little less chagrined. No one was paying her the least amount of attention. Apparently her graceless descent had gone unnoticed. She brushed the dirt from her skirt.

Trudging back up the stairs, she waited patiently for Miss Poulet's arrival.

After a few minutes the door cracked open, revealing nothing but a beakish nose. "You the one who put the reward in the paper?"

"Are you Caroline Poulet?" Sarah met her question with one of her own.

"I am if you're the lady put that ad in the paper about your pa."

"Then we have both found whom we are looking for."

As the woman opened the door wide enough to allow entry, her tone became more friendly. "Come on in. I'll take you up to my room so we can talk private-like."

Sarah was forced to swallow a smile upon her eyes' acquaintance with Miss Poulet in her entirety. With her pinched features, frazzled blonde hair, and bony figure, the name "Miss Poulet" suited her perfectly. Her drab orange dress hung limply on her gaunt frame, clashing with the scarlet paint she had applied liberally to her lips.

Sarah followed Caroline through the dimly lit parlor, her curious eyes taking in the overabundance of mirrors, a faded red upholstered tête-à-tête, and a bevy of scantily clad soiled doves reclining upon various and sundry baroque furniture.

The garish decor was an affront to anyone of sensitive taste, but Sarah was sage enough to deduce the clients of this establishment were not of genteel persuasion.

As they ascended a dilapidated staircase to the second floor, they passed several large paintings. They resembled each other in style and dress, or rather lack of dress of the subject, but each was of a different woman.

Noting her interest, Caroline queried, "Like 'em? Marty was doing one of each of us girls. Only charged six pokes a painting. Marty was real soft-hearted. Could have got twice that, easy. Always regretted him getting shot to death 'fore he got time to do me."

"Yes, I can see how that would be disappointing," Sarah commiserated, praying her face would not betray her lack of sincere sympathy. She lowered her eyes, pretending to concentrate on the placement of her feet. There was no doubt about it, she was out of her element, but she was bound and determined not to be priggish. Sarah smiled wryly. When she had awakened this morning, she'd had no idea the day would turn out to be so "educational."

"Here it is." Miss Poulet ushered her into a room at the top of the stairs. "It ain't much, but it's home."

"Home" was an eight-by-eight-foot room with a bare wood floor and equally bare walls. A single-width bed stood unmade against one wall, a mirrored dresser against another. The golden contents of a chamberpot filled the air with an astringent odor.

Upon noting the wrinkling of her guest's nose, Miss Poulet crossed the room with long strides. " 'Scuse me while I do a bit of housekeeping." Pushing up the window sash, she sang out a shrill "gardyloo" as she tossed the contents of the pot out onto the street below. The pot was returned to its place by the bedside.

She straightened the coverlet on one corner of the bed and motioned for Sarah to sit. "Now, about your pa . . . what is it you would like to know?"

"What is it you have to tell me?" Sarah countered.

"I know where he is," she stated matter-of-factly.

Excitement lit Sarah's eyes despite her best efforts to remain blank faced. "Where?"

"Do you have the reward money with you?"

"No. As a precaution against fraud, I have left it in my bank. If your information is genuine, we can walk straight from here to the offices of Wells Fargo."

Miss Poulet scrutinized her from head to toe, cocking her head this way and that, as if trying to view her

59

from every angle. Finally she shrugged her shoulders. "You look like an honest sort. I suppose I can trust you."

"Yes, you can," Sarah assured her.

"Your pa, he used to come here real regular-like. Tuesdays and Saturdays, just like a clock. 'Bout a month ago he stopped coming. Told me he was moving up north. Up in the Washington Territory is where you'll find him — a place called Tacoma."

"When he came here, did he come alone?"

Miss Poulet shuffled her feet and pulled nervously on the lobe of her ear. "What'd you mean?"

"I was just wondering if my brother was with him," Sarah remarked casually. "I expect you'd remember. Tall, well made, with green eyes and dark brown hair like mine. He was injured in the war, so he walks with a pronounced limp. He has a tiny scar over his left eye." She drew her finger over her own brow to mark the spot.

"Yeah," Miss Poulet nodded eagerly. "Never forget a face like that. Right good-looking man."

"Was it just the two of them?" Sarah continued.

"You got other relatives you're looking for?" Miss Poulet asked in dismay.

"Another brother. If I could find all three, why I'm sure my heart would be so overfilled with joy, I'd be moved to double the reward money."

"He was with them too," Caroline confirmed.

Sarah raised a fine brow. It was obvious Caroline Poulet was lying. She should stand up and march out of the room. However, she was curious to discover just how far her hostess would carry the game. Besides, grilling her was good practice. "Perhaps you could describe him to me," Sarah prodded.

Miss Poulet scowled. "Well now, I can't remember the finer details of every man who comes and goes in this place. That other brother of yours used to like to take his pleasure on Tilly. She'd know what he looked like better than me."

"I'd like to talk to her, if I may."

"Can't do that. She ain't here no more, and nobody knows where she's gone."

Sarah feigned disappointment. "Oh, I wish you could remember something. How else will I know you have really seen him?"

Miss Poulet shifted uncomfortably as she struggled to find something to say to satisfy her guest without risking the prize. Finally she blurted out, "He was handsome. Real handsome."

"And my father. How did his health seem to you?"

"Fit as a fiddle."

Sarah smiled in mock relief. "I was worried. A man going on seventy can't be too careful. But I suppose if anyone is in a position to judge his vigor, you'd be the one."

"Yep. Amazing man that pa of yours. Now, about my reward . . ."

Sarah rose to her feet. "I'm sorry, Miss Poulet, but I am convinced you never knew my father."

"Think he's too good to be sharing the sheets with the likes of me?" Caroline snapped.

"That's not it at all," Sarah assured her. "You see, I don't have any brothers, and my father will not reach the age of fifty for another year. I was testing you, and you failed the test."

The thin shoulders sagged in defeat. "I always was a

poor liar." She sighed wearily, her eyes cast to the floor as she rearranged the dust with the toe of her slipper. "Can't blame a girl for trying to better her lot in life."

Sarah's gaze drifted around her at the drab little room. Despite Caroline Poulet's deceit, she felt more sympathy than anger toward her. It really was a dreadful life she led. "No, I suppose I can't blame you," she consoled, half wishing she had pretended to believe her. "How long have you been working here?"

"Mother sold me into the trade when I was fourteen. I'm twenty-one now," she counted on her fingers, "so I guess that makes seven years."

Sarah's eyes widened with surprise and pity. Caroline Poulet looked twice her age. The similarities in their situations did not elude her. They were two young women given over to men for their mother's profit. The only difference was that she had escaped. Maybe Caroline could too. "Have you ever thought of doing anything else?"

"Nah, what would I do? I work best on my back."

"But you said you wanted to better your lot," Sarah reminded.

Caroline looked up. "I do. All my life I've dreamed of having my own little place where I wouldn't have to give half my profits to some woman who does nothing but open the door to the lusting hordes. I want to be the one opening the door."

"What if someone was willing to finance a new start in a legitimate business?"

Caroline shrugged. "I'd still be a whore. It's in my blood. Some of us just ain't cut out for living proper."

She did not fully understand, but Sarah nodded her head. Though she considered her newfound self a progressive woman, her altruism stopped short of a willingness to finance a brothel. "Well, I'd best be going."

"No hard feelings?"

"No hard feelings." Sarah held out her hand.

Caroline escorted her down the stairs and out the front door.

Blinking at the bright sunlight, Sarah started down the street. She had gone less than a block when she did an abrupt about-face and marched back to Miss Poulet's door.

"What are you doing back here?" Caroline queried when she answered her knock.

Sarah stepped over the threshold. Reaching into her reticule, she pulled out a small wad of bills. "Here." She thrust it into Caroline's hands. "Go buy yourself a pretty new dress. I think a deep shade of blue would suit you."

Caroline stared at the money in disbelief. "But I lied to you."

"I lied too," Sarah reminded her.

"But . . ."

Sarah silenced her protest with a finger upon her lips. "Take it. And if you ever change your mind about starting over, come see me."

"But why would you want to help me?"

"Maybe because we share similar histories. You were sold into prostitution. I was sold into a loveless marriage. I don't really know. All I know is if Henry's money can help you start afresh, I'd like to share a little of it with you."

Caroline's eyes welled with tears, and she sniffed loudly. "I'll buy the dress, but I ain't going to take any more of your money. Thanks for the offer anyway. It's about the nicest thing anyone has ever tried to do for me."

Sarah smiled.

The front door slammed open, and an irate man closed the distance between them with purposeful strides. The two women faced him open mouthed. How he had known she was here Sarah had not a clue; the why of his presence was easier to guess.

He turned his full wrath upon her. "I couldn't believe my eyes when I saw you step through that door," he bellowed, gesturing wildly to the aforementioned portal. "It's a lucky thing I just happened to be walking down the street when I was. Do you know what this place is?"

"It's a house of prostitution," Sarah answered him calmly.

Tyler Bennet sputtered and spewed several ungentlemanly expressions as he grabbed her by the arm.

"Hey, you unhand her. She's a lady, not one of us girls." Caroline positioned her scrawny body between the two of them. Her eyes narrowed. "If you don't leave peaceable-like, I'll get the bouncer to throw you out on your ass."

"Sarah, tell this woman who I am," Tyler demanded.

"Caroline Poulet, this is Tyler Bennet, my lawyer." Sarah's lips twitched with amusement as she introduced him. "He's a nuisance, but really quite harmless."

He ignored her insult and gently pushed Caroline aside. "Come on. I'm getting you out of here."

Sarah planted her feet firmly in place, her amusement quickly replaced with irritation. "Maybe I'm not ready to go."

"Don't press me, Sarah," he warned.

"You are not my warden."

"Hey, Poulet," a shrill voice assaulted them from above stairs, "Tell yer friends to take their caterwauling out into the streets, or that's where you'll find yerself. The parlor is for paying customers only."

For the sake of her new friend, Sarah started for the door without further urging, dragging Tyler in her wake. "Don't forget what I told you. If you change your mind about the money, you know where to find me."

"I won't forget," Caroline assured her. "And thanks again."

"What money?" Tyler demanded when they reached the street.

"I'm contemplating investing in a local business," Sarah replied curtly as she peeled his fingers off her arm.

He fell into step as she started up the street, glaring at her as if she was a madwoman.

"I am not thinking of financing my own bordello," she answered his unspoken accusation. "You really should do something about your overwrought imagination."

"What else was I to think?" he defended himself. "Ladies do not consort with prostitutes. What were you doing in there?"

"Miss Poulet left a message in response to my newspaper advertisement."

He stared at her, his expression blank. "You promised you would let me handle that."

"I promised no such thing. What I said was, if I felt any trepidation I would consult you. I didn't, so I didn't," she informed him coolly as they turned a corner. "Caroline and I had a very interesting conversation."

He growled. "I'll bet you did. How much did she bilk you for?"

"Not a dime. During the course of our conversation I ascertained she did not know my father after all."

"It is a relief to discover you have *some* good sense," he said, his words falling well short of a compliment.

Sarah was doing her best to maintain a civil air, but she was starting to lose the battle. "I don't believe I care for your tone."

"If you did not insist on exasperating me, my tone would be quite pleasant," he countered. "Today you were lucky — I happened along before you came to harm. Next time you may not be so fortunate."

"I was not in any danger," Sarah insisted.

"Your naive belief in your own statement is more than enough evidence to sway a jury. It's not safe for you to conduct this investigation yourself."

"I'm going to do it anyway."

"No, you are not."

"Yes, I am. And I would appreciate it in the future if you would not burst in on the scene like an avenging knight. It's embarrassing."

Tyler saw by the set of her jaw that now was not the time to try to reason with her. Perhaps he had overreacted just a trifle, but damn it, the idea of her traipsing up and down back alleys alone and unprotected made his blood run cold. He couldn't help himself.

The Grand Hotel loomed ahead, and he softened

his tone. "The city streets are not the place to discuss matters of a delicate nature. I think we should drop the subject."

"That's fine with me."

They walked in silence to the door. Tyler knew he had lost ground with Sarah, but he forced a congenial expression to his face. "Until this evening," he said cheerfully, tipping his hat.

Sarah couldn't believe her eyes and ears. "I think I'd rather not," she stated firmly.

He pulled her out of the path of foot traffic. "You're still angry with me?"

"Yes."

"But I've forgiven you," he said sweetly, hanging his head in repentance. He lifted one eyelid to judge the effect of his altered posture on her mood.

Sarah caught the covert gesture. "I didn't do anything for which I need forgiveness. I really prefer my own company tonight."

"Tomorrow night?" he asked.

She glared at him. A part of her was ready to end their brief acquaintance here and now. The last thing she needed in her life was an overbearing man. Still, she was intrigued by him. The idea of never seeing him again was somehow as repugnant as the thought of subjugating her will to his.

"Please," he coaxed when she did not respond. "I think we will find we can be the best of friends once we get to know each other better."

When he looked at her that way, his eyes warm with promise, it was hard to say no. "Tomorrow night," she agreed with a tentative nod of her head, then turned on her heel and left him standing alone on the sidewalk.

The next morning Sarah rose early, eager to be on her way before Tyler Bennet found an excuse to stop her. There were still four names on her list, the two men who had not been at home yesterday and two she had yet to seek out.

She retraced her steps from the day before. Today Amos Boggs was at home, but a brief conversation determined that the Elijah Jenkins he knew was a different man. No deceit had been intended.

The second door she knocked on still yielded no answer.

The chill of the early morning fog was beginning to seep into her bones, and Sarah pulled her cloak about her shoulders as she stepped back out onto the street. She checked her list of addresses. Her next stop was an office building in the heart of the factory district.

Though she had yet to glean one bit of useful information, she continued on without pause. Surely she would not encounter worse than she had in Caroline Poulet's unsavory little room, and though Tyler Bennet refused to acknowledge her achievement, she had handled that situation with aplomb.

It was his refusal to take her seriously that had compelled her to take to the streets this morning. She wanted to continue their friendship but she couldn't, wouldn't, unless he was willing to accept her as an equal and worthy partner.

Tonight over supper she would recount her activities and quietly judge his reaction. If he didn't pass muster, she would seriously consider taking her business to another lawyer.

Sarah's next interview boosted her spirits. Mr Ross, a man in his mid fifties, had clearly known her father. They had panned for gold together on the Placer River, and after they'd gone their separate ways, had exchanged occasional letters. Though they had lost touch about twelve years ago, Mr. Ross gave her a chronological list of addresses up to that date.

From the moment she had stepped through the door, Sarah had had no doubt that Mr. Ross was a man of integrity, and his refusal to accept the reward she offered confirmed her opinion.

Sarah's last stop led her even deeper into the factory district to an area close to the waterfront. Even with the help of her map, she was forced to weave her way up and down the narrow streets, scanning the tall, dark stone and brick buildings until she found the address for which she was looking.

Inside a cramped little office, a stout man sporting a flowing mane of steel gray hair sat behind a huge desk piled high with ledgers and stacks of loose papers. He pushed back the spectacles perched on the tip of his nose as she entered his domain.

"How may I help you?"

"Are you Mr. James Cory?"

"Yes."

"My name is Sarah Williams. You left a message at my hotel that you might have some information about my father."

The interview with Mr. Cory was brief and to the point. He had known her father in the years spanning 1855 to 1859. Though he had no new information to offer her, his account of the acquaintance did confirm

Mr. Ross's assertion that her father had been living in San Francisco during those years.

Mr. Cory exhibited no reluctance to accept the reward money, and they made arrangements to meet at the Wells Fargo Bank the next day.

As Sarah stepped back out onto the street, her stomach grumbled noisily, reminding her that in her eagerness to be out and about before Tyler Bennet had a chance to interfere, she had forgone breakfast.

"A fair morning's work," she complimented herself. "And not a hint of trouble. Mr. Tyler, I do believe you have overstated the case against your city."

Now that she'd accomplished what she'd set out to do, she was free to enjoy a leisurely morning meal.

There was not a hack in sight as Sarah retraced her steps, or she would have chosen the speedier mode of transportation back to her hotel and a hot meal. Her neglected stomach continued to complain stridently as she strolled along, and she decided to relieve her hunger at the first diner she passed, no matter how inelegant.

On the next block she found what she was seeking, and stepped through the doors of Mary's Café.

Inside the floor was crowded with bare wooden tables, and a plain bar stretched along one wall. Lace curtains hung limply across the windows.

There was no one else waiting to be served, but Sarah noted the absence of other patrons without concern, attributing it to the lateness of the hour. This being the factory district, no doubt Mary's patrons were already hard at work.

It wasn't Delmonico's, but Sarah could credit Mary with keeping her establishment relatively clean, and she took a seat at a table near the window.

A few moments later a thickset man wearing a grease-stained apron stepped out of the kitchen and approached her table.

"What will ya have?" he demanded, running his hand through an unruly shock of blue-black hair.

Sarah straightened under his too-familiar regard. "A menu, if you please."

"We ain't got no menus."

"Then could you tell me what you have to offer?" she queried, her tone still polite.

"Venison, mutton, Hangtown Fry, soup. Hot coffee or whiskey to quench yer thirst." The corners of his full lips curled upward as he frankly ran his gaze up and down her frame. "If ya want bread with yer meal, ya got to pay extra."

She smiled wanly, wishing Mary would make a timely appearance. She would feel better with another woman in the place. Still, it would never do to let this man know his hovering bulk intimidated her. "What kind of soup?"

"Persnickety little thing, ain't ya? How the hell should I know what kind of soup we got?"

"You could ask the cook," Sarah ventured.

"I am the cook," he stated jabbing at his chest with a meaty finger. "Now what'll ya have?"

"Coffee and a slice of bread."

"Nothing else?" he pressed, leaning so close she was assaulted by his tobacco-tainted breath.

Sarah forced herself not to recoil. "I think not."

"Ya don't eat more than that, yer going to stay a skinny little thing. Better plump up, or the men ain't going to want ya."

"I like myself just the way I am, thank you."

"Well, that's good, being content with what God gave ya, but put a few pounds on ya," his eyes took on a lecherous gleam, "why, not a man in town'd be able to keep his hands off ya."

"Then I will be careful not to gain a pound," Sarah assured him, staring at him with what she hoped was a reproving glare. He shrugged.

"Suit yerself, just trying to give ya a bit of free business advice."

"Business?"

"Yer one of them uptown whores, ain't ya?"

Sarah looked startled. "No. I'm a widow."

"That explains why ya ain't too savvy." His small brown eyes met her large green ones. "Damn, I wish I wasn't such a soft-hearted gull, but widows need work too, don't they. Tell ya what, we'll go upstairs and I'll try ya out. If you ain't half bad, you've got a job here. Room, board, and half of whatever ya bring in from the gents. Ya can have Mary's old room at the top of the stairs." He held out his hand to seal the deal.

"I just lost my appetite altogether." Sarah rose to her feet and started for the door.

"Hey, ya insulting old Macky?" He advanced on her, pinning her between his meaty arms against the wall.

Sarah's heart pounded against her chest as she looked up at his ruddy face. His breath wheezed with his anger. Tyler's words came back to haunt her: "There are neighborhoods where a lone lady would be seen as easy prey." She swallowed hard. Apparently there was some truth in his warnings. Despite her revulsion and growing fear, for expedience sake, she did her best to assume a confident expression. "Insult you? Heavens no," she assured her assailant. "I believe what we have here is merely a silly misunderstanding. You see, I am not looking for work. My husband left me well off. I am just recently arrived in San Francisco . . ."

"How well off?" he interrupted her agitated explanation.

"I'm comfortable," she answered cautiously.

"Then ya wouldn't mind sharing a little with me."

She stared at him. "Why would I want to do that?"

He pressed closer. "Yer all alone in the world, no one to look after ya, right? Seems to me ya could use a protector."

"You are the last man I would call on to fill such a position," Sarah hissed, disgust overcoming discretion.

"Now, that ain't smart, 'cause I got ya caught like a helpless little ol' rabbit, and I ain't letting ya go till ya pay my price," he cooed.

"Unhand me!"

Sarah's eyes flashed with indignation, and he planted a slobbering kiss on her lips. He pulled back, grinning in satisfaction.

Sarah erased the smirk with a hearty slap, followed by a swift kick to each shin. Ducking under his arms, she ran to the door, pulling chairs over in her wake to impede his progress should he decide to pursue her. She dashed out the door into the sunlight.

Lifting her skirts, she sprinted down the streets, unmindful of the spectacle she provided. Glancing over her shoulder, she could see Macky in hot pursuit. She continued to run for all she was worth.

Sarah ran some distance before she risked another

glance over her shoulders. He was still following her, but he was slowing.

Her own breath was coming hard, but she did not slacken her pace until she had put the distance of twenty full paces between them. By then the milieu of the neighborhood had improved considerably.

Macky stopped, raised his fist in the air, and shouted a string of expletives. Then, much to her relief, he spun on his heels and stomped back the way he had come.

Sarah slowed her pace to a brisk walk, but did not relax until she was safely closeted in her hotel room.

Chapter 5

By the time Tyler Bennet came to collect her for their evening at the opera, a nap and a long bath had erased the taint on Sarah's spirits caused by the unfortunate affair at Mary's Café, and Sarah could not think of any reason why she should mention her encounter with Macky to him.

On the other hand, she could think of plenty of reasons she should not. He was bound to blow the event all out of proportion and use it against her when the facts, weighed by a mind impartial to her sex and station, would judge her as canny, resourceful, gritty. She shuddered. Perhaps she was being a bit profuse with her self-praise, but she had learned her lesson and would be more careful in the future.

Before she had set foot outside her hotel she had known Mr. Bennet would not approve of her continuing to conduct the interviews alone. But meeting the vile Macky had nothing to do with her search for her father, she argued. No, in the interests of preserving the peace, silence on the matter seemed most rational. If he asked, she would give him an edited version of the day's events.

She dressed with care in a gown of moss-green satin brocade with underskirt of pale blue faille. The sleeves puffed at the shoulders, then cascaded in lace ruffles past her elbows. In contrast with the burgundy dress, this gown's neckline was modest.

She had resolved that what had gone on between her and Tyler Bennet as they dined at Delmonico's would not be repeated tonight. He was so attractive it took little effort on his part to make her lose her head. Simply recalling the evening spread delicious tingles up and down her spine.

She schooled her expression to one of determination. For the first time in her life she was in control of Sarah Jenkins Williams, and she didn't want to surrender even a modicum of that control. Like a moth to a flame, she felt her attraction undeniable; but if she wasn't careful, she might singe her wings. One minute he was rebuking her for her lack of good sense, the next he was offering equality, the next he was spouting provocative compliments. How did a woman understand a man like that?

"You're looking lovely, as usual," Tyler greeted, leading her out to the waiting carriage and handing her up.

So, he was playing the charmer tonight. That put her at a disadvantage. She found the professional Tyler far less disconcerting. When he gazed at her with his warm, gray-blue eyes, she found it terribly difficult to think. *But* . . . she told herself that tonight she would not be caught off guard. Forewarned was forearmed.

He continued, "I shall be the envy of every man in the theater."

Sarah smiled winningly. "I'm sure you shall, but it will be your glib tongue that causes their envy, not my beauty."

He assumed an injured air. "You cut me to the quick. My adoration is profoundly sincere."

"Perhaps you need to be fitted for a pair of eyeglasses," she quipped.

To her surprise, he pulled a pair of wire-rimmed spectacles from his breast pocket and settled them on his nose. Running his gaze up and down her person, he pretended to study her intently.

"Where on earth did you get those?" she asked, admiring his scholarly appearance despite her best intentions.

"My pocket."

Sarah rolled her eyes heavenward. "Why have I never seen you wear them?"

"Vanity," he admitted. "Besides, the only time I really need them is when I stay up half the night reading briefs. But we digress. On close inspection *with my spectacles firmly in place* I see you are even more beautiful than I originally assessed." He slipped the glasses from his nose and back into his pocket. "You will excuse me if I don't wear them, but I fear I may be blinded by your beauty."

"You, sir, are an unrepentant flirt."

"Laying it on too thick?" he queried with a grin.

"Most decidedly."

"Then I apologize."

Sarah laughed gaily. "Oh, don't do that. I have

never been courted, sincerely or otherwise, and I am finding the experience most enlightening."

"Wooing you is not wholly playacting with me," he said, his tone more serious. "I think it only fair to warn you, you have found a place in my heart."

"Oh." She didn't know what else to say, having no idea whether she wanted to encourage or discourage him. She wanted . . . she wanted to change the subject. "Did you have any trouble getting tickets for tonight's performance?"

"I had to pull a few strings, but it was easy enough to exchange the tickets." He followed her lead. "How did your day go?"

"It was interesting." There was enough hesitancy in her voice to rouse his curiosity and suspicion.

"Would you care to elaborate?"

"I conducted more interviews today."

"And . . ." he prodded, his expression darkening.

"Two were genuine, and one turned out to be a disappointment."

"I thought we agreed the interviews would be conducted through my office."

"No. I find it odd you are still laboring under that misconception. Could it be that wishful thinking is blinding you to the facts?" She met his gaze with a challenging glint in her emerald eyes. "I handled the interviews myself, just as I said I would. And quite well, I might add."

Careful, Tyler cautioned himself . . . she's baiting you. Since his goal was to continue to enjoy Sarah Williams's company, it would be unwise to repeat yesterday's mistake. "Did you learn something?" he asked solicitously.

"Yes. I now have a list of addresses where my father has lived."

"How do you know the information these people gave you is accurate?" he pressed.

"Mr. Ross refused to accept the reward money, and Mr. Cory's information corroborated Mr. Ross's," she informed him.

"And the disappointment?"

"It turned out the man Mr. Boggs knew was not my father. No fraud was intended."

Tyler fingered the tips of his mustache. "So you had no trouble."

"The interviews went smoothly," she confirmed truthfully.

"I'm glad, but in the future, as a favor to me, I wish you would let me help you." He chose his words with purpose. "A man likes to feel useful."

"I'm sure your days are already filled to overflowing with other duties," Sarah countered.

"Which I would gladly surrender in your favor. I place myself at your beck and call."

"Why?"

"Because I like you." His eyes gleamed bright with lusty promise.

Sarah shook her head in bemusement. She had been certain he was going to be angry and was prepared to fight to defend her position. Instead he was being most pleasant. He didn't berate her intelligence. He didn't issue orders. He didn't frown at her. "You're not going to scold me?"

"I would if I thought it would do me any good, but I don't. Besides, if I ruffle your feathers now, it might spoil our evening together."

She could think of no adequate words of reply and let a chary smile serve as her response.

They had reached the opera house, and Tyler handed her down from the carriage, his hand lingering overlong on hers before he tucked it under his arm and led her through the doorway. It took several minutes for them to mill through the crowd and find their seats.

Elegant was the only fitting word for the theater as Sarah perused the interior from her balcony seat. She had been here before, of course, but everytime she came her eyes caught fresh details. Mr. Maguire had spared no expense; then, she had expected he would not. She was fast learning San Franciscans did nothing in half measures.

The rest of the evening did nothing but add to the confusion Sarah had felt in the carriage. Tyler played the part of the gentleman rogue to perfection. He anticipated her needs before she thought to voice them. Dulcet words poured from his handsome mouth like honey from a pitcher. And his hands . . . strong, broad, masculine hands . . . took advantage of every excuse to linger upon her.

The old Sarah would have dutifully chastised him for his familiarity, but the new Sarah was fascinated by the feelings his touch evoked. Warmth radiated from his hands through her arm and waist wherever they touched her, causing her to feel feverish with excitement. Her blood coursed through her veins, and she felt wonderfully alive.

The opera gave her good reason to keep her eyes averted and checked all conversation. Supper did not. The meeting of their gazes across the table felt like a caress. Tyler continued to pour out compliments as freely as he did the wine. Before she had even realized what was happening, they had made plans to share dinner the next night, for a picnic on the weekend, filling every evening in the interim.

Whatever this feeling was between them, Sarah realized she was as eager to explore it as Tyler seemed to be to foster a close friendship between them.

When their carriage pulled to a halt before the Grand Hotel and he gathered her in his arms for a goodnight kiss, she did not put up even token resistance.

His gentle kiss was warm and delicious, transporting her out of herself. She sighed blissfully, tilting her head back to receive another. He obliged her, his lips playing love songs upon hers until she was limp with pleasure.

"Thank you for a lovely evening," he breathed against her ear.

"Thank you," she replied earnestly as she leaned against him.

"And Sarah . . ."

"Yes?"

He continued to speak in a seductive whisper, "Don't go to any more interviews without contacting me. Please."

Sarah sighed again. "Whatever makes you happy, Tyler."

Tyler accompanied Sarah the next day when she met Mr. Cory at the Wells Fargo Bank to pay him the money she owed him. He then arranged membership for her at the California Historical Society and left her to search their collection of documents and memorabilia for some mention of her father.

Each day dawned into another. Sarah judged the "partnership" moderately successful. Though Tyler had insisted on changing her advertisement, he had not complained overmuch when she insisted she be present at every interview. Her only real complaint was his tendency to maneuver her into spending her time researching newspaper archives or some equally insipid task when he knew he wouldn't be about to watch over her. His artifices were subtle, but each time she acquiesced to his wishes, it bothered her more. She began to long for an opportunity to assert her independence.

In contrast to her days, her evenings were entertaining and highly stimulating. She and Tyler argued politics, compared opinions on various forms of literature from Shakespeare to dime novels, and flirted both publicly and privately. Sarah judged Tyler an expert in the art, but with practice she was beginning to hold her own.

The kiss they had shared the night of the opera was oft repeated. Tyler was always discreet, and always a gentleman, and he always set her blood on fire.

She knew she really should sit down sometime soon and contemplate the expediency of the path she was traveling, but at present she preferred to live for the moment, and she made a determined effort to avoid all thoughts of a serious nature.

After spending another morning at the California Historical Society, Sarah ate a light lunch. The day had grown warm, and she decided to stop at the

Grand to leave off her cloak before she did a bit of shopping.

Upon returning to the hotel, she was handed a note. Tucking it into her pocket, Sarah climbed the stairs.

After hanging up her cloak, she settled in a chair and pulled the note from her pocket.

Sarah frowned at the coarse handwriting scrawled across the slip of paper. Another informant eager to make her acquaintance, and he wanted to meet with her this afternoon. Why was it she was always out when these people came to see her?

The address in the advertisement had been changed to Tyler's office over a week ago. This Smitty Hughes was obviously answering the original ad. It was odd he had taken so long to step forward.

The place he asked her to meet him was in the heart of the Barbary Coast district, and worse, a saloon. Despite her desire to reaffirm her autonomy, she was not eager to go alone.

Sarah argued the pros and cons of contacting her "partner" and at length decided in his favor. Pluckiness was a virtue, brazen stupidity was not. The lesson of Macky was not completely forgotten. Besides, she had given her word. Retrieving a piece of hotel stationery, she wrote a brief note and rang for a messenger.

Three hours had elapsed since she had sent her message to the offices of Johnson & Bennet, and Sarah had not seen hide nor hair of Tyler Bennet. She had made it quite clear her request to see him was immediate, and his continued absence annoyed her. Beck and call, indeed. It was not that she felt she deserved special privilege above his other clients. He was the

83

one who had given her that status. She paced the perimeter of her room. Why had he made the promise if he wasn't going to keep it?

She was tired of waiting, and the day was growing old. Grabbing her reticule, she strode out the door. Her feet carried her swiftly toward the offices of Johnson & Bennet.

Upon arriving, she smiled at Agnes. "I would like to speak with Mr. Bennet, if I may."

"I'm sorry, he's not in, Mrs. Williams," Agnes informed her, her voice tinged with apology.

"Do you know if he got the message I sent earlier today?"

"It's on his desk waiting for him."

"Oh." Sarah was only moderately successful at hiding her disappointment. She had been half hoping they had missed each other en route and he was on his way to her hotel.

"Is there something my father or I can do for you?"

The father Sarah dismissed outright. She had had her fill of censorious old men. The thought of enlisting the timorous Agnes Johnson's services as a bodyguard caused her to grin. "No. I think I can handle the matter myself."

"Are you sure? Mr. Bennet isn't expected back till late."

"I'm sure. If you would let me leave another message for him, I'll be on my way."

Sarah leaned, pen poised over paper, as she contemplated her options. She could wait till the morrow to answer the summons to the saloon, but she had no idea if this Smitty would be there the next day or how to contact him if he was not. She could hope Tyler returned from whatever business he was conducting early enough to escort her today. She could go alone. Thoroughly bored with cooling her heels, she reluctantly settled on the latter.

After leaving a note informing Tyler of the location of the interview and inviting his presence should he return sooner than expected, she took her leave.

As she walked back to the hotel, she began to formulate a plan. The trouble with Macky had resulted from the fact that she was a member of the fairer sex and therefore perceived as vulnerable. A man would have been served his meal and allowed to go on his way. Her eyes began to sparkle. Perhaps a man should go to the Barbary Coast this afternoon?

Tyler's laughter echoed in her mind as she recalled his words when she had first contemplated such a masquerade. She pressed her lips together. Could she pull it off? She would need baggy clothes to conceal her figure, a hat to cover her hair, a bottle of bay rum to give her a manly scent. A few well placed smudges of dirt would mute the fineness of her features and complete the disguise.

The more she meticulously went over every detail of her appearance, the less tentative she felt. As long as she didn't become careless, there was absolutely no reason it shouldn't work.

Having settled the matter in her mind, Sarah stepped into the first clothing store she passed and made the necessary purchases. A stop at a general store procured the rest of what she would need. Retiring to her hotel room, she spread her purchases out on the bed.

A half hour later "Jake" was ready to step out into

the hall. Sarah had settled on the name as she rubbed out the rose of her cheeks with a combination of talc and common street dirt. It had a tough, no-nonsense sound to it. A person would think twice before tangling with a Jake.

She was rather pleased with the transformation she had wrought with the oversized brown wool trousers, waistcoat, and frock coat. She had padded the front of her shirt with linen from the bed to conceal the curve of her breasts and add girth to her frame. Her hair had been pinned high upon her head and a billycock pulled down low so only the tips of her ears peeked out. To insure herself against any untimely mishaps, she had subtly secured the hat to her head. Even the stiffest of winds could not budge it. A bow tie ringed her neck.

Taking a deep breath, she mentally prepared herself to face her first test: the hotel lobby.

Upon reaching the main floor, she boldly sauntered across the room.

Several heads turned her way, and more than one eyebrow raised, but she wasn't sure if it was because she was recognized as female or because her rumpled appearance was at odds with the elegance of the hotel. To be on the safe side, she purchased the biggest cigar available from the hotel vendor.

Though it was getting late, rather than hail a hack, she decided it might be wise to further test her disguise by observing the reactions of the people she passed on the street. Being careful to maintain a jaunty gait, she set off in the desired direction.

She had not gone more than a few yards when she recognized Thaddeus Johnson stepping down from a carriage. He was directly in her path. There wasn't time to cross the street, so she quickly bit off one end of her cigar and stuck the other end in her mouth. She grimaced at the foul taste but managed to keep the cigar firmly clenched between her teeth until she had hastened past him.

Sarah raised her chin a notch. She was sure he hadn't recognized her, and her confidence soared. Resuming a more leisurely gait, she continued on her way. Here on the streets, no one paid her the least attention.

Fingering the slip of paper in her pocket, she grinned. It appeared being a man was going to be easier than she first assumed. She made her posture soldier-straight. She could hardly wait to tell Tyler Bennet of her triumph. More important, she need not fear a repeat of the type of insult she had suffered at Mary's Café. In less than an hour she would be safely in her hotel room, no worse for wear.

It was not long before she was crossing Broadway and entering the heart of the Barbary Coast district. As she approached the waterfront, the smell of the sea became stronger, and the neighborhood became increasingly seedy.

The streets were filled with men, most wearing the trappings of a sailor. Others were more elegantly garbed, in dark suits and ruffled shirts with diamond studs, pockets bulging with a variety of weaponry. A coarse version of English was spoken in a cacophony of accents.

Bevies of soiled doves lounged in doorways or congregated on the street corners. One beckoned to her, but Sarah adamantly shook her head and scurried down the street.

She found the Blue Wheel Saloon wedged in a jumble of similar establishments, its namesake nailed on the wall to the left of the door. Built on stilts over the sea, it was a single-story clapboard affair. Once it had boasted a coat of white paint, but the coastal winds and rain had worn off all but a few faded patches. The windows were thick with grime, obscuring a view of the interior.

Sarah cocked her head to one side, trying to determine if it was the sign over the door that hung askew or if the entire building leaned. She could hear someone playing a tinny melody on an out-of-tune piano. She grimaced. The condition of the piano was of little import, as the pianist had a habit of hitting the wrong notes with distressing regularity.

Most every eating establishment devoted at least one corner to the imbibing of strong spirits, but Sarah had never been in a saloon proper. To all appearances, the Blue Wheel was starting at the bottom of the barrel.

If not for her disguise, she would have turned tail and run, but the security of her costume provided along with an unhealthy dose of curiosity propelled her through the doors.

Sarah strode to the bar with a falsely confident swagger. Clearing her throat, she asked in a gravelly voice, "Smitty Hughes said I could find him here. Do you know him?"

"I know him," the burly bartender replied. He cracked the knuckles of his right hand over and over, his dark eyes peering at her from beneath bushy black brows.

"Could you tell me which one he is?" Sarah gestured to the crowd when he did not offer the information.

" 'Pends on how much it's worth to you."

Damn, Sarah cursed under her breath. As a precaution against having her pockets picked, she hadn't brought an extra dime with her. The only thing in her pocket was the smelly cigar and cabfare back to her hotel.

"Now, I'd like to oblige you, but I'm afraid I'm a little down on my luck. Poker game cleaned me out," she blustered. "How about doing a fellow a favor out of the kindness of your heart?"

"The only heart I got is black as coal."

Sarah frowned. She could well believe it, by the looks of him. His square, stubbled face emitted not a whit of human warmth. "Guess I'll have to find him on my own." She turned from the bar. "Anyone here know where I might find Smitty Hughes?" she shouted above the din, her vocal cords beginning to ache with the strain of keeping her voice deep.

The saloon went dead silent as everyone turned to stare at her.

Sarah held her breath, fearing she had not disguised her voice well enough and she was found out. Her heart pounded erratically. After an excruciatingly long minute, the men slowly began to return their attention to their whiskeys and games of cards and dice. No one stepped forward to harm her . . . or help her.

Frustrated, she turned back to the bar, fixing her gaze on the rail while she tried to determine what to do.

"You're new in these parts, ain't you?" the barkeep queried.

She glanced up, reminded herself to keep her voice deep, and replied, "Yes."

"Thought so." He grinned. "Bet you haven't been welcomed to the city proper, either."

"I don't know what you mean."

"Here at the Blue Wheel we have a little tradition." As he spoke he reached under the bar, setting a shot glass and a bottle of whiskey on the bar. "New man comes to town, he gets a free drink on the house."

"Thank you but I don't dri . . ."

He whipped a pistol from beneath his vest and waved it under her nose. "Everybody drinks at the Blue Wheel. To refuse is an insult, and I don't take kindly to insults."

Sarah swallowed hard. "I intended no insult," she croaked.

"Good." He filled the glass to the brim with the amber liquid and pushed it toward her. "To your health."

There was no doubt in Sarah's mind that the gun was very real and her continued good health was in imminent danger if she did not drink the whiskey. Lifting the glass to her lips, she took a timid sip. The fiery alcohol burned down her throat, then settled in a flaming ball in the pit of her stomach.

"What are you, some kind of goody-goody?" the barkeep gibed. "A man don't sip his whiskey. He tosses it down."

Sarah's eyes flashed with contempt, but she picked up the glass and drained the contents in a single swallow. Her eyes began to water, and she lost the ability to draw sufficient breath, but she remained on her seat.

"That-a-boy." Her tormentor reached across the bar and slapped her on the back, adding to her misery.

Sarah blinked at him. She knew beyond all doubt it was past time to admit to herself it was a mistake to come here alone, she should leave before she got herself into any more trouble; but she couldn't seem to make her legs obey her command. She shook her head as the room began to dim and the floor to sway.

The whiskey must be terribly strong if it's already going to my brain, she thought in panic. I've got to get out of here.

With a Herculean effort of will, she managed to rise to her feet. The blackness was closing in on her and she couldn't see the door, but she pointed herself in what she hoped was the right direction. One step . . . two steps . . . her knees began to buckle. Sarah felt a sharp pain at the back of her head, then nothing.

Chapter 6

"Hey Nat, drop him down easy-like. Last time ya damn near flipped me over," a bedraggled ruffian answering to the name Frankie called up at the barkeep as he and a confederate lowered Sarah's inert body through a trapdoor in the floor to the waiting dinghy bobbing in the surf below.

"Quit bitchin'. I provide you with a steady supply of merchandise to deliver, and you get a fair share of my profits fer your trouble," Nat replied.

"Helluva lot a good it'll do me if I'm drowned in the briny drink." Grabbing Sarah's trouser-clad legs, Frankie braced her weight on his shoulder, then dumped her in the bottom of the boat. "Hey, there's something not right about this guy," he hollered.

"Only gave him a little tap on the head. Mug didn't even lose his hat."

"Hell, that's not what I mean. His body feels like . . ."

"You taken to feelin' up the goods, Frankie?" Nat derided. "God damn, I'll have to watch my ass when you're prancin' about."

Frankie sputtered in outrage. "I ain't no Miss Nancy."

"Then stop standin' there gripin' like an old woman. The captain don't pay us till we deliver the goods."

"Suit yerself." Frankie made a rude gesture; then, settling himself in the boat, he put his sinewy muscles to the oars.

"What the hell is Nat trying to pull?" Captain Slodds roared.

Sarah heard the angry words through a painful haze. She tried to focus her thoughts. The smell of the sea was ripe in her nostrils. There was weathered wood beneath her cheek. The world was heaving to and fro.

It was dark. No . . . there was a dim light coming from somewhere. Was it a lantern, the moon? She blinked her eyes: *lantern.*

Shivering as a damp breeze blew across her skin, she instinctively hugged herself against the cold. Her hands touched bare flesh. Where were her clothes? The realization she wore nothing but a chemise and drawers startled her back to full consciousness. She sat up abruptly, then fell back to her hands and knees.

Someone kicked a bucket in her direction. Clutching its sides, she retched up the contents of her stomach. When she was finished, she stared up into the faces of the strangers standing over her. Terror welled in her breast.

Both were loathsome-looking examples of humanity. Clad in the clothes of a workman, the shorter of the two was thin and swarthy. His red hair hung in oily strands to his shoulders. A bulbous nose sat at an odd angle on his narrow, pockmarked face. The other wore the uniform of a sea captain. A long scar split his face from his left eye to his bearded chin. His eyes were dark and held no warmth.

"Welcome to the *Delilah*," he greeted icily, causing the hairs on the back of her neck to rise.

"May I please have my clothes?" Sarah squeaked.

"Throw her the jacket."

She scrambled to cover as much of her person as possible with the brown wool jacket. The garment was wholly inadequate, leaving her lower limbs exposed. She was too frightened to complain. She was too frightened to think. She continued to shake uncontrollably.

"Do you have a name?" the captain demanded.

"Yes." She pushed the word past her lips.

"Well, what is it?" he growled.

"Sarah."

"Do you know where you are?"

Her wide-eyed gaze darted about frantically, searching for some evidence to give lie to what she already knew to be true. She found none, and her gaze returned to the captain. "On a ship," she replied with a tremulous voice.

"Do you know why?" he continued to interrogate her.

Sarah shook her head.

"This idiot here shanghaied you," he bellowed, shoving his hand hard against the chest of the second man.

"I ain't no idiot. I told ya I tried to tell my boss he was a she, but he wouldn't listen," the man whined.

"That's not my problem," the captain informed him.

"I want my part of the money just the same." Frankie held out his hand. "Ya can settle up with Nat anyway ya see fit."

A harsh sound distantly related to laughter rose in the captain's throat. His lips remained in a grim line. "You'll not get a cent out of me. You're lucky I'm letting you leave with your life."

The outstretched hand balled into a fist, then unfurled, one grimy finger pointing in Sarah's direction. "What am I suppose to do with her?"

"Drown her," the captain ordered as he turned on his heel and strode back toward his quarters.

"Okay, up on yer feet," Frankie commanded.

Sarah stayed planted firmly on the deck, staring up at him with horror in her eyes. Her mind was clearer now. She remembered going to the Blue Wheel Saloon, drinking the whiskey, trying to get back to the hotel . . . then waking up here, half-naked and threatened with death. A numbness settled over her heart as she contemplated the gravity of her situation.

"Come on. I ain't got all day." He tried to prod her to her feet.

Sarah shook her head and clung to the deck in desperation. "I don't want to die," she murmured.

"Hell, who does?"

"Please, Mr. . . ."

"Frankie," he supplied the missing name. "Just Frankie."

"Please, Frankie," she pleaded, her eyes meeting his in an attempt to elicit a drop of sympathy. "You don't have to kill me. Just take me back to shore, and we can both go our separate ways."

"Yer way would be straight to the police."

"No. You have my word. If you'll let me go, I won't say a word to anyone," she promised.

"Yeh, and I'd trust ya to keep yer word just as far as I can spit. Ya take me for a fool?"

"Of course not," she hastened to reassure him, her need to survive beginning to override the numbing fear. She furiously searched her mind for something to say that would convince him to let her go. "It just seems . . . well . . . you have obviously gone to a lot of trouble, and it seems a pity you won't get paid. I'd make it worth your while to let me go."

His left eye narrowed. "How much?"

Finally, she sighed, relieved, she had his interest and a modicum of hope. Her life was worth everything, and she quickly decided to offer what she thought would be an irresistible sum to assure his cooperation. "A thousand dollars."

"Ya got that much?"

"Yes."

He rubbed his chin as he considered her offer. "All the money in the world ain't going to do me a bit of good if I'm swinging from a rope."

"But I've already promised I wouldn't tell."

"Hey lady, I learned early in life not to trust no one, 'specially a sweet-faced female . . . but ya've given me an idea." His eyes took on a lickerish gleam as they traveled over her bare limbs.

"What kind of idea?" Sarah asked, hope muted by trepidation.

"Ya get to live another day, and I get to line my pockets. But ya got to cooperate, otherwise it's the deep blue sea for ya. Now, get on those trousers so I can get ya where we're going without causing no heads

96

to turn."

"This could be a trick," she voiced her suspicion.

"Could be." Frankie shrugged. "I'm going. Ya can come or stay as suits yer fancy. But I'll tell ya one thing, ya stay and yer dead fer sure. Cap'n Slodds ain't as generous a man as sweet Frankie."

Sarah scrambled to her feet and pulled on the trousers. She had no more confidence in Frankie than she'd had a moment before, but at least with him she might have a chance. She had not a whit of doubt the captain would kill her without a second thought if he found her on his deck. He had ordered her death nonchalantly, with no sign of remorse. How many others had gone to a watery grave at his bidding? Instinct told her the toll was too monstrous to contemplate.

Cinching her belt around her waist, she faced Frankie squarely. "I'm ready," she said softly.

Frankie climbed down the ladder to his dinghy first, letting her see to herself. With the end of an oar, he indicated a spot at the opposite end of the boat for her to sit.

Sarah mutely followed his directive, clutching the wooden plank that served as her seat with white-knuckled resolve. If Frankie decided to push her overboard, she would not make an easy task of it.

The slap of the waves and creak of the oars filled the silence between them. She sat stiffly, trying to divine what plan this man had for her. His face betrayed nothing. Possibility after possibility filled her head in rapid succession, each more disturbing than the last.

She brought her fingers to her throbbing temples. Whatever his plan, she doubted it would be to her liking.

"The headache'll go away in a day or two," Frankie consoled.

Sarah flinched at the unexpected sound of his voice, but his words afforded some relief. They told her she would be allowed to survive at least another forty-eight hours. But under what conditions? At the moment she was too afraid to seek the answer and decided to sate her curiosity with a less volatile question. "How do you know when my headache will leave?"

"It's from the opium Nat put in yer whiskey."

Sarah looked startled. "I was drugged?"

"Yep, and bopped on the head for good measure," he informed her conversationally.

"Why?"

"Nat figured ya for a man." He eyed her up and down. "Mind telling me why yer dressed the way ya are?"

"I thought it would be safer," Sarah admitted morosely.

A peal of hoarse laughter burst forth from his lips. "Hell lady, the Blue Wheel ain't safe fer man nor beast. If the press gang don't get ya first, the whiskey will do ya in right quick."

"I'll remember that in the future."

He continued to chuckle. "You do that."

She nodded. What she really wanted was to ask him where they were going and what he had in mind to do with her.

Sarah gnawed on her bottom lip. Her unsavory companion lapsed back into silence as he pulled on the oars. Dare she ask him? He didn't emanate the same kind of evil the captain did, and she was growing more used to his company. Her gaze was involuntarily drawn to the cold sea, ink-black under a moonless sky. No! It wasn't worth the risk. Her questions would wait until she had her feet firmly planted on dry ground.

Her eyes measured the distance between the dinghy and the gaslights flickering on the shoreline. If they didn't reach land soon, she feared she wouldn't have to worry about her future as her heart's rapid pounding would wear the vital organ out.

Sarah fervently wished Frankie would volunteer some bit of information. Any conversation would be welcome.

She tried to console herself with the knowledge that when she came up missing, Tyler Bennet was sure to set out in search of her. When and if he found her, he would rant and rave like a madman, but at the moment the prospect of being scolded by his deep voice sounded wonderful.

Her comforting thoughts were replaced by another: she had no idea how long it would take him to realize something was amiss. She hugged herself. She was cold and miserable, and she wanted to be back in her hotel room. Please Tyler, she silently pleaded, forget what I said before about not appreciating your interference. I could use an avenging knight right about now.

An eternity passed before they reached the shore, but when they did, Sarah's spirits revived somewhat. A dash for safety struck her as the best idea she'd had all day, but as the thought formed in her mind, Frankie pulled a long, thin knife from his belt and pressed it into her ribs.

"Now, I want ya to walk real quiet and casual-like

next to me. We're friends, see." He ran a callused hand down her cheek. "Real good friends."

Sarah recoiled from his touch. A warning glare and the point of the stiletto discouraged further retreat, and she fell into step beside him. He grinned. "Thought ya'd see things my way."

Visions of Macky and Mary's Café blended with those of Frankie and the dark alleyways. Fearing she was about to be forcibly inducted into the army of Barbary Coast prostitutes, Sarah felt her mind reel. Horrible, dirty men touching her night after night . . . despite the knife at her ribs, Sarah halted abruptly. "Where are we going?"

Frankie scowled, pushing her deeper into the shadows, but he answered her. "To the Silk Stocking."

"Is it another saloon?"

"Naw, it's a dance hall . . ." he paused in mid sentence. "Ya can sing and dance?"

Performing in a dance hall sounded like heaven compared to what she had been imaging. Surely there would be ample opportunity to escape. Trying to hide her relief, Sarah stated, "I'm sure I can manage."

Frankie snorted. "Hell, don't really matter. Yer other assets'll be enough to suit the purpose. Now get a move on or I'm going to have to kill ya."

"What purpose?" Sarah ventured as she fell back into step.

"Why, to make me a rich man, of course."

"I've already told you I'll pay you handsomely if you'll let me go," she reminded.

"You'll not be goin' anywhere. Got to cover my arse in this mess, and the only way I can do that is to put ya where I can keep an eye on ya. Ya do yer part without complaining, and I'll let ya keep ten percent."

"And my part is to sing and dance for money on a stage," she sought confirmation.

Frankie nodded his greasy head. "That, and provide private entertainment for those that likes what they sees up on the stage. Easy work," he cackled, "Ya can do most of it lying on yer back."

Sarah froze, her face paling. "But . . ."

This time Frankie was not so patient, and he pressed the knife against her hard enough to cut through her clothing and draw blood. "Listen lady, it's the Silk Stocking or a swim in the sea. I thought I'd do ya the favor of letting ya live but," he shrugged his shoulders, "makes no difference to me which ya choose."

Sarah clamped her mouth shut and started walking. She was letting revulsion override logic. No matter what Frankie had planned for her, the Silk Stocking would be her salvation. She would not have to tolerate his company much longer, nor would she have to submit to strange men. She judged him amazingly stupid not to realize once she was onstage all she need do was scream for help, but she had no intention of bringing his lack of foresight to his attention.

When they reached the Silk Stocking, she was not surprised to find it met her expectations. The establishment was as seedy as her companion, but the waves of raucous laughter spilling out into the night air heartened her. Surely at least one man within harbored a vestige of gentlemanly pride and would come to her aid. In no time she would be snug in her own bed.

Leading her around to the back door, Frankie

pushed her down a dimly lit hall into a windowless room. He slammed the door behind her.

Sarah was left alone in the darkness, her tenuous optimism evaporating at the sound of the harsh scraping of a heavy bolt.

Chapter 7

"Are you sure she's not in her room?" Tyler barked at the footman.

"I knocked twice, sir."

"Fool woman," Tyler muttered to himself as he turned and started for the door. The sun had set hours ago.

He reminded himself her absence could be completely innocent. She could be at the theater, enjoying a late supper with a friend . . . but his instincts told him differently.

She had come to him as he had asked, and he hadn't been there. Granted, it wasn't his fault. His other clients had needs to be met; still, he couldn't help feeling culpable.

He crumpled the note in his pocket. Why in the hell hadn't she just waited?

Hailing a hack, he climbed into the conveyance. "Take me to the Blue Wheel Saloon," he ordered.

The driver hunched his shoulders. "I don't like going near them sort of places after dark," he protested.

"You know the place?" Tyler asked.

"Never been in it, but I've heard tales. Why don't you do us both a favor and quench your thirst someplace else?"

"I wish I could," Tyler murmured as much to himself as the driver. There was a cold feeling of dread in the pit of his belly. He didn't know how he knew, but Sarah was frightened and she needed him, and the Blue Wheel was the most logical place to start his search for her. "Are you wearing a gun?" he asked the driver.

"No, sir."

"Here, take this." He handed him one of the pair of six-shooters he had strapped to his hips before leaving the office. "I'll pay you double fare to take me."

The driver hesitated.

"A lady's life may be at stake," Tyler explained impatiently.

"Climb in."

Tyler's agitation increased as he rolled toward his destination. He didn't need the driver's warning to guess what kind of place the Blue Wheel would be. The address told him more than he cared to know.

His thoughts were filled with Sarah. He hated every minute he was away from her and loved every minute he was with her. He understood his admiration for her beauty, her mind, her childlike enthusiasm for life. What defied logic was the intensity of his attraction. Here he was, out of his mind with worry, as if they had been lifelong lovers. Tyler flexed the muscles of his hands. He was thoroughly besotted, and he didn't know whether to laugh or cry.

The Blue Wheel came into view, and it was every bit as bad as he'd imagined it. Jumping from the carriage, he handed the driver a wad of bills. "Stay here. If I don't come out in twenty minutes, call the law."

"Yes, sir."

Tyler covered the distance between the carriage and the saloon doors with rapid strides. His hand rested on the butt of his revolver as he burst into the noisy, smoke-filled room. "I'm looking for Sarah Williams," he shouted, careful to keep his back to the wall.

The raucous activity inside the saloon came to an abrupt halt. Every eye focused on Tyler.

"Who's asking?" Nat, the bartender, asked, reaching under the bar. He lay his own gun on the counter within easy reach.

"I am. Where is she?" Tyler demanded.

"Don't know no Sarah Williams."

"The lady was to meet someone here this afternoon."

"Ain't been a *lady* stepped through those doors in years."

"I have friends in high places and can have this saloon closed down permanently within the hour," Tyler warned. "She's a small woman with a pretty face, dark brown hair, and large green eyes. My guess is she would have come here sometime between four and five o'clock."

"Never seen her."

The two men measured each other's mettle from across the room. Though the bartender was coarse in appearance and speech and probably guilty of any number of crimes, something about his tone and carriage made Tyler believe the man wasn't lying. He didn't know if he was more relieved or distressed. If Sarah had never been here, it increased the likelihood she was simply out for the evening and her absence was not cause for concern.

"Is Smitty Hughes here?"

"I'm Smitty." A ragged man staggered to his feet. "And no, I ain't seen her. She was suppose to meet me here, but she never showed up." As a precautionary afterthought he added, "Don't matter though, 'cause I realized I don't know the fella she's looking for after all."

"Now why doesn't that surprise me? If you do see her, it would be in your best interests to contact my office immediately," Tyler tersely advised Smitty and the bartender. "The firm of Johnson & Bennet has a reputation for never losing a case, and if I find you've had anything to do with the lady's disappearance, I'll see that you rot behind bars. I assume we understand each other?"

"Yes, sir!" they assured him, their deferential tenor evincing they were both men who knew the stakes.

"Good."

"That goes for the rest of you, too. Any of you see or hear anything about Mrs. Williams's whereabouts, come to me. I'll make speaking up worth your time. On the other hand, if you know something and keep silent . . ." His menacing look as his gaze traveled around the room said all that needed to be said.

Confident that he had made his point, Tyler backed out onto the street.

He wasn't sure what he should do next. He could spend the night searching every restaurant and theater in town, but that seemed ill-advised. Their carriages could pass each other on the street and he would never know. He wasn't even sure he should trust his intuition. Was he just imagining this feeling that Sarah needed him? Probably . . . he couldn't think dispassionately where she was concerned. Perhaps the most intelligent course would be to go back to her hotel and wait a while longer.

"Take me back to the Grand," he instructed the driver.

Tyler sat stiffly in the lobby of the Grand Hotel, cursing alternately himself and Sarah as the minutes ticked by. If she had changed her mind about going to meet Smitty at the Blue Wheel Saloon, where did she go? It was true he hadn't made arrangements to call on her this evening, but her female intuition should have told her he would. Did she have other friends in the city? She had never mentioned any by name.

By midnight Tyler was convinced his initial gut feeling that Sarah was in trouble had to be true. Now his problem was where to look next.

If he held to the notion she never made it to the Blue Wheel, she must have been waylaid. She could be anywhere, including lying dead in some back alley in a pool of her own blood. He pushed the thought from his head before it could take root and completely unnerve him.

Other possibilities came to mind: she could be injured, on a ship a victim of white slavery, been robbed and become disoriented, at this very moment being pressed into service at a Barbary Coast brothel . . . His mind supplied him with an endless list of woeful fates.

Now was not the time for contemplation; it was the

time for action. Tyler seized control of his emotions. He would rouse Thaddeus, instructing him to hire every available detective in town while he began a methodical search of every inch of the city forthwith. Leaving a message at the desk that Sarah should contact his office immediately should she happen to return on her own, he set off.

Though Thaddeus voiced the opinion that Tyler's reaction to Sarah's absence was overwrought, he grudgingly agreed to do as he was asked.

Tyler began his search at the waterfront, checking every alley, stopping in every dive, questioning everyone he met. By dawn he had been joined by a legion of detectives. Organizing the city into sections, they searched throughout the day, following flimsy leads that proved false in every instance. The detective who was posted at the Blue Wheel learned nothing.

Tyler concentrated his efforts in the Barbary Coast district. Exhaustion was stayed by anxiety. He continued to comb the streets as the sun lowered into the sea.

Hours later he had yet to rest, and the slump of his broad shoulders evinced his growing frustration and fatigue. He stepped into yet another brothel.

Sarah stared numbly at the scanty red corset, black garter, stockings, and silver shoes Frankie thrust into her hands. She had spent a miserable night and equally miserable day locked in this room, and her mood was black.

Every time she had been brought what passed for food in this establishment, she had been explained her duties at the Silk Stocking in terms both explicit and vulgar. She tried to blank out the words, fantasizing her escape to buttress hope and shield herself from reality, but when she had not eagerly responded to his instruction, Frankie had made it clear if she failed to attract a man to her bed tonight, he would initiate her into her new life himself. The mere thought was enough to make her tremble.

"Well, put it on," he urged when she made no move to don her costume.

She continued to stare at him. "Where are the rest of my clothes?"

"That's it, darling."

"You can't expect me to go out on stage half-naked," she stated, despite the fact she knew full well that was exactly what he expected.

"Now, don't be shy," he cajoled. "If ya'd like, I can get something to shore up yer nerves."

"No, thank you," Sarah responded civilly, doing her best to cultivate an air of resigned acceptance of her fate lest she rouse suspicion. She had every intention of continuing to do so until she was in a position to get away.

Frankie's gaze traveled over her. "Are ya sure? Most of the girls take a little something before they go onstage."

"I'll manage just fine on my own," she assured him, despite the temptation to insulate herself from her imminent humiliation. If she was to have a chance of escape, it was crucial she be in full control of her wits.

"Suit yerself. Be ready in five minutes and remember, me and my friend," he waved a gun under her nose, "will be watching in the wings. Embarrass me and you'll be breakfast for the sharks."

"I'll remember," she avowed.

As soon as the door closed, Sarah set about changing her clothes. She wanted to be done before Frankie came back. She tried to think of the garments he had given her as a disguise, just like the male raiment she now removed; however, there just wasn't enough of her new costume to disguise much.

She pulled at the top of the corset in hopes of better covering her bosom only to expose more of her derriere.

After playing tug-of-war with the garment for several minutes to no good effect, Sarah sighed in frustration. It was hopeless. Whatever charms she possessed would be viewed by many tonight.

She paced the perimeter of her cell. The walls of her spartan chamber boasted no mirror in which to peruse her reflection, and Sarah thanked Providence for the small blessing.

Having had more than ample time to contemplate her situation, she reminded herself she had no one but herself to blame, and for the moment she also had no one but herself to depend upon. Her thoughts spontaneously turned to Tyler. Surely he was out there somewhere, looking for her. Thinking of him comforted her, bolstering her flagging spirits and courage.

A few sweet kisses were not enough. She wanted the chance to get to know him better. She wanted to feel his touch, hear his warm, honeyed compliments. . . . She must find a way to escape.

Knitting her fingers together, Sarah tested her voice. A series of pathetic squeaks assaulted her ears. "Please, we're going to get shot if you don't manage better than that," she scolded her throat. She tried again and produced a more recognizable melody.

"Not bad," Frankie opined as he threw open the door. "Come on, songbird. Yer on next."

He stepped aside, allowing her to go first. Sarah knew he did this not out of gentlemanliness, but so he could put himself and his weapon between her and the back door. They walked down a long, dimly lit hallway, then up a short flight of stairs.

Frankie clamped a restraining hand on her arm as they stood waiting in the wings for a befeathered redheaded creature warbling a bawdy ditty to finish the last notes of her song.

Despite the off-key nature of her performance, she was rewarded with thunderous applause and a goodly amount of coin, which she greedily gathered and deposited into her bodice.

As the redhead approached the wings, Frankie gave Sarah a hearty shove in the direction of center stage. Regaining her balance, she walked with what she hoped passed for dignity to the X painted on the wooden stage.

Her heart pounded as her eyes scanned the audience. It was all male, with the exception of a sprinkling of prostitutes, and appeared to subscribe to the same code of cleanliness, or lack thereof, as Frankie. Everyone stared at her bare limbs with rapacious eyes. Sarah felt the heat in her cheeks move down her throat and bosom and the trickle of perspiration under her arms turn into a flood.

The pianist struck a few chords, then began to play a tune unfamiliar to her. She stood mute, not knowing what to do. Out of the corner of her eye she saw

Frankie raise his gun.

"I don't know the words of the song," she hissed as panic seized her, earning herself a roar of laughter from the motley crowd.

"Play something the lady knows," one fellow shouted and was quickly joined by several others.

The pianist started to play another tune, then another as Sarah continued to shake her head and shrug. His hands crashed on the keyboard. "What song do you know?" he demanded in exasperation.

"Sweet Genevieve," Sarah offered meekly.

"Well, why the hell didn't you say so from the beginning?"

He struck the first note. Sarah glanced nervously in Frankie's direction. He cocked the hammer of his firearm. Without hesitation she burst into song.

"But still the hands of mem-ry weave the blissful dreams of long ago . . ."

To her profound relief, her voice cooperated admirably. As she sang, Sarah tried to think. She had to solicit help before she was whisked offstage, but there was not a face in the crowd that inspired hope.

"Move!"

She jumped, halting in mid note at the sound of Frankie's hoarse whisper.

"What?" she whispered back.

"Don't stand there like a stick. Wiggle yer arse!"

The exchange was easily overheard by the entire audience, and they whistled and stomped their feet to second Frankie's command.

Sarah took a deep breath and began to timidly swing her hips from side to side as she once again took up the words of the song.

"You've got the right idea, but you got to put your heart into it, honey." Three men near the front stood on their seat and ground their hips in a circular motion.

"And shake yer titties," another advised between long pulls on his bottle of whiskey.

Sarah fought back the urge to scream back at them that she was doing the best she could and tried to give them what they wanted.

"Sarah!"

She heard her name being shouted from the back of the room, and her eyes immediately picked out Tyler's horrified face from the crowd.

"Tyler! I'm so glad to see you," she shouted back, so relieved to see him she momentarily forgot about Frankie's gun. A bullet whizzed past her ear, pricking her memory. She dived from the stage into the crowd and was immediately lost in a tangle of limbs.

Pandemonium broke loose all around her. There was more gunfire. Sarah dropped to the floor, crawling on her belly under the seats and between the legs of the patrons toward the back of the dance hall.

The roar in her ears was deafening as the audience took sides, shouting encouragement to both her and Frankie. She was stepped on more than once, but she crept on determinedly.

Concern for herself was muted by her fear for Tyler's safety. She would never forgive herself if something happened to him because of her.

Her hands and knees filled with splinters from the floor, and the stench that assaulted her nostrils was unbelievable. She gasped for breath in small, painful gulps.

113

Where was he? She couldn't hear his voice above the cacophony of the crowd.

She had almost reached the door when a pair of rough hands picked her up off the floor.

"Lookie what we have here," her captor shouted, raising her above his head.

Sarah caught a glimpse of Tyler running toward her before she was unceremoniously stuffed back under the chair and allowed to continue on her way.

She traveled a few more feet and was grabbed again.

"Tyler," she cried in relief as she fell into his arms.

Shielding her body with his, he pushed her through the crowd and out the door. He bustled her into a waiting hack, shouting at the driver to crack the whip as the crowd spilled out behind them onto the street.

Sarah collapsed against the leather seat of the carriage as they left Frankie and the patrons of the Silk Stocking in a cloud of dust. She pulled in long drafts of fresh air as Tyler covered her with his coat.

"You don't know how relieved I was to see you," she said, smiling wanly as she gazed up at his welcome visage. "Thank you for rescuing me."

"Are you all right?" he asked anxiously.

Sarah took quick inventory of her person and nodded. "Yes."

"Good. Then you can tell me what the hell were you doing in there!" His voice exploded, hitting her like a slap in the face. Gone was the look of concern, and in its place was the face of a man filled with quivering rage.

"I was kidnaped," Sarah replied with a start.

"But not from your hotel room," he stated.

"No. It happened while I was in the Blue Wheel Saloon."

"Damn you!" He made a mental note to begin legal proceedings against Smitty Hughes and the lying owner of the Blue Wheel first thing in the morning. "Why couldn't you have waited for me to go for you? Do you realize how long it has been since I've seen my bed? Or that I've been exposed to more human vice in the last twenty-four hours than most men experience in a lifetime?" He paused for breath. "Half the detectives in town are out combing the streets for you."

Sarah lowered her gaze to her lap. "I'm sorry."

"Sorry? You're *sorry?* That's *all* you have to say for yourself? I told you it wasn't safe for a woman to traipse the streets alone, but did you listen?"

Her head snapped up. She was tired and upset and still weak from fear. He had no right to add to her misery by yelling at her. "I didn't go as a woman. I dressed as a man," she informed him.

"And they saw through your disguise in a minute, just as I warned you they would. You're not naive. You're beefbrained."

"They did *not* see through my disguise," Sarah argued, her voice rising to match his in volume. "And neither did your partner Thaddeus Johnson, whom I strolled right past less than a block from my hotel. In fact, it was not until they stripped me down on that ship that they realized I was not a man."

"Stripped you down on a ship?" Tyler repeated in horror.

"Yes. I was shanghaied, whatever that means," she continued tersely.

His jaw dropped. When he spoke, his voice had

115

regained a normal volume. "You're lucky you're still alive."

"Yes, I know," Sarah agreed softly, her anger leaving as quickly as it had come. "Captain Slodds wanted Frankie to drown me, but he took me to the Silk Stocking instead."

"Frankie?"

"The man who was shooting at me on the stage."

Tyler shook his head in an attempt to order his thoughts. "Where does he fit into all this?"

"I think he works for the bartender at the Blue Wheel."

As she answered him, Tyler noticed the strong odor of bay rum rising from her person, and he stiffened. "Did he or anyone else," he swallowed hard before he forced himself to finish his question, "molest you?"

"No," Sarah reassured him. His nostrils twitched, and she realized what had brought on his question. "I splashed on a generous amount of bay rum as part of my manly disguise," she explained.

"At least I was able to find you before you suffered that indignity," Tyler said more to himself than her.

"How *did* you find me?"

"Caroline Poulet. When no one could find a trace of you, I asked her to keep her eyes and ears open. She heard a rumor that a new girl was debuting at the Silk Stocking." He captured her gaze with his, drinking in the sight of her. "Lord, I'm glad you're all right."

"You really do care what happens to me, don't you?" she asked, a little awed by the depth of feeling emanating from him.

"When the strong take advantage of the weak, I always care."

116

Her eyes darkened. "Is that why you care what happens to me, because you see me as weak?"

"No. You're not weak, just misguided."

The first part of his answer pleased her, and though the second part did not, "misguided" was definitely an improvement over "beefbrained." She decided to make another stab at offering the olive branch. "I'll admit I was wrong to go alone in this instance, and I hope this time you will accept my apology. I truly am sorry for the trouble I've caused you."

"Apology accepted." Gathering her in his arms, he tucked her against his side. "Nevertheless, I am not letting you out of my sight again."

"Won't that make it rather hard to see to the needs of your other clients?" she teased, snuggling against him.

"I've nothing pressing on my calendar, and I'm long overdue for a vacation. Thaddeus can handle things for a while."

She cocked her head so she could see the expression on his face. "You're serious, aren't you?"

"Yes, ma'am."

"I don't need a nursemaid," Sarah objected.

"No, you need a keeper." He rubbed at a smudge on her chin. "God help me, but I've taken a fancy to you, and I would just as soon you didn't get yourself killed before I work up the nerve to propose."

Sarah's eyes widened and she sat straight up. "Propose? As in marriage?"

Tyler was rather startled himself at the words that had passed his lips, but as he sat gazing into Sarah's upturned face, he knew he was going to make her his wife. "That's the kind," he assured her.

My God, was he serious? She couldn't tell. She prayed he wasn't. Schooling her tone to reflect light-hearted skepticism, she commented, "Don't you think you're rushing things? After all, we've known each other less than two weeks."

"Of course I know I'm rushing things but, damn it, you've forced my hand," he replied. "I want you for my wife, and I'm not going to risk losing you. Before I met you, I believed in long, slow courtships, but you won't allow a man to behave sensibly." His manner changed and his eyes took on a molten glow. "Besides, after seeing you dressed as you are, I don't want to wait."

Pulling the borrowed coat up to her chin, Sarah glared at him. *Marriage.* She instinctively recoiled. She didn't want to ruin their friendship with marriage. She liked things just the way they were. "No," she stated adamantly.

"No, what?"

"No, you can't propose marriage to me."

"Why not?"

"I've been married."

He chuckled at her objection. "I assure you it is perfectly legal for a widow to remarry."

"I know that. I mean . . . I don't want to get married . . . *to anyone.*"

Tyler looked crestfallen. "Oh."

"It's not you." Sarah tried to smooth the frown from his face with her fingers. "Honestly. If I did want to get married again, you would be first on my list. But I came out here to escape marriage, not to contract one." She took his hand in hers. "I want you to know I like you more than I have ever liked any other man, and I am immensely flattered by your offer."

His expression remained morose, and she struggled to find the right thing to say. Tyler Bennet was a fine man. Any number of women would jump at the chance to marry him. She just wasn't one of them. Her eyes brightened as she warmed to an idea.

"You know what I think? I think you're giddy from worry and lack of sleep. You don't really know what you're saying. Yes, I'm sure that's it. Go home . . . get a good night's sleep. In the morning I bet you won't even remember this conversation."

"And if I do?" he queried.

"Ah . . . let's handle one crisis at a time," Sarah replied a bit too ebulliently.

Tyler's frown deepened. "We *will* talk about it in the morning," he assured her.

Sarah focused her gaze out the window. "I'd rather not."

"When do you want to talk about it?"

"Never."

"Can't agree to that." Tyler shook his head. "But you do make one valid point: I'm too tired to carry on this conversation right now. Let's just go to bed."

"What?" Sarah squealed.

"In case you haven't noticed, the carriage has stopped, and we are sitting in front of the Grand Hotel," he explained patiently. "Give me your room key, and I'll bring down some clothes."

Sarah glanced down at herself. She had forgotten she couldn't just walk into the lobby. "I lost my key," she said.

"I'll get another at the desk. I need to send a message to Thaddeus to call off the search anyway."

119

Tyler returned a few minutes later with a plain skirt and blouse. He handed them and the new key to her, then closed the door of the carriage.

Sarah quickly dressed, then stepped from the vehicle.

"Come on." Tyler offered his arm. "If I don't walk you to your room within the next minute, I can't guarantee I'll have the strength to make it up the stairs again."

"It really isn't necessary to escort . . ."

"I'll decide what is necessary."

The poor man did look exhausted. Rather than waste time arguing, Sarah allowed him to do as he pleased.

The lobby of the Grand was nearly deserted, and no one except the doorman and the bespectacled clerk behind the front desk paid any attention to them as they ascended the stairs together.

Unlocking her door, she turned to tell Tyler goodnight, but he had already stepped past her into the room. He mumbled something unintelligible, threw himself across her bed, and fell into a deep sleep.

Chapter 8

Sarah scowled at Tyler's recumbent form. "And just where do you suggest I sleep, Mr. Bennet?" she asked him.

The sound of his steady breathing answered her.

"I'm tired too, you know," she continued to carry on a one-sided conversation. "I was the one who was drugged and kidnaped. I was the one who was forced up on that stage. Then, just when I thought my life was back to normal, you had to propose. Now this. I'm sorry, but it's too much for one evening. You'll have to go home."

Marching to the bed, she gave him a hearty shake, but he only moaned in his sleep and curled into a ball.

Sarah stared at him, her arms folded across her chest. "Fine. Be uncooperative." She turned her back on him, muttering in a most unladylike manner.

Determined to ignore him, she focused her attention on herself. She was a mess. Calling for a bath at this late hour was impractical, so she settled for sponging off the thickest layer of grime with the water provided by the porcelain pitcher and bowl in the washstand. While she bathed, she stole frequent glances over her shoulder, but she need not have worried. Her roommate did not stir.

Pulling her most modest flannel nightgown over her head, she tended the splinters in her hands and knees. Her ministration was interrupted by frequent yawns; still, when she was finished, she found herself searching for some task to give her legitimate reason to avoid her bed.

After tidying her clothes and brushing her hair, there was nothing left to be done.

She approached the bed and gave Tyler another shake. He didn't budge. Sighing in resignation, she pulled off his boots and turned down the light.

In the morning he would probably name her wanton, but she was not going to spend the night perched on a chair. It was her bed, and she had been pining for the warmth of its downy softness too long to deny herself its comfort. Besides, nothing untoward could possibly happen. Tyler was sleeping as soundly as a hibernating bear.

She smiled at him fondly. His clothes were wrinkled, and dark circles ringed his eyes. She really had put him through a lot. Sarah could not deny she was touched by the intensity of his concern.

"All right, Mr. Bennet, move over," she forced a flippant tone. Knowing full well he was too deep into sleep to obey her command, she immediately set to rearranging his limbs on the far side of the bed. When she was satisfied there was enough distance between them, she covered him with a quilt and slipped under the covers on the opposite side.

Within minutes, she too was sound asleep.

Sarah awoke slowly, stretching her limbs like a contented cat. She nestled closer to the warm body lying beside her, nuzzling her nose into the fabric of his shirt. What a lovely dream she had been having. She smiled with remembered pleasure.

"Have a nice sleep?" A deep masculine voice penetrated the fog of serene slumber.

She bolted upright, but an arm across her shoulders held her down.

"Don't get up yet," Tyler cajoled. "I'm having too much fun holding you in my arms. A man could get used to waking up with you in his bed."

Sarah managed to free one arm enough that she was able to push a strand of hair from her eyes. He was right, of course. Lying abed together was a most pleasant experience—*as long as one didn't think about it.* She met his gray-blue eyes with a less-than-steady gaze.

"First, this is not your bed, it is mine," she reminded. "Second, you are here by squatter's rights, not invitation. When you crashed to the mattress like a felled redwood, there was simply nothing I could do about it."

"Third," he pressed his fingers to her lips, "I'm going to kiss you."

Before she could protest, he captured her lips with his, caressing them slowly, gently, until she melted in his arms. As he pulled her against him, the kiss deepened. His lips demanded, begged, worshipped all at the same time, leaving her breathless and blushing.

He teased her with his tongue, sending delightful

shivers up her spine. His hands massaged her. Sarah clung to him, drinking in the passion he offered.

If he had asked for more, in that moment, Sarah could not have said if she would have said yea or nay, but she did not have to face the choice. Abruptly releasing her, he swung his legs over the side of the bed, coming face-to-face with his reflection in the mirror atop the dresser.

"God, I look a wretch." He combed his fingers through his blond hair. "Our first stop this morning will have to be my house, so I can change."

Sarah stared up at the ceiling, her bottom lip protruding slightly. Why had he stopped? Did he find her undesirable? She felt lonely without his arms around her.

Dismissing her wayward thoughts, she sat up. There were other, more important matters to consider. She was not deaf to the casual way he assumed she would accompany him. It wasn't that she didn't want his company. After her recent experience with the underworld of San Francisco, she would be more than willing to have him close by her side. It was the way he took her compliance for granted instead of requesting her society that disconcerted her. She tried to conjure up genuine feelings of rancor at his high-handed manner but found she could not. Still, she felt compelled to challenge him.

"Why don't you go on without me?" she suggested in the same casual tone he had used with her. "What I really want to do this morning is take a long soak in a hot bath."

"Fine with me," he replied courteously. "Would you like breakfast before or after you soak?"

Her stomach rumbled noisily at the suggestion of food.

"Before," he answered for her as he pulled on his boots. "I'll see to it at once."

Without so much as a fare-thee-well he was out the door. Sarah stared after him. "Well, it was easy enough to be rid of him," she congratulated herself.

She told herself she should be relieved he was gone, but unfortunately the only emotion she could lay claim to was confusion. Last night's proposal, this morning's kiss, his sudden departure . . . she certainly couldn't make any sense out of his behavior.

Her own behavior was just as incomprehensible. Why hadn't she tried harder to eject him from her room last night? Why had she let him kiss her like that? Why had she liked it so much?

With a determined shake of her head, she set about making up the bedclothes.

She had just finished the task when a knock on the door sent her spinning around. Without waiting for her to answer, Tyler stepped back into the room.

"What are you doing back here?" she demanded.

"I just left to order breakfast and a bath," he informed her, bemused that she need ask the obvious.

Sarah frowned. "I thought you were going home to change."

"I am. After we have breakfast and you bathe."

It was patent she wasn't up to puzzling out the motives behind his actions this morning. A strategic retreat to solitude seemed the wisest course.

"You can't stay here," she insisted, searching her mind for something to convince him. "What will people say?"

"The same thing they will say when it becomes common knowledge I slept in your bed last night. They'll say we are lovers."

"But we're not," Sarah protested, though the idea was not wholly repugnant.

He grinned. "I'm willing to remedy the situation any time you say the word."

She presented her back to him so he couldn't read her expression. "You know very well that's not what I mean."

Laying his hands on her shoulders, he turned her so she faced him again. A good night's sleep had not changed his mind; it had strengthened his resolve. "If you're worried about your reputation, my marriage offer still stands."

Sarah's gaze rose to meet his. "So you remembered."

"Didn't I say I would?" His eyes twinkled merrily.

"We barely know each other," she reminded him.

"I know all I need to know about you, but if you need more time to feel secure in your decision, I'll do my best to accommodate you. How long do you need? A week? A month? Two months?"

"I told you last night, I don't want to get married."

"I love you," he cajoled, kissing the tip of her nose.

Her chin dropped to her chest, and she pretended great interest in her toes. "I wish you wouldn't say that."

"Why? It's true," he stated confidently.

"Because I love my freedom."

He kissed the top of her head. "I won't put fetters on you."

"Yes, you will." She sighed in frustration, willing him to understand. "You won't be able to help your-

126

self. It's human nature."

"You make marriage sound like a prison."

"It is. You forget — I have been married, whereas you have not. I told you before, I came out west to escape marriage. My mother had another man halfway to the altar and was intent on dragging me there to join him. Greed can bring such misery to one's life." She shuddered at the memory. "A woman gives up everything when she marries."

"Not in California," he contended. "A woman may retain property in her own name. I'm financially successful in my own right. I am not proposing marriage to get my hands on your money, if that's what's worrying you."

She eyed him reflectively. "The thought never crossed my mind. What I'm trying to explain, and I'm obviously doing a very poor job of it, is: I don't want to have to answer to anyone ever again."

"Not all ties that bind are constricting," he promised. "I want you, and quite honestly I fear I won't be able to keep my hands off your creamy flesh much longer." His eyes glowed as he stroked her arms from shoulder to fingertip, clasping her hands in his. "Even in that virginal nightgown you're wearing, you make my blood run hot. Gentleman's honor demands I make our union legal."

Though his touch titillated her senses, she remained steadfast. "I appreciate your sterling sense of honor, but I'm not willing to sacrifice my freedom for your honor's sake."

He was afraid she might be obstinate. Though aided in his purpose by overwhelming exhaustion, he had spent last night in her room by design. He smiled roguishly. "But you're forgetting the issue of your reputation. I *did* spend the night in your bed."

"I care not a whit for my reputation," Sarah informed him.

"Then why are you worried about what people will say?"

"I'm not," she admitted. "The question was merely a ploy to get you to leave. *You're* the one who cares about that sort of thing."

"Ah, but a man is allowed a certain amount of license when it comes to amorous exploits."

"Here in the wild wild west, so are widows with enough money to take care of themselves." Sarah met his thrust with one of her own.

"Not as much as the gossip columns might lead you to believe," he warned, his tone becoming serious.

"That is neither here nor there. *I* don't give a whit."

"Fine." But his taut expression revealed that the results of their conversation were far from fine with him. "Then I shall enjoy your private company without compunction."

"Fine."

For a few minutes, frustrated silence reigned. Tyler knew he had gone about presenting the idea of marriage all wrong, but hell, he had been dead tired last night and couldn't be held responsible for anything he said or did. This morning, when he had awakened with Sarah in his arms, he'd naturally thought everything was going to work out just as he'd hoped. And the kisses they shared . . . Sarah most definitely did not kiss like an indifferent woman.

Any other female would be demanding marriage after a man spent the night in her bed, but not Sarah.

If he could convince himself she found him repulsive, he could understand her aversion to marrying him. But damn it, he knew she found him attractive. He had waited thirty-two years to fall in love. If he had known it was going to be such a complicated matter, he would have waited another thirty-two.

Believing there was nothing to be gained in stoic silence — and much to be lost — he took a deep breath and extended his hand. "I know you're not ready to be my wife, but can we be friends again?" he queried.

Profoundly relieved he had decided to be sensible, Sarah smiled and shook his hand vigorously. "Friends," she repeated, as eager as he to bury the hatchet. She knew she didn't want Tyler Bennet to walk out of her life — not yet. Despite her love of independence, she was fast coming to the conclusion she needed his help to find her father. Experience might be the best teacher, but her last experience nearly proved fatal. Besides, they needed more time together to . . . enjoy their relationship, she finished the sentence with a vague promise that intimated future fun — as long as she could hold his nesting instinct at bay.

Breakfast came, and they both consumed it with relish. Conversation, though minimal, was pleasant. The maid had barely cleared away the dishes when the hot water for Sarah's bath arrived.

The tub sat in an open alcove, and once the men had left, Sarah ushered Tyler toward the door. He allowed her to push him to the threshold; then he stood his ground.

"Good day, Mr. Bennet," she hinted firmly.

"I told you last night, I am not letting you out of my sight," he reminded, refusing to budge.

"But I want to take a bath."

"Then take it."

"Not with you here." Sarah put her hand on the knob. He covered her hand with his.

"I'm afraid you'll have to, because I'm not going anywhere."

If it wasn't one thing, it was another with him this morning, she sighed. Schooling her expression, she sweetly suggested, "You could wait in the lobby."

He nodded affirmatively. "I could, but I'm not going to."

"Tyler," she complained. "I really am trying to be patient with you."

"And I appreciate your forbearance."

"Leave now, before I have you thrown out." She raised her voice, setting her lips in determination.

"No," he replied calmly.

She changed tactics. "Please . . ."

Tyler released her hand and strolled across the room, putting a goodly distance between himself and the avenue of exit. "I'm sorry, Sarah, but having spent most of the last two days worried sick about you, I have no intention of leaving you to your own devices."

"All I'm going to do is take a bath." She spoke slowly, emphasizing each word.

"So you say."

"You act as if I'm some scheming hoyden."

He answered her with an elegant shrug.

"I want you to leave," she demanded, tapping her foot impatiently.

"Why?" he asked, maintaining his maddening calm.

"Because I can't take my clothes off with you here."

"You didn't seem to have any trouble standing naked on that stage in front of a room full of men."

"My kidnapper had a gun pointed at me," she reminded in exasperation. "I'm sorry to disappoint you, but I didn't prefer death to dishonor. Besides, I wasn't naked, only half so."

"Quite true," he conceded. "But I am only an audience of one, so you should have no trouble dealing with the elimination of a few scanty undergarments."

"Tyler Bennet, I don't find this funny," she warned, her knuckles itching to wipe the grin off his handsome face. Why was he making an issue of a perfectly natural request? Certainly after her reaction to his previous advances, he should understand her reluctance to place herself in such a vulnerable situation.

Reading the reason for her reluctance, he magnanimously offered, "Would it help if I closed my eyes?"

"No."

"What if I turned my back?"

"Still, not good enough."

"Then I'm afraid we are at an impasse," he stated. "I've made my final concession, and your bathwater is growing cold."

The set of his jaw convinced Sarah that trying to reason with the stubborn man was pointless. She could call the house guards, forgo her bath, or tolerate his company. She glowered at him. What was she afraid of, anyway? It wasn't as if she feared he was going to ravish her. Despite his flowery flattery, earlier when she had lain willingly in his arms, he had fled the bed as if she had the plague. It was the principle of the matter more than the compromising nature of the situation that bothered her.

She eyed the inviting water filling her bathtub. Her

first option would cause a scene, and her water would grow cold before she could make use of it. The drawback of the second was obvious. After a few more moments' contemplation, she reluctantly judged her last option as the least of three evils.

"Turn around," she ordered tersely.

"Always willing to oblige a lady," Tyler replied in a thick drawl as he turned his back to her.

"Hah! And you wonder why I won't marry you."

He winced as the remark hit home, and Sarah wished she could take it back.

"I'm sorry, that wasn't a very nice thing to say," she apologized as she quickly slipped out of her clothes and stepped into the tub.

"I deserved it," he said, his tone unreadable.

Sarah stared at his back. He was right, but she hadn't the heart to tell him so.

The warm water was soothing, and she began to relax a little.

At first she kept a careful eye on Tyler, but it was soon apparent he was as good as his word and would not turn around.

Despite his gallantry, Sarah felt compelled to finish her bath as soon as possible; however, if she did, he would know he had cowed her, and that was something her pride could not allow. She determined to stay in the tub until the water grew unbearably tepid. Raising one leg from the water, she slowly drew the washcloth over her bare skin, working the soap into a rich lather.

Tyler swallowed hard as he watched Sarah's naked reflection in the mirror. God, she was beautiful! No doubt about it, he was going to make this woman his wife.

He imagined the ecstasy of the washcloth as it caressed her skin and a low moan escaped his lips.

Startled, Sarah sank deeper into the tub. "Is something wrong?"

"No, nothing at all." He was quick to reassure her. "You just go on and enjoy your bath."

"Are you sure?"

"Nothing would give me greater pleasure."

There was something not quite innocent about the way he made the statement, but Sarah decided to let the matter lie and returned her full attention to scrubbing every inch of her skin—a task she accomplished with slow, sensuous strokes.

Though his blood coursed hot in his veins, Tyler managed admirably until she began to soap her breasts. In the mirror he watched them bob below the water's surface, peeking out to tease him, then slip from view again. Her nipples were pink and taut, and he mentally smacked his lips.

He knew the mirror was a cheap trick, but his long-range intentions were honorable, and he had little trouble justifying his lapse in manners in his own mind. Granted, he would kill any other man who dare try taking advantage of Sarah's naiveté in this manner, but as her future husband a man had certain rights. Besides, the engaging view afforded him by the mirror was not procured by sly cunning but was the result of fortuitous fate. A man couldn't refuse such a blessing.

His mental conversation came to an abrupt halt as Sarah rose from the tub and began sudsing the soft, rosy cheeks of her buttocks, allowing him fleeting, tantalizing glimpses of the triangle of curly hair marking the apex of her womanhood.

The pressure in his loins turned from pleasure to bittersweet pain, and a thin film of perspiration coated his brow.

Maybe this wasn't such a good idea after all, he chided himself. A few more minutes of this and he was going to be undone. Snatching his coat from the bedpost, he faced her squarely. "I'll be in the lobby if you should need me."

Sarah barely heard his words over her own sputtered gasps as she retreated under the surface of the water.

Chapter 9

It took a long while for Sarah to work up the nerve to peer down into the lobby. If she hadn't been absolutely sure Tyler would be up to fetch her, she might not have come down at all. But since he had stubbornly committed to sticking by her side, and she was not fond of the idea of being alone, she had no choice but to brazen out the day.

She wasn't sure which bothered her more, the fact he had seen her in the altogether or her own reaction.

Her initial embarrassment was comprehensible, but after he had left she had been positively obsessed with wondering what he had thought about what he had seen. She hoped he found her attractive. Not that it mattered. She had no desire to go to bed with him. Physical relations between man and woman were not something for which she harbored fond memories. It was one of those chores of married life she was more than glad to leave behind.

Still, she could not completely squelch her curiosity. Henry, after all, had been an old man, and Tyler was young and virile. Coupling might be more tolerable with him. He did kiss nicely.

His words came back to her: "I fear I won't be able to keep my hands off you much longer . . . you make my blood run hot." A surge of primitive feminine elation raised the temperature of her own blood. It made her giddy to think she might be capable of wielding that kind of erotic influence over a desirable male of the species.

She reminded herself that despite his passionate prose and the pining look he had given her as she stood naked in the bath, he had not taken advantage of the opportunity to make love to her earlier. Was it his gentlemanly honor or a lack of genuine ardor that propelled him from her bed?

She grinned a puckish grin. It might be more comfortable to cling to a belief in the second reason, but she didn't think a man proposed marriage on such short notice unless lust was a compelling factor. She quivered with anticipation, fully acknowledging the carnal energy that flowed between them whenever they were together. Perhaps she should leave the door open to the possibility of testing the waters of passion with Tyler Bennet. She would not pursue the issue, but neither would she avoid it. She would let fate and the vagaries of whim settle her course, if and when the opportunity presented itself.

Fortified with this notion, she faltered only twice as she descended the stairs. When she spied Tyler waiting patiently in a chair, a copy of the *Chronicle* held open in his hands, she took a deep breath and crossed the room to him.

Lowering his paper, he watched her approach, a gratified smile on his lips. After his faux pas upstairs, he had half feared she wasn't coming down at all. Her presence proved she must feel something for him.

"I was just about ready to come up and check on you," he greeted her nonchalantly. "I was beginning to think you had given me the slip again."

Sarah stared at him. He had forgotten about the bath incident just like that? No words of apology were forthcoming? It maddened her that he could be so cool when she was fighting the blush threatening to stain her cheeks. Ever so subtly she ground her heel into the toe of his boot.

He grimaced.

"Good morning, Mr. Bennet." She smiled sweetly. "Any interesting headlines?"

"Only one."

"And what might that be?"

"Prominent Local Lawyer Lamed by Vengeful Widow."

"Do tell." She lay her hand above her bosom, feigning curiosity. "Anyone I know?"

"Yes, as a matter of fact, and if you don't get off my toes this instant I'm going to turn you over my knee, brat."

She called off her assault. He rose, offering his arm. After giving him a scathing look, she accepted it.

"Do you prefer to walk or take a carriage?" he queried solicitously.

"Walk," Sarah replied without hesitation, feeling a strong need to work off a little nervous energy.

Tyler escorted her out the door into the bright light of day.

"Sorry about this morning," he begged pardon as

they started down the street.

She nodded her approval. "I was wondering when and if you were going to get around to apologizing."

"I was not at my best this morning," he confessed.

"You broke your word," she charged, unwilling to let him off the hook too easily.

"The circumstances were dire."

"Nevertheless, you should not have turned around when you promised you would not."

He averted his gaze, a guilty blush coloring his cheeks. "Turning around was the least of my sins."

Sarah looked perplexed. "I don't understand."

He cleared his throat. "You'd be wise to drape your mirror the next time you take a bath."

A mental picture of where he had been standing while she took her bath flashed in her mind, and comprehension was instant. She yanked her hand off his arm. "You scoundrel!"

"I was tempted beyond my capacity to resist," he explained, his expression contrite except for the dancing fires in his eyes.

"You feign innocence?" Sarah glared at him in wide-eyed consternation. "I dare say you had the whole ordeal planned out from the start."

"No, but I would have had I thought of it," he admitted. "As F. E. Smedley said, 'All's fair in love and war.'"

"Mr. Bennet, if we are going to continue this friendship you are going to have to . . ."

"Yes?" he prodded.

"You are going to have to . . ." What? What was it she wanted him to do? "You're going to have to tell me the rules."

"But that would spoil the game."

"And what game are we playing?"

"Seduction."

Chagrin and excitement battled for supremacy as the rose in Sarah's cheeks turned to scarlet. If she had any sense at all she would turn tail and run, but doing the sensible thing had gained her little she was proud of in this life. Running now would be like throwing away a rousing novel just when the adventure reached its climax. She just had to know what happened next no matter what the outcome.

She wished she had a flippant comment to give him in answer, but her wit seemed momentarily to have deserted her, and she remained silent. To fill the void she pretended great interest in the local architecture.

The many-storied clapboard houses nestled next to each other along the hill. The higher up they went, the more expensive and elaborate the homes became. The sun sparkled off ornately designed leaded glass. Cornices crowned porch pillars. Turrets, towers, and bay windows abounded.

Sarah kept up a brisk pace, refusing to spare even a glance for the man walking beside her. Though she did her best to banish him from her mind, it was futile. How was it possible for her thoughts to be constantly filled with him when two weeks ago she had barely known he existed? When she had stepped into his office, she certainly hadn't expected this strange turn of events.

Despite having been married, she felt more ignorant and inexperienced than the greenest of schoolgirls when it came to matters of romance. She didn't want to play the fool; still, she wanted to play.

Tyler's hand on the small of her back guided her into a well-groomed yard. The house bespoke the pride of its owner. Built of clapboard and brick, with a wealth of gables, it rose two stories. It was painted olive, the trim dark terra-cotta. Windows were numerous, well-placed, and French in design. Stairs led up to a wide veranda spanning the entire front. As Sarah surveyed the many angles of the residence, she thought the home an accurate reflection of the man who lived there — appealing to the eye and possessing many facets.

"I'll just be a few minutes," Tyler promised as he ushered her through the door. "You can sit in the parlor or wander around if you like. I don't keep live-in servants, so you'll have to see to yourself."

Sarah nodded.

"Cat still got your tongue?" he teased. "Don't worry, I'm not going to force you to do anything you don't want to do."

"Just because I don't choose to fill my every waking moment with inane conversation does not mean you have unnerved me." She waved him away with a regal flourish of her hand. "Your physical person has suffered much neglect. Since that is why we are here, see to it."

Tyler chuckled as he started up the stairs. Halfway up he turned. "Be careful you don't play the role of the shrewish wife too well, or I may reconsider my offer of marriage."

Before she could respond, he bolted up the rest of the stairs and disappeared into the upper hallway.

"At least when I'm a guest in someone's home you don't see me panting up the stairs making excuses so I can gawk at his naked person," she hollered after him.

Tyler poked his head around the corner. "Too bad. You're welcome to gawk to your heart's content." He disappeared again.

"Pompous ass," she muttered to herself.

A disembodied voice floated down the stairwell. "I heard that."

"Good!" she shouted back.

Sarah waited for a reply, but apparently Tyler had grown tired of carrying on conversation at a distance She shrugged and decided to explore the lower story of the house. The more she learned about the man, the more chance she had of turning the tables to her advantage. Though she found their verbal sparring oddly exhilarating, thus far she felt Tyler was making all the points.

The first floor consisted of the main hall, parlor, dining room, kitchen, and library. Sarah explored each room in turn. The parlor was comfortably furnished with a forest green sofa and two matching chairs. Doilies and bric-a-brac covered the tables. The dining room housed a huge cherrywood table with sturdy straight-backed chairs. A leaded glass hutch was built into one wall. A bay window spanned the breadth of another.

Moving to the kitchen, Sarah found it boasted every modern convenience. It was clean and tidy and bore little evidence of recent use.

Her explorations had taken her in a circular path, and the last room between her and the hall was the library. She smiled as she stepped over the threshold. The room was cluttered with papers and books. A bottle of brandy sat on a shelf, an empty teacup on the window sill. An oak desk was placed at an angle toward the middle of the room. All four walls were lined floor to ceiling with bookshelves. Sarah perused the titles. An eclectic mix of fiction and nonfiction shared the shelves.

She pulled a volume of poetry from the shelf and settled down in the chair by the window. She had read only a few pages when she heard footsteps in the hall.

When Tyler appeared in the doorway of the library, he had transformed himself back into the sophisticated San Francisco lawyer. "I knew I'd find you in here."

"How?" she queried, rising to her feet and returning the book to its place.

"It's my favorite room in the house," he stated cryptically.

Sarah made an attempt to appear serene and failed. "What are we going to do now?"

"Stop by my office. I need to make some arrangements with Thaddeus about taking care of my other clients for a while." He placed his hand possessively on the small of her back and escorted her toward the front door.

"It really isn't necessary for you to neglect your other clients because of me," Sarah protested.

"As your lawyer, I will decide how best to handle your case."

"And how much are you going to charge me for all this attention?"

"Ah, a very canny question. I think considering the nature of our relationship, I should wave any fee."

Sarah gently removed his hand from her back. "I don't like the idea of accepting something for nothing. It will make me feel obligated."

"Oh, I intend to be well compensated for my trouble."

She raised her chin a notch, hoping to project far more confidence than she felt. "Just what *is* the nature of our relationship?"

"We're friends, right?" He returned his hand to her back, his eyes glowing with promise. "And . . . Who knows what else may follow."

"What you really are saying is you intend to bed me," Sarah quietly contended.

His grin confirmed her statement before his words. "Your quick intelligence is just one of the many things I love about you."

"What if I say no?"

"Then I'll have to persuade you to say yes." As he drew his finger lightly from the lobe of her ear to her collarbone, Sarah shivered. "You're dealing with a man whose profession has allowed him to perfect the art of persuasion."

"I see. So procuring a lover *is* your ultimate goal," Sarah stated uneasily.

"No. Our marriage is my ultimate goal, but being a man of law has also taught me a slow, steady hand is required for delicate negotiations." His hands roamed over her to illustrate his point.

"Is that why you didn't take me this morning in my bed?"

"This morning, when I had hopes you would marry me before the day was out, I didn't mind stoically bearing the pain of playing the gentleman. Now . . ." He continued to stroke her. "I had some time to think on our situation while you finished your bath. Since even a gentleman has only so much fortitude, until you agree to be my wife, we will be lovers."

Sarah stood stock-still, willing her heartbeat to moderate and the tingling excitement coursing through her veins to cease. Desire unadorned was titillating, desire with the added offering of emotional passion was stimulating beyond belief. She swallowed hard and squeaked, "I am not going to marry you."

His grin widened. "Whatever you say. Now, come on. I have business to tend."

Sarah was more than happy to abandon their conversation, and it took a supreme effort of will to keep from bolting out the door. As they strolled from Tyler's home to his office, she kept up a running conversation, launching with enthusiasm into each new topic that came to mind no matter how banal. Her only requirement was that her subjects prevent all possibility of any comment of a personal nature.

Tyler willingly cooperated, feeling he had pressed his suit enough for the moment. Sarah Williams was coming around quite nicely.

It was only a short distance to his office, and they soon stepped over the threshold. They barely had time to exchange greetings with Agnes when her father's gruff voice interrupted from the top of the stairs.

"So, I see you brought her with you," he addressed his words to Tyler.

"Yes."

"I trust she is no worse for wear."

Sarah loathed being talked about in the third person, as if she didn't have ears or a voice of her own, but she held her tongue with ease, having had years of practice.

"Sarah escaped relatively unscathed," Tyler confirmed, "though there were a few tense moments. Agnes, why don't you get my friend some tea while I have a word with your father upstairs?"

"Yes, Mr. Bennet," she replied as she rose to do his bidding.

Tyler joined his partner in his office, and they closed the door. Almost immediately angry voices began to drift down the stairs. Sarah waited, hands folded in her lap, on a chair in the reception area for Agnes's return. She could not hear enough to follow the argument going on above her head, but she could understand enough of the words being shouted back and forth to recognize herself as the subject of the heated conversation.

She frowned. She certainly had no need of Mr. Johnson's good opinion, but it bothered her that he had taken such an instant and intense dislike to her for no apparent cause.

"Here we are, Mrs. Williams." Agnes entered bearing a cup of steaming tea. "A teaspoon of sugar, no cream, right?"

"You have a good memory," Sarah complimented her. "Thank you."

Instead of responding with a polite "You're welcome," Agnes said, "Tyler's in love with you, you know."

Sarah choked on the cautious sip of tea she had just taken. What was this? Sweet, shy Agnes calling her employer by his first name and announcing the secrets of his heart. When she had regained her composure, she met Agnes's gaze head on. "He told you?"

"Not in so many words. You know how lawyers dance around a definitive statement. But he makes no bones about how taken he is with you, and when you turned up missing . . . he was not himself. There's not a jury on earth wouldn't convict him of a smitten heart. Congratulations."

"I'm a passing fancy, nothing more," Sarah replied with unsteady conviction.

"You're wrong. I've known Ty all my life. I'd be willing to bet my good name he proposes marriage before the month is out."

"He already has," Sarah admitted.

"See?" Agnes smiled knowingly. "I knew I was right."

"But I don't want to marry him," Sarah stated.

"Why not?" Agnes demanded. "Ty would make a wonderful husband."

If she had met Tyler before her marriage to Henry, Sarah knew she might feel the same way, but she had not. Her eyes widened in dismay as Agnes continued to look piqued. It was bad enough that she must deal with Tyler; now she began to fear she had inadvertently been drawn into a love triangle. It would explain Agnes's sudden familiarity and her concern, but it would also complicate an already sticky situation. "Are *you* in love with him?"

"Heavens, no." Agnes laughed. "I'd marry him if he asked me because it's what my father wants. And I daresay, we might get along famously, except the very idea makes me a nervous wreck. We've known each other too long and too well to fall in love."

"Are you sure?" Sarah pressed, sincerely worried. "I wouldn't want to come between the two of you if you have given him your love."

"To be honest, I was immensely relieved you came along and captured his heart. I'd much rather be a

146

sister to Tyler than a wife." Her voice became wistful; her countenance transformed from plain to pretty. "There is a man I pass in the park each day. I don't even know his name . . . but it would be nice to get the chance to know him better." She sighed. "I realize I'm being foolish, but I secretly dream of a marriage founded on a grand passion rather than expediency."

"You are not the least bit foolish," Sarah assured her. "I married to please my parent and paid a heavy price. Don't let your father or anyone else push you into anything."

"The only thing my father wishes for me is marriage to Tyler, and you have saved me from that fate." Agnes smiled conspiratorially. "Perhaps now he will be more willing to let me make my own choice."

"Let us hope so," Sarah concurred.

Agnes's smile began to fade. "But I am forgetting Tyler. If you don't marry him, I may have to. I don't want him to get hurt."

"Neither do I," Sarah promised her. "But I intend to follow my own advice. I will not be pushed into anything."

"Tyler's the sort of man who's used to getting what he wants," Agnes warned.

Sarah pursed her lips. "Is he now?"

"Yes," Agnes pronounced with sisterly pride.

"Well, maybe he's about to meet his match."

Agnes eyed her thoughtfully. She had instinctively liked Sarah Williams from the first and despite her father's rantings and ravings had not revised her good opinion. Besides, she trusted Tyler's judgment, and if he wanted Sarah Williams, it was what she wanted for him. "Perhaps." She smiled enigmatically. "Or perhaps you have just met yours."

Above stairs in the office of Thaddeus Johnson the issue of Tyler's love life was also the topic of discussion.

"I really don't see how it is any of your business," Tyler complained.

"Don't be dense man! A wife's behavior will most certainly reflect upon this firm. I don't understand what you see in the woman. Sarah Williams is flighty, irresponsible, and a poor influence on you. Your father would roll over in his grave if he knew you were allowing that comely face to blind you to her true character. He taught you better than that."

"Sarah's face, comely though it might be, has nothing to do with my feelings for her. It is her intelligence and warm heart that attract me. And I think Dad would approve of her wholeheartedly."

"Hrmph! It seems to me if all you require in a wife is intelligence and a warm heart, you would do well to look closer to home."

"And who do you suggest?" Tyler asked, meeting the older man's gaze.

"Anyone would be preferable to the wanton widow Williams." Johnson pretended to search his mind for a name. "Take my Agnes for example. She would make a marvelous wife. She understands the business of law and is not given to wild escapades, and there is not a woman alive who possesses a warmer heart. In my opinion, her pale looks are far superior to your dark-haired widow."

"Agnes is a very lovely lady," Tyler agreed, completely oblivious to the veiled purpose behind his partner selecting his daughter as an example. "But why compare her to Sarah?"

"Because I don't want you to ruin your life!"

"I am a grown man," Tyler reminded, "fully capable of making my own decisions."

"Until two weeks ago I would have agreed with you, but this widow has bewitched you."

It was true he had never before neglected his work for the sake of a woman. He didn't understand it any better than Thaddeus and when he thought about it, it made him a little uneasy. But, damn it, he was entitled. "I repeat, my relationship with Sarah Williams is my own affair."

"And those who care about you are supposed to stand by and do nothing? Are you forgetting what happened to Alexander Crittenden?"

Tyler took a deep breath, praying for enough patience to hear his partner out. "What has he to do with me?"

"Everything," Johnson stated. "He was a lawyer of high reputation who allowed himself to become smitten with a widow. Where is he now? In a cold grave. Put there by Mrs. Laura D. Fair's own hand."

"Crittenden was a married man who pretended he was not. When he was found out, he continued to string Mrs. Fair along with false promises. Though I grieve for his wife and children, he got what he deserved."

Johnson growled. "Whatever Crittenden's faults, the fact of the matter remains that he was laid low by a widow. Surely you can see you are embarking on a parallel road to disaster."

"Your logic is not sound," Tyler argued.

"The words of a lovesick puppy if ever I heard them."

"You may think what you like. All I require of you is that you cover for me while I take a leave of absence. You can have no objection to doing that since you have been urging me to take a little time off to enjoy life for years."

"Now is not a good time," Johnson protested.

"Why not? Our caseload is light."

"Because, damn it! I don't want you cavorting about the countryside with that widow."

"If that is your only objection, I can't oblige you, Thaddeus." Tyler strolled to the door. "I'll check in periodically, but otherwise you can assume I am on extended holiday. Good day."

Thaddeus glared at the retreating back of his younger partner in frustration, muttering to himself, "Everything was going perfectly until that widow showed up on the scene, and now my sweet little Agnes is being left out in the cold. I'll make you see the error of your ways . . . before it's too late . . . for you and my daughter."

Chapter 10

A visit to the sheriff's office was their next order of business. Under Tyler's direction, Sarah recounted her experiences at the Blue Wheel, on board the *Delilah*, and at the Silk Stocking in minute detail.

Tyler's lips thinned on hearing the whole story for the first time, but otherwise he maintained a businesslike mien throughout her narrative.

Formal complaints were filed, and the sheriff promised prompt action.

For the remainder of the day Tyler stayed close by her side. They took a drive in the country, ate a picnic on the grass, strolled along the beach.

They spoke of nothing of great importance, and Sarah was able to relax completely and give herself over to the simple joys of the day. When uncomfortable thoughts threatened to disturb her peace, she pushed them out of her mind. Living in the moment afforded her pleasure, and she embraced the moment enthusiastically.

There was no denying she was happy in Tyler's company. He was charming, intelligent, considerate. As long as they both continued to be honest with each other, she could see no harm in maintaining the friendship. Even if it did neither of them any personal good, Agnes would benefit. She would be free to pursue her grand passion. And, having no illusions about Thaddeus Johnson's opinion of her — and a good notion that whatever he had said about her to Tyler when they were closeted in his office was not kindly — she found that the idea of thwarting him was not without its appeal.

If she had not wanted to pursue the acquaintance for her own pleasure, she would not have carried it on for the sake of spite, but since one purpose served the other, she did not feel more than a twinge of guilt about Mr. Johnson's discomfort.

Tyler's appraisal of the day was even more favorable than Sarah's. He could see she was enjoying herself as much as he, and that fit into his plans for this evening perfectly. He wanted her soft and mellow, so he could further his own cause.

Under normal circumstances he would feel some compunction for what he was about to do, but in this case the end justified the means. If the woman wouldn't accept a straightforward proposal of marriage, a back door one would have to do.

He licked his lips in anticipation. A little friendly persuasion was what was needed to achieve his ends. He would convince Sarah he could be a most pleasurable companion.

As evening settled upon the city, Tyler took Sarah back to his home. Leaving her with a pot of tea in the parlor, he retired upstairs.

He returned shortly, dressed to the nines in a coat of black superfine with velvet collar and matching trousers that hugged his long limbs. His hair was parted on the side and neatly combed, his chin freshly shaven. His blue-gray eyes twinkled with promise.

As he approached her, her nostrils detected a hint of musk. Her heart quickened. "And what do you have planned for this evening?" she asked, smiling broadly.

"Dinner."

"At Delmonico's?"

"No, but someplace equally as elegant. Come along." He held out his arm. "We need to stop at the hotel so you can change. Wouldn't want to miss our reservations."

"When did you have time to make dinner reservations? We've been together all day."

"I had the hotel make them for me this morning while you finished your bath."

The unwelcome reminder of the morning's incident caused a blush to stain Sarah's cheeks. "When we reach the hotel, you are not coming up to my room," she said, folding her arms across her chest.

"I wouldn't think of suggesting such a thing." He feigned shock at the very notion. "I will wait in the lobby while you dress."

"I just want to be sure we understand each other." Keeping an eye on him, Sarah placed her hand on his offered arm.

The trip from Tyler's door to the hotel was accomplished with the aid of a carriage. Sarah retired upstairs to change, selecting a gown of ruby velvet with underskirt of pale blue satin. The scooped neckline fell off the shoulders but revealed only a hint of cleavage. The sleeves were short and puffed. Every edge and seam was trimmed to profusion as was the fashion of the day.

In less than a quarter hour she presented herself downstairs.

"I admire promptness in a woman. Combined with your beauty, it's irresistible." He planted a furtive kiss behind her ear before presenting his arm.

"Behave yourself," she admonished in a whisper, though a tingle of excitement ran through her veins.

"I am." He grinned. "Are you hungry?"

"A little."

"Good."

His single syllable spoke of something more than dinner, but she was not unduly alarmed. She knew the course this evening would take. They would exchange hungry looks over the dinner table, whisper provocative compliments, then share a few feverish kisses in the carriage when Tyler took her back to her hotel. He might hint at a desire for more, but she would politely demur, and he would go home.

"You still haven't mentioned the name of the place you are taking me," she remarked casually.

"The Poodle Dog Café."

The name did not evoke images of elegance or romantic intrigue, and Sarah's face clearly expressed her confusion.

"I don't think you'll be disappointed," Tyler pre-

154

dicted. "I understand the place was originally called *Poulet d' Or*, or something similar. The miners Americanized the name. It's run by a French family from New Orleans and boasts all the amenities."

"Really. How interesting. Still, I hope we're not overdressed."

"I thought you were impervious to the opinions of others," Tyler continued in a low, seductive whisper.

"I am, but I see no reason to go out of my way to make a spectacle of myself."

"Rest assured, we shall be the very soul of discretion," he promised with a devilish twinkle in his eyes as he ushered her out the door into the waiting carriage.

As she sat beside him on the leather seat, Sarah kept her hands folded primly in her lap, but that did not prevent Tyler from covering her hands with his. She glanced up at him. He was smiling with boyish enthusiasm, and she found herself returning his smile.

Instead of stopping in front of the five-story Poodle Dog Café, Tyler had the driver take them around to the back. After paying the hack, he placed his hand on the small of Sarah's back and guided her to a staircase.

"Why are we going in this way?" she asked.

"Discretion."

"I'm really not that upset that we might be overdressed," Sarah protested in bemusement. "I was merely making conversation."

"The first floor is reserved for family dining, the second for banquets," he explained. "The upper stories are set aside for private dining."

"How private?"

He smiled serenely. "Very private. I think you'll be impressed."

Before Sarah could reply to his comment they had reached the door and were being greeted by a waiter and ushered into private chambers. He closed the door and they were alone.

Sarah took a cautious step away from her dinner companion and surveyed the room. Dark red velvet curtains hung across the windows, and a thick-piled Persian rug covered the floor. A fire crackled on the hearth. There was a table for dining, but by far the most prominent piece of furniture in the room was a long couch large enough to double as a bed. Pillows were everywhere. There was only one word to describe the mood intended by the designer of the room: sensual. She swallowed hard and slowly turned to face Tyler.

"Just why have you brought me here, Mr. Bennet?" she asked warily.

"Why, to enjoy your company, of course," he drawled. "And the name is Tyler, remember. You agreed to call me Tyler."

She retreated another step. "That was before I knew you well enough to realize you might be more rogue than gentleman."

He closed the distance between them. "I thought you came to California looking for adventure."

She wasn't a stupid woman, Sarah reminded herself, and if she stayed here, she knew where it would lead. His intentions were clear, hers were not. "I did . . . I think."

He gifted her with a slow, seductive wink. "Well, I

guess it's up to me to help you make up your mind. I vow that what I have in mind will be more enjoyable than tangling with the Barbary Coast lot." He ran his fingers over her lips. "Would you like a glass of wine?"

"Yes, very much," she replied, greatly in need of additional fortitude from any source.

He walked across the room and pulled a cord hanging on the wall. As if by magic, their waiter appeared at the door.

"We would like a bottle of your finest white wine," Tyler instructed.

Turning back to face her, he met her gaze. His eyes were dark with desire.

Sarah shifted uncomfortably. He said not a word. Did she want this? Yes . . . no. She scolded herself for not taking his declaration that they would become lovers more seriously. She had thought she would have more time. She had thought . . .

The wine arrived and Tyler promptly poured them each a glass. "To our future," he proposed.

Sarah raised her glass to meet his, then drained the contents in an effort to shore up her flagging nerve. The warmth of the wine spread from her belly to the tips of her fingers and toes. She smiled wanly.

"Another glass?" Tyler offered.

"No, thank you."

"Good. I want you to be fully cognizant of all that goes on this evening." As he advanced, Sarah retreated until the back of her knees bumped against the seat of the couch.

"Aren't we going to have dinner first?" she gasped as he leaned over her.

"There are other kinds of hunger that need satisfying, my dear Sarah." His warm lips met hers in a slow, lingering kiss, sending waves of heat through her. Tentatively she returned the kiss and in the giving increased her own pleasure. As the impassioned movement of their lips continued to sap her strength, Sarah was forced to wrap her arms around his neck to keep from falling. Tyler tightened his hold on her and gently lowered her to the couch.

She opened her mouth to protest, but her words were cut off by the invasion of his tongue. She could feel her heart pounding within her breast, the fire surging through her veins. Henry had never kissed her like this. Curiosity overpowered prudence. She tested the effect of her own tongue on him. A low groan of animal satisfaction rose from his throat, startling her back to reality. The step she was about to take suddenly seemed enormous.

"Tyler, we shouldn't." She pushed against his chest.

"Why not?" he demanded as he continued to ply her with kisses.

Distracted, she spoke the first words that came into her mind. "Someone might come in."

"I took care of that when I let the waiter out. There's a lock on the door."

"But . . ."

"But nothing. I have wanted you from the first moment you stepped through my door. And you want me. I can feel it in your response."

"I . . ."

"Shhh." He pressed his lips to hers. "Let me kiss away all your worries. I won't hurt you. I love you. I want you. Please let me have you."

Sarah clung to him in her confusion. He sounded so sincerely needful. As he continued to beseech her with feverish kisses, she tried to come up with some good reason to put a stop to this before it went too far, but logic worked against her. Her reputation would not suffer. Tyler had already spent the night in her bed. Even though nothing had happened, people would assume the worst. She certainly couldn't claim fear of pregnancy. Even the fact that she found physical intimacy awkward and uncomfortable didn't stand. She had endured the act for Henry's sake, and she felt closer to Tyler Bennet after knowing him two scant weeks than she had after years of marriage to Henry.

"All right," she managed to blurt out between intoxicating kisses.

Tyler expressed his gratitude with worshipful kisses upon her neck and shoulders, driving all possibility of further consideration beyond her reach. At length he allowed her to rise from the couch so they might shed their clothes.

Sarah lingered over the buttons of her bodice while he shed his coat and vest with enthusiasm. His shirt, trousers, and undergarments followed them to the floor. Sarah stared wide-eyed at his nakedness.

"Heavens." She swallowed as she ran her eyes down his thickly downed chest to his flat belly and beyond. "I didn't expect you to be so . . . attractive."

He grinned. "I'm glad you like what you see." He waited with strained patience for her to deal with her own garments, but when little progress was made, his smile began to wane. He reached for her. "You need help with those buttons."

Sarah stayed his eager hands. "I can manage."

"I know you can, but there's no harm in accepting a little help from a friend." He brushed her hands away and made quick work of the remaining buttons.

Sarah stood tense as he slipped her outer skirt to the floor. His touch was tender as he eased off each successive garment—her shoes, petticoats, crinolette. Tyler said nothing, but his smoky eyes spoke of his intense desire for her. The beating of her own heart thundered in her ears.

As he unlaced her corset, his fingers brushed her breast and her cheeks bloomed with color.

Tyler murmured his appreciation. Taking his leisure, he removed her garters and stockings, stroking her legs with his broad hands, then following their ministry with reverent lips.

Having never been undressed by a man, Sarah found the experience both titillating and provoking. His touch was driving her wild. She didn't know how to deal with it. When at last her chemise and drawers floated to the floor, she sighed.

"I know," Tyler commiserated. "I want you too, but we should go slow this first time, savor the experience." Gathering her in his arms, he began kissing her lips again, saving her the trouble of coming up with a reply.

Sarah was undone by the sensation of bare flesh against bare flesh.

Tyler felt her quiver and lowered her to the couch, covering her with his weight. She could feel the firm length of his sex pressing against her legs.

Bracing herself, Sarah became starch-stiff.

Bemused but undeterred, Tyler let his hands knead her breasts, his tongue drawing lazy circles around the pink tips, urging them to bud. He caressed every inch of skin from her neck to her belly, first with his hands, then with his lips and tongue. When she remained unpliable, he began to run his hands slowly down her inner thigh then up again, each time, inching closer to the heart of her passion.

Sarah squeezed her eyes tight against the sensations his touch evoked. Letting him make love to her was exquisite torture. She was going to humiliate herself. She tried to remain in control of herself but finally could bear no more. "Tyler, please! If you don't stop doing that I will never be able to lie still."

The sincerity of her plea startled him. He braced himself on his elbows. "What on earth are you talking about?"

"If you keep touching me that way, I am not going to be able to lie still as I am supposed to," she reiterated.

Tyler stared at her in consternation. "You're supposed to do no such thing. I want you to abandon yourself to our lovemaking."

"But Henry always scolded me if I moved. He said it was depraved."

"Good God!" he sputtered. "Henry was a fool. Lovemaking is a game for two. You share yourselves with each other."

"I'm afraid Henry did not concur with your views."

Tyler groaned. It was damned difficult carrying on a conversation in their present position. He had not invited Henry's ghost into this room, and he resented the influence Henry had on Sarah. She was his now.

161

"I don't care what Henry believed or did not believe." He toyed with a wisp of hair at her temples. "I don't mean to pry, but I know you to be a woman of passion. What did you do all those years you were married?"

"Just as he instructed," she assured him. "Henry was quick about it, so doing as he asked wasn't really much of a problem. Since he came to my room every Thursday night and the cook liked to have the weekly menus Friday mornings, I distracted myself by planning our meals in my head."

Tyler chuckled at the mental picture of this.

"It really wasn't funny," Sarah protested.

"I know, sweetheart," he sympathized. "Let's not think about old Henry ever again." Taking her earlobe between his teeth, he playfully nibbled it and her neck until she began to squirm beneath him. "That's better," he murmured his approval.

"Are you certain you won't be repulsed if I return your affection?" she queried, her desire to please unmistakable in her emerald eyes.

"Quite the opposite," he promised, pausing to caress her lips. "The fact is, I was beginning to question my masculine prowess when you were lying there without moving a muscle."

"Oh."

While Sarah took a moment to digest this information, he continued, "And if I find you are thinking of anything but me, I shall beat you."

She blinked at him. "You wouldn't."

"Of course not, but I would be compelled to make love to you again and again until you know how much I want your impassioned response. Weeks from

162

now they might find us, two fleshless corpses locked in passion's embrace."

Sarah made a face. "Is it necessary to be so morbid? I daresay you will frighten me from this couch, and my curiosity will remain forever unsated."

"Curiosity?"

She nodded, her eyes glowing with passion. "You make me feel all tingly with want of you. I would hate to leave this room without discovering why."

"And you won't," Tyler vowed enthusiastically as he turned his attention back to his original purpose for bringing her here.

Sarah met his kisses with unrestrained ardor, reveling in her newfound freedom of expression. She kissed his eyes, his neck, his shoulders, any place she could reach, returning again and again to his soft, warm lips to drink in heady draughts of the passion they offered.

Tyler's arms tightened around her as he eased his tongue between her lips, stroking the sensitive skin that lay beyond. Sarah hungrily tasted him, using her own tongue to delight him as he did her. As she writhed against him, she could feel the evidence of his arousal grow harder and hotter against her thigh. He moaned in pleasure, and Sarah was awash in a wave of pure euphoria.

Spurred on by the realization that she was capable of casting the same sensual spell upon him as he worked upon her, she maneuvered herself to sit atop him. Reaching up, she pulled the pins from her hair. It fell to her shoulders, framing her face with loose curls.

She leaned forward, allowing her hair to form a

dark curtain as she claimed his lips again and again. Tyler's mouth slowly curved into a grin beneath hers.

"Having fun?" he queried.

"Maybe," she teased, lowering herself for another kiss.

Before her lips could capture his, he eased her upward, closing his mouth around one pink-crested nipple. He suckled as his tongue laved the areola.

"Tyler, please," she gasped as rivers of fire coursed through her veins.

"I please you?" he murmured against her burning flesh as his lips trailed to her other breast.

Her legs tensed around him, and she answered him with a sharp intake of breath.

The rapid pounding of her heart against her ribs caused her color to rise, painting her skin warm and rosy with passion. She felt apart from herself, floating to dizzying heights on a cloud of sensual celebration.

Tyler continued to work his magic with his hands and mouth. She clung to him, giving him passion for passion. When he rolled them so he once again lay atop her, her thighs opened and she eagerly received him, pulling him deep within her.

Echoing the rhythm of their hearts, they strained together. Sarah's hips rose to meet each thrust. Each time he filled her, she sighed in contentment. Each time he withdrew, she cried out her need of him.

She was lost to herself; yet, she prayed the exquisite sensations evoked by flesh caressing flesh would go on forever.

The heat between them built, radiating from the coupling of their flesh to every toe and fingertip. It felt as though he was searing not only her physical body but her soul with his lovemaking. The erotic tension was becoming unbearable; then, without warning, her senses exploded into a thousand shards of unparalleled pleasure, leaving her limp and exhausted. Moments later she felt Tyler's shuddering climax within her. He rolled his weight from her, but kept her cradled firmly against him.

Contented thoughts drifted in and out of her head as she lay within the circle of his arms. Their union felt right, good, a natural extension of their friendship. She did not regret succumbing to him, quite the opposite. She briefly wondered at her lack of moral compunction. Did it make her wicked? She didn't care. Making love to Tyler Bennet was the most gratifying thing she had done in a very long time.

She nuzzled her nose in the hair of his chest as her consciousness wavered in the twilight between sleep and full wakefulness.

"So, what are we going to eat this week?" Tyler purred in her ear.

Her expression confused, she opened her eyes and stared at him. "How should I know?"

His lips curled into a cocky grin. "Just checking," he said, as much to himself as her.

Understanding dawned, and Sarah pushed at his chest in mock reproach. "If you are fishing for compliments, I will be more than happy to give them to you. I have never experienced such passion in a man's arms. Thank you very much for introducing me to such pleasures."

"You're very welcome, my love." He kissed her

rosy lips. "Perhaps you would be willing to discuss the permanent solicitation of my services?"

"Hm," Sarah sighed her approval, drifting into dreamy repose.

"Care to set a date?"

"For what?" she murmured.

"Our marriage."

She opened her eyes again. She didn't understand this need of his to marry her, but apparently it must be firmly dealt with or he would give her no peace. Sitting up, she retrieved three pillows, arranging them over the more distracting parts of their bare anatomy. "I have already told you I'm not interested in marriage."

"I was hoping lovemaking would change your mind. Just think, if we were married, we could indulge ourselves day and night without a thought to the consequences."

"Why can't we go on as we are?" she argued without rancor.

"Because I want you for my wife."

Hugging the pillow covering her breasts, she gazed down at his recumbent form. "I can't think of one good reason why. To hear you tell it, I have been nothing but trouble to you since the day we met."

"You are a lot of trouble," he confirmed. "But I love you any way."

"Why?"

"Now who's fishing for compliments? No. No." He pressed his finger to her lips when she would have made reply. "I fully intend to answer your question." His finger trailed from her lips to the swell of her breasts. "There is the physical attraction, of course.

166

I've wanted you like this, all soft and naked in my arms, since the first moment I laid eyes on you. But a rational man knows lust is not a sound foundation for a marriage." Tyler toyed with the corners of his mustache, his expression one of a man pondering a weighty matter. "I love you because you are sweet, funny, intelligent, charmingly naive, and God protect me from the repercussions of admitting this to you, I admire your bravado. You're extremely comely. I feel good when I'm with you. Shall I go on, or have I given you enough reasons?"

Sarah shook her head. "I'm glad you hold such a high opinion of me, but it does not change my mind about marriage. I would be honored to be your lover, but I have no intention of being any man's wife."

"And if I get you with child? What then?"

Sarah's eyes clouded with pain. Her barrenness was the one failing with which she had never completely been able to come to terms. She disliked being reminded of it. "I am unable to conceive children," she said softly.

"I'm sorry . . . I didn't realize." As he pulled her into his arms, Tyler silently cursed himself for his inadvertent insensitivity. He searched his heart. He had assumed there would someday be children in their lives . . . but having Sarah by his side was more important to him than a house full of progeny. He loved her. He needed her. If she returned his love, he would live his life a fulfilled man. He pushed back a strand of hair that had fallen across her face. "It doesn't matter to me."

"It does matter. Every man wants children."

"I'm not every man."

"Oh, Tyler, what am I going to do with you?" She smiled wanly. "You are exactly the kind of man I would wish for a husband. But I can't marry you. I have been free such a short time. I can't give that up. Not yet. *Please* don't ask it of me." She gently stroked his cheek with the back of her hand. "I don't fully understand it myself, but freedom is a need in me." She sighed. "Perhaps if you were a woman you would understand."

"If I were a woman, marriage would not be an issue between us." He chuckled in an attempt to lighten the mood. He was disappointed, to be sure, but shared intimacy had brought new closeness and insight. Deep down he did understand.

The specter of Henry was still in this room standing between them, and by his side stood Elijah Jenkins. If he had listened with his heart instead of his head, he would have realized from the beginning that Sarah was afraid to marry him. What did she know of marriage except a father's desertion and a husband's oppression? If he truly loved her, he would give her the time she needed.

Capturing her hand, he brought it to his lips. "Spread your wings, my little swallow. Just promise you'll come home to me should you get the urge to nest."

Her eyes gleamed bright with gratitude. "I don't want you wasting your life waiting for me to do something I may never do."

"I have no intention of frittering away my time," he assured her. "If you will recall, you have agreed to be my lover. I would prefer to give our relationship the stamp of respectability, but I am not fool enough to cut off my nose to spite my face. Lovers we are, and lovers we shall stay until the day you are ready to give me your hand in marriage."

Chapter 11

Tyler and Sarah spent the rest of the night making love again and again. They were sometimes playful, sometimes serious. They made love with the leisure of a Sunday afternoon stroll. They made love with the wild enthusiasm of lust-filled youths. They explored the many moods of physical intimacy until both were too exhausted to do anything but lie limp in each other's arms.

The Poodle Dog Café provided everything: blankets, pillows, an eight-course dinner. The quality of discretion was as excellent as that of the food.

Sunlight tickled the lids of Sarah's eyes until she slowly blinked them open. Tyler's face was inches away, and she smiled. He looked like a little boy, with his hair all rumpled and his lips relaxed in a reposeful pout. She resisted the urge to kiss him lest she disturb him. Heaven knew, the poor man needed his rest. Her smile widened.

Until last night she hadn't known places like the

Poodle Dog Café existed. Until last night there were a lot of things she hadn't known. "Thank you for the lovely evening, Mr. Bennet," she whispered to her peacefully sleeping companion.

She watched him a while longer before the call of nature compelled her to ease herself from the couch. She wasn't surprised to find her muscles stiff and sore. When she returned from the water closet, Tyler was sitting up.

"You left me," he lamented.

"Only for a minute," she replied, slipping under the covers beside him. She snuggled up to him, pillowing her head on his chest.

"Are you hungry?"

"Are you offering breakfast, or another demonstration of your masculine prowess?" she asked charily.

"Whatever your heart desires."

"What I desire is a long soak in a hot bath. I fear you have worn me out."

"I didn't hear you complaining last night," he teased, running his hand over the curve of her breasts.

She captured his hand and brought it to her lips. Her green eyes sparkled with impish fires. "Oh, I'm not complaining," she assured him as she kissed his palm. "But though the spirit is willing, the flesh is weak."

"Not mine." He grinned as he lifted the sheet.

Sarah stared at his rigid sex in mock consternation. "When I signed on to be your lover, I had no idea you would be such an exacting taskmaster. Don't you ever need to rest?"

"Not around you."

She laughed. "I'll take that as a compliment."

"It was meant to be." Rising from the couch, he crossed the room and pulled the bell rope.

Sarah sat up. "What are you doing?"

"Ringing for your bathwater."

"But what about . . ." She gestured in the direction of his nether region.

"The matter will resolve itself."

"Are you certain? I'm perfectly willing to . . ."

"It is a commonly held myth, perpetrated by the male of the species for his own benefit, that a man once aroused must be immediately satisfied or he will come to some grave harm. Your bath comes first; then we will discuss other matters." He smacked his lips, his eyes taking on a feral gleam.

"You almost had me convinced you were a gentleman," Sarah rebuked.

"Another myth. If I were a true gentleman, I'd have insisted you marry me before I bedded you. Last night I proved myself a rogue, as I will today and tomorrow and the next day and . . ."

"Being a lover is much more exciting than being a wife," Sarah interrupted, her eyes glowing warm with affection.

"Ah, but you have yet to be *my* wife."

Sarah frowned at him. "Tyler, I thought we disposed of the notion of marriage last night."

"I did say I'd give you time," he brusquely reminded himself. He combed his fingers through his hair. "It's going to be difficult, but I promise I'll do my best not to harp on the subject. But you must *promise* me that when you are ready to make an honest man of me, you won't hesitate to say the

172

word."

"*If* I decide I have changed my mind about marriage, you'll be the first to know," Sarah promised.

A politic knock at the door interrupted their conversation. The request for bathwater followed by a light breakfast was made, and Tyler returned to his place beside her on the couch.

"We may as well make good use of our time while we wait." He gathered her in his arms. Their lips met gently at first, but the passion between them quickly escalated. Their tongues tasted and titillated; their hands moved over each other with abandon. They barely heard the knock at the door.

"Your water has arrived. We'd best cover ourselves," Tyler whispered in her ear.

"Tell them to go away," Sarah purred as she nipped his shoulder.

"Are you certain?" he asked, trying not to sound too hopeful. "I didn't intend to do anything but steal a few kisses."

"I want you now," she pleaded, arching herself against him. "Tell them to go away."

"Come back in half an hour," Tyler hollered huskily in the direction of the door.

"Very good, monsieur."

Showering his face with kisses, Sarah straddled Tyler's hips. He eased himself into her. Though he would have been gentle, she rode him with gusto, bringing them both to a swift, shuddering climax. They clung to each other as they struggled to catch their breath.

"You are a hazard to my health," Sarah scolded as she nuzzled his neck.

"I only did your bidding, my lady. If you feel you must chide, chide yourself."

"I'd rather blame you." She chuckled. "You intoxicate my senses."

Tyler gave her an affectionate squeeze, then repositioned her so she lay cradled in his lap. He leaned his head against the back of the couch and they both rested.

When her water arrived again, Sarah eagerly sought out its soothing warmth. She played with the water, dripping it down her bare limbs and sighing repeatedly.

Tyler watched with undisguised appreciation, his looks warming her as much as the steaming water. When she finished, he took a turn in the tub.

"You lingered so long the water is barely tepid," he teased as he lathered himself from head to toe.

"Do you want me to ring for more hot water?"

"No, this will do. It will be noon before we get out of here the way it is."

"Have I been keeping you from pressing business?"

Tyler's expression evolved from thoughtful to mirthful as he realized for the first time in his adult life he didn't have someplace he needed to be. Being on holiday was going to take some getting used to, but he would persevere. "There's not an appointment on my calendar," he answered her. "And since I have all the time in the world," he crooked his forefinger and smiled seductively, "why don't you come here and scrub my back."

Sarah and Tyler spent the next three weeks in each

other's constant company. Part of each day was devoted to sifting through city records or scanning issue after issue in the archives of the *Examiner, Morning Chronicle, Alta,* and *Bulletin* in hopes of gleaning clues to Sarah's father's present whereabouts, but engaging in pleasure was their primary pursuit.

It had not taken Sarah long to discover that when Tyler Bennet set his mind to entertaining a lady, he spared nothing. Each day was filled to the brim with new and exciting experiences.

Visiting Chinatown was like stepping into another world. The streets were filled with brightly clad, pigtailed men chattering in their own language. Tyler treated her to her first Chinese meal, and she was immediately enamored with the cuisine.

The next day they picnicked on the grounds of Mission Dolores, exploring the decaying, late Baroque-style church and indulging in the more secular amusements that had grown up around the abandoned mission.

He introduced her to Mr. Ghirardelli and his chocolates at his home and factory at 415 Jackson Street.

They spent Sunday in Woodward Gardens, meandering through the lush landscape and visiting the private zoo and art gallery. Sarah played the elegant lady as she leaned back in the boat Tyler had rented, twirling her parasol while he rowed her around one of the many artificial lakes. Later, she made a less than elegant tableau as she tried her hand at rollerskating. Though her buttocks bore evidence of her many falls, her dignity remained unbruised. She was having too good a time to spare a thought for anything as inconsequential as the snickers of the more accomplished ladies.

He took her to Cliff House, the fashionable meeting place of politicians and a favorite trysting spot for fine gentlemen and their ladyloves. Sitting in a corner where they could discreetly observe the comings and goings of the patrons, Tyler amused her with a primer course on local scandals.

Another day, they took a ferry to New Sausalito, where Tyler held membership in the San Francisco Yacht Club, and they spent an afternoon sailing on the bay. Upon returning to San Francisco, they stopped at Abe Warner's Cobweb Palace at the foot of Meiggs' Wharf for hot toddies. The eating house was filled to overflowing with exotic animals and bric-a-brac, including a collection of carved sperm whale teeth. Dust-laden cobwebs draped every corner, and Abe — garbed in a black suit, high topped hat, and white apron — presided over the whole with pride.

Each night Sarah returned to Tyler's home tired but happy and full of anticipation of the joy to be found in his arms. Since the night they had dined at the Poodle Dog Café, she had made his bed her own. She humored his gentlemanly instincts by keeping her room at the Grand Hotel for appearance sake, but if she had had her way, she would have lived with him openly. Even so, their names had appeared twice in the gossip columns, a fact that pained Tyler and amused her.

"Well, what have you planned for today?" she asked over the brim of her morning cup of coffee.

"I received a message that I'm needed at the office

while you were taking your bath," he said, his voice tinged with annoyance. This was the third time this week he had received such a message. "Just in case it's important, I'll have to stop by and see what has come up; then, I thought we might drive out to Point Lobos."

"You really should start thinking of spending a little more time at the office. Though I have had more fun these past weeks than I have had during the whole of my previous life, I am coming to agree with your partner, Mr. Johnson. Our friendship will be your ruination."

Tyler looked vexed. "Who told you he said that?"

"No one. I overheard him arguing with you the day before yesterday when we stopped in to pick up those papers that needed your signature, and I gathered from his words that it was not the first time he had told you as much."

"If I want to take a hiatus, Thaddeus has no right to make a peep. He's been toying with the idea of running for congress for years and often goes back east to visit relatives and check out the political climate in Washington. Last time he was gone nine months. I'm not going to feel guilty for taking a little time for myself," Tyler informed her.

"I'm not recommending a bout of guilt," Sarah assured him. "But a little more business and a little less pleasure might appease him. I fear our friendship is driving a wedge between you and your partner."

"Thaddeus just can't bear to see a man in love," Tyler discounted her concern. "It doesn't make much sense, either, since he has been extolling the virtues of settling down with a wife for some time now."

"I think what Mr. Johnson can't stand is me," Sarah said bluntly.

Much as he wanted to, Tyler could not argue with her statement. He had never seen Thaddeus take such an instant dislike to anyone. It bothered him more than he cared to admit. Thaddeus was his friend as well as his partner. He wanted him to like Sarah, and he wanted her to like him. "He's never taken the time to get to know you. Maybe we sho'' invite Agnes and him to dine with us tonight, suggested pensively.

Sarah was tempted to explain to Tyler why the dinner would do little if any good, but she did not feel she had the right to betray Agnes's confidence. The poor girl was in an uncomfortable enough situation with her father intent on fostering a romance between her and Tyler when neither of them desired such a liaison.

She wondered how Agnes's budding romance with the gentleman in the park was progressing and determined to ask her at first opportunity. Sarah brought her wandering mind back to the matter at hand. Maybe it would help the situation if Mr. Johnson saw them all together. He could see how devoted she and Tyler were to each other and how Agnes supported the romance. Of course, if she were willing to marry Tyler, it would put an end to the issue once and for all, but she had no intention of making that sacrifice. "Dinner with the Johnsons sounds like a fine idea," she agreed.

The long pause between his presentation of the idea and her acceptance did not go unnoticed, but

Tyler chose to ignore her hesitancy. "I'll stop and make reservations on my way to the office."

"If you'd rather, I could cook something for them here," Sarah offered, thinking seeing her and Tyler in a domestic setting might further her purpose.

"It might be better to meet on more neutral territory," Tyler mused out loud.

Sarah bit her lip. Mr. Johnson's opinion mattered not a whit to her, but she knew it did matter to Tyler. He had to work with the man every day. She did not like to see him torn between the two of them. It was hard for her to sympathize with the meddling man, but for Tyler's sake she would do her best to nurture more congenial relations.

"If you think Mr. Johnson would be more comfortable in a restaurant, so be it."

Dinner was a disaster. Though Sarah did her best to foster a favorable impression — dressing in a demure gown, practicing the excruciatingly correct manners taught her by her mother, smiling until her jaw ached — Mr. Johnson crowded the boundaries of civility. He asked pointed questions about her parentage, her schooling, her plans for the present and future. She felt as if she was a defendant trapped in the witness box by a tyrannical prosecutor.

Tyler and Agnes did their best to deflect his questions, but to little avail. Even when they did manage momentarily to steer the topic of conversation to matters less personal, Mr. Johnson continued to stare at her, shaking his head as if he couldn't believe anyone so wretchedly inadequate as she was allowed to walk the city streets, let alone share his table.

By mutual consent the evening ended early.

Tyler had scheduled an interview the next day with the latest newspaper ad respondent at his office. Though he had taken her in his arms the moment the Johnsons had left them and had done his best to erase the taint on her spirits with chivalrous love-making, she preferred to avoid a chance encounter with his partner. Rather than participate in the interview, as was her habit, Sarah opted for a stroll in the park.

She had not gone far when the sound of rapidly approaching footsteps captured her attention.

"I finally caught up with you," Agnes said between breaths as she fell into step beside her. "Tyler said I would find you here. I wanted to apologize for my father's behavior last night."

"It wasn't your fault," Sarah consoled.

"In a way it is. If I didn't get so tongue-tied when I try to talk to him, I would have a better chance at convincing him to give up this foolishness about Ty and me. I thought last night would help, him seeing how it is between the two of you, but obviously it didn't."

"I had hoped much the same," Sarah admitted.

Agnes startled to alertness, her cheeks blooming with color. "Look, he's coming our way!"

Sarah's gaze followed the direction of Agnes's and alit upon a tall, dark-haired gentleman. "The man you were telling me about?" she queried.

"Yes. Don't you think he is quite the handsomest man you have ever seen?"

While the man approaching them was pleasant in

appearance, compared to Tyler she found him rather lacking. But Sarah kept her opinion to herself. She had never seen quiet little Agnes so vibrant. She was positively aquiver with anticipation.

"Have you discovered his name?"

"No," she replied ruefully. "All I know about him is that he walks in the park this time every day, and when we pass, he tips his hat and smiles at me."

So, an apology was not the only reason Agnes had come dashing into the park. Sarah was thoroughly delighted to see that Agnes was looking out for her own interests. Still, it was obvious she was in need of a gentle nudge in the right direction. "Agnes, you cannot hope to nurture a romance if the two of you never speak," she advised in sisterly tones.

Agnes's repining expression evinced her complete agreement. "But we haven't been properly introduced."

"I can take care of that," Sarah assured her.

The gentleman in question was almost abreast of them. Sarah let about a yelp and crumpled to the ground at his feet. "Oh dear, I fear I have twisted my ankle," she breathed, bringing the back of her hand to her forehead as she grimaced with pain. "Do you think you might assist my friend and me, kind sir?"

Agnes's complexion went scarlet. Sarah allowed herself a secret smile as the gentleman's gaze moved between her and Agnes. Unless the man was dense, he would realize for whose benefit this little charade was being enacted. His brown eyes gleamed golden with delight as he continued to gaze at Agnes, and she knew she need not fear a lack of intelligence or interest.

"I would be honored to assist you ladies," he replied, straight-faced.

Leaning down, he attempted to help Sarah from the ground, but she stayed him with an outstretched hand. "Wait. We have yet to properly introduce ourselves."

"How remiss. I am Clayton Bevington," he presented himself. "And you?"

"I am Mrs. Sarah Williams, and this is my dear friend Miss Agnes Johnson."

"Charmed."

Agnes had yet to say a word, but Sarah was undeterred. "You know, Mr. Bevington, I'm sure that if I could be helped to that bench, I would feel much better."

"Of course." He and the still-mute Agnes helped her hop to the nearby bench. "Would you like me to call you a carriage?" he queried solicitously.

"Oh, no. I'm sure all my poor ankle needs is a little rest. It's such a lovely day. Why don't you two take a stroll around the park? I'm sure I'll be much recovered when you return."

A mortified groan escaped Agnes's lips. "I must beg pardon for Mrs. Williams's behavior. I'm sure you have never before been subjected to such a blatant piece of overacting," she gave Sarah a pointed look, "and want nothing better than to escape our company."

"Your assessment of your friend's acting ability is quite correct, but I have not the slightest desire to escape your company." He offered his arm. "Miss Johnson, would you do me the honor of a turn around the park?"

"I'd love to," she replied.

Sarah grinned like a Cheshire cat as the two strolled off arm in arm under the canopy of trees. She approved of Mr. Bevington wholeheartedly and was willing to do what she could to promote the romance.

The wheels of her mind began to turn. She would ask Tyler to make discreet inquiries into the man's background to be sure he was not a snake in gentleman's clothing; then, if he passed muster, she would throw herself into the campaign.

Twice this afternoon Agnes had taken responsibility for another's behavior. The similarity to her old self was too conspicuous to ignore.

Though Agnes's happiness was her prime motivation, she was honest enough to admit to herself that the opportunity of foiling the father was added incentive. Managing parents were a blight on true love. She would make sure Agnes did not make the same mistake she had.

The letter from her mother arrived on Tuesday. It was the first she had received since coming to San Francisco. The opening page was devoted to probing questions in regard to the progress of her search for her father. The remaining four pages were a litany of complaints, all of which could be remedied if only Sarah would come home and do her duty.

Sarah crumpled the letter into a ball, her gay mood spoiled. She could feel her mother's long fingers stretching across the distant miles, snatching at her liberty. She was an emancipated woman. She would never go back!

She began to pace. It was apparent that anyone living in San Francisco with honest information about her father had already come forward. They had seen nothing but frauds for the past two weeks. The newspaper archives and public records had been thoroughly combed. What little information they possessed seemed to point north, to the state capital, but it was years old and questionable at best.

The letter made her feel restless. Living and loving in Tyler's home was rewarding, to be sure, but it was becoming a little too comfortable.

She didn't regret being sidetracked from her search. No woman in her right mind could regret the last few weeks. But she did still want to find her father, if for no other reason than to experience the thrill of the hunt.

She supposed many would think it unnatural of her, after her ordeal in the Barbary Coast, to continue to crave excitement. Perhaps it was. But the facts of the matter were that she had escaped unharmed; the men responsible were behind bars awaiting trial; and she felt too adored to have any room in her heart for fear.

"I don't think we are going to learn anything more about my father's whereabouts here in San Francisco," Sarah commented that evening as they sipped wine in Delmonico's.

"I agree."

She smiled broadly. "So, when do I start packing?"

Tyler shifted uncomfortably. He had been expecting this conversation for some time. In fact, he was rather surprised at her lack of zeal to find her father, but he had said nothing. He was not a man to question his good luck, and try as he might, he couldn't foster any enthusiasm for the quest. He didn't want Sarah hurt, and he was sorely afraid that Elijah Jenkins, when and if he was found, would hurt her. "The north country is rugged territory. I think now would be a good time to call in professional help," he suggested casually.

Sarah set her drink down on the table. Tyler had been so obliging of late that she could hardly believe he was bringing up that issue again. True, she had not performed very well in the Barbary Coast, but that was practically ancient history. She had been the very model of prudence since that unfortunate affair—except when she was in Tyler's bed, and she certainly hadn't heard anything resembling a complaint about her activities there. Had his opinion of her competence not changed one whit since he first met her? She decided to test him.

"Do you think me unequal to the task?"

"Unprepared is a better word," he answered diplomatically. "You have no idea where your search will lead you. Life on the road is sometimes brutal and in the very least requires certain skills I do not believe a woman of your upbringing would possess."

"Perhaps you are right," she mused. "First thing tomorrow morning I shall see about hiring someone to teach me to ride a horse properly, and as poorly as they are paid, for a fee, I'm sure one of the soldiers from the Presidio would be willing to teach me how to use a gun."

"I am not thrilled with the idea of employing jockeys and soldiers to turn you into a wild west sideshow. Sarah, you know I love you, and I'd do almost anything for you . . ."

"You have been very sweet and understanding," she assured him. "But this is something I need to do for myself."

"Why? We could stay here, comfortable in San Francisco, while someone else does the dirty work."

"We could, but then I wouldn't get to see much of the world, would I? I'm sure there is a lot to see that is worth my time and effort."

"Could I interest you in something less taxing?" he asked. "Say, a grand tour of Europe?"

Sarah patted his hand and smiled indulgently. "Someday I would like to travel to Europe, but for now I prefer a less cosmopolitan journey. Being city born and bred, I find that the wilderness holds much fascination for me."

Tyler began to stroke his mustache as was his habit when he was deep in thought. "I suppose if I am there by your side to watch over you, you can't come to any real harm."

"I welcome your companionship, but do not think I will allow you to treat me as a child," she warned.

"Surely you can't claim I have treated you like anything but a woman these past weeks," he chided, an amorous gleam in his eye. "But just like you, I have needs to be filled. One of those needs is to have you for my wife someday, and I can't have a wedding if I let the bride get herself killed before she comes to her senses and realizes what an admirable husband I would make." He reached under the table and squeezed her knee.

She blushed. "Tyler, you are the most provoking man I have ever met."

"But you love me anyway, right?" he cajoled.

Sarah pursed her lips and toyed with her earring as she thought about the question. "As long as you understand admitting my fondness for you doesn't mean I'm going to marry you," she began. "Yes, I do like you very much."

"Good enough for now," he quipped, retreating behind his menu so he could veil his disappointment that despite his best efforts to woo her, she was not yet ready to accept his offer of marriage.

Chapter 12

Considering his devotion to her company, she should have guessed Tyler would insist on teaching her himself how to ride and use a gun.

Over the weeks he hadn't fulfilled his vow to "not let her out of his sight" quite as vigilantly as he had those first few days, but she certainly couldn't claim a want of attention.

Sarah stroked the velvety nose of the sorrel mare he had hired for her, eyeing the sidesaddle in consternation. "I should feel far more secure if you let me sit astride the animal," she told her handsome teacher.

"And what would you do with your skirts?" he queried. "Hike them up above your ears?"

"I could split them."

"Dress appropriately and I will teach you to ride astride, but for today you will have to make do. Now, come around and I'll give you a hand up."

Sarah slipped her foot into the stirrup formed by Tyler's hands. Using his shoulders to steady herself, she hefted herself up on the horse. The mare whinnied and pawed the ground.

"All right. Remember what I told you," he instructed as he handed her the reins. "Don't jerk on the reins. A steady hand lets the horse know you're in control."

Sarah nodded. When Tyler was engaged in business, as he was this morning, he was all business, and she found him rather high-handed. However, he exhibited the same single-mindedness when he pursued pleasure, and he did so often, so she could hardly complain.

She was still opposed to the idea of their marriage, but in her weaker moments, the idea of someday—in the distant future—becoming Tyler Bennet's wife was tempting. He wasn't at all like Henry.

Though he was far more enamored with convention than she, he was willing to forgo it when it suited his purpose. His motivation seemed to stem from a genuine concern for her comfort and welfare and not an arbitrary love of rules.

Could they be happy together? She was happy now. The mare shifted, and Sarah tightened her grip on the reins. The future would have to look after itself. She had a horse to ride.

Tyler mounted a second horse and signaled her to lead the way.

Her position felt precarious, but after a few minutes she began to accustom herself to the steady roll of her horse's gait.

The countryside surrounding San Francisco was composed of low-lying grass-covered hills piled one on top of the other. Red-orange poppies, lavender lupine, and wild daisies dotted the slopes with color. The fingers of fog that lay over the city did not reach this far inland, and the sun shone brightly in a brilliant blue sky.

She smiled as her eyes surveyed the scenery. If a lady was going to be thrown to the ground, she couldn't have chosen a more lovely setting.

Despite her prediction of an ignominious fall, Sarah kept her seat. Tyler called out instructions to her, and she followed them without calamity or complaint. Though their pace had never gone above a slow walk, by the end of her first lesson Sarah was convinced she had the makings of a skilled horsewoman, and she told him so.

"You're not bad for a greenhorn," he agreed, earning himself a sunny smile.

"Thank you."

Keeping to the side streets, they rode their mounts to the stables. Tyler made arrangements to hire the horses every morning for the next week.

Afternoon found them at the target range. Tyler placed a Winchester rifle in her hands.

She weighed the weapon. "I was thinking of something a little smaller."

"You'll learn to use a derringer later," he promised. "Rifles are more accurate and a helluva lot more deadly. If you ever get in a situation where you need to pull a trigger, I don't want whatever is coming after you to be able to get up."

Sarah looked a bit startled. "Just what do you think is going to come after me?"

"Bear, bandit, wildcat, a man who's been without

a woman's company too long. If you are going to insist on conducting this search yourself, I want you to be prepared for anything."

Rather than frighten her, as she knew he hoped they would, his words brought a gleam of anticipation to her eyes. "Do you really think we will get to see wild animals?"

"Depends on how far north we go."

"And Indians? I would hate to have come all the way west and not see a single Indian."

Tyler sighed in exasperation. "We're not going looking for trouble. I just want you to be prepared if we happen upon any. I hope you'll never have need to use a gun."

"I didn't mean to sound bloodthirsty," Sarah apologized. "I would like to meet an Indian so we could exchange notes on our respective cultures."

Tyler roared with mirthless laughter.

"What's so funny?" Sarah demanded.

"You don't go waltzing into an Indian camp the same as you would a neighbor's parlor. Quite a few of them are more than a little miffed that the white man has taken the land they believe to be rightfully theirs."

She frowned. "I didn't know you still had Indian wars in California."

"For the most part that era of our history has passed, but there are still pockets of violence in the north country." His expression became introspective. "I find it hard to blame the Indians for fighting back. We've broken our word so many times, the treaties we make with them have become an insult to anyone who places honor on a man's word."

"Who is responsible?"

"Indian affairs are controlled by the United States government, but we're all responsible. The law of the west has always been that the strong survive and the weak perish. The Indians are weak, and they stand in the way of progress. The army is intent on wiping them out."

Sarah cast her eyes earthward, feeling shamed by her own shallowness. Back east she had been far removed from the problem and had never spared it a thought. "Can't anything be done to help them?"

"Be upright in your own dealings. Write letters to your congressmen, though I can tell you from bitter experience, more times than not, protest falls on deaf ears. There is little else you can do."

"It was wrong of me to view them as nothing but a curiosity."

"A common mistake of Easterners. Now you know better," he consoled. "The fact that you care at all puts you a cut above the majority of the citizenry."

He ran his finger along the rifle and began naming the parts and their functions.

When Sarah did not give him her complete attention, he tapped her on the nose. "If you're truly concerned about the plight of the Indians, I've plenty of literature on the subject in my library. Just remember, when we're out in the wilderness, no matter who you believe is right or wrong, if you have to shoot to save your life, you do it."

"I don't think I could kill a man," she protested.

"Then think again. I'll not have you going anywhere unless you're willing and able to defend yourself."

"But . . ."

He threw up his hands in disgust. "But nothing. Make up your mind here and now. There's no point in wasting my time or yours if you're too squeamish to use a gun."

He was goading her and she knew it. Worse, she could not deny that what he said made absolute sense. Gritting her teeth, Sarah shook her head. "What did you say was the name of this part?"

Her first attempt to hit the target was a dismal failure, as were the second and third. Every time she squeezed the trigger, the rifle jerked upward and the bullet sailed skyward.

Tyler stepped behind her and encircled her with his arms so he could help her steady the weight of the firearm. "Try again."

She took careful aim and squeezed the trigger. The bullet skimmed the outer ring of the target.

"Better," Tyler pronounced. He helped her fire off several more shots, then stepped back.

"You're on your own this time. Remember how the gun should feel, and don't forget to use your shoulder to brace the butt."

Sarah did as she was told. The lesson continued until her arms were so weary they refused to lift the rifle. Despite her best efforts, her progress was less than spectacular. First she was too high, then too low, too far right, too far left. She was thoroughly frustrated with herself, and she frowned as Tyler took the weapon from her aching arms.

"Tomorrow you'll do better."

"I hope so," she said with feeling.

"Dinner, a hot bath, and a good massage will put you back in fine spirits," he promised. "And I know just the man to provide all three."

The change in his tone and manner signaled he was through playing the role of teacher and ready to be her beau. She gave him a crooked smile and placed her hand in his.

Rather than dining out, as was their habit, they stopped at the California Market for a loaf of crusty bread and the ingredients necessary to fix oyster stew. Tyler prepared the stew while Sarah sliced the bread and poured the wine.

"This is delicious," she complimented as she tested the cream-laden broth directly from the pot on the stove. "I didn't know you could cook."

"One of my many hidden talents," he replied.

"Who taught you?"

"I taught myself." He carried the pot to the table and ladled out steaming portions into their bowls. "Men who are condemned to be bachelors are forced to desperate measures."

"I hardly think your single state is the result of a lack of willing females. I daresay, you could sweet-talk the wings off a butterfly," she commented wryly. Before she could stop herself, she found herself asking a question that had bothered her for some time. "Why haven't you married before now?"

"Never met a woman I wanted to marry until I met you." His eyes glowed as they met hers. "Of course, now that I have, I have every intention of remedying my single state."

"Have some bread." Sarah pushed the plate under his nose to silence him. He lifted a slice and slathered it with butter.

Sarah covertly studied him. She couldn't really accuse him of breaking his promise to her. The turn of the conversation was as much her fault as his. Besides, he hadn't exactly pressed her to succumb to his invitation to wedded bliss. Still, the reminder that all was not as he wished it would be was not appreciated. It made her feel culpable for being so happy with things the way they were.

There was a long silence while she searched her mind for some other topic of conversation.

"I almost forgot to tell you. We're going to church tomorrow," she announced when she settled upon one to her liking.

"We are?" Tyler asked, his interest piqued. Heretofore Sarah had not exhibited the slightest sign of religious zeal. Being a man who preferred a private relationship with God, he had assumed she was of like mind.

"Yes, I promised Agnes," she explained.

"Why?"

"Surely you haven't forgotten Mr. Bevington?" Sarah queried.

Tyler managed to look properly shamefaced. "To be truthful, I haven't given him a second thought since I looked into his background for you."

"Well, if you will recall, you found him to be unattached and a gentleman. On my own I discovered he attends St. Patrick's Church on Mission

Street."

"I see you two ladies are still scheming to catch the poor fellow." He reached across the table and tapped the tip of her nose with his finger. "Don't you think laying a trap in the house of God is a bit blasphemous?"

"It is no such thing," Sarah promised. "I'm sure God, in his infinite wisdom, would approve of my aiding the course of true love."

He chuckled. "I should have guessed this was your idea."

"Agnes is shy. She needs a guiding hand in these matters," she earnestly reasoned.

Tyler groaned good-naturedly. "If being with Mr. Bevington makes Agnes happy, I am more than willing to play your game for her sake. Perhaps we can find some reason to invite the pair to join us for an evening on the town."

"My thoughts exactly." Sarah beamed at him. "When do you think we can arrange it?"

Agnes and Mr. Bevington continued to dominate the conversation as they did the dishes. Sarah was so enraptured with devising various stratagems to get them together, Tyler could not resist commenting, "For a woman who claims to have an aversion to marriage, you certainly are eager to see others walk down the aisle."

"It wouldn't be right for me to impose my sentiments on Agnes. Whether or not she wants to go so far as to marry Mr. Bevington is up to her. I am only intent on providing them with the opportunity to get better acquainted." She paused for breath.

"Besides, I have nothing against marriage in general, it is only for myself in particular that I don't approve of the conjugal state."

Tyler opened his mouth to inform Sarah that despite her professed opinion concerning herself, her days as a single woman were numbered, but he bit his tongue. Why put her on her guard? She was enjoying the role of matchmaker, and he was enjoying her company. Though he craved the emotional security of marriage, he was ever cognizant that if he pressed his suit too hard too soon, he risked losing her altogether.

He wanted to proclaim his love for Sarah to the world, but for now he would have to content himself with the occasional subtle reminder of his honorable intentions and the enthusiastic practice of the art of lovemaking.

Sunday was such a smashing success, Sarah felt no qualms leaving Agnes and Mr. Bevington to their own devices while she concentrated on her riding and shooting lesson.

Every morning she looked forward to her riding instruction. The purchase of a split skirt put an end to the issue of the sidesaddle, and Sarah came to love the feeling of freedom that galloping along the hillsides, the breeze ruffling her hair, afforded her. Tyler seemed to look forward to the daily outing as much as she.

The hours they spent on the firing range were a different matter. Though Tyler was a patient teacher, each day Sarah left the field so frustrated she could scream. It took a full week of daily practice before she began to hit the target with anything approaching consistency. The bull's-eye eluded her completely.

If she had not been so eager to start on the trail, she could have accepted her lack of aptitude with grace, but Tyler had said he was not going to let her go anywhere until she had proven she could take care of herself. He took advantage of every opportunity to remind her of the harsh realities of trail life. Since in this case his demands made sense, and she found his companionship too engaging to wish to strike out on her own, she was determined to become accomplished with a gun.

To that end she secretly returned to the firing range for more practice when he was occupied elsewhere. Her ears had begun to ring constantly, but she would not give up. Finally her efforts began to pay off, and he pronounced her ready to graduate to a handgun.

Coward that she was, she had hoped they'd be on their way by now. She had received another letter from her mother—this one intimating that she was contemplating a visit to San Francisco to "personally escort her back to Baltimore and the bosom of her family." If she could believe her mother lonely for her company, she would feel compassion for her, but as the majority of the letter was taken up extolling the virtues of several wealthy and aged bachelors, she didn't have to guess at her mother's true purpose for wanting her home.

But there were reasons other than her slow progress on the firing range for postponing the beginning of their journey. The men who were responsible for her abduction were being brought to trial, and her presence was required in court to see the miscreants did not escape retribution.

Sarah and Tyler both agreed that bringing these men to justice took priority over a speedy commencement of their journey. It was her duty to protect the lives of others who might fall victim to a similar scheme if the men were allowed to go unpunished.

Though she had no clear date for their departure, she sat down immediately and replied to her mother's letter, informing her that a trip to San Francisco would be futile as she would no longer be in the city by the time her mother arrived. She did not mention that the very thought of her mother invading the new life she was trying to create in California filled her with panic.

As soon as she mailed the letter, she began to feel better and was once again able to accept the necessity to delay her journey with relative calm.

Sarah savored the fragrant fresh country air as she waited for Tyler and his horse to catch up with her. They had gone farther afield today, and with not a soul in sight, she pulled the pins from her hair, letting it fall to her shoulders in loose waves.

Although she was unable to escape San Francisco, she had discovered she could escape the lingering fear that her mother would momentarily descend upon her by the frenzied pursuit of pleasure.

When Tyler was almost abreast of her, she nudged her horse in the flank and set off at a run, leaving a trail of dust and laughter in her wake.

"So you want to play games, do you?" he called after her. He urged his mount to a faster pace and raced after her.

Her hair flew behind her like a dark, daring flag. In his mind's eye Tyler could see the flush of exhilaration on her cheeks, the mischievous sparkle in her green eyes. When he caught her, he would teach her a lesson that had nothing to do with horses. He would teach her about the folly of provoking a lustful man.

Sarah was gripped with a powerful excitement as she pitted her horse against his. The rhythm of the horse, the rush of the wind, the thrill of issuing a challenge combined forces and sent her spirits soaring.

She managed to keep a healthy distance between them for quite some time before he began to close the gap. The sound of horse's hooves thundered in her ears as he came ever closer.

They were racing side by side now; then, suddenly, she felt herself lifting in the air. Tyler whooped for joy as he threw her across his lap.

Reining in his horse, he loomed over her.

"How'd you do that?" she squeaked from her undignified position.

"Another one of my hidden talents," he proclaimed as he shifted her to a more comfortable position. She immediately caught the feral gleam in his eye. "And now, my sweet lover, you are at my mercy."

Sarah looped her arms around his neck. "Out in the open? In broad daylight?" she asked in mock horror.

"Yep," he drawled.

"What if someone comes upon us?"

"You should have thought of that before you tempted me beyond reason. You have made your bed, madam; now you must lie in it."

His lips claimed hers, and Sarah gave up all pretense of protest. Lowering her to the ground, he dismounted and hobbled his horse.

"What about the mare?" she asked.

"She'll wander back this way when she has a mind to. In the meantime, I suggest," he took her hand and led her under the shade of a nearby oak tree, "we entertain each other while we wait."

Eagerly shedding their clothes, they formed a makeshift mattress of their garments and lay down together. The sunlight filtered between the canopy of leaves, dappling their flesh.

Their lips met in a series of brief kisses as their hands explored the contours of each other's limbs.

Sarah ran her fingers through the hair covering his chest, teasing his nipples with her tongue.

He suckled her breasts until she squirmed with want of him; then he claimed her lips once more.

This time his kiss was slow, lingering, building the heat between them until it matched that of the sun overhead.

"You're beautiful," he whispered into her ear as he nibbled its perimeter.

"So are you," she returned the compliment.

He nuzzled her neck. "You smell like roses."

"You smell like a horse."

A chuckle rumbled up from deep within his chest. "A horse, is it? Your insult has earned you the honor of doing all the work." He rolled so she lay atop him.

"But I'm lazy," she demurred.

She found herself back on her back. "Then I guess I'll have to do the riding." Parting her thighs, he eased himself into her.

Sarah bucked playfully.

"Whoa, girl," he soothed. "This old cowpoke isn't going to hurt you. He just wants a sweet little ride."

She boxed his ears, and they rolled off their blanket onto the grass, giggling like children.

Their twinkling eyes met. Words were abandoned, and the looks they exchanged became smoldering as they arched together. They moved slowly at first, then built to a headlong rush toward the crest of passion and shuddering release.

Their skin glistening with perspiration, they lay panting with exhaustion, still wrapped in each other's arms.

"This feels decadent," Sarah murmured against his chest. "We'll have to do it more often."

"Pagan!"

Paling, she abruptly sat up, tucking her knees under her chin. "I knew it. Deep down you disapprove of me. Though you are willing to make use of my passionate nature, you would prefer I was prim and proper."

Tyler pulled her back down, covering her bare

flesh with his weight. "Now what the hell put that idea in your head?"

Sarah gave him a pointed look. "You called me a pagan."

He rolled his eyes heavenward. "I was teasing, you goose. I love you just as you are."

She studied him intently. She tested him with a passionate kiss. He responded enthusiastically.

Still not completely convinced, she nervously drummed her fingers against his temples. "Much as I like you, Mr. Bennet, I cannot figure you out."

Tyler looked dumbfounded. "I don't know why not. I'm a straightforward sort of fellow."

"Hah! One minute you're a priggish gentleman, the next a seductive rogue. You quote Shakespeare and Bierce in the same breath. You beg for my hand in marriage, but are willing to take me like a stallion takes a mare in a field."

He shrugged. "I'm adaptable."

"You're confusing me."

"Good. Confusion is a step in the right direction."

She frowned at him. "That is exactly the kind of statement that leaves me at a loss as to your meaning."

"So don't think, just enjoy me."

"I like to think. It stimulates me."

"Then think about how stimulating life as my wife would be. You could spend the rest of your life trying to puzzle me out."

"Tyler Bennet, remember your promise," she admonished.

"Sorry. It just slipped out." He didn't look at all

sorry; then, his expression changed to one of attentiveness, and he cocked his head to one side. "Speaking of stimulating, I hear the sound of approaching hoofbeats, and I don't think it's our mare. Might I suggest it stimulate a hasty retreat back into our clothes."

Tyler laughed as Sarah scrambled for the brush, clothes in hand. She need not fear he would ever seriously mistake her for a hedonist. Underneath her carefully cultivated cosmopolitan exterior, Sarah Williams had a streak of propriety a mile wide.

Chapter 13

It took another week for the Blue Wheel case to be settled. All involved had been convicted of various and sundry crimes. Only Captain Slodds had escaped the reach of justice, but a warrant had been issued for his arrest when and if he ever returned to the Port of San Francisco.

Now, nothing stood in the way of their departure.

"When do we leave?" Sarah asked eagerly as they walked away from the courthouse.

"Tomorrow. Knowing how anxious you are to get started, I took the liberty of booking passage on the late ferry. I assume you'll have no trouble being ready by then."

"I've been ready for weeks," she replied with a grateful grin. "And thank you for being so efficient."

"Just part of my never-ending effort to prove I would make a life's mate nonpareil."

Having long since grown used to these occasional slips of the tongue, Sarah ignored his remark. She sometimes found it vexing to be reminded of the ultimate purpose behind his companionship, but most of the time he was very good about avoiding the subject of matrimony. Besides, experience had taught her that if she brought his faux pas to his attention, the matter would escalate into a full-blown conversation. Silence is golden, she mused.

After a quiet dinner at home, they spent the night making love in Tyler's big four-poster bed. As always, the experience was highly rewarding.

The next morning they went their separate ways: Tyler to his office to tie up loose ends, and Sarah to the Grand Hotel to remove the last of her belongings and officially check out.

Returning to Tyler's home, she packed what she thought she would need for the journey in a large valise and stored the rest in a guest bedroom. Rummaging through the closets, she found a leather traveling bag and proceeded to pack for Tyler.

When he rejoined her later that afternoon, he was pleasantly surprised.

"It's nice to have a woman do for me." He pulled her into his arms for a passionate kiss. "Be careful you don't treat me too well, or I shall abandon my resolve to be patient."

"Then I shall abandon you," she warned, but her expression was such that her words did not carry much sting. "Did you get everything settled at the office?"

"Everything is in order," he replied, reluctantly letting the subject of their marriage fall by the wayside. He had weeks ahead of him to press his suit, and he fully intended to take advantage of every opportunity to do so. Protecting Sarah from harm was not the only reason he was going on this little venture. "I'll carry the bags down, if you'll double-check the doors and windows to make sure the house is locked up tight."

Sarah nodded her agreement and set about her task. A few minutes later, she presented herself in the entry hall.

The hired carriage had arrived, and the men had already loaded their luggage. Tyler locked the front door behind her, then handed her up into the hack. As soon as both his passengers were settled, the driver flicked the reins and they were off.

Sarah was filled with a delightful sense of anticipation as they rolled along the streets. Would she find her father in Sacramento? Though she was eager to find him, she knew a part of her would be disappointed if her search came to fruition too quickly. To her mind, the whole affair was something akin to a treasure hunt, and she was looking forward to the journey as much as to the results. The uncomfortable knowledge that at the end of her particular rainbow she might find an old boot instead of a pot of gold shaped her attitude. She had ample reason to fear her father would not be happy to see her, and from the beginning her fervor to find him had run like the tide, rising and ebbing with her moods. Besides, it would be a pity if she was never afforded the opportunity to test her newfound skills.

She glanced in Tyler's direction. He wore a pleasant expression, but she could not read his thoughts. She hoped he shared some of her enthusiasm for this trek. He was so good to her, and even she sometimes viewed her behavior as self-absorbed.

Reminding herself he was here because he had invited himself, not because she had requested his presence, she tried not to feel culpable for taking him away from his other responsibilities. It was not her fault he had yet to let her pay him a penny for his services. No matter how much he protested, she intended to settle accounts when her father was found. She further reminded herself she was not his keeper any more than he was hers. The decision to come had been his. Just because she was glad he would be by her side did not mean she need feel obligated to him.

The side-wheeler belched great clouds of steam as it gently rocked in its berth. A scaled-down version of a Mississippi paddle wheeler, it was painted white with bright blue trim. Already its decks were aswarm with passengers — some dressed in silks and fine woolens, others garbed in sturdy denim and flannel.

Tyler paid their driver, arranged to have their baggage carried aboard, then guided her to the gangway. Pulling their tickets from his pocket, he presented them to the boarding agent.

"Welcome aboard, Mr. and Mrs. Bennet. Pleasant journey," he greeted.

Sarah scowled at Tyler as he ushered her onto the boat. "What is the meaning of this?" she demanded in a low whisper.

"Since I could not bring myself to book separate cabins, for your reputation's sake, we are traveling under the guise of man and wife."

"Why wasn't I consulted?"

"Because I feared you'd object."

"I do." Twice in one day was too much for even a tolerant woman like herself to overlook, and this contrivance wasn't even subtle. She drummed her fingers on the ship's railing as she stared out over the city, her lips drawn tight with annoyance.

"If it will make you feel better, I can ask the captain to make fiction fact," Tyler offered magnanimously.

"I am not going to be coerced into marrying you. I can't believe you would stoop so low." Before he could defend himself she continued, "How long have you been hatching this ill-conceived scheme?"

"Actually, less than thirty seconds. If the truth be known, a riverboat captain has no authority to marry."

"Then why on earth did you suggest it?"

He grinned coyly. "First thing that popped into my head?"

"You're obsessed with the idea of marriage," Sarah chided. "One would think you would be more than happy with things the way they are. After all, you have all the advantages of marriage with none of the responsibility."

Tyler shook his head in disagreement, covering one of her hands with his. "A sense of responsibility, my dear lady, is born of affection, not a piece of paper."

Sarah pulled her hand from his and tucked it into the pocket of her skirt. "Nevertheless, I still say our present arrangement is the most advantageous for both of us," she argued.

"But I'm selfish."

She stared at him slack-jawed. Of all the things she had expected he might say, a declaration of self-centeredness was not among them. "What do you mean? You're the most selfless person I have ever met."

His pleasure with her high opinion spread across his face. "I don't want to share you with any other man," he explained, his expression becoming slightly less exuberant. "If we were married, I could openly proclaim to the world that you are mine and no other's."

"The way you hover over me, I think your fears are groundless. Even if I desired to do so, which I don't, I haven't enough time or energy to nurture another romance. There is absolutely no reason for either of us to put fetters on our relationship, and I would appreciate it if for the duration of this journey you let me worry about my own reputation." Sarah made her speech, then turned toward him, waiting expectantly for his reply.

"If you would worry about yourself, I wouldn't be compelled to do it for you. Besides, I'm smitten and therefore shouldn't be held wholly accountable for my behavior." His eyes widened innocently as he gazed down at her with a look of pitiful longing. He was becoming quite adept at adopting such a mien at will, and he congratulated himself. He found it very effective. "Would you really condemn a man for loving you too much?"

"Yes," she replied, but a smile had crept to her rosy lips. "It's beyond me why I put up with you."

"Maybe you're smitten too."

"But *with what* is the mystery."

He laughed at her pained expression and once again took her hand in his. "Come on, let's check to see that our luggage made it into our cabin; then, I'll show you around the ship."

Having no desire to spend the trip arguing, she did not belabor the issue of traveling as man and wife. Though it made her uncomfortable, it was probably a sensible way to avoid trouble with the captain about their sleeping arrangements should he subscribe to any old-fashioned notions of propriety. As long as Tyler and she both knew where they stood, what the captain and other passengers thought was of little consequence.

Their cabin was on the upper deck and comfortably appointed with a wide berth, built-in wardrobe, and an escritoire to accommodate traveling businessmen. They stayed just long enough to ascertain that their luggage had indeed arrived, then set off on their tour of the steamboat.

While the cabins were comfortable, the public lounge, dining rooms, and promenade stopped nothing short of luxurious. Opulently furnished in the latest Victorian decor, it boasted marble-topped tables, gilt-framed mirrors, and red plush upholstery. The molding was exquisite, the railing skirting the mezzanine elegantly turned. A trio of musicians provided entertainment.

If this was Tyler's idea of hardship, Sarah could only wonder at his standards for the soft life. She started to quiver with amusement.

"Are you feeling unwell?" he queried solicitously.

"I am merely quaking with fear at the sight of all this frontier rustication. How I shall manage, I simply do not know," she panted, bringing her hand to her bosom as if to quiet an agitated heart.

"We will see how flippant you are should our search take us beyond the state capital," he retorted.

Sarah's eyes flashed. "I look forward to the challenge."

"I know you do. That is why I booked us on the most luxurious steamer plying the river. There is no telling where you will drag me before you allow me the comfort of my own soft bed again."

In her zeal for adventure she had not even considered that his dissertations on the hardships they could be called to face might be motivated as much by concern for his own comfort. Not every man was enamored with the rugged life, even if he chose to make his living in the west. She had simply made the assumption that he would view such things as facing desperadoes and living off the land as routine. "Is it really going to be so bad for you?" she asked with true distress.

"Rest assured, I shall survive the experience far better than you," he quipped. "Though I am a man who likes his comforts, I can live perfectly well without them." His eyes twinkled merrily. "The more interesting question is: Can you?"

The trip up the quarter-mile-wide American River was peaceful. They talked and teased as they strolled about the deck, taking in the scenery as it floated by. At dusk they ate a sumptuous meal, then returned to the deck to bask in the moonlight. Later that night they made passionate love in the cozy confines of their private cabin.

Sarah initiated their lovemaking, as she often did, giving her sensual nature full permission to express itself.

Tyler abetted her with lickerish glee. Though the prize of marriage might still elude his grasp, compensation was not without its merit. He would pretend patience for as long as it served his purpose, but if a more direct approach was called for, he would not hesitate to toss Sarah Williams over his shoulder and physically carry her to the altar. He wanted her for his wife, and he would have her for his wife. If she was naive enough to think it would be otherwise, she was in for a big surprise.

Thaddeus Johnson ushered the thin, bewhiskered man into his office and closed the door. "I have another job for you, Mr. Sneed." He motioned for the gentleman to take a chair.

"Always glad to help bring a criminal to justice. Has the fellow skipped town, or are you just looking for information to seal your case?"

Johnson hesitated before he replied. "This has nothing to do with any criminal case. It is a private matter. I called you here because you are one of the best detectives in the business, and in the past I have been able to depend on your discretion."

Mr. Sneed accepted the compliment with a nod. "What is it you want me to do?"

"There is a woman, a Mrs. Sarah Williams. I'm sure you remember her from the massive search my partner instigated on her behalf. I want you to find out everything you can about her." Johnson handed him a packet. "I've compiled everything I know. If you find something I can use, I'll pay double your usual fee."

"Just exactly what kind of information would you find useful?"

"Anything that can be used against her. She has bewitched my partner. He's with her now, running around the countryside on a fool's errand." Johnson pursed his lips in disgust. "I need evidence to convince him not to throw his life away for his ladylove."

Mr. Sneed shifted uncomfortably. "He's a grown man. What business is it of yours?"

"Since his father's death, Tyler has been like a son to me. Until *she* came along, he has always been a sensible man. Now, he is hell-bent on ruining his future. I can't stand idly by and do nothing," Johnson argued passionately.

"Well, it's not my usual case, but I've never known you to hire me without good cause." Sneed offered his hand. "When do you want me to start?"

"As soon as possible. You can catch up with them in Sacramento."

"Do you want me to follow them both?"

"Yes, but if they split up, stick with her. Report back to me on a regular basis. I have another man working in Baltimore. Between the two of you I should have no trouble setting wrong to right."

A deep whistle cut through the early morning air, signaling the steamer's arrival in Sacramento. Stretching the languor of sleep from their limbs, Sarah and Tyler hurried into their clothes and stepped out on deck.

The city was bustling with activity. Having briefly stopped there on her way to San Francisco, Sarah was not completely new to Sacramento, but her bright green eyes took in the wooden sidewalks, brick streets, and whitewashed buildings as if seeing them for the first time. The trees around the wharves had been cut down long ago, but further downriver grew mighty oaks. Willow trees dipped their branches towards the river's surface with each puff of breeze.

Inland there was no fog to plague the morning hours and the sun sparkled on the water, promising a warm day. Sarah shaded her eyes against the brightness with her hand as they waited to disembark.

The first order of business was to check their belongings into a hotel. Tyler had wired ahead from San Francisco for reservations, and there was a room waiting for "Mr. and Mrs. Bennet." Sarah said nothing, but her look was less than approving.

As soon as they were settled, they set about visiting newspaper offices to place advertisements and going to government offices to pour through their records.

* * *

Sarah pushed back her chair and stood, rolling her shoulders to alleviate the tension in them. "I have got to get out of here for some fresh air. The words are starting to swim before my eyes."

Tyler glanced up, pushed his glasses up the bridge of his nose, and smiled sympathetically. "Do you want me to come with you?"

"I'm not really planning on going anywhere. I was thinking a brisk walk around the block to wake myself up; then it's back to work." She indicated the stack of county records on the table with a sweep of her hand. "But you're welcome to come if you like."

"Instead of waking yourself up, why don't you go over to the hotel and have a catnap," he suggested. "I can finish up here."

"That hardly sounds fair to you," she protested.

"Consider it my penance for keeping you up half the night." He twirled the ends of his mustache, his eyes gleaming with roguish delight. "I really don't mind."

Sarah blushed at the remembered pleasure of lying naked in his arms. "If memory serves, last night was my doing."

"So it was," he conceded, grinning broadly. "Nevertheless, I think you have earned a nap."

She covered her mouth with her hand to stifle a yawn. "Are you sure you don't mind?"

"Positive. There are still a couple of hours of work left in me, and I'd like to get through as many of these records as possible." He lowered his gaze to the document before him.

Though a nap sounded just the thing, Sarah was reluctant to abandon Tyler in the stuffy little room when there was still work to be done. There was absolutely no adventure to this aspect of her search, and she feared he found it as dull as she did.

Sensing her hesitation, Tyler rose to his feet and ushered her to the door. "Make it up to me tonight," he suggested in a low whisper. "Now scat!"

Sarah walked out of the building into the sunlight. Almost immediately she began to feel revived, and she decided she was more in the mood for a stroll than a nap.

She meandered aimlessly, looking in shop windows and pausing to watch construction on the state capitol building. A replica of the nation's capitol, it was magnificent even in its unfinished form.

Her wanderings took her towards the outskirts of town, and her eye was caught by another wonder. There, rising from the middle of a field, was the red and blue silk of a hot-air balloon.

She had read articles and looked at sketches of them but had never seen a real balloon. It was fascinating and beautiful. Picking up her skirts, she hurried across the field.

As she came closer, she could see the huge balloon was still tethered to the earth, and a man and a boy were bustling about it. A horse-drawn wagon stood a short distance away. "Excuse me . . . do you mind if I watch?" she called as she approached them.

"Be my guest," the man invited. "The name is John Giles, and that's my boy Billy."

"Pleased to meet you." Sarah held out her hand.

"My name is Sarah Williams."

Mr. Giles accepted her extended hand, but Billy ducked his head and stepped away.

"Don't mind him. He doesn't get on well with strangers. Keep thinking he'll grow out of it, but he's coming up on fourteen and still barely says a word." He lay his arm on his son's shoulders and gave him a hearty squeeze. "But he's a real good boy. Ain't you, Billy?"

Billy nodded his head affirmatively and busied himself checking the rigging. His father joined him.

Sarah shaded her eyes to get a better look. The whole of the balloon was covered with a netting of rope, the ends of which were secured to a wicker basket. Ballasts were tied around the basket. Between the basket and the mouth of the balloon hung some sort of burning apparatus. It flamed brightly.

"What does flying feel like?" she asked the elder Giles.

"Nothing like it in the world," he replied.

"Have you been doing it long?"

"Learned how during the war, and it got in my blood. After my wife died I sold the farm, and me and my boy have been doing exhibitions at county fairs and such ever since."

Taking a deep breath, Sarah continued, "Do you ever take passengers up?"

He eyed her curiously. "Why? Are you interested?"

She knew a fleeting moment of trepidation, but it was overwhelmed by a wave of ebullience. "Yes."

"It'll cost you," he warned. "Coal to keep this thing burning doesn't come cheap, and it takes more to keep two aloft than one."

"I'm willing to bear the expense."

"Well, I guess you've just bought yourself the ride of a lifetime." He ceased his labor and extended his hand to seal the deal. "Couple things you ought to know though before you climb in this basket. First, once you go up you don't come down until the balloon is ready for you to come down, and I don't have perfect control over where that will be. Second, we won't be going very high."

"I'm not frightened," she assured him.

"I can see that, and I like a lady with spirit, but fear has nothing to do with it. The air's too warm. The way these things work, the air on the outside of the balloon has to be cooler than the air on the inside, or it doesn't go up. It's the wrong time of year and the wrong time of day to set any height records."

Sarah nodded. "Well, it certainly sounds like you know what you're doing. When do we go up?"

"It'll take a few more minutes to heat her up proper."

While they had been talking, a steady stream of curious souls had followed her path across the field and a sizable crowd had gathered. They too began to ask questions. Sarah listened attentively as Mr. Giles continued to explain the aerodynamics of ballooning.

She was so enamored with the idea of drifting among the clouds, the bubbling excitement filling her was almost enough to lift her off the ground without aid of the balloon.

When Mr. Giles climbed into the wicker basket

and held out his hand to her, she followed without hesitation.

"Ready?" he asked.

"Ready," she confirmed.

Billy untied the ropes from the stakes that kept the balloon earthbound. Mr. Giles increased the flame, and the balloon drifted slowly upward. The basket swayed gently under Sarah's feet as it left the ground.

"Oh, no," she exclaimed.

"Too late for second thoughts," he informed her, his expression kindly.

"I'm not having any. I just remembered I have a friend on the ground who thinks I'm napping at my hotel." She leaned over the edge of the basket. "Will someone please get word to Mr. Tyler Bennet that I am cloud-bound?" she shouted. "He's staying at the City Hotel. Leave a message if he's not in."

Several hands signaled her request had been received and would be honored, and she relaxed.

As they rose above the ground, Mr. Giles was occupied with the tasks of ascension. Sarah was consumed with the sensations of flight. Mr. Giles was right: there was nothing in the world like it, and she could not find words adequate to verbalize her feelings.

They leveled off and began to drift eastward. Below the crowd had shrunk to the size of insects. Trees and houses appeared as miniatures. The sense of exhilaration, of total freedom, was magnificent.

"I can see why you abandoned the farm for this," she commented, her smile radiant.

"A born aeronaut, heh?" He grinned. "Glad you're enjoying your ride."

"Yes, it's even more wonderful than I imagined it would be. I'm curious, though—why can't I feel the wind?"

"Because we've become a part of it," he explained. "If you look real close, you can see little wisps of vapor and motes of dust. Watch them and you'll know which way we'll go next."

Sarah's gaze followed his, focusing on the nearly invisible airborne particles of dust. He continued to enlighten her on the intricacies of flight, answering her many questions and asking a few of his own. Mr. Giles was as congenial by nature as Sarah, and they got along famously.

As they continued to float above farms and grasslands, occasionally one or the other would disturb the quiet with a comment or question, but mostly they privately reveled in the celestial silence.

Tyler Bennet bolted out of the hotel lobby and stared skyward. On the horizon he could see a dot of color drifting across the azure blue sky.

"How could she?" he muttered to himself. He crumpled the slip of paper in his pocket. The desk clerk had told him he had missed the messenger by only a few minutes.

Friend up in balloon. Doesn't want you to worry. What the hell kind of message was that? The woman he intended to marry was dangling in some straw basket in the sky and he was supposed to just sit back and enjoy a pot of tea?

He frowned so fiercely his face hurt. "Where's the best place in town to rent a horse?" he demanded of the first passerby.

"The livery right down the street." The man pointed. "Can't miss it."

"Thanks." Tyler raced down the street, glancing skyward every few steps so he would not lose sight of the balloon. It was a lucky thing he had decided to call it a day early. His lips set in a grim line. He was going to throttle Sarah when he got his hands on her.

He secured a horse and gave chase, keeping to the roads whenever possible so his progress would not be hampered by fences.

Using the red and blue balloon as his beacon, he followed, pushing the horse beneath him as hard as he dared. As long as he could see the balloon in the air, he knew she was still all right and the roll of his emotions calmed to a mild tempest.

Just as his mind was beginning to win the battle with the panic gnawing at his gut, the balloon suddenly began a rapid descent and dropped out of sight. He kicked his mount to a breakneck pace.

As he rode, he mentally rehearsed what he would say to Sarah when he caught up with her, using anger to mask his harrowing fear for her safety. Still, hideous visions of her mangled, lifeless body haunted the edges of every conscious thought.

It took a full half hour before he caught sight of the balloon hanging from the branches of a huge oak tree. The joy that leapt into his breast upon seeing

Sarah unharmed, standing in the dangling basket, was quickly replaced by a towering rage.

He galloped across the open field, startling off the small herd of cattle grazing under the shade of the tree.

At first, he was too infuriated to say anything to her as he stood staring up at her and the stranger who shared the basket, but Sarah could feel his displeasure rising from the earth.

"Hello, Tyler," she ventured meekly.

He opened his mouth to speak and clamped his lips shut several times before he managed a barely controlled, "Hello, Sarah. Did you have a nice nap?"

"I'm afraid I got distracted on the way to the hotel."

"Yes. I can see that," he mewed.

His deadly tone caused Sarah and Mr. Giles to exchange nervous glances.

"I don't think your gentleman friend is too happy with you," Mr. Giles whispered under his breath.

"He does seem a bit miffed," she returned in equally low tones. "But don't worry, he's not given to acts of violence."

Giles nodded his thanks for this piece of information.

Despite her reassurances, Sarah leaned close and whispered, "I suppose there's no way you can get this thing to go up again, is there?"

The mischievous twinkle of a guilty co-conspirator was so bright in her eyes, Mr. Giles burst out laughing. Sarah joined him in his amusement.

"What the hell is going on up there?" Tyler demanded. "Sarah, can't you tell I am livid! You could have got yourself killed! If you have a death wish, at least have the decency to give me the pleasure of relieving some of my frustration by wringing your neck."

"Sorry, I didn't mean to start laughing," she apologized between trills of ill-muted merriment. "You know what would really make you feel better. A ride in this balloon."

"It doesn't look to me as if that balloon is in any shape to go anywhere."

"Sure it is," Mr. Giles warranted. "It's only the rigging got caught in the tree. Replace a few ropes and she'll be good as new by tomorrow or the next day."

Tyler scowled at him. Damned friendly fellow. How dare he lure Sarah into taking a ride with him in his balloon? The unhappy thought she might not have been lured at all followed quickly on its heels. "Sarah, I want you to come down from there. We can continue this discussion at the hotel."

She held up her hands in a gesture of helplessness. "I'd oblige you if I could, but as you can see, we're stuck."

He could not argue the point. Surveying the situation, he searched for some way to remedy it and found none. "What will it take to get you down?" he asked tersely.

"The chaser wagon," John Giles answered him. "It's got everything I need to extricate myself from unfortunate landing situations. Won't be too much longer. I can see my boy coming up the road now. Don't know if it will make you feel any better, but the lady was never in a moment's danger."

"Yes. I can see your skill at maneuvering that thing is without equal."

"Tyler, stop being a stick-in-the-mud," Sarah scolded. "I asked Mr. Giles to take me up. We had a lovely time. We landed awkwardly but safely. End of adventure."

"You and your adventures will turn me gray before my time. Next time you say you want a breath of fresh air, I'll know you're talking about a whole damn sky full of it."

"It was all quite spontaneous. Really," she soothed. "If I'd have known I was going to make Mr. Giles's acquaintance, I would have asked you along."

"Can't take more than one up at a time," the aeronaut interjected a note of practicality.

Tyler ignored Mr. Giles's comment and responded to Sarah. "The fact that I might believe you in no way affects my opinion of this incident. I am doing my best to understand this need you have for adventure, but can't you curb it with at least a little concern for your safety?"

"There is not a scratch on me," Sarah reminded him gently.

Tyler clamped his lips shut. What she said was true. The balloon ride had not harmed her one whit; in fact, with her brightly sparkling eyes and rosy cheeks, the woman positively radiated good health.

He frowned. Was her other statement also true? *Was* he a stick-in-the-mud? It gave him pause. He thought back over the last few years of his life, and his frown deepened. When his father had died, he had thrown himself into his work to help cope with the pain of his loss. He rose early in the morning, hurried to the office, worked late, then returned home to work some more. There was the occasional sail on the bay or night on the town, but they hardly signified.

With a flash of insight, he seized upon the solution to the mystery that had been plaguing him since the moment Sarah Williams walked through his door. He was the kind of man who liked to know why he felt and acted as he did. Though few but the poets attempted to understand love, he needed to understand it to fully accept it, and the reasons he had given himself thus far, as numerous and persuasive as they were, had not wholly satisfied him.

Now he felt he knew why he had been not only willing but happy to turn his life upside down for the widow Williams. She was heaven-sent to save him from a life of stale sobriety.

He raised his gaze, studying the balloon from a fresh perspective. "Is it really as much fun as you say?" he asked.

"More so. I can't describe the feeling to you, but I've never experienced anything like it. Are you seriously thinking of going up?" Sarah asked, her voice bubbling with excitement.

"If Mr. Giles has his balloon in operating order before we leave Sacramento, I'll go up." His lips curled into a grin. "Can't let you go on thinking I'm a stick-in-the-mud."

The arrival of Billy with the chase wagon brought

a halt to their conversation. Tyler stood back as the boy tied the end of a rope ladder to the line his father dropped to him. The ladder was long enough to reach to the ground, and as soon as it was secured, Mr. Giles helped Sarah climb over the edge of the basket.

Once she was safely on the ground, Billy joined his father in the tree and the two men began to work to free the balloon.

"We may be up here a long time," Giles called down. "Feel free to take the lady back to town."

Tyler nodded and started to usher Sarah toward his horse. She turned back toward the tree.

"What about the money I owe you?"

"Where are you staying?"

"The City Hotel."

"I'll come by for it tonight or tomorrow. We can settle on when your gentleman friend wants to go up then too if you'd like."

"I'd like that very much. Oh, I almost forgot, when you come to the hotel, ask for Sarah Bennet. I'm registered under that name." She and Tyler exchanged mutually damning glances.

Giles raised a brow, his expression curious, but his reply did not pry. "I'll do that. Thanks for the fine company."

"Thank you for a lovely experience." Sarah waved as she turned away.

"We're going to have to walk awhile," Tyler warned. "I practically killed this poor horse chasing after that balloon."

"I don't mind," she replied, taking the leads from

his hands and stroking the animal's nose. "I hope you didn't suffer too much."

"Are you talking to me or the horse?" Tyler queried.

Sarah looked sheepish. "The horse. But I'm sorry for any suffering I caused you too," she added, her face expressing an excess of sympathy.

They started across the field toward the ribbon of road winding through the countryside.

"Do you really think I'm a stick-in-the-mud?" he probed.

She studied him a long moment before she replied, "Sometimes. . . . But you are improving upon acquaintance." Laughing, she scampered out of reach when he would have chucked her chin.

Darkness had settled upon the city by the time they had gained its streets. After returning the horse to the livery, they stopped in the hotel dining room for a supper of steak and potatoes, then retired to their room.

When they lay under the covers, Sarah reached for his hand. "Are you tired?" she asked, guiding his hand to her breast. She gently massaged his fingers.

The moonlight streaming through the window caused his teeth to gleam white as he grinned from ear to ear. "Not so tired I can't show a lady a good time." He rolled on top of her and kissed her enthusiastically. "Is this what you had in mind?"

"Exactly." Her arms came round his neck. "The perfect ending to a perfect day."

The next morning they were back to business, sifting through old records as soon as the city hall opened.

Mid morning Sarah came upon a deed with her father's name. "Look, my father bought a house here in 1860. He sold it again in 1861, but I can't find any record of a subsequent sale. If Mr. Carl Mattson, the new owner, still lives there, maybe he can tell us something."

"That would be a piece of luck." Tyler reached for the deed and scanned the document as he spoke. "Do you want to go over there now or keep looking to see if we find anything else?"

"Let's go now," Sarah replied, already halfway to the door. "We can always come back later if we hit a dead end."

They had to stop and ask directions several times before they finally found the address for which they were looking. The one-story clapboard house sat squeezed between two larger homes in an unassuming neighborhood on the south side of town. Tyler knocked on the door.

"If you're selling something, go away!" a gravelly voice called from behind the closed door.

"We're not selling anything," Tyler assured him.

"Are you sure?"

"Yes, we're sure," Sarah chimed in.

The door was opened by an ancient man who smelled of mellow brandy and Cuban cigars. He looked them over from head to toe before he spoke. "Can't abide them traveling sales folk. Ought to be a law against them. If I have a hankering to part with

229

some of my hard-earned cash, I got two good feet to take me down to the general stores. Now, what can I do for you?"

"My name is Tyler Bennet and this is Mrs. Williams. Are you Carl Mattson?"

"Yep."

"I understand you bought this property from Elijah Jenkins several years ago," Tyler continued.

"Sure did."

"We're looking for him."

"Why?"

"Mrs. Williams is his daughter. They lost touch and she would like to find him."

"Do you have any proof you're who you say you are?"

Sarah and Tyler each handed him a calling card.

He glanced at the cards and handed them back. "Those things can be made up in any name. How do I know you don't mean Jenkins some harm?"

"So you do know where he is?" Sarah pressed, her eyes lighting with excitement.

Mattson stroked his beard. "Not saying I do; not saying I don't. Not until you give me better proof."

"I don't have any proof," she lamented, her joyful expression wilting. "I suppose I could send back east for certification of my parentage but that could take weeks."

"My credentials are more easily produced," Tyler informed him. "Wire any judge in San Francisco. He'll tell you who I am."

Mattson's dubious expression moved back and forth between the two; then it settled on Sarah.

"Well, you got his green eyes and you look honest. I'm going to take a chance on you," he addressed his words to her.

"Then you *do* know where he is," she replied.

"I know where he went after he left here. Whether he stayed put or not is anybody's guess."

"Where did he go?" Tyler prodded.

"Virginia City. Thought he'd try his luck in the Comstock."

"Thank you very much." Sarah shook his hand enthusiastically. "What's the fastest way to get there?"

"You can take the Central Pacific as far as Reno. After that you got to switch to the Virginia and Truckee line. Now, if you're through with your questions, I got an old hound dog who's waiting for his ears to be scratched."

The door slammed in their faces.

Tyler and Sarah exchanged amused grins as they listened to Carl Mattson's rapidly retreating footsteps; then they turned in unison and started up the street.

Chapter 14

As a precaution against overlooking some pertinent fact, Tyler and Sarah returned to the stuffy little room that housed the county records. By mid afternoon they had combed every piece of paper in the place.

"I'm glad this task is complete," he commented as Sarah refiled the last deed.

"Me too. What would you like to do with the rest of the day?"

"I suppose we should stop by the hotel to see if anyone has answered our advertisement. If not, we can purchase tickets to Virginia City."

"Shouldn't we wait a day or two to be sure we don't miss anybody?" she asked as they stepped out the door.

"We can if you like, but I don't think it's necessary. My gut tells me Mr. Mattson has already told us what we need to know."

Sarah nodded her agreement with his assessment of the situation. They strolled along, stopping to peruse the merchandise displayed in shop windows and buy a dish of ice cream from a street vendor.

They had almost reached their hotel when Sarah commented, "What about your balloon ride? If we leave tomorrow, you'll miss your chance to go up in Mr. Giles's balloon. It's a chance of a lifetime."

"What about your father?" Tyler queried. "Back in San Francisco you were practically chomping at the bit to be on the trail."

"After all these years, I don't think another day or two is going to matter," Sarah assured him. A thought struck her and she stopped in her tracks, her expression one of serious concern. "I'm sorry, in my eagerness to share my experience, I haven't been thinking of your feelings at all. If you're afraid to fly, I don't want to force you."

"I am cautiously optimistic I will not be killed by indulging your enthusiasm for ballooning," he replied. "And in truth, my curiosity is piqued. I was speaking from a habit of putting business before pleasure. I keep forgetting you subscribe to the opposite philosophy."

"That's not wholly true," Sarah protested.

He flicked a wisp of hair from her forehead. "I didn't mean it as a criticism. Don't forget, I'm here of my own free will. Has it never occurred to you this 'old stick-in-the-mud' was ready for a holiday from duty? You showed up on my doorstep and . . ." He simultaneously shrugged his shoulders and turned his palms upward.

"I wish you would stop bringing up that term. I would never have made the comment if I had known you would take it so much to heart."

233

"It is you I have taken to heart." He brought her hand to his lips and kissed it. "I don't think I would have fallen head over heels in love with you so quickly if you weren't exactly the kind of woman I needed to shake up my life."

"What's that supposed to mean?"

"It means I am more determined than ever to have you for my wife. Care to capitulate now and make our union legal?"

Despite his auspicious treatment, marriage and oppression were so kindred in her mind she instinctively lashed out. "I will never be a subservient wife to you or any other man."

Tyler remained even-tempered. "Good. That's the last thing I want from you."

She stared at him, feeling both relieved and confused. "What is it you want?"

"Adventure, romance, lovemaking," he announced. "And I'm getting all three in spades."

When Mr. Giles stopped by their hotel for his money, arrangements were made for Tyler to go up the next morning. They ascended and descended with nary a hitch.

Tyler found the experience as exhilarating as Sarah, causing him to further cement his recently embraced opinion that he had been on the road to the land of humdrum before Sarah had come to his rescue with her joie de vivre.

He and Sarah were good for each other. He was as certain of her need for him as he was of his for her.

Love was what had been missing from her life, and he was more than willing to provide a lifetime of adoration.

No one came forward to answer their newspaper advertisement, and the next day they boarded a Central Pacific train bound for Nevada.

When she had last passed this way, going in the opposite direction, Sarah had been too tired to pay much attention. Today, with a friend by her side to share her thoughts and feelings, she saw the countryside with fresh eyes as they began the seven-thousand-foot climb out of Sacramento into the granite and tree-covered mountains of the Sierra Nevada.

"This is beautiful country," she commented as she gazed out the window. "I can see why California lured so many to her."

"It's not the beauty of the mountains but what lay in their streams that enticed so many to come. Like it or not, California was built on greed."

"Gold was why my father came," she admitted.

"I wouldn't hold that against him. He had lots of company."

Her expression became thoughtful. "When I was a little girl, I used to pretend some tragedy had befallen him and he couldn't come back for us—that one day he was going to show up on our doorstep bearded and bedraggled and full of love for his family." She abruptly straightened her shoulders. "I'm sounding melancholy, aren't I? Can't have that."

He squeezed her hand. "There's no reason you shouldn't talk about your father if you feel the need."

"No. There'll be time enough to think about my

father when and if we find him. Besides, it wouldn't be fair to judge him before I meet him for myself." She tidily dismissed the subject. "Have you noticed how plush this rail car is? It wasn't so long ago, pioneers were struggling over these mountains in ox-drawn wagons."

His gaze followed hers as it drifted over the crimson curtains striped with gold, silver lamps hanging from the ceiling, and Axminster carpet. "The wheels of progress churn at an amazing rate," Tyler agreed, respecting her wish to move on to a less personal topic. He continued to cradle her hand. It was curious . . . searching for her father in the abstract fascinated Sarah. The idea that there would be a flesh-and-blood man at the end of their quest she seemed to accept with less enthusiasm.

As the train puffed its way up the steep mountainside, Tyler pointed out wildlife and places of interest, giving her a brief history lesson and entertaining her with colorful tales of varying degrees of believability.

The time passed quickly, and before they realized, they had reached the summit and were on their way down the other side, following the serpentine tracks leading down to Carson's Sink.

At Truckee Meadows they switched to the canary yellow coach cars reserved for passengers on the ore trains operated by the Virginia and Truckee line.

The terrain on the east side of the mountains was dry and desolate. The only evidence remaining of the forest of piñon trees that had once covered these slopes were stumps poking through the alkaline dust. After the lushness of the western slopes, the contrast

236

was startling.

Stepping off the train at Virginia City, Sarah looked around her with a mixture of amazement and dismay. The city of twenty-five thousand was built on the slopes of a barren mountain, its streets steep and buildings built so close the members of one household could reach out the window and shake hands with the members of the next. Sluices wound down the mountainside like giant snakes. The sun beat down, hot and merciless, without the shade of a single tree to provide relief. The deep, rhythmic thunder of mills reverberated through the dry air.

"Not exactly paradise," Tyler commented as he reached into his pocket for a handkerchief to wipe the sweat from his brow.

Sarah nodded her agreement as a driver for hire loaded their bags in his vehicle. She and Tyler joined their luggage.

"Take us to the International Hotel," Tyler instructed.

"You've been here before?" Sarah asked in surprise.

"Yes. Business often takes me in this direction."

It was too hot to talk, and they lapsed into silence.

As they moved into the heart of the city, Sarah could see Virginia City was not without amenities. There were public buildings rivaling the splendor of those in San Francisco and more than one palatial home. Tom Maguire had established a theater here, and church spires rose above the rooftops. She also noted the overabundance of saloons.

Though the ride was short, she felt thoroughly

wilted by the time they reached the hotel.

"Tyler Bennet. Who'd have thought I'd see you here?" a nattily dressed gentleman called from across the lobby, waving to catch their attention. He covered the distance between them with long strides. "Who's the lady?"

"Sarah Williams." Sarah extended her hand. He bowed over it, then turned a speculative gaze on Tyler.

"Mrs. Williams is a client, a respected client," Tyler informed him tersely. "Mrs. Williams, this is Harry Harrison, a lawyer of dubious reputation and character."

"Still the kidder, I see." Harry guffawed. "What brings you to this part of the country?"

"Privileged information," Tyler replied, covertly nudging Sarah toward the front desk. "Good day, Mr. Harrison."

Tyler booked separate rooms, and Sarah followed the bellboy up the stairs without comment.

As soon as he left, she opened her blouse and threw herself across the bed.

"Tempting, but I'll have to decline your invitation for the moment."

Sarah sat up with a start, staring at Tyler. "How'd you get in here?"

"Side door." He indicated the open portal behind him with a gesture of his hand. "I booked adjoining rooms. Just because I have a penchant for protecting your reputation doesn't mean I'm a devotee of deprivation."

Sarah smiled, undid a few more buttons, and lay

down again. "For your information, I have no intention of inviting you to join me in this bed. I can barely draw sufficient breath the way it is."

He chuckled. "We can haggle over sleeping arrangements tonight. I just stopped in to tell you I'm on my way out to visit the office of the *Territorial Enterprise* to place the usual ad. I get the feeling you'd just as soon move on to cooler climes as soon as possible."

"Give me a minute to freshen up and I'll come with you," she offered but made no move to rise from the bed.

"You needn't bother. Be back in less than an hour." He turned to leave then faced her again. "A word of warning. If you leave the room, try to stay away from Harrison. If he corners you, be polite or rude as suits your fancy, but don't divulge any information about yourself, our relationship, or why we are here."

"Why, don't you like him?"

"He's as crooked as the railroad track that brought us here. At the moment I can't figure out any way he could profit by causing us trouble, but if there is one, you can bet he'll find it."

"I'll avoid him like the plague," Sarah promised, having no particular desire to further the acquaintance.

Striding toward the door, Tyler spun on his heels once more. "Almost forgot, no matter how thirsty you get, don't drink the water while we're here or you'll live to regret it."

"Why is that?"

"It's full of arsenic and a few other unpleasant

extras. Not enough to kill you, but enough to make you sick."

"Thanks for the warnings."

"You're welcome." He closed the door behind him, and she was once again alone.

Though the wary part of her mind argued she should stop pampering herself and get up lest Tyler think less of her resolve to be an equal partner, the heat made her too lazy to care. If they didn't find her father here, the next town she would insist she be the one to visit the newspaper office while Tyler rested. The thought was enough to quiet the warning bells ringing in her head, and she closed her eyes.

Sarah awoke to a darkened room. She hadn't meant to sleep at all, and she was rather disconcerted with herself. Padding on bare feet across the floor, she entered Tyler's room, an apology on her lips, only to find it empty. Her brows knit with worry.

Even without a clock to tell her the time, she knew he had been gone far longer than an hour. She contemplated going out in search of him, but concluded such action might be dangerous and would probably be self-defeating anyway. The newspaper office would be closed by now, and she hadn't a clue where to start looking for him.

When he finally returned, Sarah had had more than ample time to refresh herself with a sponge bath and change into a clean set of clothes. He gave her a husbandly peck on the cheek when he found her waiting for him in his room. "Our advertisement will be in the morning paper," he informed her, turning his attention to the improvement of his own appearance.

"Did you run into some kind of trouble with Mr. Harrison?"

"None in the least. In fact, I had the pleasure of seeing him board a stage out of town."

"Then what took you so long?" A note of censure had crept into her voice. "I was worried about you."

He started to apologize, then stopped, a wicked gleam entering his eyes. "Don't like it when the shoe is on the other foot?"

"I never purposefully try to cause you anxiety," Sarah protested, her outrage growing with her suspicion that he was trying to teach her some object lesson.

"Not guilty," he pleaded. "The truth is, I came back here just as I said I would and found you asleep. I left a note."

"Where?"

"On your dresser." He crossed the threshold to her room. The dresser top was empty. "I know I put it here." Searching the floor, he picked up a slip of paper that was half hidden behind the armoire. "What little breeze is coming through the window must have blown it off. Sorry."

"No, I'm the one who should be sorry. Next time I'll go along with you instead of lying abed like some limp rag," Sarah said. Feeling a strong need to reassert her competence and independence, she continued without pausing for breath or deliberation. "I was thinking, since this is the silver-mining capital of the world, and my father was a miner at least at one time . . . I was thinking it would be most enlightening to tour one of the mines."

Tyler's first inclination was to protest. He held stocks in several mines and had personally toured every one before he had invested. To his mind they were hellish places. But he knew that no matter how noble his intentions, if he tried to dissuade her, she would hold it against him.

Why not turn the situation to his advantage, he asked himself. Here was an ideal opportunity to indulge Sarah's lust for adventure and to prove to her he could be a true egalitarian. She, of course, would be so impressed she could not help but agree to marry him. "I'll arrange it," he promised.

"You will?" Sarah asked in surprise.

"If it's what you want." He smiled reassuringly. "It will probably take a day or two to set up, but I think I can pull it off. In the meantime, try to keep your enthusiasm to yourself; otherwise, I may not be able to get you in."

"Is there some sort of problem?"

"Yes, but leave its solving to me."

Her curiosity was piqued, but Sarah thought it unwise to press her luck by probing. She waited for him to volunteer more information but when he did not, she reluctantly moved on to another subject of conversation. "So, how have you been entertaining yourself while I slept?"

"I've been playing detective. Your father had a claim here."

242

"He did?"

Tyler continued, "Seems the fellow who handles the advertisements for the *Enterprise* knew him. He says your father sold out to the Silver Kings when they were putting on the pressure. Gave me the names of a couple of fellows he thought might know where he went from here."

"And did you talk to them?"

"Yes. One is sure he moved to Eureka; the other is just as positive he moved up to Boise. Of course, it has occurred to me the Elijah Jenkins we're following might not be your father at all."

"But Mr. Mattson said the man he knew had my eyes," Sarah reminded.

"So he did. I'd forgotten about that." Tyler exchanged one white shirt for another. "I can't imagine there are too many men with eyes as green as yours and even fewer with the surname of Jenkins."

"What do you suggest we do?"

"Wait and see if anyone answers our ad, tally the votes, and decide which direction we go." He finished buttoning his vest and reluctantly donned a dinner jacket. "Now, I don't know about you, but I'm starved. How about we finish this conversation over a nice juicy steak?"

With the initial clues leading in two different directions, they had no choice but to wait for another party to step forward. The first day they occupied themselves by poring over records of claims and deeds, a necessary task, but one Sarah was coming to loathe.

With the help of tall glasses of lemonade and the elimination of all but the most essential undergarments, Sarah found herself rapidly acclimatizing to the heat, and she was almost able to function at her usual high level of energy. That evening they attended the theater at Maguire's Opera House.

Shortly after they were seated, a thin man sporting a trim beard took the seat next to them. As the performance began, Sarah had the uncanny notion that his eyes were upon her, not the stage, but every time she turned to confront him, his gaze was steadily fixed forward. She shrugged it off as imagination.

Early the next morning, Tyler's voice roused her from a deep sleep. She reached for him but found nothing but empty air and a dent in his pillow.

"Come on, sleepy. Don't want to be late, do you?" he prodded cheerfully.

"Late for what?" She sat up rubbing the sleep from her eyes.

Tyler grinned appreciatively as the sheet fell from her bare breasts. "For your tour of the mine."

Sarah's eyes opened fully. Tyler was standing at the foot of the bed, already dressed, with a brown paper-wrapped package in hand. She scrambled out of bed.

"Here. Put these on." He tossed her the package. "You can borrow one of my hats."

"What is going on here?" she asked as she untied the string binding the package and found a set of gentlemanly attire.

"I could never get a woman into the mines. The miners believe it brings bad luck," he informed her casually. "For today you are my rich client, *Samuel* Williams. You're thinking of buying stock in the mine."

"So I am," she commented in a deep voice, holding the shirt to her as she puffed out her chest.

"Yes. And I suggest you do the looking and I do the talking."

She considered reminding him that her imitation of a man's voice had fooled everyone at the Blue Wheel Saloon, but thought better of it. His willingness to take her into a mine at all, let alone disguised as a man, was so unlike him she wasn't going to risk spoiling his mood over such a trivial matter. Sarah laughed gaily as she began to dress. "So, I am to be a silent partner."

"If you don't want to be found out, you will be," he confirmed. "You're going to look like an effeminate fop the way it is. We don't want to give anyone reason to look too closely."

"I can't believe you are being such a good sport about this," she commented as she pulled on the trousers.

"Neither can I," he replied sardonically. "But I have my reasons."

Sarah spared him a quizzical glance. It would be ever so convenient if she could read his mind.

Enjoy this while it lasts, she advised herself. Who knows how quickly he will come to his senses?

As soon as Sarah was properly masculinized, Tyler guided her out into the hallway. She stopped before they had taken more than three steps and gingerly removed his arm from around her waist.

"If you don't want people taking a hard look, I suggest you remember to keep your hands to yourself," she cautioned.

He colored slightly, a bit mortified at making so stupid a blunder. "Sorry, force of habit."

Sarah smiled sympathetically.

A fine buggy was waiting for them when they stepped out of the hotel. "The owner is courting us," Tyler explained in a low whisper, then forced himself to stand back while she got herself into the vehicle.

They set off immediately, traveling up a steep road.

The hillsides and canyons were filled with men dressed in blue flannel pants, gray shirts, brogans, and narrow-brimmed felt hats. Some were going to work. Others, begrimed from head to toe and looking as if they would drop in their tracks at any moment, were on their way home after working the night shift.

"What on earth!" Sarah exclaimed, pointing off into the distance.

As the first word left her lips, Tyler was seized with a convenient coughing fit, and between his diversion and the loud grating of the buggy wheels upon the rough road, the driver seemed not to notice her mistake.

Tyler followed her gaze to the camel lumbering its way down the hillside. "Haven't you ever seen an Arabian mule?" She nodded negatively as he went on to explain. "They brought a whole herd out here during the early days of the boon. The beasts will carry up to eight hundred pounds without complaining, and they were born to the desert. That man leading it is probably a small-claim miner who doesn't fancy or can't afford more modern modes of transport."

There were a thousand questions she would have liked to ask, but Sarah held her tongue.

They arrived at their destination: a gaping hole in the earth. Clouds of steam rose from the mouth of the mine.

The man in charge came over to greet them as they alighted from the buggy. "You must be the San Francisco gentleman the boss told me about." He held out his hand.

Sarah shook it with exaggerated vigor. Tyler was a little less enthusiastic. "I'm Tyler Bennet, and this is my client, Samuel Williams."

"Pete O'Conner, superintendent." He faced them both squarely as he introduced himself.

"My client requests you address any and all conversation to me," Tyler informed him curtly.

Wearing the expression of a man who was used to accommodating himself to the idiosyncrasies of the rich, the superintendent nodded. "Are you ready to go down?"

"Yes," Tyler answered.

They were led to an open wire mesh cage with wooden floorboards. "Hold on to that safety bar," O'Conner instructed when they had climbed in.

Peering down into the blackness below her feet, Sarah clung to the waist-high bar without further urging. O'Conner joined them in the cage, then signaled the engineer to lower them down.

The mine was a honeycomb of timber-braced tunnels lighted by sputtering miner's candlesticks at one-hundred-foot intervals. Eerie-looking fungi hung from every surface.

She could hear the sounds of men working, but except for a lone miner manning the shaft at each one-hundred-foot vertical station, they saw no one.

The lower they went, the hotter and wetter it got. The smothering air was filled with the noxious odor of sulfur and other less identifiable toxins.

Sarah could feel herself sickening, but she forced herself to stand ramrod straight as their guide explained the many features of the mine.

A call of "Fire!" rose up the shaft, and suddenly the tunnel was reverberating with thunder, followed by the sound of raining debris.

Sarah's knuckles went white.

"No cause for alarm," the super comforted. "Just one of the powder monkeys setting off a little Riggoret in the lower level. Give you a chance to take a sample for the assayer from right where we're working. The boss don't believe in playing tricks on the investors."

"That's good to hear. As you probably know, one of the reasons we insisted on coming down is because of the rampant fraud practiced by more than a few would-be millionaires," Tyler commented as he covertly watched over Sarah. She didn't look well at all, and he began to doubt the wisdom of bringing her here. Unfortunately, it was too late to reconsider his decision.

The two men continued to carry on a business-

248

oriented dialogue while they descended into the bowels of the earth. Sarah was more than happy not to be required to add anything to the conversation. She wasn't exactly frightened, but she was extremely ill at ease in these dark, dank surroundings.

They arrived at the thousand-foot level. "Better make this a fast tour," O'Conner advised as he climbed out of the elevator. "Your client's not looking too good. I've had more than one city bred fellow keel over down here. Temperature's a hundred and twenty degrees."

Tyler turned to Sarah. "Do you need to go up?" he queried solicitously.

She made a lame gesture to signify her wish to stay and followed the superintendent out of the wire cage.

He led them down a horizontal tunnel filled with men swinging pickaxes and hoisting shovels. Their guide referred to them as *hard-rock men* and *muckers*. Stripped to nothing but loincloths and boots, their muscular bodies gleamed with sweat in the flickering light.

Sarah felt a blush spreading across her cheeks as she stared at their masculine nakedness, but it was dark enough so that no one noticed her reaction. This is like a scene from Dante's *Inferno*, she thought to herself. Why her father, or any other man, would choose to make his living in this manner was beyond her comprehension.

She was rather in a daze as she walked between the two men to the end of the tunnel and was relieved when they collected their ore sample and turned back toward the cage elevator.

The cable creaked as they began their ascent, causing her to wince, but as they moved toward daylight, the tension in her limbs began to slowly dissipate. Despite the red sun beating down overhead, the air on the surface felt positively balmy, and she drew in deep breaths of fresh air as she climbed out of the cage.

"Thank you for the tour," Tyler said. "My client will be in touch with the owner soon, should he decide to invest."

It was hard for Sarah to remain mute on the ride back to the hotel, but she managed. She had so many questions and comments, she felt as if she would burst. The instant they attained the privacy of their rooms, she turned to Tyler and rattled off a series of questions so rapidly that he found it difficult to squeeze in the answers. At length her curiosity was satisfied.

"Well, I'm glad I went, but that is one experience I do not care to repeat," she said as she began to peel off her sweat-drenched clothes.

"Silver mining not your cup of tea?" Tyler chuckled. "You had me worried. I was sure you were going to swoon on me a time or two, and if O'Conner had gotten to you before I did, we'd have been caught."

"You could have warned me about the heat . . . and the naked men," she chided amiably.

"And spoil your fun?" he quipped. "Half the pleasure of a new experience is the excitement of discovery."

"Well, I certainly discovered a lot about mines and men."

Tyler's smirk began to fade. "Just how closely were you looking at those brawny fellows?"

"Close enough. Their attire left nothing to the imagination." Sarah feigned great delight.

His brows lowered and his bottom lip jutted forward as he stared at the floor, contemplating an appropriately derisive response.

She threw her shirt at him. "Hey, I'm just twitting you. I was too busy concentrating on trying to breathe to make a zealous study of the masculine physique. Besides, even if I had scrutinized them from head to toe, I'm sure you would have put them all to shame."

"Prove it," he demanded, pushing her onto the bed. He towered over her, grinning broadly.

"Prove what?" she asked with false innocence.

"That you still think I'm the most desirable man you have ever laid eyes on."

"Hmmm." She drew out the sound as if she were weighing the matter.

He jumped on the bed, growling ferociously.

"We really should have a bath first," Sarah protested as she wrapped him in her arms.

"Why? We'd only get all sweaty again."

She kissed his eyes, then his nose and lips. "All right, my insecure lover, I won't make you wait for your proof." She kissed his lips again, this time with ardent passion. "It is you I want and no other."

* * *

By the end of their second day in Virginia City they had received five replies to their newspaper advertisement. All five men claimed to have worked with Elijah Jenkins and to know him to have moved from the area. All five claimed his subsequent residence to be in a different city. There was nothing to determine the veracity of any story over another.

At week's end they had tallied three votes for Boise, three for Portland, and one each for Eureka, Lovelock, Susanville, St. Louis, Laramie, and New York City. One man claimed her father was dead.

"What do you want to do?" Tyler queried.

Sarah sighed loudly. "I haven't the slightest idea."

"Logic says we should bet our money on either Boise or Portland," he advised.

"I agree, but which of the two?"

"It's up to you," he offered her the choice.

She thought for a long while. Having no good reason to choose one over the other, she pulled a coin from her purse. "You call it."

"Heads Boise, tails Portland," he ordained.

With a flip of her thumb, Sarah sent the coin skyward.

Chapter 15

The wheels of the train ground against the track as it pulled out of Virginia City on its way north to connect with the Central Pacific Line.

Sarah and Tyler settled themselves on their seats for the long ride to Winnemucca, where they would catch a stage north to Boise, Idaho.

They chatted, read, and played guessing games to pass the time. Sarah stole frequent glances out the window, but the scenery was depressingly similar. Sandy clay and sagebrush greeted her in every direction.

Winnemucca was a dry, dusty little settlement at the base of a barren, mine-scarred hill. Vegetation consisted of cheat grass and sagebrush. Though a few visionary residents had planted a scattering of trees, no tree had attained sufficient stature to provide much shade.

The buildings were predominantly clapboard of the unpainted variety.

Immediately upon disembarking, Sarah and Tyler sought accommodations at the Winnemucca Hotel.

As Sarah managed to introduce them by their rightful names before he could stop her, Tyler was forced to book separate rooms. They deposited their luggage and went to the station to buy tickets on the early morning stage.

That evening they enjoyed a delicious Basque dinner in the hotel and retired to separate rooms.

Sarah lay naked in her bed, listening for the sound of familiar footsteps in the hall. She was not disappointed.

"Adjoining rooms are a lot more convenient. Next time I'll wire ahead to make sure two are available," Tyler commented as he slipped into her room and locked the door. "I thought the traffic in the hall would never abate."

Sarah laughed as she sat up and opened her arms, beckoning him to her bed. "You may not like sneaking up and down the halls, but I think the thrill of intrigue rather charming."

"So you think forbidden fruit will taste sweeter?" he teased as he shed his clothes. He adopted a scholarly mien. "In the interest of science, I am willing to sacrifice my honor and test your theory."

"How very noble," she quipped as she stared pointedly at his fully erect manhood. "I suppose you are going to claim the reason you sneaked into my room was to share a cup of cocoa or some equally chaste activity?"

His gaze followed hers, and his expression became coy. "Don't think I could pull it off?" he queried.

Her green eyes danced with fiery lights. "No, I do not."

"Well, in that case . . ." Tyler pounced on the bed. Rocking back into a cross-legged position, he pulled Sarah onto his lap. Their eyes met and darkened in anticipation. "Hi," he whispered seductively as he stroked her breast.

"Hi," she replied, looping her arms around his neck.

They abandoned wordplay and set about the very pleasurable task of titillating each other's senses.

While Tyler massaged her breasts, Sarah nipped at his neck and earlobes. Their lips embraced, gently at first, but as the heat built between them, so did the force of their kisses.

Warm moist tongues curved around each other, sliding in . . . and out . . . in . . . and out, in a mimesis of the union of man and woman.

He stroked the mound of dark, curly hair that hid the entrance to her womanly cleft—the place he would soon bury himself, his own private garden of earthy delights—gently probing the moist, soft valley until she writhed against him.

Shifting her to her back, he positioned himself between her legs. His mouth caressed her belly; then he leisurely worked his way upward, pausing to give her budding breasts an extra measure of loving attention.

When he had raised himself so his sex lay above hers, he plunged into her, then withdrew.

Sarah gasped. Tyler grinned.

He entered and withdrew again, this time slowly. Sarah's knees rose as he echoed this movement again and again, entering and withdrawing until she could bear the exquisite sensation no more and her legs clamped around him.

They brought each other to the pinnacle of passion, then collapsed against the mattress and slept in each other's arms.

The next morning they were up early to catch the stage. To her mind a stagecoach ride promised all the romanticism of the old west, and throughout breakfast Sarah chatted enthusiastically about the upcoming journey, quoting many of the professed virtues of such travel from bills of advertisement. Tyler only smiled.

The Concord stage was constructed of oak, with basswood panels and elm hubs. Pulled by four horses, it had room for six passengers within, three facing forward, three facing back. The seats were leather and padded.

Sarah settled herself on the forward-facing seat. Tyler slid in beside her. Three men and a little girl filled the remaining seats.

As the stage set off down the road out of town, the passengers covertly eyed each other, assessing one another as traveling companions.

From his dress, Sarah guessed the man traveling with the little girl to be a farmer. He was short and stocky, with weathered skin and pale brown hair and eyes. The little girl resembled him in coloring, and like him, her palms bore the calluses of a hard laborer, but her facial features and figure were delicate. Sarah guessed her to be five or six years old.

The second gentleman was dressed in a black suit and white ruffled shirt. He wore diamond studs at his cuffs. His hair and full mustache were dark. His face and figure were admirable.

The last passenger was a grisly old man with stooped shoulders. His snow-white hair cascaded down his back, and most of his face was obscured by a flowing beard and mustache. His blue eyes twinkled from their deep set, wrinkle-lined sockets. He wore the clothes of a miner. He was the first to speak.

"As long as we're going to be stuck with each others' company for the next couple of days, we may as well introduce ourselves. The name's Ray Simpson."

"I'm Mrs. Sarah Williams and this is . . ."

"Mr. Williams," Simpson supplied the name as he offered his hand. "Pleasure to meet you."

"Mr. Tyler Bennet," she corrected. "I'm a widow. Tyler is my lawyer."

Tyler flinched at her use of the familiar address, but said nothing. Anything he did say would only aggravate the situation. He didn't mind pretending he was Sarah's husband, and he didn't see why she should mind pretending she was his wife. Didn't she realize this penchant she had for honesty called question upon her character and put them both in an untenable position?

It was safer if she pretended she was his wife. A woman of tainted virtue was considered fair game, and he had better things to do with his time than spend it beating off hordes of woman-hungry men. He hid his prodigious frustration at her continued unwillingness to marry him for her comfort. She should be more willing to do this small favor for his.

"John Murkens and my daughter Elly," the farmer informed them tersely as they continued the introductions.

The well-dressed gentleman smiled at Sarah, offering her his hand and a slow smile. He ignored the others. "Lewis Fraser. What brings a fair lady like yourself to these parts?"

Sarah colored slightly under his ardent regard. "I'm trying to locate my father. And you?"

"I'm trying to locate my fortune."

"You're a miner?" she asked in surprise.

"No, I'm a gambler." He reluctantly released her hand. "I prefer to leave physical labor to those possessing less intellectual and financial acumen."

Murkens voiced his opinion of Fraser's statement with a guttural growl.

The stage rolled over a large rock, jostling them so hard for a moment that the interior of the coach was a jumble of flaying limbs; then the vehicle regained its normal, rough sway and the passengers regained their seats.

Murkens opened his mouth to say more, then clamped it shut, glaring at Fraser with ill-concealed contempt. Sarah and the others watched the two men covertly.

"Cheatin' honest folk out of their hard-earned money," Murkens grumbled loudly. "Hangin' from a rope is where you'll end your days, fancy man."

"I'm a gentleman gambler," Fraser corrected amiably.

"Ain't no such thing."

"Mr. Simpson, what do you do for a living?" Sarah chimed cheerily, hoping to avert a violent argument.

Simpson grinned crookedly. "Oh, I'm one of those stupid fellas Fraser was just telling you about. I've prospected about every mineral find from the Rockies to the Pacific. Got a hand full of blisters, a belly full of rotgut, and a head full of tales to tell my grandchildren. 'Cept I ain't got any."

"I'd like to hear some of your stories."

"Would you now? Well, if nobody else's got any objections, I guess I could spin a few yarns for you."

Elly's eyes lit at the prospect.

"If it makes the ladies happy, I've no objections," Fraser said.

Folding his arms over his chest, Murkens stated, "The only thing I hate more than a gabby woman is a gabby man."

"This is a democracy. Let's put it to the vote," Tyler suggested, deciding he had played the silent observer long enough. "All those in favor of hearing a tale or two, raise your hand."

Everyone but Murkens raised his hand. Murkens gave his daughter a killing look, and she quickly lowered her hand to her lap, lacing her fingers tightly as she squeaked an apology for her act of disloyalty.

Tyler threw the little girl a comforting wink, earning himself a tentative smile. "Four in favor, two against." He tallied the votes. "Tell your tales, Mr. Simpson."

Murkens muttered something unintelligible under his breath, then fell silent.

Despite their brief acquaintance Sarah was rapidly forming an unsympathetic opinion of Mr. Murkens. The lines of discontent were firmly etched at the corners of his pursed lips. She knew his type well — a puritanical misery-monger who would make their journey a hell if given half a chance.

Simpson cleared his throat several times, stroking his snowy beard as he leaned back on his seat. "Well, the year was forty-nine, the day so bitter cold that spit froze before it hit the ground . . ."

Mr. Simpson proved an avid storyteller, and he entertained them for hour upon hour. Murkens remained morose. Elly did her best to appear disinterested, but was frequently betrayed by ariettas of tinkling laughter. Sarah was openly fascinated and besieged Mr. Simpson with questions which he answered magnanimously. Tyler and Fraser smiled indulgently at Sarah.

The latter did not confine himself to smiles and flirted with Sarah at every opportunity. She accepted his compliments with guileless grace, rewarding each phrase of flattery with a winsome smile. Soon, Mr. Simpson joined in the game.

Tyler bore the gentlemen's attention stoically for a time but, at length, could not prevent himself from reaching for Sarah's hand and cradling it possessively in his own. Simpson took the hint. Fraser did not.

When they reached the first stage station, while the horses were changed, they ate a hurried meal consisting of greasy stew, stale biscuits, and weak coffee.

The sun had risen high in the sky, and the passengers of the stage, who had had to contend with the dust and violent jostling from the start, could now add hot stuffy air and sour stomachs to their list of discomforts.

Reboarding, Tyler · suggested they shift positions and Elly sit by Sarah and him awhile.

Murkens's expression evinced he was more than willing to surrender his traitorous offspring to their care.

Elly was well pleased with her new position and though she kept a heedful eye on her father, she gradually allowed Tyler and Sarah to draw her out of her shell. Tyler seemed to know how to ask just the right questions.

Elly told them she was going to Boise to visit her aunt, recited simple sums, and instructed them quite extensively on the proper care of chickens, announcing with obvious pride that the henhouse was her responsibility.

Her father ignored her, but anyone observing Tyler would have concluded he had never been treated to such fascinating discourse. He gave the little girl his full attention.

Sarah exhibited like interest, though her attention divided equally between watching Tyler interact with the child and the child alone.

As they rolled along hour after hour, the adventure of stagecoach travel began to pale even for Sarah. She felt as if every limb had been jarred loose from its joint. Perspiration trickled down her heat-flushed face, stinging her eyes. She could smell the men sweat.

The male members of their party had long ago closed their eyes and appeared to be dozing. Simpson and Murkens evinced they had achieved escape through sleep by filling the stage with their sonorous snores. For a time, Sarah busied herself reciting nursery rhymes and playing finger games with Elly, but eventually her young playmate tired and began to whine.

Without opening his eyes, Tyler reached an arm around the child and guided her head to his lap. He stroked her thin back lightly, as one might do to soothe a cosseted pet. Elly snuggled against him for a nap without complaint. Her light snores soon joined those of her father and Simpson.

As Sarah watched Tyler and the little girl, her heart constricted. Though she was not ready to settle down yet — in all probability would never be — in the back of her mind a part of her was enamored with the possibility of becoming Tyler's life mate at some future date. She slammed the door on the thought.

Without conscious intent, her mind began to recall incidents that at the time she had given little attention: Tyler stopping to play a game of toss with some boys in the park when their ball had rolled past his feet; Tyler slipping a penny into the palm of a little girl who stood staring wistfully at the jars of candy displayed in the window of a general store; Tyler stooping to help a stable boy recover the grain he had spilled from a bucket so the boy would not be scolded by his employer.

Her eyes misted as she gazed at him. His broad lips were curved into a contented half smile, and his arm rested protectively over Elly's shoulder.

In her mind's eye she could see herself with Tyler, standing in the yard in front of his house, a brood of blond and brunette offspring clamoring about their feet. Sarah inched as far as she was able from the man and child. Most times she was adept at confining her longing for a baby deep within her subconscious.

Henry's querulous comments had made it difficult, but she had managed well enough, partly because he had eventually become resigned and partly because Henry desired an heir to carry on the family name, not a flesh-and-blood child to love. With Tyler it was different. Though they had spoken of her barrenness but once, he offered sympathy, not censure. His children would be showered with affection. It was far more difficult to dismiss her condition when he would be the one to share her burden.

She blinked several times, clearing her eyes of the vision and their excess moisture. It was not to be and she would not torture herself with visions of a false future.

What a goose I'm being, Sarah mentally scolded herself. I don't want to get married in the first place. Considering the circumstances, I should view my inability to conceive children as a blessing. I am free to be a devil-may-care lover, which is just what I want to be.

She silently lectured herself until she was convinced she was happy with things exactly the way they were.

And she was happy, happier than she had ever

been in her life. She was not going to waste energy fretting over things she could not change. She was going to direct her energy to having fun.

Turning her attention to the passing countryside, she banished the subjects of marriage and children and sought to occupy her mind elsewhere. The Santa Rosa range rose to the east, the flat, relentless desert stretched to the west. There was scant to excite the imagination.

The stage rolled on.

Despite the poor food at every stop, Sarah began to look forward to each opportunity to stretch her tired, aching body with something akin to a religious zealot's fervor for the second coming.

Though she did her best to maintain witty and congenial conversation between the members of their party as they exchanged histories and opinions on various topics of interest, it was becoming increasingly difficult to accomplish. Mr. Murkens was invariably the culprit. Whereas Sarah was determined to make the best of a bad situation, he seemed born with the ability to cast a pall over the brightest of circumstances.

If she commented the food at one station was an improvement over the last, he predicted they would all come down with the gripes momentarily. If she remarked upon the smoothness of a particular stretch of road, he launched into a terse dissertation on the next mile ahead, promising it would rattle the teeth from her head.

Sarah vastly preferred his silent scowls and guttural growls to his attempts at social intercourse, but the constant jostling seemed to have loosened his tongue and with each passing mile the man became more loquacious.

Tyler and the other two gentlemen did their best to counteract his unpleasantry, but civility was sorely strained. By the time they had passed Fort McDermitt, Mr. Fraser suggested, in a dead serious tone, that they tie Murkens to the top of the stage with the luggage for the rest of the journey.

If not for Elly's wide-eyed look of fright, Sarah would have wholeheartedly seconded the motion. Instead, she and Tyler squelched the idea, calmed the little girl's fears, and turned the topic to the weather.

A tenuous peace reigned until Murkens, spotting a lone cloud in the sky, decided it was his duty to convince them all they were about to be trapped by a torrential deluge. When he failed at that, he began to predict the temperature today would be twice as hot as it had been the day before.

Tempers flared again.

The terrain slowly changed to red clay desert valleys dotted with boulders, huge basalt spires . . . and more sagebrush. It flattened and grayed as they neared Boise. The city came into sight not a moment too soon.

The town of Boise squatted at the base of a huge brown mountain. To the east was flat-topped Table Rock. Barefoot children played in the dusty streets, dogs yapping happily at their heels. Painted signs advertised the various services to be bought in the clapboard buildings lining the streets.

The city had seen boom and bust, but its future

265

was secured by its selection as the capital of the Idaho territory and the influx of farmers and ranchers.

The stage came to a halt near a cluster of hotels, and the passengers eagerly disembarked. Murkens grabbed his traveling bag with one hand and Elly with the other and set off down the street without a word of farewell.

Sarah wished she could do something to soften the little girl's future as she waved her on her way, but knew there was nothing to be done. She consoled herself with the knowledge that she had survived a similiarly grim childhood. Perhaps Elly would grow into a happy adult despite her father.

"Your company has been my only pleasure on this thoroughly wretched journey," Lewis Fraser's voice intruded on her musing. He doffed his hat and offered his hand. "Good luck finding your father."

"Thank you." She smiled at him. "Good luck finding your fortune."

He grinned broadly, said his farewells to Tyler and Simpson, then turned to retrieve his carpetbag from the dusty street where the driver had dropped their luggage.

"Good-bye, Mr. Simpson," Sarah said.

"Good-bye, Mrs. Williams," he replied.

He turned toward Tyler. "You take good care of this lady, or old Ray will have to come after you with a gun," he quipped, a canny gleam in his eye. "Never shot a man yet, and I'd hate for you to be the first."

"I'm doing my best to take care of her," Tyler assured him.

"When are you going to marry her?" he demanded.

Sarah started at the remark.

Tyler ignored her reaction. "I haven't convinced her to take the trip to the altar, but I'm working on it."

"Excuse me, Mr. Simpson, but I don't see . . ."

"How any of this is my affair," he finished her sentence for her. "It ain't, but one of the advantages of old age is speaking your mind. Couldn't do it in front of the kid. Widow or not, you can't go traipsing around the country together without causing talk. A woman needs a husband."

Sarah squared her shoulders and recited the familiar argument. "Not this woman. I like the freedom of relying on myself and no one else."

"I'm sure you do, honey," he patted her hand sympathetically, "but you're going to end up lonely just like old Ray."

"I appreciate your concern, but . . ."

"Hoe your own row," he interrupted her again. "Good advice. Be seeing ya." Hoisting a small trunk to his shoulder, he crossed the street and stepped into a saloon.

Tyler stood, a smug expression on his handsome face, watching Sarah. She knew he was expecting her to say something, and she remained defiantly mute.

"Man's got a good head on his shoulders." He broke the silence. "Sees a situation that needs setting right and doesn't mince words proposing a solution."

"Of course the fact his remedy abets your scheme to shackle me has nothing to do with your favorable assessment of his mental prowess," Sarah retorted.

"If you don't want free advice, you shouldn't be so eager to offer unsolicited information. I would have bore the title 'Mr. Williams' stoically."

"We shouldn't have to pretend we are something we are not," she stated succinctly.

He continued to tweak her with his words. "You don't feel even a twinge of guilt that you've driven the poor man to drink?"

"I suspect he would have retired to that saloon at the end of this journey whether or not he had met either of us. I hate to disappoint you, but I'm not going to lose any sleep over our friend."

"You're a hard woman, Sarah Williams."

Though he spoke the words in jest, they hit a tender nerve. Sarah was happy pursuing the path she had chosen for herself, but the longer she kept company with Tyler, the more important his feelings became to her. He was kind, gentle, intelligent, charming. She did not want to hurt him.

She was fast discovering there was a price for self-indulgence, just as there was for self-sacrifice. If she did not like Tyler so well, it would be easier to enjoy his company.

Sarah pursed her lips. Though she disliked thwarting his wishes, she could see no help for it. If she gave in and married him, her life would never be her own. *Wives, submit yourselves unto your own husbands.* How often had Henry recited that scripture for her edification? He had even required her to stitch it into a sampler. As Tyler's lover, she cast herself outside the realm of respectability and was therefore free to go her own way. As a wife she feared she would feel compelled to become dutifully submissive.

She had spent twenty-two years compromising her own desires for the comfort of others. It was someone else's turn to do the compromising.

As much to stave her conscious as she did because she believed it was the truth, Sarah reminded herself she had been cursed with a certain deficiency that made her unsuitable to be Tyler's wife in any case. He was entitled to a full life complete with wife and *children*. She couldn't give him a family even if she embraced domesticity with open arms.

Though embracing domesticity was the last thing she wanted to do, the knowledge that that avenue was closed to her should she ever want to make the choice made her angry.

Seized by a restless mood, she felt the urge to assert herself. She turned to Tyler. "Why don't you check us into the hotel. I'm going to visit the newspaper offices."

"Do you know where they are?"

"No, but I'll find out."

Before he could reply, she set off down the street at a brisk pace. Burdened with their luggage, Tyler had little choice but to let her go.

The offices of the *Idaho Statesman* and the *Boise News* were located with little effort, and Sarah concluded her business in short order.

She started for the hotel, then stopped. She needed to distance herself from Tyler Bennet for a little while, but she didn't want to be alone. She needed someone to distract her from her disquieting thoughts.

Spying Lewis Fraser stepping through the double doors of a saloon, she decided to follow him.

When she entered the bar, she found him sitting alone at the table, thumbing a deck of cards.

"Mrs. Williams, what a pleasant and unexpected surprise," he greeted.

"Do you mind if I sit?" she asked.

"Not at all." He rose to his feet and pulled out a chair for her. "Where's your friend?"

"Back at the hotel."

"Does he know you're here?"

"No," she replied a bit too brusquely.

Fraser's lips curled into a puckish grin. "Is this the start of a love triangle?" he queried, a hopeful gleam in his eye as he leaned close. "I'm sure I needn't tell you how attractive I find you, or that I'm willing to oblige your romantic fancy in anyway I can."

Sarah blushed. Though Lewis Fraser was an appealing man, taking him as a lover was the furthest thing from her mind. She merely wanted congenial company and had thought him a likely candidate to provide it. She smiled wanly. She couldn't blame him for forming the wrong impression. Ladies didn't follow men into bars. The knowledge she had done so without compunction made her realize she no longer *was* a lady, and the discovery startled her.

Since she was no longer a lady, there was nothing to stop her from doing exactly as she pleased.

For a moment she half-seriously considered his offer. If one lover was a pleasure, would two be a double delight? She and Tyler were bound to part

270

company sometime. What better way to exorcise him from her head and heart?

Try as she might, she couldn't conjure even a shadow of enthusiasm for the idea. She didn't want to exorcise Tyler from her head or heart and though she might no longer be a lady, she was not so wanton she was willing to fall into bed with every man she met. Then there were Tyler's feelings to consider. He had told her quite plainly he did not want to share her, and she had assured him he need have no fear he would ever have to do so. It would be cruel to go back on her word, and she knew she would not do so even if it had been her desire. Fortunately, it was not. "I'm sorry, Mr. Fraser, but one man is more than I can handle," she informed him.

Weighing the lapse of time between his offer and her reply in his favor, Fraser's expression remained optimistic, and he captured her hands in his. "Sure I can't change your mind?" he cajoled.

"I'm sure. I don't think it would be in either of our best interests."

"Bennet's got a nasty temper, does he?"

She did not confirm or deny his assumption but remained silent, having no desire to discuss the true reasons for her rejection of his offer.

Fraser studied her expression and drew his own conclusion. "In that case, you're probably right." He shrugged elegantly. "Not too fond of the idea of being shot with my pants down."

Sarah's blush deepened.

Fraser chuckled and released her hands. "Well, if you won't let me bed you, perhaps you'd be willing

271

to part with some of your cash. Have you ever played poker?"

She shook her head.

"Well, there's no time like the present to learn."

He'd been cooped up on that stage too long to be content to do any more sitting, and Tyler decided there was no point in waiting around the hotel for Sarah's return.

He wondered what she would say when she discovered he had once again registered them as man and wife. Probably nothing he wanted to hear, but he had done it anyway. A mock marriage was preferable to none at all, and there were the cost and convenience factors to consider. If she balked, he would use them as his arguments.

Leaving a note, he stepped out into the sunshine. A brisk walk up and down the streets afforded him an overview of the city, stretched his cramped limbs, and provoked a powerful thirst. He stepped into the next saloon he passed.

Blinking his eyes, he stood in the doorway. Sarah was here with Fraser. He growled under his breath. He wasn't particularly keen on the idea of finding her in a bar, but what rankled him far more was the company she was keeping.

He did not wish to deny Sarah other friendships, but he drew the line at handsome, itinerant gamblers. He already knew Fraser to be a smooth tongued devil, and he guessed his game to be just as slick. He certainly had wasted no time beguiling

Sarah into this saloon.

Despite the cards on the table, Tyler was not convinced the game Fraser was playing with Sarah had anything to do with a deck of cards. Jealousy raged within him, but outwardly he maintained a calm mien. He closed the distance between them.

"Sarah, Fraser." He pulled up a chair without waiting for an invitation and motioned for the bartender to bring him a whiskey. "Mind if I join you?"

Having regained her good humor, Sarah replied, "Not at all."

Fraser nodded his consent.

"Are you enjoying yourself?" Tyler continued casually.

"Yes. I'm learning to play poker," Sarah informed him, showing him her hand. "And I'm winning."

"Good for you." He leaned back in his chair, taking a sip of his whiskey. "Don't let me interrupt your game. I just came in to quench my thirst."

The hairs on the back of Sarah's neck rose. Tyler was being too perfect. She was grateful he wasn't scolding her for being in a saloon, but his lack of any peevish reaction was odd. She took a nervous sip of her lemonade. "Are you all right?"

"Couldn't be better. Why do you ask?"

"It's nothing," she demurred, forcing her attention back to her cards.

"Care to join in the hand?" Fraser invited, his gaze covertly shifting between the two as he measured the situation.

"No, thank you. I'll just watch." Tyler ordered another whiskey. Sarah was squirming. Good. He hoped she was every bit as uncomfortable as he was. It was taking every iota of his self-control to maintain his genial mien.

Every time his teeth started to clench, he reminded himself that a jealous display would not be to his benefit. Sarah appeared to be interested in nothing more than the card game. Whatever womanizing schemes Fraser might be hatching, he owed her the benefit of the doubt.

That was the only benefit he was willing to give her. If she would be sensible and marry him, it would prevent situations like this — situations where other men entertained ideas of playing free and easy with his woman. If she desired no other man but him, as she claimed, why wouldn't she marry him?

The numbing effects of the whiskey was welcome. He ordered another.

"That's your third whiskey," Sarah commented with concern.

"Are you counting?"

"Yes."

"I'm a thirsty man," he retorted.

"You're going to be a drunk one," she warned.

"My choice." He dismissed her dismay with a nonchalant shrug and ordered another drink.

If he wasn't concerned, she shouldn't be either, Sarah told herself. He was a grown man and knew what he was about. She pushed her concern to the back of her mind.

Fraser and Sarah played out another hand, and she again found herself with the higher cards. "Sorry," she apologized to Fraser as she raked in her winnings. "I can't seem to do anything wrong."

"Gambler's trick. He's letting you win a few hands to build your confidence," Tyler curtly informed her. "You get cocky. Bet more. He cleans you out."

Sarah frowned. "Is that so, Mr. Fraser?"

Fraser grinned. "I'm afraid it is."

"Darn! And here I thought I was playing brilliantly."

"Hey, you're not half bad for a beginner," he consoled.

Her face brightened a little.

Fraser gathered his cards in his hand and continued, "Though as a gentleman, I'd have to advise you not to try to make your living at cards. Your face reads like a book."

Sarah digested this piece of information with grace. "Well, I'm disappointed but not devastated. After all, I have accumulated a tidy sum and you have not a penny of my money." She collected her winnings and dumped them in her reticule. "Thank you for the lesson. I consider my time profitably spent."

"Normally I hate to lose, but with you it's been a pleasure." He tipped his hat as she rose to her feet.

Tyler remained in his seat, staring at the two of them with annoyance as their friendly banter grated on his ears.

Sarah waited patiently for him to follow her lead. When he did not she asked, "Tyler, are you coming?"

"Yes." Downing the rest of his whiskey, he slammed his glass on the table and pushed himself to his feet. When Sarah did not accept his proffered arm fast enough for his liking, he grabbed her hand and planted it on his arm.

"Tyler?"

"Say good-bye to Mr. Fraser," he instructed.

"Good-bye, Mr. Fraser," she said, hoping to humor him.

"Good-bye, Mrs. Williams, Mr. Bennet," Fraser replied with ill-concealed amusement as he watched Tyler pull Sarah toward the door.

Chapter 16

Sarah was not pleased when upon arriving at the hotel she was greeted as "Mrs. Bennet," but she said nothing. Tyler's persistence was both flattering and vexing—a combination of emotional responses she found almost as discomforting as his desire to marry her. The self-restraint he had exercised in San Francisco was dissipating far too rapidly for her peace of mind.

He remained grumpy the rest of the day and was given to long discourses on the glories of matrimony, pointing out every smiling couple who crossed their path. Sarah assumed it was the liquor talking and did her best to ignore him. It took a night of passionate lovemaking to break his maddening mood.

They spent the next five days leaning over stacks of old newspapers, deeds, and mining claims. The name of Elijah Jenkins was nowhere to be found. Not a soul stepped forward to answer their newspaper advertisements.

"There is nothing to help us here in Boise," Sarah said when they had retired to their hotel room at the end of another long, unproductive day. "I guess it's off to Portland."

"I'll book a stage," Tyler offered.

Sarah cringed. The memory of their last stagecoach ride was still fresh in her mind. The constant jostling was enough to put her off, but the thought she might be forced to share the close confines with another passenger of Mr. Murkens's ilk was what decided her. "Let's hire horses instead," she suggested. "We've been on the road nearly three weeks, and I have yet to have opportunity to put my skills as a horsewoman to use."

"We're less likely to run into trouble traveling by stage," he reasoned.

She leaned against him, smiling seductively as she looped her arms around his neck. "Please. I don't want to be trapped in a stuffy old stage with God-knows-who for company." She ran her tongue across her lips. "If we travel alone, we can indulge ourselves in private pleasures along the way. It would make the journey ever so much more enjoyable, don't you think?"

"It will take us longer," he argued.

"I'm not in any hurry." She continued to rub against him. "Are you?"

He moaned. "Sarah, it's not nice to strike a man at his weakest point."

She ran her hand across the crotch of his pants, testing the fullness, and smiled. "But it's effective."

"Damn right it is," he agreed.

Sarah was relentless. "Remember the day we made love under the oak tree?" She stroked him boldly. "I do. It seems a pity to let all that wide open country-side and fresh air go to waste."

A damned pity, he thought to himself. Having Sarah all to himself with no one like Fraser to distract her from his wooing . . . it did seem a golden opportunity to further his suit. Of course, in these sorts of situations, it never did to give in too easily.

Scooping her up in his arms, he tossed her upon the bed. His fingers eagerly disposed of the buttons fastening her bodice.

"Tyler, I want my answer first," she protested between fervid kisses.

"I need more persuasion," he murmured, burying his face in the valley between her breasts. "I'm almost convinced, but not quite."

She was on fire for him, and she squirmed beneath him, wriggling out of her clothes. "What will it take to convince you?"

She could feel the laughter rumbling within his chest as he raised his head from her breasts. "Darling, see if you can guess."

The road from Boise to the ferry at Boomerang was serviceable and the horses they had hired well-tempered and steady of gait. Even with the hot summer sun beating down on her back, Sarah judged their new mode of transportation vastly superior to a stagecoach. She smiled at Tyler.

Dressed in denim pants and a long-sleeved cotton shirt, a wide-brimmed hat perched on his head, he looked more cowboy than lawyer. She had adopted a similarly practical style of dress — split skirt, cotton blouse, and western-cut felt hat to protect her eyes from the sun.

"What are you smiling at?" Tyler queried.

"Us. I think we look . . . cute."

He wrinkled his nose at the word.

Sarah laughed. "Perhaps 'cute' isn't the appropriate word. What I meant to say is that the rustic look becomes us. Felt hats, bedrolls, saddlebags—I feel positively pioneering."

"A city-girl observation if ever I heard one," he drawled.

"You're from a city too," she reminded him.

He chuckled. "So I am."

The morning stage sped past them, hit a rut in the road, and bounced wildly. Though she could not see through the cloud of dust in its wake, Sarah could imagine the distress of the passengers within the coach.

"Aren't you glad you decided not to be stubborn about taking the stage?" she commented when the dust had cleared enough to allow her to speak without harvesting a mouthful of grit.

"I am never stubborn," he protested.

"Hah!"

"Just because a man holds firm when he knows himself to be right doesn't mean he's stubborn. You're good on a horse. These roads are well traveled. I really didn't have any strong objections to forgoing the stage in the first place." He gifted her with a provocative wink. "I just played the devil's advocate with you because I found your particular method of persuasion most gratifying."

"Have I ever denied your straightforward requests for lovemaking?" Sarah demanded in mock reproach.

"No. Have I ever denied yours?" he countered.

"No," she admitted, her green eyes sparkling with merriment.

"Has it occurred to you that this insatiable desire we have for each other's person might contain a hidden message?" The lights in his eyes reflected hers and something more. "I'm speaking theoretically, of course, but for argument's sake, let's say there is a beautiful widow who is trying to decide whether or not she is going to marry a certain gentleman. Physical compatibility should not be discounted."

"Neither should the folly of obsession," Sarah retorted.

It took the majority of the day to reach the Snake River ferry crossing. Once on the western side they turned northwest. The first night out they camped under the wide open sky, but as they continued to wend their way north, temperatures became cooler and the sagebrush gradually began to be supplanted by grass and conifers.

They had been covering an impressive number of miles each day, but upon reaching the foot of the Blue Mountains, progress slowed. The horses had to be rested more often and saddles readjusted.

"Have any objections to stopping a little early today?" Tyler queried as he sat in the saddle looking down on a cool mountain stream. "This looks like a good place to make camp."

"You'll not hear a word of complaint from me," Sarah assured him as she dismounted and automatically began the routine chores of setting up camp. Much as she preferred a saddle to a stagecoach bench, sitting astride all day did make her weary. The chance for a respite was welcome.

Within the hour they had the horses tended, firewood gathered, and a rabbit stewing in the dinner pot.

"I came upon a pool a few yards upstream when I was gathering wood for the fire. I'm going to take a bath. Care to join me?" Sarah invited.

"Wouldn't miss it for the world."

Soap and towels in hand, they headed the short distance upstream.

After discarding her clothes, Sarah tested the temperature of the water with her toe.

Tyler watched her with unabashed admiration. Her face had taken on a pale golden glow from the sun, her cheeks bloomed with color. She looked at home here in the forest, a siren of the stream.

Love at first sight was but a weak shadow of love upon second and third and . . . All the attributes that had initially attracted him were more valued upon further acquaintance, and traits that annoyed seemed less significant, almost charming. He couldn't imagine his life without Sarah's daily companionship.

She was not only his lover but his best friend. Someday soon she would be his wife. . . .

"Have I told you you're beautiful today?" he asked, coming up behind her and pressing his warm naked flesh against hers.

Sarah smiled. "As a matter of fact, you have."

"Do you mind if I do it again?"

She turned in his arms and gazed up into his eyes. "Not in the least."

"You're beautiful."

Her smile widened.

"And I want you."

"Before or after our bath?" she queried blithely.

"Both."

Leading her to a soft patch of meadow grass, he lowered her to the ground. Wildflowers perfumed the air as their fragile petals were crushed under the weight of the lovers' clinging bodies.

Their lips joined again and again, gentle, playful, as tongue teased tongue. Arching her body away from his, Sarah slid her breasts up his chest, then down again. She rained kisses on his belly, hips, thighs.

Tyler was hard and ready, but when she moved her body to cover his, he protested huskily, "Not yet. I haven't had my turn."

Rolling so he lay atop her, his weight cradled in the valley of her thighs, he captured her breasts in his hands, pressing them together so he could suckle both nipples simultaneously. Rivers of fire coursed through Sarah's veins.

He lifted his weight from her, retreating as far as her toes, which he kissed one by one; then he began to trail his lips slowly, methodically, upward. No inch of her was left unkissed. By the time he claimed her lips with his, she was begging for him to enter her.

He eased himself into her, then rolled so he lay upon the ground. Sarah moved her hips against his, filling herself with him with each thrust.

Senses already titillated to the bursting point exploded in erotic waves of shuddering release. Her own heartbeat hammering in her ears, Sarah went limp against him.

It was a long while before they stirred themselves to

take the bath, and they might not have at all if a bee had not begun to buzz persistently about them. Reluctantly they abandoned their spot on the grass.

"It's cold," Sarah warned as Tyler lowered his foot into the stream.

A quiver wracked his lean frame, but he waded out, chest deep, into the middle of the pool, soap in hand. "We'll have to make love again just to thaw ourselves out," he commented.

"Cleanliness is a virtue. Its price should never be judged as too steep," Sarah quipped.

"Some prices are gladly paid. Now quit spouting maxims. I recognize a stall tactic when I hear it."

"But the water is so cold," she protested.

He chuckled. "It's not going to warm up no matter how long you stand there talking."

Sarah eyed the rippling water. What he said was true, of course, and if she intended to attain the desired state of cleanliness, she had to brave the water sometime.

Stepping onto an outcropping of rock, she closed her eyes and, without warning, leapt into the center of the pool. When she came up gasping for breath, Tyler was sputtering a few feet away.

"Was that really necessary?"

"Yep," she drawled. "No sense in prolonging the agony."

"Hrmph!" He shook the water from his hair. "Turn around and I'll scrub your back."

Sarah did as she was told, but instead of performing the offered service, Tyler pushed her back under the surface of the water.

"You villain!" she accused, her eyes gleaming with

vengeance. Skimming the heel of her hand across the surface of the stream, she engulfed him in a wave of icy water.

Pandemonium ensued.

"Truce," Sarah finally begged.

Tyler eyed her suspiciously.

"This isn't a trick," she cajoled, but the moment he let down his guard, she caught him square in the face.

"That's the last time I trust you," he promised. Exacting his revenge with a barrage of water waves, he smiled smugly and began soaping his skin.

Sarah hated to let him win, but she feared if she protracted the war, she would freeze clear to the bone. Already her teeth had begun to chatter.

"Here, you'd better go first." Tyler offered her the soap.

Scrubbing herself from head to toe, she was out of the water in less than a minute. Tyler quickly followed.

Using their towels as blankets, they huddled together, rubbing each other's skin and stamping their feet until circulation returned to normal.

Sarah reached for her clothes, but Tyler stayed her hand.

"Huh-hum," he cleared his throat, looking down on her expectantly. "Aren't you forgetting something?"

Sarah stared up at him with wide, innocent eyes and shrugged. "Can't think of a thing."

"Maybe this will stimulate your memory." He dropped to his knees and began kissing her feet, slowly moving up her ankles, calves, knees. . . .

Sarah quivered with delight as he splayed his broad hands across her buttocks, pillowing his head on the soft curve of her belly. "Tyler."

"Yes?"

"If we lie on the ground, we'll get dirty again," she murmured.

"Now, why would we want to lie down?" he queried between feather-light kisses.

"It's how it's done," she reminded him.

"Not always." Rising from his knees, he gathered her in his arms and pulled her against him. His lips took hers in a searing kiss that left her weak and breathless.

Clinging together, they played love songs upon each other's senses, tongues tantalizing, hands roaming with abandon, their orchestra the babbling of the brook and the whisper of the wind through the tree-tops.

They joined their flesh in a celebration of primitive passion, moaning and straining against each other until both went limp with release.

"Lord, I love you," Tyler whispered as he cradled her in his arms.

Sarah opened her lips to return a like sentiment when her eyes fell upon *him*. Squealing, she stiffened in fright. Tyler shoved her behind him, shielding her naked flesh with his.

Sitting upon a dappled horse on a low rise, not more than fifty feet away, was an Indian. He was clad in a fringed buckskin shirt and leggings, breechcloth and moccasins. Two braids framed his face. The rest of his dark, shoulder-length hair was worn loose. A hunting rifle rested in his hands. He stared at them. They stared back

"What are we going to do?" she whispered.

"Nothing," Tyler hissed as his eyes covertly searched the ground for something he could use to defend them should the Indian choose to attack. There was nothing, not even a rock to throw.

Sarah's awareness of their vulnerability caused her heart to pound so hard it nearly deafened her. How long had the Indian been sitting there? Had he seen them making love? Did he mean them harm?

No one moved a muscle. Minutes ticked by.

"He's starting to smile. What does it mean?" she asked softly.

Tyler spared her a glance out of the corner of his eye. "Hell if I know."

For a few more minutes the Indian just sat there grinning at them; then, as suddenly as he had appeared, he was gone.

For a moment Tyler and Sarah stood stock-still. Tyler cautiously scanned the countryside and found it empty. He turned to Sarah. "Get dressed," he ordered.

"Do you think he'll be back?" Sarah asked as she scrambled into her clothes.

"I doubt it. If he meant to harm us, he would have done so. We were defenseless and he knew it."

She breathed a sigh of relief.

"Nevertheless, it might be a good idea to move our camp down the road a mile or two and keep our weapons close by our sides."

Sarah wholeheartedly concurred. She had not forgotten their conversation, nor did she dismiss the material she had read on the subject. The encroaching whites had treated the native population abominably on numerous occasions. It would be difficult for a thinking person not to understand any yearnings for revenge, but she had no desire to offer herself up as a sacrifice.

The remainder of the day passed without incident. That night, when Tyler took her in his arms, he made no attempt to make love to her.

They lay in silence, comfortable yet tensely alert to every sound of the forest. An owl hooted, and Sarah burrowed deeper into the shelter of Tyler's arms.

"Nervous?" he queried, stroking her hair.

"A little," she admitted.

"I'll watch over you," he promised.

Sarah smiled. "I know you will." She stifled a yawn. "Tyler, I want you to know how much I appreciate you. You're the best friend I ever had."

To his heart her words were like tinkling raindrops falling on parched desert sands. Though Sarah showered him with physical affection, she rarely translated her feelings for him into words. "Can I ask you something without ruffling your feathers?"

"Of course."

Though she might not often say it with words, she often said "I love you" in other ways. God knew he loved her. He should have been content, but he wasn't. He wanted to make their union legal, binding, something he could depend on for the rest of his life. "Have you thought any more about marrying me?"

"Tyler . . ." she rebuked gently.

"I know. I said I wouldn't pressure you, but the waiting is hard." He brought her hand to his lips, kissing the base of the finger that would one day wear his ring. "Marry me. I promise you won't regret it."

"Yes, I would."

"No, you wouldn't," he vowed. "You accuse me of

being stubborn, but you are the one who refuses to be reasonable. You're going to marry me eventually. Why not humor me and do it now?"

"I don't want to marry you," she insisted.

"All right, then let's become engaged," he offered a compromise.

The temptation to say yes was nigh onto irresistible. An engagement would appease him, make him happy.

He was slowly chipping away at her initial reluctance to marry by proving a sensitive and loving companion, but a far more impervious barrier than her fear of oppression stood between them. If she told Tyler the truth, he would insist it didn't matter, but it did. It would be easier on them both if she pretended her refusal to marry was fueled wholly by an aversion to domestic life.

Somewhere out there was a wife for Tyler Bennet. A woman who would take her place in his bed and fill his house with children. The thought hurt, but it was what she wanted for him.

He was not the sort of man who would keep a mistress, and she was not the sort of woman who would bed a married man.

There might be other lovers in her life, but she knew this affair would be the one she would hug to herself to keep her warm on cold winter evenings. She shook her head to clear it of its melancholy musings. In the meantime, she was going to squeeze in as much fun as she could. She sat up abruptly.

"Let's play poker."

"What?"

"As long as neither of us is going to get any sleep, I thought we might as well entertain ourselves with a game of cards," she explained, carefully keeping her gaze averted from his.

Well, he had his answer, Tyler silently complained as she abandoned their bed to search for a deck of cards. His fists balled in frustration. How much time did she need? From the start they had connected in a unique way. He was certain she felt it too. Why postpone the inevitable? A man and woman met, fell in love, got married. It was how things had been done for centuries. They had managed the first two steps without a hitch. Why did achieving the third one have to give him so much trouble?

Sensing the futility of voicing his questions out loud, he resigned himself to a few more weeks of private purgatory.

Of all the days they had spent on her father's trail, the time they traveled from Boise to the Columbia River were Sarah's favorite. Civilization was sparse, and she loved being surrounded by nothing but untamed beauty. They were free to do and say anything they liked, and the rhythm of their days was ruled by nature and inclination rather than rigid rules of conduct dictated by an ever so polite society.

Deer and elk roamed the valleys in large herds; birds and squirrel chattered in the trees overhead. Spotting new species became a game, and the day Sarah spied her first black bear, her squeal of excitement was such that she frightened the poor animal. It disappeared into the forest at a dead run. In retrospect, their encounter with the Indian had more an aura of comedy than drama.

Though they had been in the saddle for five straight days, she was disappointed when they reached the landing on the Columbia River and boarded a steamboat bound for Portland. As far as she was concerned, she could spend the rest of her days wandering the vast and pristine wilderness, Tyler by her side, and never want for a thing.

She was tempted to suggest to him they forego the speed and luxury of river travel for a few more days' reprieve from civilization, but he had already been away from his office over a month and she feared he might be getting anxious to bring this search to an end.

Sarah considered her own lack of fervor to bring this venture to a speedy conclusion. When she thought about it, it was rather odd to travel all the way across the country, then lose interest. It's because I'm afraid I might not like what I find, she reasoned to herself before a wave of insight forced her to consider the more likely reason. Once she found her father, she no longer had a convenient excuse to continue her acquaintance with Tyler, and she wasn't ready to step out of the picture yet.

Whenever she allowed herself to think of the future, her emotions became so entangled she had no hope of sorting them out. It was far more comfortable not to think of it at all.

During her marriage to Henry, she had learned to face each day as if another was not fated to follow. She called on that skill now and vanquished the shadows that threatened her present pleasure with her life.

Portland proved more rewarding than Boise. The information they gathered there led further north.

They followed it and each successive clue — Sarah grasping at every new experience with zealous glee, Tyler watching over her, biding his time, doing his best to prove he was no more akin to Henry than sugar was akin to vinegar.

Weeks turned into months. Tyler could not claim he was unhappy. Having never been a man to do things halfway, he had committed himself to the venture for as long as his resources allowed. Most times he greeted each day with the same enthusiasm as Sarah.

They were like two children seeing the world for the first time. He came to respect her carefree spontaneity, and she came to respect his ability to think a situation through before he took action.

It was only when the subject of marriage arose that an underlying discontentment surfaced. Tyler was beginning to fear Sarah would never agree to their marriage, and despite his vow to carry her to the altar by force if necessary, he knew he couldn't really spirit her off like a marauding pirate. His frustration at his inability to bring about the desired end grew daily, but he was becoming as adept at hiding his vexation as Sarah was at turning down his proposals.

Sarah continued to rate the single state above marriage, and she argued so passionately in favor of personal freedom she could almost forget that she *couldn't* choose marriage.

The new year had come and gone when they found themselves in Portland once again. Their second day there, Tyler sent a telegram to Thaddeus informing him of their present whereabouts. Within hours, he received a reply stating it was imperative he return to San Francisco immediately.

Tyler ran his hand through his hair as he fingered the telegram. "I wish he had mentioned why my presence is so necessary."

"Perhaps the matter is too complicated or private to explain in a wire," Sarah suggested.

"You sound as if you're telling me to go," he said, and Sarah could tell by his tone that was exactly what he wanted her to tell him.

"You have been gone a long time," she reminded. "Though I would be content to wander the world forever, someday we have to face the fact that you have other clients."

His eyes met hers, and she could read relief in them. Not once had he complained about her taking him away from his other duties, but his expression confirmed an underlying suspicion that he was beginning to miss the drama of the courtroom, and her conscience tweaked her for being so selfish for so long.

"Then you don't mind returning to San Francisco for a time?" he queried.

"No, I don't mind." She smiled. "The steamer we were going to take to Eureka goes on to San Francisco. We'll just change your ticket."

Tyler's expression of relief changed to one of consternation. "What about you?"

"I thought I'd stay in Eureka a day or two and do the usual checking," Sarah explained. "I doubt I'll find a thing, but it's the only lead we have left."

"I'm not going to abandon you," he insisted.

Sarah sighed. Sometimes she wondered if he had changed at all. No, that really wasn't fair. He was amazingly supportive of her activities most of the time.

She had done a lot of changing in these past months, too. She had gained a confidence in herself she had never had before and knew she could hold her own no matter what the situation. Even marriage no longer seemed intimidating. If not for her barrenness, she would gladly accept Tyler's offer to wed her.

Though she knew the absence of his company would be sorely felt, she could see no harm in a few days' separation. It was the practical thing to do.

"Your presence is needed, not mine," she said. Hoping to pacify him, she added, "Two days, three at the most, and I'll follow you to San Francisco."

"I don't like it. Come back with me to San Francisco, and we can go back to Eureka together."

"It would be a waste of time and money," Sarah argued. "I think I have proven I am capable of handling myself."

"I am not questioning your competence."

"Then what is your objection? One would think you'd welcome a holiday from my constant company."

"Why would I do that? I love you."

"If you love me, then you must also trust me."

He folded his arms across his chest. "I do trust you. It's other people I don't trust."

They argued over the matter for well over an hour before coming to a settlement neither one liked but with which both could live.

Sarah agreed to confine her activities to searching the halls of records and to using Tyler's San Francisco office address in any newspaper advertisements she placed. Tyler agreed to leave her behind in Eureka.

Chapter 17

"So, the prodigal lawyer returns. I'm glad to see you haven't completely abandoned your sense of responsibility," Thaddeus Johnson greeted his younger partner. "And the widow Williams isn't tagging along behind you. Dare I hope you have recovered from your adolescent infatuation?"

"Sarah is in Eureka and will be along in a few days," Tyler answered his question with ill-concealed ire. "And if I had known this was the kind of greeting I was going to get, I would have stayed there too."

Johnson smiled tightly. He had feared it was too good to be true. Neither Mr. Sneed nor his man in Baltimore had found a thing he could use against Mrs. Williams; however, his own observations were enough to condemn her. No decent woman would prefer an affair to marriage. Tyler deserved better. He deserved someone like his Agnes. He squared his shoulders before giving reply. "A few days away from her won't hurt you any. Might even help you regain your sanity."

"Thaddeus, be careful you don't push the bounds of

friendship too far," Tyler warned. "I am growing tired of being harangued on this subject every time I step through this door. If you can't like Sarah, kindly learn to keep your opinion to yourself. I will no longer accept your lack of common civility towards her. She is my client. When you speak of her, show her respect for that reason if you can't for any other."

"You used to respect my opinion," Johnson complained.

"I still do, but where Sarah Williams is concerned, you've behaved like a stubborn old goat from the first moment I mentioned her name."

Johnson remained unmoved. "It puts me off when a grown man waltzes into a room like a demented poet waxing eloquent about some female he barely knows. I knew she was trouble then, and experience has proved me right. If not for me, this law firm would be on its way to ruin."

There was enough truth in what he said to cause Tyler a twinge of compunction. He had never expected to be gone so long, had never expected Sarah to be so recalcitrant about marrying him. Still, their long courtship had intensified, not lessened his desire to wed her. He sympathized with Thaddeus's vexation. He could hardly expect the man to understand the situation when he himself was at a loss to explain Sarah's continued resistance; however, he did expect him to accommodate him. "I've covered for you plenty of times, so you could pursue your political ambitions in Washington, and *I* didn't begrudge you the favor. Your lust is for power. Mine happens to be for a woman."

Johnson expelled a long, mournful sigh. "You argue as well out of the courtroom as you do in. Always were better at it than me. That's why this law firm depends on you, my boy. We can't get along without you."

"False flattery won't get you any further than nagging me like an old woman, though I must admit I like it better. You and Dad taught me everything I know. There's nothing I can handle you can't."

"If I'm so good, then why can't I talk you out of this 'attachment' you have developed for the widow Williams?"

"No man can thwart the course of true love," Tyler quipped. Sarah had honed thwarting love to an art form, but she was a woman and he wasn't about to supply fuel for Thaddeus's fire. He continued, hiding the frustration caused by his own thoughts, "Not even a great jurist like Thaddeus F. Johnson."

"Hrmph!" Johnson snorted, but his chest puffed at the backhanded compliment.

Tyler smiled fondly and turned the conversation. "Now, what business is so urgent you saw fit to call me back to San Francisco?"

Though they had been separated only a few days, it took every ounce of Sarah's self-control not to run from the steamer dock to Tyler's doorstep. The minute she stepped over the threshold into his private office, she closed the door and threw herself into his arms.

"I missed you," they spoke in unison as they greeted each other with feverish kisses. Several minutes passed without further comment while they sated their need for each other's touch. At length they released each other, and Tyler pulled up a chair for her to sit.

"Did you learn anything in Eureka?"

"No. It was a complete waste of time," Sarah replied, sighing in frustration. "We've run out of clues. I'm beginning to think I may never find my father."

"It is a possibility you should face," he advised, squeezing her hands sympathetically.

"Is everything all right here?" She indicated his office with a sweep of her hand.

"Just fine," he assured her.

"I'm glad."

He turned to his desk and shuffled through the papers until he found a small packet of letters. "You received these while we were away."

Sarah frowned as she read the return address on the top envelope. "They're all from my mother?" she queried without looking at the rest.

"Yes."

She tucked them in her pocket. "I'm in too good a mood to face them right now. I'll read them later."

Tyler raised a brow. "You act as if you already know what they say."

Sarah took a deep breath. Her relationship with her mother was something she preferred not to discuss. She preferred to think of her new life as totally disconnected from the old, but she knew that was childish; reality did not change just because she chose to ignore it. "I do know. They will say she wants me to come home. They always do."

"And what will you say?"

"No."

"Have you told her about me?" he queried, keeping

his voice nonchalant.

"In a roundabout sort of way." She shifted on her chair, focusing her eyes on various objects around the room. "I mentioned that I hired a lawyer, and that we were working closely together to find my father."

"But you've said nothing about the true nature of our relationship," he stated.

"No," she admitted.

He hesitated before voicing his next question. Sarah was obviously uncomfortable with their conversation, but curiosity made him ask, "What would she do if she knew about us?"

Sarah shuddered. "I don't really know and I have no intention of finding out. Three thousand miles separates us, and if I have anything to do with it, I'm going to keep it that way."

"You're not the least bit homesick, are you?"

She shook her head. "Apparently my mother was right. I am just like my father." She changed the subject. "How is Agnes? I didn't see her when I came in."

Tyler respected her wish to abandon the topic. Sarah was born to be gay. He didn't like to see her frown, and his questions had conjured a thoroughly petulant expression. "Agnes is fine. She must have stepped out to run an errand. She was here a minute ago."

"And Mr. Bevington?"

"Can't wait to be filled in on the local gossip?" he teased. "I'm afraid you'll have to ask Agnes about him. I'm not as nosy as you."

"Very funny. Don't seek to cover for your lack of concern by discrediting mine," Sarah rebuked him with a grin. "You should take more interest in your employees' future."

"Speaking of the future, since we seem to have run out of leads, would you have any objections to conducting our search by less personal modes for the time being?"

"What are you proposing?"

"We have covered the north pretty thoroughly and come up empty-handed. It's a long shot, but I thought we could blanket the cities in the southern part of the state with newspaper advertisements and see if we get a nibble. I have a couple of friends I can call on for assistance. It would be far less costly than going ourselves, and it would give me a chance to put in a little time at the office."

Sarah was perfectly willing to accept his advice, not only because it was sound, but because she feared Tyler's professional life would suffer irreparable damage if she did not.

When and if they received a worthy lead, she could decide what she wanted to do, but for now Tyler's need to apply himself to the practice of law superseded her desire to see the world. The world would still be there, waiting for her, tomorrow and the next day. If he neglected it much longer, his career in law might not be so enduring.

"That sounds like an excellent idea," she replied.

He smiled, grateful she had not objected. "Did you have your things brought round to the hotel or the house?"

"The house," she answered.

"Come on then, I'll walk you home."

The next morning, though he offered to spend the day with her, Sarah insisted Tyler maintain regular business hours. He put up a token protest, securing a promise that she would join him for lunch, but Sarah could tell he was relieved she did not take him up on his offer. She sent him off with a kiss and the assurance that she would meet him at noon.

Wanting time to chat with Agnes, Sarah arrived at Tyler's office well before the appointed hour.

"Agnes, I'm glad you're in," she greeted her.

"Sarah." Agnes smiled. "Tyler said you were back."

"Do you have time to take a stroll in the park?" Sarah asked. "I'd like to talk with you about . . ."

"Mr. Bevington," Agnes finished for her. "Tyler warned me. I'm afraid you are not going to be very pleased with me."

Sarah's brows knit. "Is something amiss?"

"Between the two of us, no. Between my father and me, yes." Agnes placed some papers into a folder and filed them away. "I can't speak freely here, but I'll tell you all about it while we walk."

As soon as they had escaped the office, Agnes launched into her tale of woe. Clayton Bevington had asked her father's permission to court her, and he had turned him down flat, explaining his daughter's affections were occupied elsewhere. Clayton had been devastated, and she had had to run after him. After she had explained the whole complicated affair, he had been much relieved, but try as they might, they could not convince her father to give their romance his stamp of approval. A few days ago, he had forbidden her to continue to see Clayton.

301

"What am I going to do?" she moaned.

"You have to decide that for yourself," Sarah told her.

Agnes smiled tentatively. "I was hoping you might solve my problem for me."

"I don't see how I can do that. Unless your father's opinion of me has changed radically since I last saw him, he certainly isn't going to listen to anything I say to him."

"But if you married Tyler, there would be no reason for my father to refuse Clayton."

"Agnes, really!" Sarah exclaimed, her face clearly displaying her displeasure.

"It was just a suggestion," Agnes demurred. "I mean, I am not so stupid I haven't realized the two of you are lovers. Marriage does seem the next logical step."

"The logical step is for you to tell your father plainly that you do not love Tyler and he does not love you," Sarah informed her.

"I have told him, but his opinion that we are a match made in heaven is unshakable," she whimpered. "Apparently he has been nurturing the notion since the day of my birth. Until you marry Tyler and put him out of my reach, he will not give me leave to turn my affections elsewhere."

Sarah wished she could help her, but knew she could not. "I have my reasons for not marrying Tyler."

"I would have thought you've had more than enough time to fall in love with him," Agnes argued.

Sarah's expression became wistful. "Sometimes love does not lead to marriage. Sometimes it prevents it."

"That doesn't make sense."

Taking her emotions firmly in hand, Sarah continued, "Yes, it does, and if you fully understood, you would agree with me. However, I prefer to keep my own counsel. If you want Mr. Bevington, you are going to have to get him for yourself."

"But I have never defied my father in anything," Agnes protested.

"Do you love Clayton Bevington?" Sarah asked.

Agnes's cheeks bloomed. "Yes, with all my heart."

"Does he love you?"

"Yes."

Reaching for her friend's hand, Sarah squeezed it tightly. "Then my advice to you is to listen to your heart."

While Tyler devoted his days to his other clients, Sarah devoted herself to charitable works. It was far more satisfying to give of herself than of her pocketbook, but she did both and with a generosity of spirit that won her many friends.

The nights they reserved for each other. Tyler had given up the pretense of propriety, and they lived together openly. San Francisco society was far more tolerant of erring widows than it was of virgins who were led astray, and the affair soon became stale news.

They settled into a pleasant sort of domesticity that had nothing in common with the life she had lived under Henry's roof. Disagreements were settled by discussion rather than oppression and ridicule, and Tyler solicited her opinion as frequently as she did his. Moreover, if her advice was sound, he followed it instead of trying to find some way to discredit her intelligence just because she was a woman and a few years younger than he.

Often Sarah found herself wishing she could accept Tyler's proposal of marriage, but she never let him see her waver.

She might be selfish enough to continue to keep him as a lover, as long as he wanted her, but she was not so selfish that she could marry him. In this she wavered also, but every time she had herself convinced they loved each other enough to compensate for her barrenness, a child would cross their path and Tyler would smile or perform some act of kindness, and she just couldn't bring herself to let him make the sacrifice.

Even if he was willing to do so now, in the coming years he would feel the emptiness in his life and his love might turn to hate, or worse, indifference. Long before that day came she intended to have extracted herself from his life for his sake as well as her own.

She began to scrutinize the women of San Francisco, looking for her own replacement, and though she found many who measured up to standard, she judged none as precisely suitable. Besides, after a few days of conducting her noble quest, she found she was becoming so depressed that Tyler started asking probing questions, and she abandoned the idea of finding him a fertile mate. He would have to do it himself after he had tired of her.

Using force of will and an overfilled schedule, brick by brick Sarah built a wall between her conscious mind and her emotions. She loved and laughed and threw herself into each day's activities with feverish determination.

Tyler was not a man who was used to defeat, and the fact that he could not fathom the reason for his failure to secure Sarah's hand in marriage added to his frustration. She showed no sign of leaving him, showed every sign of loving him, but he felt no closer to tying the knot than he had the day she'd first refused him. He couldn't make any sense of her behavior. She had no more freedom now than she would have as his wife.

He told himself he had two choices. He could go on as he was, hoping that some day she would agree to marry him, or he could give it up. Since he couldn't bring himself to give her up, he was stuck with things the way they were; however, each day his patience wore a little thinner.

His proposals were starting to sound desperate even to his own ears, and he didn't like it one bit. Worse, despite her perpetually gay exterior, he sensed an underlying sadness in Sarah. He tried his best to cheer her, but the harder he tried the more distant she seemed to become.

"I have something that might please you," he announced over dinner one evening late in March. "At one time, at least, your father resided in southern California. I received a letter at the office about a week ago from a fellow in Los Angeles. He claimed your father worked on a cattle ranch and was involved in some sort of ruckus over water rights. I wired an acquaintance in the area and just received his reply this morning. The story checks out. Apparently, it was quite a fight and made all the local papers. Your father was shot, but the papers listed his injury as a minor wound."

"My father is living in Los Angeles?" Sarah asked, her enthusiasm proportional to the relief she felt at having a new activity to help her run away from her feelings.

"No. The incident happened almost five years ago." He continued to explain, "He quit the ranch and moved on, but the new information gives us a place to start looking again. Do you want me to hire someone to do some additional checking around the area or book passage?"

"Book passage," Sarah replied without hesitation.

"Still haven't had enough of travel I see," Tyler commented.

"No," she replied even though that was not the real reason she jumped at the chance to escape San Francisco. Though it made no logical sense, her growing contentment made her discontent. She wasn't even sure she wanted Tyler to accompany her. "What about you? Do you want to come? Can you afford the time away? If the trip will interfere too much with some pressing business, I can go alone."

"I've been caught up for quite some time now. I prefer not to be gone months, but I can afford a week or two away."

"Are you certain? I really don't mind if you have more important things to do."

"I can be ready to leave tomorrow if you can," he assured her, thoroughly vexed. He was right to believe something was amiss. She sounded almost eager to go without him. What was it she wasn't saying?

306

The weather was fair and the trip down the coast idyllic. They spent their days basking in the sun and enjoying the sea breeze, their nights closeted in their cabin making passionate love.

When they docked in San Pedro harbor, a line of bright red coaches were waiting to carry the passengers the last twenty-one miles of their journey to Los Angeles.

The trip into town was a hair-raising race as each driver sought to outdo the others. When their coach finally careened to a halt before the Bella Union Hotel, Sarah thanked Providence they had arrived in one piece.

After checking into the hotel, they deposited their luggage and stepped back out onto the street.

Los Angeles was a sleepy little town of five thousand residents. Surrounded by orange orchards and farmland, its principal industry was cattle. With the exception of a handful of two-story structures in the center of the commercial district, it was a community of one-story adobe buildings. The roofs were flat and covered with tar, the streets choked with dust.

Two brown, half-naked children passed them leading a burro up the street. They were followed by a mongrel dog that detoured to chase a fat rat down an alleyway.

Though Spanish was the predominant language spoken on the streets, subtle signs of Yankee encroachment were evident at almost every turn.

"Are you sure you don't want to eat something before we get down to business?" Tyler queried.

307

"Positive. I left my appetite several miles down the road. I'm afraid it's going to take awhile before it catches up with me," she explained, laying her hand on her roily stomach. "But you needn't starve on my account. Go ahead and eat if you're hungry."

Rather than sit down for a meal, Tyler stopped to buy a tamale and a beer from a street vendor. At the offices of the *Los Angeles Star* and the *Los Angeles News* they found the articles they were seeking.

Lady Luck, who had eluded them for so long, smiled upon them. After less than twenty-four hours in the city, they had directions to two cattle ranches her father had worked on shortly after the time of the water rights dispute. There was no telling if he was still at either ranch, but they felt they were one step closer to finding him.

It was two days' hard riding to the first ranch, another day past it to the second. The weather was comfortable, the terrain hilly. Trees were sparse and grass abundant.

Her mind occupied with the search for her father once again, Sarah quickly regained a healthy measure of her blithesome spirits.

Upon questioning the owners and cowhands at the two ranches, they came up empty. Her father had talked a lot about buying his own spread, and it was generally assumed Elijah Jenkins was probably living somewhere in the area, but no one knew where.

They decided to return to Los Angeles and see what else they could turn up there.

A few hours into the second day of the return trip, Sarah's horse began to limp. Inspecting the hoof, she found a sharp rock had buried itself in the pad. It was not easy to remove, and her horse continued to limp as she led her around in circles to test the foot.

"It doesn't look good," Tyler commented. "Looks like we're going to have to camp out a few extra nights while we wait for the foot to heal."

The sound of a horse approaching caught their attention. When the rider came abreast of them he halted, covertly running an appraising eye over them—checking Sarah's ears, neck, and wrists for jewelry, and their hands for wedding rings.

Sarah shaded her eyes so she could better see the man.

Dressed from head to toe in black cloth heavily embroidered with silver thread, with silver spurs on the heels of his ornately tooled riding boots, he cut a startlingly romantic figure. His hair and eyes matched the fabric of his suit. White teeth gleamed from beneath a long handlebar mustache.

There was something vaguely familiar about his face, but she was sure they had never met before, and Sarah dismissed the sensation of recognition. She returned his smile.

"It looks like you are having a bit of trouble, señorita, señor." He tipped his fringed flat-topped hat. "Perhaps Carlos can be of assistance?"

"My horse has injured her foot," Sarah started to explain.

"We were discussing where to make camp for a few days," Tyler continued for her, his expression less friendly than hers. "Do you know a good place?"

"A lady should not be forced to sleep on the ground. Why don't you come with me to my brother's rancho? It is just over the rise."

"We wouldn't want to impose," Tyler demurred.

Carlos directed his words to Sarah. "It is never an imposition to give assistance to a beautiful señorita. We would be honored if you would grace our house. I am returning home for fiesta. Come join the party. It will be far better than sitting here in the dust," he cajoled.

She turned to Tyler.

His eyes met hers. Californios were well known for their hospitality. Just because this Carlos fellow was as handsome as the devil himself and Sarah returned his silky smiles was no reason to take an instant dislike to him. Sarah enjoyed flattery, but she never took it seriously. She was friendly to everyone. She couldn't help it. It was her nature. "It's up to you," he answered her questioning look, trying his best to sound unbiased and hide the jealousy that was as much apart of his nature as friendliness was hers.

"I have never been to a fiesta," she answered Carlos, her voice effervescent with enthusiasm. "We would love to come to your party."

The sun sparkled off Carlos's pearly teeth. "My brother will be so pleased. Come here, my pretty one. I will share my horse with you, and we can get better acquainted as we ride to the rancho."

Tyler was all for being a reasonable man, but he wasn't *that* tolerant. He recognized a smitten look even if Sarah did not. His own eyes reflected such a look every time they fell upon her. Already he was regretting letting her make the decision to stay. He frowned fiercely at Carlos. "She'll ride with me," he tersely informed him, reaching down his hand and lifting Sarah from the ground.

"Of course, of course. There will be time to talk later." Carlos flourished his hand. "Follow me."

While they rode, they exchanged names and engaged in conversation of a general nature. Carlos had no knowledge of her father, but he explained he did not live at the rancho and promised to ask his relatives if they knew of him.

El Rancho Robles was built of adobe and tile and looked to have stood for many years underneath the shade of the large oaks that ringed it. Water-stained and pockmarked, it had clearly seen better days. Corrals were built a short distance from the house. A handful of children chased a fat pink pig, scattering chickens and ducks in their wake.

"Niños, look what I have brought, another señorita to dance at our fandango," he greeted them as he dismounted.

They laughed and clapped their hands. "Hola, señorita," they said, the boys bowing and the girls curtseying.

"Hola," Sarah returned the word of greeting.

"Pedro, take the horses to the stable. Tell Juan to see to the mare's injured foot at once," he instructed. "Señor, señorita, come with me. I must tell Doña Maria to prepare your rooms."

From the outside the house looked like a large adobe square, but upon following Carlos through a set of wide wooden doors, Sarah discovered the home to be a series of connecting rooms arranged around a central plaza.

Here there was no sign of the poverty she had seen without. Statues of the saints stood sentry about the quad. A fountain graced the center. Pots of bright multicolored flowers hung from every eave.

Carlos stepped into one of the rooms, easily identified as the kitchen from the delectable aromas wafting through the open door, gesturing for them to wait in the courtyard.

"Doña Maria . . ." The rest of what he said was in Spanish, and Sarah could not understand it. A few moments later he rejoined them, followed by a smiling, late middle-aged woman dressed in black silk and an apron. "This is my aunt, Doña Maria. Doña Maria, mi new amigos Señor Tyler and Señorita Sarah." He continued to use the unmarried form of address even though he now knew Sarah to be a widow. "I am sorry but my aunt refuses to learn English, so you must speak to her through me."

They exchanged greetings through their interpreter and followed the woman across the patio. She ushered Sarah into one room and Tyler into another at the opposite end of the wing. Shutters were opened and clean linen put on the beds. The rooms were dark, cool and well kept.

After Sarah and Tyler stowed their gear, they rejoined Carlos. He took them on a brief tour of the rancho, introducing them to relatives and ranch hands alike. The ranch traded mainly in cattle, but it was readily apparent that Carlos's enthusiasm was for the horse stock. He and his brother had bred some beauties which he showed them with pride.

Though Carlos did not live on the rancho, he clearly took great interest in its success and held his brother in high regard.

They did not meet their esteemed host until the mid afternoon meal. Pablo Rameriz was an older version of Carlos and showed a like generosity of spirit. He promised Sarah's horse would receive the best of care and offered the hospitality of his home for as long as they wished to stay.

After dinner, yielding to an atypical drowsiness, Sarah availed herself of the custom of siesta.

Throughout that day and the next a steady stream of guests arrived until by nightfall every room was filled. Though the conversations that went on around her were in Spanish, through observation and the occasional comment in English directed her way, Sarah learned most of the guests were in some way related to their host.

Children outnumbered the adults by an alarming margin and had to be constantly moved out from underfoot. Everyone chipped in to help, and any complaints that were heard were good-natured.

Though their hosts protested, there was much to do, and Sarah and Tyler insisted their consciences would not allow them to accept the family's hospitality unless they were allowed to help where they could.

A large family was something Sarah had never experienced. Though the noise was ofttimes deafening and chaos constantly threatened, she found herself envying the Rameriz family.

She and Tyler took their separate turns entertaining the children with the rest. As Sarah watched him through the kitchen window, running and shouting as he played tag with the boys, her eyes misted with tears.

"Señorita Sarah, is something wrong?" one of the many cousins asked.

"No," Sarah smiled through her tears and lifted an

onion from the pile she was assigned to chop. "It's just the onions, nothing more."

"I will tell Doña Maria to have someone else do them," the woman offered.

"There's no need," Sarah assured her. She blinked several times. "See, I'm already better."

The rancho was frantic with activity. Sarah loved it. Each day started early with prayers in the family chapel and a breakfast of warm tortillas spread with a mixture of mashed beans, tomatoes, and chilies. Most of the men rode off to work on the range, and the women stayed in the kitchen to prepare food for the fiesta.

Carlos was not among the men who left. He was so attentive that Sarah began to feel like she was the guest of honor. Whatever direction she turned, he seemed to be at her side—at morning prayers, at dinner, when she sat by the fountain to rest from the hustle and bustle of the preparations for fiesta. She enjoyed his company, and his attention was flattering, but she felt compelled to chide him for neglecting his duty to the other guests. It did little good, and she assuaged her conscience by continuing to lend a hand wherever she could.

At Pablo's invitation Tyler spent a good portion of each day riding the range with the elder Rameriz. When she did see him, he did not seem to be enjoying himself quite as much as she. However, when they managed to snatch a private moment and she questioned him about it, he denied anything was amiss.

Since the Rameriz family extended the same measure of hospitality to him as they did to her, she surmised his less-than-ebullient mood must be caused by the fact that they were assigned separate rooms, and he was suffering from his forced celibacy. She sorely missed their love play herself and sympathized wholeheartedly.

The morning of the fiesta dawned. Sarah was surprised to find a bright red silk blouse, black and red ruffled skirt, and lacy shawl lying on the foot of her bed. She dressed quickly, wondering who had provided them for her.

"Do you like them?" Carlos greeted, when she stepped out her door onto the patio.

She smiled. He was dressed in his usual black, but his suit was of velvet profusely embroidered with shining red thread. A bright red sash encircled his waist. "So you are the one I need thank. Yes, I like them very much." She turned so he could view her from all sides. "I feel like a real señorita."

Carlos grinned. "I am glad my gift has made you happy."

"You really shouldn't be so generous," she scolded.

"Why not? Fiesta is the time to bring smiles to the faces of beautiful women."

"I do declare, you can be as excessive with your praise as Tyler." Her eyes twinkled merrily. "It is a trait of western men I much admire."

"A scarcity of women has taught us to take good care of those we have." The sound of a door opening and closing caught both their attention. "Ah, here comes Señor Tyler now."

They waited for Tyler to join them. He too was dressed in his finest suit, but it lacked the color and

315

excitement of the Spanish costumes.

"Well, what do you think?" She modeled the skirt and blouse for Tyler when he joined them.

"You look very lovely," he assured her.

The smile on his lips did not reach his eyes. He was doing his best not to be a jealous fool, but this Carlos was really starting to get on his nerves. He buzzed around Sarah like a bee did a flower. It made him nervous.

The chapel bell called them to prayers. Doors opened all along the courtyard. The men were all dressed in a manner similar to Carlos, the women in bright skirts, blouses, and mantillas like Sarah. The older women wore ornate combs in their hair. The younger women wore their dark tresses loose. Children dressed in imitation of their parents.

Morning prayers were extended into a full service with Don Pablo presiding, thanking the Lord for his many blessings, and asking Him to continue to provide for the needs of the family. The service was conducted in Spanish, but Carlos whispered a translation as he knelt beside her.

Tyler knelt on the other side, praying for forbearance. Sarah's horse was healing nicely, and they could be gone from here by tomorrow. He could hardly wait to leave Carlos Rameriz behind.

He told himself he could trust Sarah, but his alter ego reminded him she had been acting restless of late and he had no claim on her. There was nothing to prevent her from succumbing to Carlos's charms except her love for him, and her continued refusal to marry him left the strength of that love suspect.

He had been a reasonable man for a long time, but

even a reasonable man had limits to his patience. They could not go on like this forever.

After a light breakfast, everyone chipped in to festoon the plaza with brightly colored paper flowers constructed by the older children and banners of like colored ribbons. The men carried in long wooden tables which the women covered with cloths. When the decorating was done, everyone moved out into the yard.

The unmarried men had slipped away early and sat in line atop ornately decorated horses. After parading about the grounds to show off their finery, they set about in earnest to impress the single women with a display of equestrian skills, ranging from races to trick riding. For a while the older men let them have center stage, but one by one they joined them, doing their best to outshine the youths.

The ladies cheered, shouting encouragement and offering finely embroidered handkerchiefs as prizes to their husbands and beaux.

As the day progressed, the men became more boisterous, the activities less refined. Horses had been brought in from the range. More wild than tame, they did their best to buck the riders from their backs, succeeding more often than not.

"Señor Tyler, you do not wish to ride the horses?" Carlos queried amiably as he returned to Sarah's side after a successful ride.

"Just waiting for my turn," Tyler coolly responded to the challenge. Climbing the first two rungs of the fence, he threw a leg over.

Sarah put her hand on his arm. "Do you think you should? These men are trained . . ."

"Let your friend play the vaquero," Carlos urged. "It will be entertaining."

As Tyler was already over the fence and approaching the horse, there was little Sarah could do to stop him.

Her eyes riveted on the horse. He was snow white except for his tail and mane, which were fringed in black. With each step Tyler took toward him, the animal seemed to grow by hands.

It took four men to steady the horse while he mounted. When they let go, Sarah held her breath.

The animal bucked and twisted, jumping high off the ground. Tyler held fast. The battle continued, the shouts of the crowd spurring on both horse and rider. At last Tyler began to prevail, and the animal gradually settled to an agitated gallop. Tyler rode it around the ring several times, then reined to a halt and dismounted before her. Sarah cheered wildly.

Carlos frowned.

Other men took their turns pitting themselves against the range horses. There were more races and games for the children. The boys imitated their fathers, strutting around with their chests puffed out after every victory; the girls imitated their mothers, waving lacy handkerchiefs and cheering on their favorite contestants.

As the heat of the day increased, the merrymakers began to slowly drift back to their rooms to escape the sun and refresh themselves for the evening.

At dusk the women carried out the platters of food and laid them on the tables. There were fresh vegetables and fruits, and corn and flour tortillas spread with freshly churned butter. Some were filled with mixtures of meat and cheese. Bowls of punch were filled and emptied at an alarming rate. The men filled their cups from a keg of Mexican beer.

When it was deemed everyone had had ample time to eat and drink their fill, Carlos and a cousin named Emile brought out a guitar and violin.

"Es la hora de fandango!" Carlos shouted as he strummed the first chord.

The ladies and their gentlemen formed two lines facing each other. Another chord was strummed and they began the slow, seductive movements of a contra-danza.

Sarah and Tyler watched from the sidelines.

Ever alert to their guests' needs, the Rameriz clan could not let this situation remain for long. A gentleman presented himself to Sarah, a lady to Tyler. Through observation, instruction, and an occasional hand on the wrist to pull them in the right direction, they began to catch on to the rhythm of the steps. By the end of the fourth dance, both had been transformed into respectable partners.

Though they had little opportunity to dance with each other, they danced until their feet ached, then danced some more. In between the contras were dance games where one or more members of the family had the chance to show off their skills.

Several dark-eyed beauties took turns dancing the *sombrero*. As each señorita danced, she collected hats atop her head from the gentlemen. The better she danced, the more hats she collected. At the end of the dance, each man had to pay a coin for the return of his hat.

The stately Doña Maria astonished Sarah when she

entered the arena, a glass of water perched upon her head, to dance *el son*. Not a drop was spilled.

Shortly before midnight, the children were herded off to bed. Carlos handed his guitar to a younger man who took over his task, and he walked directly to Sarah.

"Señorita Sarah, I would be honored if you would dance with me." He held out his arm.

She curtseyed and allowed him to guide her out onto the dance floor.

Carlos's feet were as skilled on the dance floor as his fingers were on the strings of the guitar. Spinning and swirling, Sarah tapped her feet in time to the music, following his lead.

One dance ended and another began. Carlos's enthusiasm for flamboyant footwork was contagious, and Sarah laughed as she tried to match him, raising her arms above her head and snapping her fingers in time to the music as she had seen the other señoritas do.

Her partner was well pleased, and he insisted she join him for another dance and then another. . . .

Tyler frowned as he watched them. While others showed signs of tiring, Sarah was unflagging. Her body swayed to the music, intoxicating his senses, making him want her so badly his loins ached. Then his eyes fell upon Carlos and possessive rage mingled with lust. She should not be dancing like that with another man. She should be dancing with him and him alone.

Crossing the dance floor, he captured her hand in his and swung her into his arms.

Tyler and Carlos took turns stealing Sarah from each other. On the surface it was all in good fun, but underneath it all, both men knew the game they were playing. Sarah, too imbued with the spirit of fandango, was blind to the narrow looks they cast each other.

The adults danced on through the wee hours of the morning, but at last even the most devoted reveler was ready to call it an evening. The musicians put away their instruments, and those remaining said their good nights and retired to their private chambers.

Tyler lay in his bed with his hands hooked behind his head, staring up at the ceiling. Watching Sarah dance had set his blood on fire—dancing with her had set his whole body ablaze. He had never known a woman to have such enthusiasm for life. He closed his eyes, picturing how she had looked, her lips smiling, her eyes flashing as she spun round and round. Her laughter echoed in his ears. He had been surrounded by beautiful women tonight, but he had only had eyes for Sarah.

He wasn't any good at sharing her. Every man she danced with stirred his jealousy. Carlos's attentions maddened him to the point that he was ready to call the man out. He told himself over and over that he was responding like an insecure adolescent, but it didn't mute his feelings.

He sat up. He was not good at sharing, and he was even worse at denying himself the pleasure of her bed. Every night he lay awake half the night wrestling with his lust. Even if he could do no more than hold Sarah in his arms, he knew it would help. It had been far too long since they had been alone.

An idea slowly formed in his head, tickling his fancy. They had been among the last dancers to seek their beds. Perhaps . . . he would wait until he was sure no one was moving about. . . . There was no reason he couldn't sneak into her room. They could quietly make love; then he would slip back into his room. No one would be the wiser.

The more he thought about it, the more he warmed to the idea. Rising from his bed, he dressed in the dark. He struck a match, checked the time on his pocket watch, then sat on the edge of the mattress — tapping out the minutes with an impatient foot.

He lit another match. Thirty minutes had elapsed. Surely it would be safe. He eased his door open and stuck out his head.

His gaze traveled slowly around the patio, then came to an abrupt halt.

"Carlos." His eyes narrowed and his teeth clenched as he muttered the name. What the hell was Carlos doing outside Sarah's door? The man stood, his back to her door, drawing on a cigarillo and blowing smoke rings in the air.

Tyler watched him, his fury growing with each passing minute. He waited for him to approach Sarah's door. When he did not, he began to worry that he had already been there.

He knew Sarah liked Carlos. Would she? Could she? Had she? He hated himself for even thinking the thought and pulled his head back inside.

Chapter 18

"Señorita Sarah, you are up early. After watching you dance the night away, I thought you would sleep till noon like the other ladies," Carlos greeted as Sarah stepped into the courtyard the next morning.

She smiled and yawned. "I seem to have acquired the habit of rising at dawn. Why are you up so early?"

"I fear I have the same habit as you. Perhaps you would like to go for a ride with Carlos? We can talk about the fun we had last night without disturbing the others."

Having no desire to tiptoe around like a mouse until the others awoke, she readily agreed. "A ride sounds lovely. Just let me slip into my riding skirt and I'll join you. Shall I meet you at the stables?"

"Sí, I will have the horses waiting."

It took Sarah less than five minutes to present herself at the stables. Carlos was waiting with his own horse and a beautiful tawny mare.

"Is my own mare still unfit?" Sarah asked in concern.

"No, she has healed nicely, but why not let her rest as long as she can. La Dama, she likes the ladies to ride her, and she is swift as the wind."

Carlos gallantly assisted Sarah onto the horse, then mounted his own. They continued to converse on a variety of topics as they rode along at an easy gait.

Sarah enjoyed the feel of the morning sun upon her face. The air was brisk, and a gentle breeze tickled the leaves of the trees.

They passed long- and short-horned cattle. Some lay in the grass. Others grazed along the streambed or stared with large, soulful eyes as they stood chewing their cud.

Carlos followed her gaze, surveying the property. "The herd is not as big as it used to be," he commented. "But we are lucky we still have our land."

"Did you almost lose it?" she asked.

"Many of the Californios were cheated out of their land by the Americanos. My father fought and won, but many fought and lost."

Sarah's brows knit. This was a side of Carlos she had never seen, a serious side. She realized with a start that she had never before seen him without his smile. "How did we cheat you?" she queried.

"With the courts. The Californios had to produce proof they owned land they had occupied for generations. Sometimes deeds could not be produced. Other times delays were used to bankrupt the family. But the Ramerizes, we survive because Carlos understands Americanos."

His words were tinged with a certain bitterness, and she felt a need to soothe him. "I'm glad. I like your family very much."

His smile returned. "And Carlos, what do you think of him?"

"I like you very much also," she replied honestly. "I can't thank you enough for inviting us to stay in your home and especially for the experience of fiesta. I shall always remember it."

His smile broadened. "Let us walk awhile."

Dismounting, he tied his horse to a tree. Sarah did the same. They walked side by side in silence, enjoying the peace of the countryside.

It was pleasant to stretch her legs. She thought about Carlos and his family and their way of life. If what he said was true, it seemed a great pity other families had been deprived of such.

His velvety voice broke into her musings. "I like Señorita Sarah very much also. She is like a gay child—always laughing. You are good for Carlos."

"But I am an Americano," she reminded.

"You are different from the others. I have seen you cooking and cleaning with the other women. You do not think yourself better than my people. You accept our ways." His caressing tone caused her to pause, and she turned toward him.

Gathering her in his arms, Carlos leaned over her, kissing her passionately.

Tyler Bennet reined in his horse. The sight that greeted his eyes made his heart sink and his blood boil. He clenched his teeth so hard his jaw ached. Sarah and Carlos were locked in embrace. Carlos covered her neck and shoulders with feverish kisses. She writhed against him as he claimed her lips again and again. Last night he had chided himself for thinking there might be something going on between Sarah and Carlos. Now he chided himself for being so easily duped.

The signs were all there, plain for him to see: the laughter, whispered words in the chapel, warm glances. Carlos was handsome, slick, smooth tongued. He realized he had been kept conveniently out of the way by Pablo so Carlos could work his wiles on Sarah.

"But, damn it, she didn't have to succumb!" He pounded his fist on the pummel of his saddle, causing his horse to lurch. Tyler deftly regained control, soothing the animal with long strokes down its shoulder.

All the frustration caused by Sarah's reluctance to marry him came to a head and no longer could be repressed. It exploded within him like a charge of dynamite. He had played the game her way, giving her the time she asked, and she repaid him with infidelity! Months had been invested in patient wooing—and it had brought him to this. He cursed his own naiveté. Either she loved him or she did not. If she did not love him, it was past time she stopped playing him for the fool and let him get on with his life.

He'd been a patient man. Too patient. His lips froze in a grim line.

They were standing close, talking now. What were they saying? Were they whispering words of love? Laughing behind his back?

He had seen enough! The horse whinnied and he spun around. He didn't want them to know he had followed them. He needed time to collect his thoughts—to decide what he was going to do.

As he rode back to the rancho, Tyler fought the impulse to turn back, to give in to the primitive urge to beat the hell out of both Carlos and Sarah.

He argued with himself against violence. He was a civilized man. He would deal with this situation like a civilized man. But damn it, being civilized was what had gotten him into this mess in the first place.

He would give Sarah an ultimatum. If she wanted him, she must forsake all others "till death do you part." It was the only way he would forgive her.

Upon reaching the rancho, he left his horse's care to the stable boy and strode purposefully towards Sarah's room.

When Carlos grabbed her, Sarah's arms instinctively flew around his neck to keep herself from falling. At first she was so stunned, she was incapable of doing anything but lying limp in his arms, while he showered her with kisses, but slowly her senses returned to her.

"Carlos!" she protested, pushing against his chest. "Please! What has gotten into you?"

"I am on fire for you," he purred, his dark eyes warm with longing. He captured her lips again.

"Don't!" Sarah wriggled against him until she gained her release. She tried to step away, but he captured her hands.

"But I want you for my *amante*," he protested.

Misinterpreting the meaning of the word, Sarah replied, rather breathlessly, "I appreciate the offer, but

327

I can't marry you. If I marry any man, it will be Tyler. I am sorry if I have said or done anything to give you the impression I felt differently, but friendship was all I ever thought to offer. You flirt with everyone, even Doña Maria. It never occurred to me . . ." She managed to extract one of her hands, and she fanned herself as she paused for breath. "I must say, you western men fall in love at a dizzying speed. It makes one wonder if you will fall out of love just as quickly."

Carlos chuckled. "I do not want you for a wife, I want you for a lover. It is what you are to him, is it not?" He gazed directly into her eyes. "I am a far better hombre than he. I would not drag you around the countryside, making you sleep in the dirt. I would keep you in a house in the city and shower you with fine silks and jewelry."

Embarrassed by her error as well as his offer, Sarah struggled to maintain her composure. Out of respect for the Rameriz family, she and Tyler had been the very essence of propriety while in their home. She had not thought it right to do otherwise. Obviously, despite their exemplary behavior, the nature of their relationship was easy to discern.

She liked being Tyler's lover, but she did not like the fact Carlos considered her fair game. He certainly hadn't been shy about asking her to be his lover.

Seeking to disguise her discomfort, she rebuked him, "Tyler Bennet does not make me sleep in the dirt. He accompanies *me* where *I* go, so where I sleep is my own choice. As to the other, I think your money would be better spent helping your family rather than keeping a mistress in jewels."

Carlos remained undeterred. "But I am the black sheep of the family."

"They do not seem to regard you as such," she argued.

"That is because I provide well for them."

Sarah studied him closely. Now that he mentioned it, despite their many conversations, there was a lot she didn't know about Carlos. He talked of his family, and the rancho, but never of himself. "What exactly is it you do to provide so well for them?"

He grinned. "You would not like the answer."

She continued to study him, puzzling out every bit of information she had, searching her mind for more. Carlos not living at the rancho but having a say in its running. The incongruity of the faded exterior and opulent interior of the house. His admission he was a black sheep. Suddenly, her eyes lit up with knowledge.

"You're a bandit!" Sarah exclaimed. "When you stopped to help us on the road, I had the feeling I had seen your face before, but I couldn't place it. Now, I remember where I have seen you. Your face was on a wanted poster." As the last word left her lips, Sarah was consumed with fear that admitting her knowledge was less than prudent. Carlos was a different brand of criminal from those she had met in the Barbary Coast, but he was still a criminal. She had misjudged his attentions towards her as platonic. It was quite possible she had misjudged him entirely. Yanking her hand from his, she took a step back.

"Do not be afraid, señorita. Carlos may sometimes be a bandito, but he is always a gentleman."

"Then you aren't angry I know who you are?" she

asked tentatively.

"Why should I be? The policia already know who I am and where my family lives."

Sarah sighed in relief for herself, but even knowing what he was, she couldn't help feel some concern for Carlos and his family. "You're not afraid of getting caught?"

Carlos shook his head, his smile still firmly in place. "I have been a bandito for many years, and always I am one step ahead of the law. A generous man has many friends."

"But you must also have many enemies," she argued.

He shrugged. "I have a deal with God. I take the money my family needs, but I never take a life. He watches over me."

Her eyes widened. "Is that what you pray about when you are on your knees in the chapel?"

"Sometimes." He twirled the ends of his mustache. "And what do you pray about? That Señor Tyler will someday marry you?"

"No."

He opened his arms and took a step towards her. "Then I have hope. Perhaps another kiss is what the señorita needs to persuade her to be *mi amante*."

Sarah took another step back, but her eyes met his. They were dark and smoky with passion. "Carlos . . ."

"Does it bother you that I am a bandito?" He continued to advance and she to retreat.

She chewed her bottom lip. He claimed he never hurt anyone, and she believed him. "I am no saint myself," she replied softly.

"Then am I to be your lover?" he pressed.

Her relationship with Tyler could not go on forever, she reminded herself. If she were a virtuous woman, she would release him now so he would be free to find the kind of woman who could give him all he deserved.

She and Carlos were better suited to each other. Neither could lay claim to a high standard of morality. With him it wouldn't matter that she couldn't have children. He wouldn't want the encumbrance.

But she didn't want another lover. She wanted Tyler, and she hadn't the strength of character to let go, even though she knew prolonging their relationship would make their inevitable parting harder on them both.

Carlos ran a finger across her lips. "Señorita? What is your answer?"

"No, Carlos. I will not be your mistress."

He looked disappointed, but far from devastated. "Do you love Señor Tyler so very much?"

"Yes, I love him so very much," she answered without hesitation.

"He is a lucky man."

She shook her head. "Not so lucky as you think. If I stay, I hurt him. If I go, I hurt him. It would have been far better for him if we had never met."

"And for the señorita?" he asked.

Sarah smiled wanly. "The señorita would not have missed these past months for anything in this world or the next."

Tyler was waiting in Sarah's room when she returned. The wait had not been long, but his rage had simmered all the while. She started at the sound of his voice, spinning to face him.

"Did you have a pleasant ride?" he asked.

"Yes, I did."

"You look like you enjoyed yourself," he said coldly. "Your cheeks are flushed, your lips rosy with passion."

Her conversation with Carlos had left her drained. He had forced her to face things she preferred to ignore. Having come to her room to be alone and patch up her tattered emotions so she could present a cheerful face to the world, she did not feel able to cope with anyone else's ill-humor. "If you are upset about something, I wish you would come to the point. I'm not in the mood for guessing games."

"I came to your room to talk to you this morning and found you were already out. Lucky for me, I saw you and Carlos riding over the ridge. I followed you."

Her heart sank.

"And?" Sarah prodded, having a good idea what he was going to say next, but unwilling to divulge the information herself on the off chance she was mistaken and she could avoid an uncomfortable confrontation.

"I saw the two of you kissing," he growled.

So much for false hope, she mentally shrugged. Pushing her own pain aside, she reached up to smooth the lines from his brow. He brushed her hand away. "You really don't need to work yourself into a dither. It's not what you're thinking," she explained gently.

"Then what was it?" he demanded.

She didn't see any point in mincing words and

answered him frankly. "Carlos asked me to leave you and become his mistress. I told him no."

The fire of fury blazed brighter in his eyes, and he captured her upper arms in his hands. "Was that before or after you kissed him?"

"Tyler, don't be obtuse. I didn't kiss him. He kissed me."

"You didn't appear to be putting up much of a struggle."

"I was taken by surprise."

"Did you slap him?"

"No."

"Why not?" He glared at her.

She glared back. "I didn't think it was necessary."

"So, you like kissing Carlos," he said, his grip tightening.

"Tyler, please. You're hurting my arms. Can't we just forget it?" she pleaded.

His hold on her did not slacken. "You are avoiding my question."

"You didn't ask a question. You made a statement—a very rude statement."

"I'm not feeling very gentlemanly at the moment. I want you to tell me just exactly what is going on between you and Carlos. I have a right to know!"

She had seen Tyler angry before, but never like this. Where was the adoring, patient man she had grown to love? "Lower your voice. Someone will hear you."

"I don't care if every cow on the damn range hears me! I want to know what is going on."

Losing her last shred of composure, she shouted back at him, "Nothing is going on! And I made it perfectly clear to Carlos there could be nothing between us in the future! As to the quality of his kisses, I was too busy securing my release to take time to notice."

"Good." He loosened his grip but did not let go. "Then you won't mind packing your bags. We're leaving."

"Right this minute?"

"Yes. And furthermore, we are going to stop in the first settlement large enough to support a preacher, and you are going to marry me."

"What!"

"You heard me. We're getting married. I'm through standing by watching other men ogle you. I'm staking my claim publicly. Expect a large and very conspicuous wedding ring."

This whole conversation was getting out of hand. It was clear Tyler had abdicated his good sense, and she struggled to fill the gap. "Don't you think you're overreacting?"

"Not in the least. Do you or do you not love me?" he charged.

"You know the answer to that."

"Say it!"

"I love you, Tyler."

"Then prove it by marrying me," he exhorted.

The color drained from Sarah's cheeks. "No."

"Why the hell not? I've wined you. I've dined you. I've indulged your every whim. I've done everything in my power to prove to you I am not the same brand of man as your late husband, Henry. God knows I love you. Why else would I be willing to believe what you are saying about your lack of feelings for Carlos?

334

It's because I want to believe it." He took a ragged breath. "I've come to the end of my rope. What is it going to take to make you marry me?"

"I've explained before why I'm not the marrying kind." Sarah feebly offered up the old excuses, "I like my freedom too much. I don't want to feel obligated to answer to anyone."

Tyler ran his hands through his hair and turned from her. "Hell, maybe I'm deluding myself. After all we've been to each other, if you still view me as some kind of ogre who will lock you away in my house and throw away the key, you can't really love me."

Sarah could feel his pain, and it tore at her heart. She lay her hand on his back and swallowed the hard lump in her throat. "I do love you, Tyler. I wouldn't say it if it weren't true."

"Then why won't you marry me?"

She opened her mouth to tell him, then clamped it shut again. He would use the truth against her, use it to weaken her resolve to put his future happiness above her own selfish desires. Tyler Bennet possessed a spirit too generous for his own good. It was because she loved him, she could not marry him. Some burdens were too great to share, and if she truly loved him, she wouldn't let him share hers even if he was willing.

"I'm waiting for my answer," he reminded her. "Sarah, I want you for my wife, but I won't go on living the way we are. I have given you more than enough time. Either you want me and me alone, or you don't. If you think I'm worth having, you'll marry me."

"I can't marry you," she protested.

"Then we have nothing further to discuss," he stated brusquely, walking towards the door. "Good-bye, Sarah Williams, it's been a pleasure."

"You're leaving me?" she called after him.

"I'm going home," he confirmed. "If you ever decide to grow up, you know where to find me."

Chapter 19

Sarah sat on the edge of her bed, her head in her hands. She rocked back and forth, crooning soothing words to herself as one might a disappointed child, but she did not cry.

Tyler was leaving her. She should be grateful he had saved her the distasteful task of leaving him, she told herself, but she didn't feel grateful. All she felt was an awful, soul-numbing cold.

She cursed fate for forcing her to deprive herself of Tyler's company. What good did it do her to be mistress of her own destiny if she could not have the one thing she truly wanted? All her life she had been lonely, and now she would be lonely again.

"Tyler, please don't hate me for what I am doing," she whispered. "I do love you, but if I can't be a satisfactory wife to you, I would rather be no wife at all."

She pressed her lips together to stay their quivering. The words of her mother and Henry resounded in her head, ghosts from her past, rebuking her for her many inadequacies, mocking her for believing even for a moment that she deserved lasting happiness.

She knew what she was doing was best for Tyler. Their parting had come to pass far sooner than she would have wished, but they had had glorious months together. She would concentrate on the happy memories he had given her and go on with her life.

She wondered how long it would be before he forgot her. One month? Two? Six months at the most, she decided. He would find another woman, someone he could love even more than he loved her, and the two of them would live happily ever after. Her heart rebelled.

Sarah shook her head vigorously to purge it of all thoughts of Tyler Bennet. Melancholy ruminations would not change her situation one whit! What she needed was a task to keep her busy. Surely Doña Maria would have something for her to do.

Tyler left within the half hour. Sarah did not see him go, but she heard him thanking Don Pablo and the *adioses* of the children as he rode away. Their happy laughter mocked her.

No one questioned her as to why he left without her, and she did not volunteer any explanations. She made herself move through the day as if nothing was amiss, smiling, laughing, chatting with the members of the Rameriz family who spoke enough English to carry on a conversation.

Despite the reticence of her hosts, Sarah could feel their eyes upon her, following her throughout the day. There were whispered conversations in Spanish that came to an abrupt halt whenever she approached.

Carlos was ever present at her side. He remained as mute on the subject of Tyler's departure as his family. In fact, from the harsh glances he cast upon anyone who accidentally started to broach the subject, she surmised him to be the author of their constraint.

Whatever the reasons behind the conspiracy of silence, she was grateful. It made it far easier to pretend her heart was not breaking and the day was like any other. Despite her rejection of him, Carlos further aided her in her charade by keeping her well entertained. She used their friendship as a shield, keeping emotions she did not want to feel at bay.

More than once she reconsidered his invitation to be his lover, but the reasons against following such a path far outnumbered those for doing so. She did not love him. She felt no physical desire for him. He was a bandit. . . .

The only argument in his favor was that spending her life constantly running from the law was bound to keep her mind preoccupied with the present so it could not dwell on the past.

Her spirits had never sunk so low, but she was not so disconsolate she didn't recognize that becoming Carlos's lover would be an act of desperation and one she would surely come to regret

One day came and went, as did another. She wanted to be certain Tyler had a generous head start, so there would be no chance their paths would cross. She could not face the pain of another good-bye, nor did she think she had the strength to resist him should he again ask her to marry him. He had not said so, but it was logical to assume he would go to Los Angeles to catch a steamer to San Francisco. She would be returning to Los Angeles also, to resume the search for her father — alone.

The next morning Carlos was missing at both morning prayers and breakfast. His absence was sorely felt. His carefree nature was diverting, and at this particular time in her life, diversion was more necessary to her well-being than food and drink. "Where is Carlos?" Sarah asked.

"He had to go away," Don Pablo informed her.

"Why?" She was perplexed that he had not bothered to say farewell.

"We hear the sheriff is coming to pay us a visit."

Sarah looked alarmed.

"Do not be distressed, señorita, Carlos will be safe."

She was not as confident as Don Pablo. She did not want to repay the Ramerizes' hospitality by causing Carlos harm, but neither did she feel comfortable thwarting the law. Whatever she said or did, she would feel culpable. "I am afraid I am not a very good liar," Sarah voiced her misgivings.

"You do not need to lie," he assured her.

"I don't?"

"Of course not. It would be rude to put a guest in such a position. Tell the truth. You will not put Carlos in danger. The members of my family will also be honest. The sheriff will leave knowing nothing because we do not know anything to tell him. Carlos does not say where he goes or when he will be back. It keeps him safe and his family also."

"Why doesn't the sheriff just post a guard here at the rancho?" she asked, then bit her lip, realizing the Rameriz family activities were really none of her affair, and the less she knew, the better it would be for her peace of mind.

340

Don Pablo did not seem offended by her question. "Once he did. The deputy stayed two months with us, but Carlos is too wise to come." His lips stretched into a slightly wicked grin that was startlingly similar to the one Carlos perpetually wore. "The sheriff and his men have many duties. He cannot afford to waste so much time on one man."

The lawman arrived as predicted. Tall in stature and graying at the temples, he wore the expression of a man who knew the outcome of his interview long before it had begun.

Don Pablo greeted him like a friend, inviting him to stay for dinner. The sheriff politely declined.

Everyone was gathered outside in the yard to answer the sheriff's questions. They did so with surprising candor.

When the sheriff came to Sarah, his gray eyes glimmered with faint hope. "What can you tell me?" he asked.

"Little that hasn't already been said," she replied honestly. "Carlos invited us here when my horse was injured. We stayed for the fiesta. When I woke up this morning, he was gone."

The sheriff glanced around the yard, but found no other face that was unfamiliar to him. "We?"

"I was traveling with my lawyer, Tyler Bennet."

"Where is your lawyer now? Is he with Carlos?" he demanded.

"No. He left two days ago. I expect he is either in Los Angeles or on his way to San Francisco."

The sheriff rubbed his chin. "So, he cannot be reached for questioning," he said suspiciously.

"If you are willing to wait a few days, I'm sure you

341

can reach him at his law office in San Francisco. He is the Bennet of Johnson & Bennet. But I can save you the time and trouble by telling you now he knows even less than I."

"I see."

"Were you aware of Carlos's unlawful activities when you accepted his invitation?" he continued to interrogate her.

"No."

"Did you know he was a thief before I came here?"

She shifted uncomfortably. "Yes. I discovered his secret two days ago."

"Why didn't you contact the law at once?"

Sarah was determined not to lie; however, she was equally determined not to discuss her broken love affair with the sheriff or anyone else. She chose her words carefully when she answered him. "I am a guest in this home . . . and my mind was preoccupied with other matters. Besides, Carlos said it would do no good—that you already knew all about him."

"Are you in the habit of taking criminals at their word?" he queried, his expression probing.

"I am not in the habit of dealing with criminals at all," Sarah replied unhappily.

"You would be wise not to do so in the future," he informed her tersely; then, his voice modulated. "What Carlos told you was true. By the time you had gotten word to me, he would have been gone, but that doesn't mean you shouldn't have made the effort."

The sheriff dismissed Sarah and directed a few more questions to Don Pablo before taking his leave. Sarah sighed in relief.

Everyone resumed their activities, laughing and

chattering with their usual enthusiasm. Sarah watched them in amazement. The dust of the sheriff's departure had yet to settle, and no one observing the Rameriz family would have been able to tell he had been there at all.

She was not able to dismiss the encounter with equal sangfroid. Despite having told the truth, she felt horribly guilty. The sheriff seemed a decent man, a man who was only trying to do the job for which he had been elected. It was impossible to reconcile her sympathy for the Rameriz family with her strongly held belief in abiding by the law.

The next day Carlos returned. He offered no apology, and she offered no censure. One dilemma at a time was enough with which to deal, and it was taking every ounce of her resources to maintain both an external and internal facade of casual acceptance of Tyler's departure.

Tyler Bennet had been gone for four days, and the routine schedule of rancho life was secure, but most of the Rameriz family had returned to their individual homes. Sarah knew it was time she moved on too.

Her desire to find her father was stronger now she did not have the comfort of Tyler's companionship. The old childish dreams of being enfolded in her father's loving arms returned double force, despite her logical mind's persistent reminders that she might never find him, and if she did, there was no guarantee he would welcome her at all. She needed some reason to rise from her bed each morning, and searching for the man who had fathered her filled that need.

The next morning after prayers, she said her thank yous and good-byes.

"Where will the pretty señorita be going?" Carlos queried as he carried her saddlebags to the stables.

"To Los Angeles."

"I would come with you if I could, but . . ." He shrugged his shoulders.

"It's not safe for you," she finished for him. "I understand."

They had reached the stable, and Carlos saddled her horse, speaking while he worked. "Do you have enough money?"

"Yes," she assured him.

"And a gun?"

"Yes."

"Good." He nodded his approval. "You must be careful. If you meet a bandito on the road, he may not be so much a gentleman as me."

"If a lady should meet a bandito on the road, what should she do?" she asked, curious as to what he would say.

"Shoot him."

Sarah smiled wryly. "Aren't you afraid I might kill one of your friends?"

Having finished securing the saddlebags, he turned to face her. "A friend of Carlos would never prey on a lone lady. You have my permission to shoot anyone who approaches you." He spoke so earnestly that Sarah was moved to genuine laughter.

It felt good after days of pretending amusement, but the moment quickly passed. "I have every intention of protecting myself, but I certainly hope there will be no need to shoot anyone. If the truth be known, I'm not terribly accurate with my aim."

His eyes darkened, and he brushed a wisp of hair from her face, the intensity of his gaze imprisoning hers. "Carlos could protect you, if you came with him. Since you have parted company with Señor Tyler, I could keep you from getting lonely."

It was the first time he had spoken Tyler's name out loud since Tyler had left, and Sarah's smile grew pallid.

"I overheard you arguing," he continued, taking her hand in his. "I know it is my fault he left you. I feel I should help you over this sadness I see in your eyes."

Dislodging her hand from his, Sarah mounted her mare. "It is not your fault," she said, her words far more stoic than her expression. "I have known from the first that Tyler and I were fated to part company. You just sped up the process a little."

"But I could make it up to you," he cajoled.

"I have thought about your offer these past few days," she admitted. "And being the lover of a bandito sounds very exciting. But I just can't bring myself to do it."

"Señor Tyler?"

"Señor Tyler," she confirmed. "Him and the fact that bandito is really just a romantic name for thief."

"You do not approve of me?" he asked, the sadness in her eyes momentarily reflected in his own.

She shook her head. "I'm sorry but I can't. I know you feel your actions are justified because of what has been done to your family and the other Californios, but two wrongs do not make a right. I hated it when the sheriff was questioning me. I would not like to live like that."

"Would you betray me to the law?"

She hesitated a moment before replying truthfully. "Probably. I think eventually my conscience would make me. It's a choice I never want to have to make."

"Then we should not be friends," he advised without rancor.

"No, we shouldn't," she agreed. "Take care, Carlos. If they catch you, there will be no one to play the guitar at the next fiesta."

"You are forgetting my nephew, Vincente," he reminded her.

"I should still not like to hear of your capture. I should like to hear you retired and took up a respectable trade."

Grinning, he lifted her hand and brushed his lips against it. Sarah returned his smile, but the light did not reach her eyes as it did his.

Reluctantly, Carlos released her; then, he gave her mare a hearty slap on the rump. "Vaya con Dios, Señorita." He waved her on her way. "If you were not so honest, we would have made a pair, you and me."

Sarah's ride back to the coast was long and uneventful. Alone, there was no need to keep up a cheery countenance for anyone but herself, and she found it increasingly difficult to do so. The dust seemed dustier, the sun hotter as it beat down upon her shoulders. When she lay on her bedroll and stared up into the night sky, the stars did not twinkle as brightly.

Concentrating her thoughts on her father helped crowd out thoughts of Tyler, but they had an annoying habit of taking over her mind despite her best efforts.

Already she missed him terribly. She didn't want to think of him. What good did it do her?

The temptation to return to San Francisco and accept his offer of marriage was great. She would do it in a minute, if only . . . if only didn't amount to much when one knew the necessary conditions would never occur.

God had seen fit to deny her the ability to have children. She could be selfish and marry Tyler, or she could prove her love and stay away.

She realized she owed her mother and Henry a debt of gratitude. Under their roofs she had had much practice coping with thwarted desires. She knew she would survive. The knowledge helped her direct her energies to matters at hand while she waited for time to work its healing on her heart.

Upon arriving in Los Angeles, she checked back into the Bella Union Hotel. Her first order of business was to visit the branch of the Wells Fargo Bank and arrange for a draft to be drawn on her account to be paid to the office of Johnson & Bennet for services rendered. The amount of the payment was a guess, but she felt better having done with the debt.

She knew she should also arrange for her belongings to be moved from Tyler's home and stored elsewhere, but she couldn't bring herself to break this last tie with him. Whatever he decided to do with her things would be fine with her.

Sarah returned her attention to the search for her father. The routine avenues of collecting information had already been exhausted. What she needed was a fresh approach.

Since her father's last known occupation was that of

cattleman, she decided to make personal inquiries at every business that dealt with the cattle industry. If her father was anywhere in the area, someone somewhere must have done business with him.

Sarah spent a week interviewing. She started at one end of the city and systematically worked her way to the other. The results were disheartening.

Thus far she had avoided the less savory sections of town, but she had only one small cattle yard on the edge of town left to check, and she must either give up or brave the worst.

More than once during the week she had had the hair-prickling sensation that she was being closely watched. Nothing had ever come of it, but she was well aware of her vulnerability and was not eager to go looking for trouble.

The cattle yard buzzed with flies and smelled strongly of hay and dung. Two men worked to repair a fence. Others were occupied moving a group of fat brown cattle from one pen to another.

"Excuse me, but do you mind if I ask a few questions of these men?" she asked a tall cowman who looked like he might be in charge.

"Don't mind at all." He wiped his hand on his pants before offering it to her. "Name's Ted Smith."

"Sarah Williams." She shook his hand.

"What kind of information are you interested in, Sarah Williams?"

"I'm trying to find anyone who might know my father. He's a cattleman, or at least he was, and I would like to locate him."

"He a Williams too?"

"No. Williams is my married name." She did not

348

mention the fact that she was a widow. Mr. Smith seemed harmless enough, but she had discovered early in the week that having a phantom husband was good insurance against overly friendly men. She had run into more than a few of this variety and was thoroughly weary of their hungry smiles and the hangdog faces that followed when she declined their offers to get better acquainted. "His name is Elijah Jenkins," she continued.

His ears pricked at the sound of the name. "I think I may be able to help you. Why don't you step into my office?"

"You've done business with him?" Sarah asked, her voice cautiously hopeful.

"I don't know him personally, and I'm sure he doesn't come round often, but the name seems vaguely familiar. If we've had dealings with him, his name will be in the files."

Sarah followed him into his office. It was a stark room housing nothing but file cabinets and a small wooden desk. One window provided light, and the door was left open to catch the breeze.

Mr. Smith turned his back to her and rummaged through the files. "Here it is. He bought a bull from us about nine months ago."

"That recently? Does it give an address in the file?"

"No, but it has a sketch of his brand and the name of his ranch. It's called the 'Lucky J.' Someone around here is bound to know where it's located."

After so many disappointments, Sarah was afraid to hope, but her fears were unjustified. The fifth man they spoke to had a brother who worked a neighboring ranch, and he was able to draw her a detailed map.

Sarah stopped at the livery to secure a horse, then returned to the Bella Union and immediately packed her saddlebags.

The Lucky J was a three-day ride, and though it was late in the day to start a journey, Sarah wanted to cover as much territory as possible before nightfall. Her need to find her father grew daily. She was sure finding him would dispel some of the loneliness caused by Tyler's absence.

Sarah made excellent time, but the closer she came to her destination, the more nervous she became. She tried to calm herself with firm reminders that the whole journey might turn into another wild goose chase, but she couldn't squelch the feeling that this trail would prove true. If it did, what then?

Sarah sat on her horse, watching the activity around the ranch house. A woman she judged to be in her early thirties stood in the yard, hanging laundry on the line strung between the house and the barn. Three children played near the porch. She could hear the faint cry of a baby coming from the basket at the woman's feet.

Her brows knit. The name painted on the board over the drive was the same as the man at the cattle yard had given her, but the ranch house was small, too small to house more than one family. Had her father sold out and moved on? The only way to find out was to ask.

She turned her horse into the drive but had gone less than a yard when she stopped abruptly and wheeled around in the opposite direction. Sarah rode back the way she had come, not stopping until she was certain she was out of sight of the house.

What if her father hadn't moved on? What if that woman was more than a stranger to him? Though there was no guarantee her father would be eager to see her in any case, if she came charging in on the scene announcing she was his long-lost daughter, she might disrupt his life so thoroughly that he would hate her on sight.

Her fear that she might commit some monumental blunder combined with the old fear that she would not like what she found to convince her to proceed with caution.

She had not seen any sign of a man around the place, and she decided the most prudent thing to do would be to wait until she did. If she could tell at a distance he could not be Elijah Jenkins, she would ride down and ask her questions. But if there was any chance the man was her father, she would wait until the opportunity to speak with him alone presented itself.

Positioning herself on a low rise where she could watch the house but far enough away that her presence would not be easily noticed, she hobbled her horse and settled herself under the shade of a tree.

The waiting was nearly unbearable. Sarah was too agitated to sit still, and she found herself pacing the hillside more often than she sat.

Toward evening she finally spotted a man. He rode into the yard from the pasture opposite, stabled his horse, then went directly into the house.

She was so far away, she had little by which to judge the man and not nearly enough to determine accurately whether or not he could be her father.

Dusk turned to dark. Not wanting to call attention to herself by lighting a fire, she chewed on an apple and some jerked beef to satisfy her hunger.

Long after the lights in the house went out, Sarah sat staring at it, wondering who it was that lived within and how long it would be before she was able to find out.

It was shortly after dawn she had the answer. The owner of the Lucky J Ranch, whoever he was, was riding straight toward her hill.

Suddenly terrified, she grabbed her brush to tidy her hair and did her best to smooth the wrinkles from her clothes. When she judged herself presentable, she stood, fingers laced tightly together, waiting for him to come up the rise.

"Hello," the man called as he approached and dismounted. His smile was friendly.

"Hello," Sarah returned, her voice shaking with excitement. She judged him to be about the right age. His hair was red. His eyes were green.

"I thought I saw someone up here when I rode in last night, and when you were still here in the morning, I figured the neighborly thing to do was ride over and introduce myself. Never guessed I'd find a woman. Why didn't you come down to the house?"

"I wasn't sure I'd be welcome."

"We'd have been glad to put you up for the night," he chided her hesitancy in the same gregarious tone. "My wife could use the company. She doesn't get the chance to talk to many other women living way out here."

He had called the woman his wife. If this man was

352

her father. . . . She shifted from foot to foot. The moment of truth had arrived. She could bear the suspense no longer. "Excuse me, but I didn't catch your name."

"Must be getting dotty in my old age," he apologized. "Ride up here to introduce myself, then forget to do it. The name is Elijah Jenkins."

Sarah stared at him, drinking in every detail. The weathered skin, the crinkles lining the corners of his eyes, his straight nose, his broad mouth. His height was average, his build broad.

"Miss? Are you okay? You look a little pale." He reached out a hand to steady her should she start to swoon.

"I'm fine, thank you," she replied softly.

"Just the same, I think you should let me take you down to the house," he argued.

"You may not want to when you find out who I am." He looked perplexed. "Why?"

How did one announce to a man that you were his daughter? Especially when he had a new family complete with wife . . . despite the fact that he already had a wife. Maybe you just said it. She took a deep breath. "My maiden name is Sarah Jenkins."

It was his turn to stare. He stood dumbstruck for a full minute before he spoke. "My Sarah?"

"Yes, I came all the way from Baltimore to find you." As an afterthought, she added, "I hope you don't mind."

"Mind!" he exclaimed. "I thought I'd go to my grave without ever having a chance to see you. This is wonderful! My little girl." His gaze traveled over her. "But you're all grown up now, aren't you?"

She smiled tentatively. "Yes. I'm all grown up."

"Sure would have liked to been there to see you do the growing."

"Why weren't you?" The question slipped out before she could stop it, but since it had, she decided to pursue it. "No one made you desert us," she said calmly.

He looked startled by her words. "What's this? I never deserted you."

Sarah scowled at him. She understood his fears, but she was not in the market for fairy stories. "I'm not going to cause trouble for you. The past cannot be altered. I learned to accept it. I'm here to satisfy my curiosity; that's all." She squared her shoulders. "Please, don't lie to me."

"I'm not lying. Your mother was the one who abandoned our marriage," he insisted.

"No. You left for California and never came back. You were supposed to send the money for us to join you, but you never did." It was a tale she had been told her entire life.

"I sent the money," he protested. "Five different times. And I came back to Baltimore twice to fetch the two of you myself. Your mother wouldn't listen to reason. She wouldn't even let me see you. The last time I tried, she hired a couple of thugs to work me over and put me on a ship back to California. That's when I knew our marriage was hopeless."

She heard his words, but their import did not fully register. The mantle of adult dispassion gave way to the hurt and resentment of the little girl who had never known a father's love. "And you never tried to see me again?" she demanded.

He shook his head sadly. "Not long after I got back to California, I received that letter from you saying how much you hated me and telling me to leave your mother alone. Didn't seem like there was any reason to keep trying."

"I never wrote a letter like that."

Their eyes met. As father measured daughter and daughter measured father, they realized they were both being honest with each other. The truth dawned.

"Amanda wrote the letter?" Her father was first to voice their mutual suspicion.

"She must have," Sarah answered. "Why did she lie to me all these years?"

Elijah Jenkins hesitated. He had no idea what the relationship between mother and daughter had been, and if they were close, he had no desire to cause a rift. Still, Sarah had asked him not to lie to her. She had gone to a lot of trouble to find him. She deserved the answers she sought. "Amanda was a funny woman," he began. "She had to have her way about everything, and when things didn't work out like she expected, she put the blame on someone else. I knew she was that way before I married her, but I was young and foolish and turned a blind eye to everything but her beauty."

"But why did *she* marry you?" Sarah queried, unable to imagine her mother caught up in youthful passion.

Her father looked shamefaced. "If I tell you, you'll know just how big a fool I was."

"I want to know."

"She told you she was raised by her grandparents?"

"Yes."

He cleared his throat. "Your mother was hopping mad at her grandfather. She wanted him to buy her a

355

prize filly she had taken a fancy to. She married me to spite him and because I was willing to buy her the horse. Funny thing is, she lost interest in the filly just about as fast as she lost interest in our marriage, and she told me to sell it." He paused, nervously running his hand through his hair. "When her grandparents died a couple years later and left her out of their will, she was furious. Don't think she ever forgave me for marrying her after that."

As Sarah listened to her father, everything began to fall into place—her mother's reaction when she had told her she was going to look for her father, the letters begging her to come home—Amanda Jenkins was afraid of being found out. And well she should be, since her livelihood was dependent upon her daughter's good will.

She was saddened and enraged and feeling a little numb. She didn't know what to say.

"The truth isn't much better than the lies, is it?" he consoled. "Since neither of us can change the past, why don't we concentrate on the present? I want you to tell me everything about yourself. What you like. What you dislike. Who your friends are."

They sat in the shade for hours, taking turns catching each other up on twenty-three years of life. Sarah found it easy to talk to her father. He seemed genuinely interested in anything she had to say.

He was everything she had wished he would be: kind, gentle, full of good humor. So often her mother had chided her for being just like her father. The accusation was meant as a rebuke, but as she got to know the true Elijah Jenkins, the insults took on the aura of praise.

Her father filled in the blanks left by their search. After selling out in Virginia City, he had drifted for a while, taking odd jobs, before settling in southern California. Cattle suited him better than mining. The drought of '64 and '65 had made land prices plummet, and he was able to purchase a small spread with his earnings. He was by no means rich, but he was his own boss and he made a decent living.

The only subject he avoided was that of his new wife and family. For a while Sarah said nothing, but eventually she had to ask. "What about your family? You have mentioned nothing of them."

"Maggie is a good wife," he said hesitantly.

"Not like my mother?" she pressed.

"Not at all."

"But you don't think she would understand if she knew you have another wife still living and the two of you are not legally married," Sarah spoke his thoughts for him.

"She knows nothing of Amanda or you. She thinks she married a crusty old bachelor," he admitted.

"How long have you been married?" Sarah asked softly.

"Less than four years."

"But the children?"

"Maggie was a widow. Her husband was killed in a stagecoach accident," he explained. "Only the youngest two are mine, but I love them all as if they were my own."

Sarah nodded. "And you love Maggie?"

"Yes. I've led a lonely life." He gazed off into the distance at the ranch house. "I missed out on a chance for a family. When I met Maggie, everything just seemed to work out between us. I wanted a family and she wanted a husband. Getting married was the natural thing to do."

"Weren't you forgetting you already had a wife?" she asked, not to be cruel but because she truly wished to understand.

He shifted uncomfortably. "I didn't forget, I just chose to ignore the fact. I didn't think anyone would ever be the wiser."

"And now I've shown up on your doorstep," Sarah stated. Their eyes met, their expressions acknowledging the predicament her arrival had caused.

Though he smiled, her father was clearly more than a little distressed. "I guess it's time to pay the piper," he announced ruefully. "I hope Maggie loves me enough to forgive me."

Try as she might, Sarah could not condemn him for marrying again. To ask him to pay for the rest of his life for the mistake of marrying her mother was too hard. Though she barely knew him, she did not wish to see him or his new family hurt. "I could go away," she offered.

He clasped her hand tightly. "No! For twenty-three years I have longed to know you. I am not going to let you ride in and out of my life in the space of a day."

"But what about Maggie?" she reminded.

"I can't say how she will feel, but I'm willing to pay the price."

Sarah's eyes misted with tears. That her father was willing to risk so much for the sake of her company was manna to a heart that since birth had been denied the sustenance of parental devotion.

Collecting her thoughts, she swallowed the lump in

her throat. She didn't want to leave any more than he wanted her to go. "Let's tell Maggie I am your niece."

"I'm not ashamed of you," he vowed. "The decisions I have made were my own, and I'll not ask you to lie for me."

"You didn't ask me to lie. I offered," she contended. "It is only a little white lie, and it will save everyone involved much pain. I do not want the destruction of your family on my conscience."

"The burden belongs on my shoulders, not yours," he protested her willingness to protect him.

Undeterred, Sarah continued, "What if Maggie cannot forgive you? Your children will grow up without a father. I have trod that path, and it is hard to do. And what of Maggie's feelings? If I were in her place, I know how I would feel . . . devastated. She might never recover her faith in you. I won't be a party to ruining your life or theirs."

Her argument was sound, and he felt a surge of pride that she was his daughter. He didn't want to see Maggie or the children hurt. They were as innocent as Sarah in all this. Perhaps the fabrication was not so objectionable. Wavering, he asked, "You're sure you wouldn't mind?"

"Absolutely. I think presenting me as your niece is an admirable solution. We will have our time together, and no one will be injured."

"It doesn't seem to make sense to cause unnecessary grief, does it?" Elijah spoke his thoughts.

"No, it doesn't," Sarah declared.

Rising to his feet, he reached down a hand to help her up. "Well, niece, let's go on down to the house and meet the family," he said cheerily; then his expression and tone became thoughtful. "But I want you to understand, if you ever change your mind about this, I will claim you as my daughter. I owe you that much and more."

Chapter 20

"Maggie, darlin', you'll never guess who I found camping on our hill," her father greeted his wife as they rode into the yard and dismounted. "I'd like you to meet my niece, Sarah Williams. She's my brother's child."

"Pleased to meet you," Maggie wiped her hands on her apron, her expression both pained and amused.

Sarah shifted, uncomfortable under the woman's frank regard.

"You'll have to excuse my stare." Maggie chuckled. "Your Uncle Elijah, God bless his soul, somehow forgot to mention he had a brother. He'd forget his own head if it wasn't screwed on tight." She paused, running her gaze up and down Sarah once more. "There's no mistaking the family resemblance, is there? Why don't you come in and get out of the sun? Can't believe your uncle kept you sitting on that hill so long when you could have been sitting in our parlor."

"It's my fault as much as his," Sarah insisted. "We started talking and just lost track of the time."

"Why didn't you just ride down here in the first

place, honey?" she asked.

"The foolish girl wasn't sure she'd be welcome," Elijah answered for Sarah. "You know I'm not much on letter writing, and I guess my being gone so long has given me the reputation of being unsociable among some of the family."

"Serves you right." Maggie smiled indulgently as she scolded him. "No telling how many relatives you have offended with your hermit ways." She turned to Sarah. "Come along, honey. Let's get you settled in."

Maggie bustled Sarah indoors, chattering all the while. "Now if your name is Williams, that must mean you're married, but I don't see any husband tagging along."

"My husband died a year and a half ago." Sarah informed her.

"Oh, I'm sorry. And so young too. Well, I assure you I fully understand what you are going through, being a widow myself before I met your uncle. Maybe you'll meet someone special before too long."

Before Sarah could respond, she continued, "I hope you don't mind sharing, but there's not an extra bed in the house. Jane doesn't toss and turn much, so I think I'll put you in with her."

"I'm sure I will be perfectly comfortable."

Maggie kept up a running conversation as she put fresh linens on the bed Sarah was to share. Sarah was saved the embarrassment of feeling her presence was an imposition in the already overcrowded household — Maggie's nonstop talking was an indication of how truly desperate she was for adult female companionship.

Having tended to the horses, her father rejoined

them. He was less awkward with his wife than Sarah had expected, and soon the entire family was getting along as if they had known each other for years.

Except for her parentage, there was no reason to lie about the rest of her life, and Sarah was reasonably comfortable with the situation in which she found herself—far more comfortable she realized than she would have been if her father had insisted he introduce her as his daughter.

She found both Maggie and the children a delight, and they returned her affection. The chores of day-to-day existence consumed most of their hours, but there was plenty of time to chat while they worked.

Maggie was a simple woman with a good heart. She loved her husband and her children, and when Sarah questioned her about her dreams for herself, she proudly proclaimed she had already achieved them.

The children were well behaved. The older ones helped with the chores with only an occasional squabble disrupting the rural tranquility. When it did, their mother's retribution was swift but just.

Sarah's affection for her father grew each day. He was so unlike her mother. In dealing with his children, he rated good intentions above good manners. He took pleasure in little things and seemed content to let the future take care of itself.

But what she liked most about him was his demonstrative displays of affection—for Maggie, for his children, for her. His home was a home in the true sense. It was a place abounding in love.

Though they were careful with what they said in front of the others, her father managed to arrange many opportunities for them to be alone. They spoke of their respective lives more openly at these times.

Her father was not pleased when she told him about the circumstances surrounding her marriage to Henry Williams, but his displeasure was not directed at her or even her mother or Henry but at himself for not being there when she needed him.

They spent much time consoling each other, expressing regret over the wasted years, but both were more inclined to focus on the positive, and their conversations provoked far more laughter than tears.

There was nothing to mar Sarah's contentment except the absence of Tyler Bennet. Every night she lay in bed longing to feel his touch, to feel a part of him once more. During the light of day, she would catch herself sharing her experiences with him through imaginary conversations. Sarah did everything she could to block him from her mind, but he wriggled his way into her thoughts at the least expected moments.

She had mentioned Tyler to her father and Maggie only in passing and in the context of their relationship as client and lawyer. Despite her father's bigamy she wasn't comfortable telling him she had taken a lover. She wasn't comfortable talking about Tyler at all.

She continued to do her best to exorcise Tyler Bennet from her heart but to little avail. More often than not little Christopher, the baby of the family, was responsible for her undoing. He was a sweet child with sparse tufts of blond hair and big gray-blue eyes. Every time she held him, she was painfully reminded of why she and Tyler could not be together.

Though she was treated as a full member of her

father's new family, the longer she stayed at the Lucky J Ranch, the more melancholy she became, and the more melancholy she became, the more impatient she became with herself.

For the first time in her life she was surrounded by love, and yet she had never felt so lonely in all her life.

No matter how much she might want to stay, she really didn't belong here. She realized she really didn't belong anywhere anymore.

Sarah began to feel restless once again.

The idea of returning to Baltimore was as repugnant now as it had always been. More so. She had no desire to confront her mother with the truth. Amanda Jenkins may have discarded her husband, but Sarah feared if she discovered him to be alive and happily married, she would be on the first train to California to "set things to rights." Sarah wasn't willing to risk her father's happiness or that of his family for the dubious pleasure of seeing her mother undone. Besides, whatever Amanda Jenkins had done in the past or present, she was still her mother, and as long as she had the financial wherewithal, she had every intention of continuing to support her.

San Francisco was a more tempting destination, but Sarah discarded it as quickly as she did Baltimore. Tyler did not want her back unless she was willing to marry him, and she couldn't. Sometimes she wondered if she was being foolish, if she should marry him despite her inability to produce children. Perhaps if she loved him enough, he would not feel cheated.

The argument fell on ground as barren as her womb. How could he not feel cheated? She felt cheated. If Tyler was the sort of man who treated children as a necessary nuisance, she might be able to convince herself her love would be enough; but if he were that sort of man, she doubted she would love him in the first place.

Her heart was not healing as quickly as she had hoped it would. She wondered vaguely how long it would take, what she could do to speed the process.

She had always said she wanted to see the world. Here was her opportunity, Sarah told herself. If she kept herself busy enough, she would not have time to think about her lost love.

Saying farewell to her father was difficult. He was not particularly pleased with her plans to travel alone; however, his objections were tempered by the knowledge that he had forfeited the right to direct his daughter's life long ago.

Many tears and kisses and heartfelt hugs preceded Sarah's departure, and she promised to write often.

Sarah filled the next few weeks with a frenzy of activity. She didn't care where she went as long as she did not stay in any place so long that she had time to contemplate what she was doing or why she was doing it.

There were wonderful sights to see and she met many interesting people along the way, but the effort to maintain a carefree outlook became more exhausting with each passing day.

Tyler Bennet sat at his desk, leaning over a contract. He went over each sentence, word by word, changing a phrase here and there to make sure every line of the document was unimpeachable. He was happiest when he could immerse himself in his work. The law made sense. It was amicable to the rules of logic. Work had helped him get over the loss of his father, and it would help him get over the loss of Sarah. At least that was what he told himself.

He had willfully stepped back into the dull rut from which he had once been convinced Sarah had come into his life to save him. Work was the only thing he had just now. As he lay awake at night pondering the unhappy course his life had taken, he did his best to convince himself a life overfilled with work was preferable to the hell of uncertainty Sarah had brought into his life.

It had been three months since he had seen her, three long, torturous months. At first anger had sustained him, but it was slowly being deposed by a dull ache.

Every night when he walked home, it took every ounce of his self-control not to keep on walking right on to the docks to catch a steamer back to Los Angeles. He couldn't stop thinking about her, couldn't stop worrying about her. He wanted to stop loving her but he didn't know how. He had been a fool to leave her, but he knew he would be an even bigger fool if he went back.

She had to come to the decision to marry him on her own. He had done all he could. He was not going to spend the rest of his life sniffing at her heels and wagging his tail whenever she deemed it convenient to give him a morsel of affection and pat him on the head. He had his pride. If his self-respect was the price, he didn't want her love. He had taken the only stand he could. He slammed his fist on his desk. Where was she? He had thought she would have come back to him by now!

"Tyler, are you all right?" Agnes asked, her face suffusing with concern as she stepped through the door.

He looked up at her, his expression haggard.

"You didn't sleep well again last night, did you?" She straightened the papers scattered on his desk. "I swear, if she doesn't come back soon, I will set off in search of her myself and drag her back."

Tyler smiled wanly. "If coercion worked with Sarah, I would have used it long ago," he assured her.

"I just feel I should do something."

"There is nothing you or I or anyone but Sarah can do. She'll return when she's ready."

"What if she never does?" Agnes voiced the question Tyler steadfastly refused to consider.

"She's coming back!" he declared harshly.

Agnes winced. "I'm sorry, I didn't mean to upset you."

His voice softened. "I know you didn't. I had no right to yell at you. It is past time I face the fact she probably isn't coming back." He straightened his shoulders and abruptly changed the subject. "How goes your love life?"

She needed a sympathetic ear, but she hesitated. At length his expectant expression and the hope that her problems might distract him from his own compelled her to answer him honestly. "Not much better than yours, I'm afraid. Father is still being stubborn, and Clayton is growing impatient. He doesn't like me sneaking out to see him and would confront Father if I let him."

"Why won't you let him?"

"Because I'm afraid if Father found out I was disobeying him, he would find a way to prevent us from seeing each other at all." She took a deep breath. "I would simply die if that were to happen."

"Do you want me to talk to your father?" Tyler offered.

"No!" Agnes exclaimed. Thus far her father had not embarrassed her by proposing to Tyler that he marry her, and she intended to keep it that way. Her life was complicated enough. She did not need an added burden, nor did he. "I have to find some way to work this out on my own," she said resolutely.

"Be careful you don't take so long you lose your beau," he cautioned. "I would not like to see you in the same position as I."

"Perhaps what we both need is an extra measure of patience," Agnes offered.

"Patience," Tyler spoke the word as if it were a curse, "is something I find I have in short supply."

Thaddeus Johnson sat across the table from Mr. Sneed in the out-of-the-way café where they had previously arranged to meet. He counted out the money he owed him and laid it on the table.

"There is *nothing* you can tell me I could use to impeach her character?" Johnson prodded.

"I'm sorry. Other than her affair with your partner,

the lady's behavior has been above reproach."

"What about this Carlos Rameriz?"

"I told you before, she left a few days after your partner—alone. Other than the one kiss, there was nothing between them. I'm sure of it."

"But he is a criminal." Johnson sought verbal confirmation of information he had received earlier in a letter.

Sneed nodded. "Yes. When I followed her back to Los Angeles, I checked him out. He is wanted in several counties."

Johnson sighed. "Well, that's something at least."

"I don't see how that can help you since she never saw him again. I know you don't want to hear this, but she seems to me to be a perfectly nice lady. Perhaps you misjudged her."

Johnson's expression evinced the displeasure Mr. Sneed had predicted. "Are you sure you didn't overlook something?"

"I know my business. If you will read the log I gave you, you will know who she was with and her exact whereabouts day and night. She spent a little more than a month with her father at the Lucky J Ranch and has been drifting ever since."

"I wonder why."

"I couldn't tell you. Maybe she has a penchant for sightseeing."

"Well, whatever her penchants, she seems to have lost interest in my partner. I knew she would prove heartless."

"It was my impression he left her," Mr. Sneed corrected.

"Whoever left whom, I think we can call an end to

this investigation." Johnson lifted the log in his hand. "Thank you for your time and trouble."

After leaving Mr. Sneed, it took Thaddeus two days to come to his decision. Something had to be done, and he was the man to do it. They were all growing old waiting for this muddle of emotions to be resolved. Though Tyler had rededicated himself to his work with a vengeance, he was but a shadow of his former self. Poor Agnes was so tired of waiting for Tyler to notice her as a woman that she had convinced herself she didn't care and that this Bevington fellow was an acceptable substitute.

He invited Tyler over for dinner three and sometimes four times a week. He ushered the most interesting cases his way. He had even gifted him with a membership at the Olympic Club in hopes of helping him fill his leisure hours, but to no avail. The man was still smitten.

If left to his own devices, his younger partner might carry a torch for years. Mrs. Williams did not deserve such loyalty. It was quite apparent to him she had no intention of ever returning.

Though his initial dislike of Sarah Williams had been fueled by his need to see Tyler and Agnes wed, he now could legitimately claim a less selfish reason. He could despise her because she had broken Tyler's heart.

It took another two days to alter the log so the small additions he made appeared to be in Mr. Sneed's hand and part of the original. He didn't like deceiving Tyler, but he had watched him pine over the widow Williams quite long enough. What he was doing was an act of kindness, he told himself. Life must go on.

No one would be hurt, and all would benefit.

The last appointment of the day had been met, and Thaddeus Johnson could hear Tyler moving about in the office across the hall, preparing to leave.

Retrieving Mr. Sneed's log from the bottom drawer of his desk, he crossed the hall and entered his younger partner's office, closing the door behind him.

"Tyler, I think it is past time we had a serious talk," he began.

Tyler continued arranging the papers he intended to take home with him that night. "About what?"

"Sarah Williams."

He stopped what he was doing and glared at Thaddeus. By tacit agreement, Sarah was a subject they both avoided discussing. He had no desire to change the arrangement. "I really don't think there is anything to say."

Johnson cleared his throat. "Yes, there is. I had hoped to avoid this. Hoped you would get over her on your own, but . . ." He laid the log on the desk. "I brought something for you to read."

Perplexed, Tyler stared at the leatherbound notebook. "What is it, and what does it have to do with Sarah?"

"We are both well aware that I had strong reservations about Mrs. Williams from the start. I took the liberty of hiring a detective."

"You hired someone to follow her?" Tyler asked in outraged disbelief, his instinct to protect Sarah momentarily overriding all else.

"I know you don't approve . . ."

"You're damned right I don't approve! What gave you the right?"

"My affection for you," Johnson replied without hesitation. "Anyway, what is done is done. I think you should read that." He pointed to the log.

"Why?" Tyler demanded.

"Because after you do, I believe you will begin to view Mrs. Williams's continued absence from your life with relief rather than regret. The notebook contains a day-by-day record of her activities." Johnson swallowed the lump of guilt that threatened to prevent him from saying his piece. "You may have loved her, but to her you were a convenient plaything."

"You sound certain of yourself."

"I am. You have refused to discuss why the two of you parted company, but I'm sure the name Carlos Rameriz is familiar to you."

Tyler flinched.

"They were lovers," Johnson said bluntly.

"Are you positive?"

Johnson shook his head, his face full of sympathy. "Yes. Even I was surprised she would stoop so low as to take up with an outlaw."

Tyler stood rooted to the spot, his expression blank except for the pain in his eyes. "Rameriz is a criminal?"

"He robs stages for a living," Johnson confirmed. "I know this is hard for you to hear, but there have been other men since him."

"How many?"

"Five have been documented. I know it is little consolation, but no one seems to be able to capture her fancy for long." He lay a consoling hand on Tyler's shoulder. "Listen, I can see this is tearing you apart. There is nothing I can tell you that isn't in that book. Go home. Read it privately. I'll understand if you don't feel up to coming into the office tomorrow."

"Yes, I'll do that," Tyler replied bleakly. He shrugged on his coat and picked up the journal. "Good night, Thaddeus."

It was past midnight when Tyler lay down Mr. Sneed's notebook. He had read it over and over, hoping the words would change, but they did not.

If Sarah had ever loved him, it was clear she no longer did. It was a bitter pill to swallow.

If he could hate her, it would be easier for him, but he didn't hate her. He found himself making excuses for her behavior. She was lonely. She needed him. He was the one who had left her.

She had found her father, and he was happy for her. He hoped Elijah Jenkins had not been too much of a disappointment. She had stayed at the Lucky J Ranch a full month before moving on. He wondered why she had left. Had her father rejected her? Is that why she had taken so many lovers in rapid succession? Had she needed him to comfort her and turned to others because he was not there?

But what about Carlos, he reminded himself. She had turned to him when he was still available. . . .

Sympathy was instantly replaced by humiliation and fury. How long was he going to play the lovesick fool? He had seen evidence of her perfidy with his own eyes. It was here in his hand. He knew Sneed's work. The man was painstaking and scrupulously honest. It was time to stop deluding himself. Sarah didn't love him, and she wasn't coming back. The damned notebook made it clear she was pursuing the oft-praised life of grand adventure with gusto.

He should have listened to Thaddeus when he'd warned him against her. He should have listened to her when she'd said she didn't want to marry him.

Tyler alternately derided himself and Sarah until he had spent his anger. A numbness slowly settled over his heart. It was comforting not to feel at all.

Thaddeus had been right from the start, and he vowed to thank him for forcing him to face the truth. One should be wary of emotions that seized one suddenly and engulfed like a tidal wave. They were dangerous.

He would not make the mistake of falling in love again.

Chapter 21

Sarah sat on the edge of the bed in her hotel room, hugging her belly. She beamed from ear to ear.

At first she had been afraid to believe it. She kept waiting for her monthly flow to begin but it hadn't, not after one month or two or three. There had been other, less conspicuous signs—a tenderness in her breasts, bouts of heartburn, and an unaccustomed lack of energy.

After four months of denying the obvious, she had worked up the nerve to see a physician. His words had been music to her ears. She was pregnant. It was almost too wonderful to believe.

It was Henry's fault she had never conceived a child, not hers. She had accepted the blame for so long, it had never even occurred to her it might not be true.

Sarah could hardly wait to share the news with Tyler, and the first thing she had done after leaving Dr. Graham's office was to buy a ticket on the first train out of town. She was going home.

Solitary travel gave one the opportunity to do a lot

of soul searching. She had discovered how truly important family was to her. She had discovered she really wasn't cut out for living alone.

She remembered all those she had met with fondness and gratitude for the lessons she had learned through them. She now understood Mr. Simpson's warning about the loneliness of the single life. Carlos had helped her realize she put more value on morality and the rules of society than she had previously been willing to admit. Her father and Maggie had showed her a conventional life could be filled with love and laughter.

She had once told Tyler she did not want to be a subservient wife, and that was still true, but she did want to be a wife. *His wife.* Marriages came in many colors, bright and dull, warm and cold. So did families. She was determined *her* marriage and family would be the very best. The individual members would provide each other with love and support, help each other grow in their own unique way.

She had floundered for so long. It was magnificent to know without a doubt what she wanted from life and finally be in a position to seek it out.

She had come to the sleepy little town of Green River, Wyoming, on a whim — to see if the river was really green. Sarah laughed gaily. She had known for a long time that what she had really been trying to do these past months was outrun her love for Tyler Bennet. Well, the river wasn't green, and her love for Tyler hopped on every train and stage she boarded and rode to the next town with her. She hugged herself tighter. Soon it would be Tyler's arms that wrapped around her. It would be such a relief to stop running, to stop pretending she was something she was not, to feel the heat of flesh against flesh and make passionate love until the ache of their separation was banished to the province of memory.

The train west pulled into the station at Green River during the wee hours of the morning. Sarah was first in line to board. Most of the passengers on board were sleeping, and she settled herself into her berth.

Though she had been up since dawn of the previous day, sleep eluded her. She was far too excited. She played her reunion with Tyler over and over in her mind. It was wonderful! Glorious! A fairy-tale ending!

She refused to even consider he might not be as happy to see her as she was to see him. Her pregnancy was a miracle, and miracles were never thwarted. Tyler loved her. He had told her so often enough. She could not stop loving him, and she was sure he had found himself in similar circumstances. True love did not wane. It fed upon itself and grew stronger everyday. She sighed blissfully.

It was but a few days to San Francisco, but to Sarah it felt like the journey was taking years. Every time the train stopped to take on new passengers, she had to fight the urge not to jump from her seat and help herd them on board. She attempted to read, but found it difficult to concentrate. She chatted with the other passengers. She tried to sleep to make the time pass more quickly. Nothing helped.

When the train finally rolled into Oakland, she was

the first one to disembark. A ferry took her the last few miles of her journey. She stood at the rail, straining for a glimpse of her final destination.

As soon as they docked, Sarah hired a hack and instructed him to drive her to the offices of Johnson & Bennet.

"You've come back?" Agnes greeted her, her eyes wide with disbelief when Sarah stepped over the threshold.

Sarah put her fingers to her lips. "Is he upstairs?"

"Yes, but . . ."

"I'm going to take your advice and marry Tyler Bennet. Isn't it wonderful?" Sarah exclaimed, her expression evincing the joy she proclaimed. It was all the explanation she was willing to spare time to give, and she sprinted up the stairs.

Outside Tyler's door, she paused a moment to catch her breath and pat a loose strand of hair back in place before proceeding through the door. Tyler was sitting at his desk, leaning over a stack of papers. He looked up at the sound of the door opening.

"Sarah?" he whispered hoarsely as he rose to his feet. All the tender emotions he had succeeded in repressing rushed through him like a flood. A surge of sexual desire followed. His eyes drank in the sight of her. She was even more beautiful than he remembered.

"I've come home," she said as she crossed the room and enveloped him in her arms. "I love you, Tyler Bennet, and I'm never going to leave you again."

His arms reflexively enfolded her, but he stood stiff, his expression taut, as a wave of reality washed through him and swept away his initial gladdening upon seeing her again. He was having a little trouble absorbing that she was here — standing within the circle of his arms, declaring her love, as he had so often dreamed she would be.

He didn't know what to say. Hell, he didn't even know what to feel. He had reconciled himself to her loss, and now she was back. Why? What had brought her back to him? Hadn't she already put him through enough? He set her away from him.

Sarah noted his drawn expression and her joyous smile faded. Still, her heart was so filled with love, there was little room for any other emotion. "Tyler?"

"What?" he asked tersely.

"Aren't you happy to see me?"

He turned his back on her. "I don't know."

"I realize I've been gone a long time, and I have a lot of explaining to do, but . . ." She gingerly stroked his back. "Please say you're happy to see me."

There was a long pause before he replied, "I missed you."

"I missed you too. Nothing was the same after you left." She tried to wrap him in her arms, but he stepped away from her. It finally hit her that something was terribly wrong. She had stayed away so he could find a new love, and the fear he might have already done so gripped her heart. "Tyler, have you found someone else to love?"

"No."

"Have you stopped loving me?"

Her first question he had answered without hesitation. The second was more difficult. He knew the answer, and he hated himself for it. His inclination was to lie, but he forced himself to respond truthfully. "No."

A smile returned to Sarah's lips. Walking around him, she positioned herself so he once again faced her. "Then why are you acting so distant?" she asked softly.

"As you said, you've been gone a long time."

"You said I could come back." She tried to meet his eyes, but he kept averting her gaze. "I'm ready to marry you."

"You've come back to marry me?" he asked dully.

She nodded. "Isn't that what you wanted me to do?"

He was almost afraid to believe his ears. If she wanted to marry him. . . . There was no point in lying to himself and pretending he did not still want her. Thaddeus's revelations had killed his hope that she would come back, but they had not killed his love. He knew nothing ever would. What he didn't know was if he could forgive and forget.

If he was to even consider taking her back, she was going to have to play the game by his rules. His eyes took on a steely glint, and he adopted an adversarial stance. "Would you be faithful?"

Sarah blinked at him. "What a silly question to ask."

"Answer it," he demanded.

"Of course I would."

"I won't tolerate anything less than absolute fidelity," he warned.

"I would not expect you to."

381

"Would you find it a hardship?"

"Tyler, I don't understand these questions." Sarah sighed in exasperation. She didn't want to stand here answering asinine questions. She wanted to throw her arms around Tyler and cover every inch of him with kisses. "I love you. I desire no one but you. If I was faithful to Henry, whom I did not love, why on earth would you fear I would be any less so to you, whom I love with all my heart?"

"When you were married to Henry, you had yet to taste temptation," he countered. "I mean it, Sarah, I cannot even consider accepting you back if I cannot be sure of you."

She frowned. He must be thinking of Carlos and the kiss. She had hoped he would have forgiven her that by now. It was her own fault, she realized. When she had refused to marry him she had not told him the true reason, but had pretended she desired freedom. Though she had denied any feelings for Carlos, it was obvious he had not fully accepted her assurances. She had been so caught up in dealing with her own pain that she had not adequately considered the pain she was causing him by her refusal to reveal the real reason she would not wed him. And it had all been so unnecessary. She silently vowed she would find some way to make it up to him. "I have never loved any man but you," Sarah promised. "And I never will."

She sounded sincere, and he wanted to believe her more than he had ever wanted anything in his life. He wanted those other men to mean less than nothing to her.

She had been widowed such a short time when he met her. Perhaps he had pushed her too hard. Perhaps he should have been more understanding of her needs. Perhaps he should not have issued an ultimatum.

In fairness, he had to accept partial blame for all that had ensued since they had parted company. He did not like knowing there had been other men in her life, but if they had helped her realize they belonged together . . . he gazed into her large, bright green eyes, staring up at him expectantly. His heart constricted. Sarah Williams was everything he had ever wanted in a wife—with one glaring exception—and she promised that was a thing of the past.

It was within his power to have her. He could marry her today, this very minute. . . .

His jaw tensed. He had rushed into love and been badly burned. They had a lifetime ahead of them. This time he was determined to proceed with caution. "I had not expected you to come back. I need time to think about this, Sarah," he informed her coolly.

Though she was disappointed their reunion had not lived up to her blissful fantasies, she nodded in understanding. His reluctance was her fault. She had been gone a long time. She had not been totally forthright with him when they had parted company.

He had said he still loved her. That was what was important. The rest of this uncomfortable conversation paled in significance. And, she reminded herself, some of her initial exuberance returning, he had not yet given her a chance to share her blessed news with him. She felt sure the knowledge he was about to

383

become a father would go a long way toward healing old wounds.

"You were more than patient with me, and under different circumstances I would be willing to give you all the time you desired," she began, smiling serenely, "but I don't think you should take too long."

"Why are you suddenly so eager to tie the knot?" he asked, his voice tinged with suspicion.

Her confidence did not wane. "Because . . ." She paused for dramatic effect, then made her announcement with unrestrained enthusiasm. "We are going to have a baby."

Tyler's jaw dropped. "I thought you couldn't . . ."

"So did I," she interrupted, smiling happily. "But I was wrong. Isn't it grand!"

He stared at her, trying to assimilate what she was telling him. A baby? His baby? Amazement quickly turned to fury as the pieces fell neatly into place. He had wondered what had made Sarah change her mind about marrying him, and now he knew. She had come back not because she loved him as she claimed, but because she needed a name for her child. She'd been caught, and now she wanted him to come to the rescue. And why not, he chided himself. He had proved himself convenient, easily manipulated, easily duped.

He was even more appalled with himself than he was with Sarah for trying to use him. He had known what she was when she had walked back through his door, and still he had entertained thoughts of taking her back.

His eyes narrowed and his lips stretched taut. He

was through playing the fool of fools for this woman.

Sarah's brows knit in confusion as she stared up at him. She had been so certain he would be as delighted as she, but his face was not that of a happy man. He was looking down on her as if she were some sort of pariah.

"You're not happy?" Her whispered question made him wince.

He glared at her. "Why would I be?"

"Because you love children, and now that I know I can give them to you, there is nothing to stand in the way of our marriage," she meekly offered, struggling to return the smile to her lips.

"Excuse me if I'm not as thrilled as you appear to be."

"You don't want to be a father?" she protested, unable and unwilling to comprehend the notion. "When you said it didn't matter that I was barren, I thought you were just being kind. It never occurred to me you didn't want a family." She studied the father of her child and saw no evidence of a loving man, only hard-edged disenchantment. Still, she refused to believe he had changed so much in the months she had been away. "None of this makes sense. I've seen the way you act around other people's children. You would make an excellent father. It's why I came back."

Tyler growled. "Now *that* I believe."

"Why do you sound so angry?" she squeaked, as she felt the walls of the room closing in on her.

"Because just for a minute I was naive enough to hope you had come back because you loved me."

She reached for him, but he stepped away as if

repulsed by the thought of her touch. Desperately, she tried to reach him with words. "I do love you. I have loved you for a very long time."

"You have a funny way of showing it. Usually when a woman loves a man, she doesn't run off for months on end. She marries him when he asks her."

"It's because I loved you that I couldn't marry you. I . . ."

"That's not the excuse you gave me," he interrupted. "According to my recollections, you wanted your freedom more than you wanted me."

"That was true in the beginning, but later I wasn't completely honest with you," Sarah admitted, doing her best to remain calm and logical. "The more I came to love you, the more I wanted what was best for you. I wouldn't marry you because I couldn't give you a family — just me. I feared if I told you the real reason, you would argue that I was enough, and I would give in and cheat you out of a full life."

He shook his head, his expression pitying. "All very noble sounding. How long have you been rehearsing that little speech?"

By now Sarah was feeling thoroughly dazed. If logic and calm didn't help the situation, what would? Perhaps she had been overly optimistic about the tenor of their reunion, but she had not expected cold hostility. The man standing before her was not the Tyler Bennet she knew and loved; he was a stranger. "Tyler, what has gotten into you?" she begged him to help her understand.

"A healthy dose of common sense," he rejoined. "There were other options to leaving me. We could have adopted children."

"You would have considered adoption?" she asked. "When I suggested adoption to Henry, he was so incensed he almost struck me. He said . . ."

"I don't give a damn what Henry said," he shouted, using his anger as armor against her entreating looks. "You're just using him as a scapegoat to cover for your deceit. You say you were not completely honest with me before. What about now? Are you telling the whole truth and nothing but the truth?" he demanded.

"Yes! Of course I am."

"How do you know I'm the father of the child you carry?"

Her eyes widened at the question, and she answered him firmly. "Because it is impossible it could be anyone else."

"I might believe such protestations from a simple-minded woman, but I know you to be intelligent. You have had many lovers. We both know any one of us could have fathered your child."

For a moment she was too stunned to reply, but eventually she found enough voice to deny his accusation. "I have had no other lover but you."

A look of revulsion passed over his face. "Perhaps I neglected to mention that a detective has been closely following your activities. I have his report here in my desk." He smiled coldly. "Now would you like to change your story?"

"I can't believe you hired someone to follow me," Sarah protested, realizing the situation was far worse than she had been willing to accept. "Why?"

"I didn't hire Mr. Sneed; Thaddeus did, and don't try to evade the basic issue."

She wanted to scream at him that she was not trying to evade anything, that she was trying to make sense of insanity. "I am not going to change my story, because I am telling you the truth," she argued passionately. "I am perfectly willing to accept the blame for the mistakes I have made, but I will not be held accountable for things I never did. You are the only man I have been with since my husband's death."

"Mr. Sneed tells a different tale."

"Then he is a liar!"

"What would he stand to gain by lying?" he demanded.

"How should I know?" Sarah shouted back. "Maybe Mr. Johnson paid him to lie. He has never pretended to like me."

Tyler brought his fists down hard on his desktop. "Thaddeus may not like you, but he would never pay to have lies fabricated about you or anyone else, and I find it offensive that you would even suggest he might do so. He is a far better friend than I once credited him with being. You only vilify yourself by insulting him."

She sucked in lungfuls of air, trying to regain a measure of composure. What was she doing hurling accusations and screeching like a fishwife? Such behavior would not help the situation. If only she knew what would help. Whatever she said was the wrong thing. Her warm gaze met Tyler's cold one, and her heart sank a little deeper into despair. "I apologize for casting dispersions on Mr. Johnson's character. I should have realized you would not be partners with a man who was less than honest. I'm just so upset I spoke before I thought the matter through. I really don't know what to think about anybody or anything, but one thing I do know is, whatever this Mr. Sneed has told you, I am not some sort of trollop who falls into bed with every man who asks me."

"I didn't have much trouble getting you there."

If he had slapped her, he could not have hurt her more than he had with those words, and she staggered back as if the assault had been physical. She could fight against the lies, but she didn't know how to fight the truth.

Had she lost his respect when she had become his lover? His behavior toward her had been that of a gentleman toward a lady. She had taken his proposals of marriage seriously, but perhaps they were all part of the game he called seduction. She had stated from the outset that she wasn't interested in marriage. Had he proposed only because he was certain she would refuse him? Had he feigned disappointment? Had he used Carlos's advances as a convenient excuse to rid himself of a lover of whom he'd grown weary? Was he just now revealing feelings that had been true from the start?

She cradled her belly as she backed away from him. It couldn't be true! None of it! She refused to believe she had so thoroughly misjudged him. She loved him. He loved her.

Yet how could she deny the evidence of her own eyes and ears? He wasn't happy to see her. He didn't even want her to touch him. He had called her a liar.

She had to struggle to form her words into a coherent question. "You don't want to marry me?"

"No," he replied brusquely.

She pressed her back to the door for support. All her hopes, all her dreams dissolved before her tear-filled eyes. "I'm sorry I bothered you with this," she said numbly as she swiped at the tears spilling down her cheeks. "I thought you would want me back. I didn't understand. It confused me when you said you loved me. I thought you felt the same thing I felt when I said the words. You did tell me I was naive on more than one occasion. I guess I should have listened. I'm sorry again for any inconvenience I may have caused you."

Turning on her heels, Sarah ran out the door, down the stairs, and into the street.

Chapter 22

"Sarah," Tyler shouted hoarsely. "Don't run away from me!"

He stood staring at the empty doorway. Sarah was crying. He had never seen her cry.

Despite his own hurt and anger, his feet carried him down the stairs and out the door after her. He reached the street just in time to see her coach careen around a corner.

"Damn!" he cursed out loud, running his hand through his hair as he turned to walk back into his office.

"Tyler?" Agnes queried. "Is there anything I can do?"

"Yes," he replied gruffly. "Cancel all my appointments for the rest of the day. I'm going home." Taking the stairs two at a time, he returned to his office, retrieved Mr. Sneed's notebook from his desk drawer, and retraced his steps.

As he passed Agnes's desk he paused. She was watching him with sisterly concern, and he knew he could turn to her for sympathy. There was often an unspoken invitation in her expression that said she would provide a willing ear should he ever need to unburden himself. He continued out the door. He had kept his own counsel thus far, and he would continue to do so. Agnes was a lady. His affairs were too sordid for her gentle ears.

As he covered the distance between his office and his home with long strides, his thoughts churned.

He wasn't sure what he would do once he arrived home, he just knew he wasn't in any shape just now to do his clients justice. He needed to be alone. Seeing Sarah again had been a shock. He had reacted badly. He should have been less emotional, more businesslike.

He had had plenty of time to come to terms with her infidelity. She had made him no promises. They had parted company. He had no right to censure her behavior. But he did have a right to protect himself, and he would not allow himself to be used.

The hell of it was, he still loved her. Worse, he had admitted it. Seeing her again and holding her in his arms had summoned up all his old feelings. He couldn't let her touch him again. The physical attraction between them was so intense he was afraid he wasn't strong enough to resist the twin salvo of love and lust.

If he thought she really loved him, that having sown her wild oats she had come to recognize what a truly special love they had shared, would it make any difference?

It was a moot point. He knew such was not the case. If Sarah had not become pregnant, she would not have come back to him. She would still be cavorting around the countryside with every Tom, Dick, and Harry she met.

The lies hurt as much if not more than the infidelity. She must think him sadly lacking in intelligence if she thought for a moment he would believe she had refused to marry him because she thought it unfair to burden him with her barrenness. They had barely discussed the issue of children. Was he supposed to believe she would blithely throw away their future without even consulting him because she wanted to protect him? No, indeed, her premise did not withstand the test of fire.

It was all too convenient, all too unbelievable. He was not going to be taken in by her winsome looks or her tears. Sarah Williams was a liar. His love for her was a ghost from his past. It was only natural that seeing her again would conjure up the old feelings. It was not natural for a man to throw away his pride and self-respect for a woman he knew to be false.

His fingers clenched around the journal. He knew the truth. He had the evidence in his hand. If he allowed her back into his heart, he deserved whatever misery she meted out.

Upon reaching his house, Tyler unlocked the door. He wondered where Sarah was staying. Though his inclination was to set out immediately and make the rounds of the better hotels until he found her, he forced himself to deny it. He had spent more than enough time chasing after Sarah Williams.

She would have to come around sometime for her belongings. He had not been able to bring himself to throw them out, and he had stored them in his attic. If he felt he had something to say, he could say it to her then.

He was determined to be strong, and if necessary, he would rely on Thaddeus's support to keep him from making an ass of himself. Thaddeus was a true friend. If he had heeded his counsel in the beginning, he could have saved himself untold grief.

Though he repeatedly told himself the less he saw of Sarah Williams the better, he wasn't happy with his decision to ignore her. He couldn't forget the sight of Sarah staring at him, tears spilling down her cheeks. Knowing he was the cause of those tears made him feel like a villain, despite the fact that he knew full well he had been the intended victim of the reunion scene.

Sarah sat in her room at the Grand Hotel worrying the ribbons decorating the hat in her lap. The weeks she had spent in this room were some of the happiest of her life, and she considered herself lucky that she was able to stay in the same room she had occupied months ago. If only her return to Tyler could have been accomplished with equal ease.

She glanced around the room without really seeing it. What a fool she had been to imagine their reunion would be a joyous affair. Lasting happiness had always eluded her grasp. What had made her think the personal state of her affairs would suddenly be different?

But things were different. She now had her baby's future to think of as well as her own. What was she going to do?

Sarah closeted herself in her room for two days. The first day she unashamedly wallowed in self-pity. The second day she pondered her problem from every angle — doing her best to comprehend Tyler's feelings as well as she did her own. On the morning of the third day she rose, dressed in her best wool dress, and set out for the offices of Johnson & Bennet.

"Good morning, Agnes," she greeted, her tone businesslike. "I would like to make an appointment to see Mr. Bennet at his earliest convenience."

Agnes shifted uncomfortably. Nobody was telling her what was going on, but whatever it was, it wasn't good. She wasn't sure what was expected from her by either Tyler or Sarah. "He has about fifteen minutes before his next client is due to arrive. Do you want me to ask if he will see you now?" she queried, deciding to emulate Sarah's formal air.

"No. I am sure our dealings will take far longer than a quarter hour. Besides, I want him to have plenty of advance notice."

Agnes looked over the appointment schedule and offered a time. "Wednesday afternoon at three?"

"That would be fine. I would also like you to deliver a message for me. Tell Mr. Bennet a man will be coming round this evening to pick up the belongings I have stored at his home. Please assure him that if he has discarded them, he is not to worry, and that I apologize for not seeing to the matter sooner. In any case, if he would be so kind as to give the man the report we discussed the other day so I might study it before our meeting, it would be much appreciated."

"Are you sure you wouldn't like to tell him yourself?" Agnes asked.

Sarah bit her lips in indecision, her cool expression momentarily melting under the heat of the emotions she repressed. She quickly stiffened her posture and continued, "No. I think it would be better if we are both prepared for our next meeting."

"Mrs. Williams." In the face of Sarah's rigid formality, Agnes instinctively reverted to the formal address. "I haven't a clue what is going on here. Tyler isn't talking. You aren't volunteering any information." Her tongue tripped over her words before she managed to blurt out, "I thought we were friends. I want to help."

The blank expression Sarah had worked so hard to foster crumbled at Agnes's offer of sympathy. "I'm glad at least you still consider me your friend." Her eyes darkened. "There is something you could do for me. Would you talk to your father and find out where I might get in contact with a Mr. Sneed?"

"Mr. Sneed, the detective?"

"Yes." Sarah replied without elaborating. "I am staying in my old room at the Grand Hotel. When you find out, you can have the information sent by messenger."

"I could bring it myself," Agnes offered.

"No. I may need to call on you later for additional help, but until I have a better idea where I stand, I don't want you to get too involved. You were Tyler's friend long before you were mine, and I don't want you to be put in a position where you might be called upon to take sides."

Agnes's eyes widened in alarm at the notion, and she nodded in agreement. "I will do as you ask," she assured her.

"Thank you. Until Wednesday."

Agnes delivered her message to Tyler, then stepped across the hall into her father's office. "Papa, I need the address of Mr. Sneed."

Johnson grimaced at the mention of the name. He was feeling thoroughly miserable, and the name Sneed an unwelcome reminder of the imbroglio in which he was presently involved. From the moment he had learned Sarah Williams was back in town, he had had no peace.

He stared at his hands. Altering Sneed's journal had seemed like such a good idea when he was certain they had seen the last of Mrs. Williams. It was a lie of convenience to help his partner get over a broken heart so he could get on with his life.

And it had worked, too. Though he was a little harder around the edges, for all intents and purposes Tyler Bennet was back to his old self. He and Agnes were spending more time together. Everyone's lives were back on track.

Now all that was changed. The widow was back, and pregnant to boot. When Tyler had come to him for advice, he had had to tell more lies to cover up for the first.

He knew Tyler would not understand his reasons for doing what he did. He would never forgive him. If he was found out, their partnership and friendship would be ruined.

"Papa, did you hear me?" Agnes pressed when he did not answer her question.

He looked up, forcing a blasé expression to his face. "Yes, I'm sorry. I'm a bit preoccupied with the Henley case this morning. You wanted to know something about Mr. Sneed?"

"Yes, his address."

"Do you need the services of a detective?" He tried to make the question sound like a joke.

"No. Mrs. Williams was here earlier and asked for it. She didn't say why and what with . . . well, we both know there is something radically amiss. Anyway, I was afraid to ask why lest she think I was prying."

Now what, Johnson asked himself. If Sarah Williams talked to Sneed, he was a gone goose. He searched his mind for a solution. There was no way he could put Agnes off without rousing suspicion. He had to tell her Sneed's address. "I have it somewhere here in my desk." He stalled for time by sifting through his papers until he hit upon a plan. "Ah, here it is." He recopied the address on another slip of paper and handed it to her as he rose to his feet. "It's lucky you caught me when you did. I was just on my way out. I should be back in an hour, two at the most."

"Will there be someplace you can be reached?" Agnes asked, reverting to the role of secretary.

"No. I have several errands to run, and tracking me down would take more time than it's worth."

Thaddeus Johnson hailed a hack and instructed the driver to take him to Clay Street posthaste. He strode into the tiny office Mr. Sneed shared with several of his compatriots and was relieved to find him present and alone.

"Mr. Sneed," he greeted. "I have a job that requires your immediate attention. Can you be ready to leave town within the hour?"

"Another out-of-town assignment? You keep directing these kind of cases my way, I might be smart to save myself the cost of renting this office."

"Can you be ready?" Johnson repeated his question.

"Are you still paying double?"

"If I can't get you any cheaper, I'll bear the added expense," he confirmed, unwilling to waste precious time quibbling.

"Then you've got yourself a deal."

"Good. I have a carriage waiting outside. I'll ride home with you and explain the details while you pack."

Sneed sifted through the papers cluttering his desk, searching for a blank sheet of paper. "I'd better leave a note."

"Fine." Johnson paced impatiently. "Just don't mention my name in it. This assignment requires the utmost discretion. It's why I have called on you once again. You're the only man I trust for the job."

Sarah was surprised at the speed with which she received Agnes's message. She tucked the address into her pocket, then set about filling the hours of the day as best she could. She did not want to confront Mr. Sneed until she had read his journal, and it was not due to arrive until this evening.

Though she would have preferred to be firmly ensconced in Tyler's arms, Sarah was feeling far better than she had a few days ago. Having gotten over the initial shock and disappointment, she was able to think clearly again.

All the horrible things she had thought about Tyler when he had first rejected her could not possibly be true. She knew him too well to believe him a villain. This Sneed fellow had convinced him he had been betrayed, and that was why he was treating her this way. If what he accused her of had been true, she could fully sympathize with his reluctance to take her back. But she wasn't a villainess any more than he was a villain. Once he had loved her passionately. If in her absence that love had waned, she would just have to find a way to make him love her unreservedly once again.

She was willing to accept the blame for their separation, but how was she to have known she was pregnant when he left? The possibility had never crossed her mind. Besides, she had let him leave because she loved him. She should not be condemned for an act of love, even if it was misguided. No matter what he believed, she knew she had been true to Tyler during their long separation.

Her thoughts turned to her baby. She was not going to let her child grow up without a father. A child deserved the benefit of both parents. Whatever mistakes she had made, her baby would not pay the price.

Evening arrived and with it her trunks. The moment she was alone, she lifted the lid of the smallest one, and found the journal within.

Two hours later she had read it cover to cover, and her rage had increased with every turn of the page. There was something decidedly off-putting about having one's day-to-day activities recorded in such detail by a complete stranger. The journal began with a chronicle of her activities in Sacramento and ended two months after she had left her father.

Her heart went out to Tyler. It was easy to understand why he had believed what he read. Except for the nature of her relationship with Carlos, the journal contained a completely accurate account of the time he had been traveling with her. Even the account of the time after they had parted company contained more truth than fiction. But the fiction it contained was appalling. Mr. Sneed had painted her to be a whore—a woman who flitted from bed to bed with less discrimination than a bitch in heat.

Her fingers fairly itched with the desire to wrap

themselves around his throat and squeeze the truth out of him. She could not come up with a single plausible reason why he would wish to ruin her life, but she was going to find out what had motivated him to do such a reprehensible thing. Then, she was going to march him over to Tyler's office, by gunpoint if necessary, and he was going to tell Tyler the truth.

First thing in the morning, Sarah tucked her derringer into her reticule and set off to confront Mr. Sneed. On her way she rehearsed what she would say to him, and the conversation was not a pretty one.

When she arrived at his office, she found it locked and empty. She clenched her fists in frustration. Mr. Sneed would not escape her wrath so easily. She waited outside his door.

It wasn't long before a whey-faced gentleman dressed in a nondescript suit of brown worsted approached the portal, key in hand.

"Mr. Sneed! I would like a word with you." She stepped into his path.

"Sorry, ma'am, but I ain't Sneed."

"Then who are you?" she demanded.

"Daniel Hinkley, at your service," he introduced himself. "I share this office with Sneed and two other fellows."

"When do you expect him in?" Sarah continued tersely.

"I don't. He's out of town on a case. Left yesterday."

"Where did he go?"

"Can't say. His note just said a case came up and not to expect him in. Didn't give any of the particulars."

Sarah's eyes narrowed and she took a menacing step toward him. "Don't you think that a little odd?"

"Pretty standard in our line of work," he explained, hoping to calm the wrathful female advancing on him. "If you want to leave a message, I can have him get in touch with you just as soon as he gets back in town."

"I am quite sure Mr. Sneed would ignore any such message," she informed him. "I would be much happier if you sent me a message when he returns—without telling him. I have the money to make it worth your while."

Hinkley shook his head. "I don't know what kind of complaint you have against Sneed, but he's a friend. I play straight with my friends."

"If you are a friend of Sneed's, then you are my enemy, and I shall feel no compunction in having this disreputable firm closed down. Good day, Mr. Hinkley." Sarah turned on her heel and started down the street.

"Hey, wait a minute." Hinkley hurried after her. "I've worked hard to build a reputation as an honest man. I wouldn't want you spreading false rumors about me."

Sarah looked him up and down, her expression one of utter disdain, then kept walking. "But false rumors are Mr. Sneed's forte. I cannot see how you can claim to have an aversion to them if you are willing to claim you are *his* friend. Or is it simply that you do not like them when you are the victim?"

"Listen lady, I don't know what Sneed has done to make you so upset, but I'm sure he'll be willing to talk to you and straighten the whole thing out. And if it makes you feel better, I'll personally make sure he does, the moment he steps through this door."

Sarah's expression remained stony, but she stopped walking. "You will understand if I have the place watched to be sure you comply."

"Suit yourself."

"I intend to do just that." Raising her chin to a patrician angle, Sarah stepped past him and marched up the street. It felt good to vent a little of her anger on someone, and she could not judge Mr. Hinkley innocent if he was Sneed's friend.

Without Mr. Sneed, the task of convincing Tyler she was telling the truth became far more complicated. However, for once in her life she was going to fight for what she wanted instead of physically or mentally retreating. Tyler had told her she knew where to find him when she grew up. Well, she had grown up. The knowledge she was going to be a mother had done more than make it possible for her to embrace her love for Tyler; it had helped her put the pain of her past behind her. She didn't have to subjugate herself to others. She didn't have to numb herself by the frenzied pursuit of pleasure. She was still discovering who the real Sarah Williams was, but she was learning to accept her strengths as well as her weaknesses, and best of all

404

to genuinely like herself. With true self-acceptance came self-confidence and the desire to be the very best she could be, not only for her child but for herself. Tyler was the man she wanted by her side as she struggled to achieve that goal.

Sarah's next stop was at the telegraph office where she sent a telegram to the Rameriz family asking them to deliver the soon-to-arrive letter into Carlos's hands without delay. She had no idea how the Rameriz family contacted each other, but she judged the wire would save her a few days time.

Retiring to her hotel room, she composed the promised letter. In it she frankly explained her situation and asked Carlos to come to San Francisco immediately and vouch for her faithfulness. If he felt it was too dangerous to come in person, he should send a letter to the offices of Johnson & Bennet.

She had no idea if Carlos would do her the favor, but she thought it worth the effort of asking. Sarah posted the letter the moment the ink was dry.

She had the rest of the day and half of the next to fill before her scheduled appointment with Tyler. Other than hiring someone to watch Mr. Sneed's office, she had nothing pressing to occupy her time. More than once she thought of going to see Tyler early, but she forced herself to stay away. When next she saw him, she wanted them both calm, and an unscheduled visit might throw him off balance.

Sarah sat on a chair near the lamp, taking tiny

stitches in the cloth she held in her hand. Stitchery was not something for which she had ever had much love or patience, but the fact that she was sewing clothes for her and Tyler's baby made the task take on a whole new character. She found it a soothing and surprisingly satisfying way to pass the time. She was glad she had given in to the urge to purchase the length of material.

That night Sarah slept far better than she had expected. The next morning she continued to sew the tiny nightgown. It helped to keep her hands busy while she waited for three o'clock to arrive. While she sewed, she mentally rehearsed what she would say to Tyler.

By two o'clock, the garment was finished and she folded it neatly and tucked it into a drawer. She then turned her attention to preparing herself for their meeting, dressing in a high-collared gown of dark blue merino and pulling her hair into an un-embellished chignon.

She arrived at the offices of Johnson & Bennet promptly at three. Agnes indicated she was to go directly upstairs.

"Tyler," she greeted as he opened the door to her knock. The sight of him set her heart to beating like a butterfly's wings, and all the painstaking re-hearsal and efforts for calm were for naught.

"Sarah," he returned her greeting. "Please come in and have a seat." Tyler covertly perused her from head to toe. He had not been able to stop worrying about her since the day she had run out of his office, but he had won the battle with himself to stay away. Still, seeing her standing before him, her eyes searching his for some sign of warmth, made him feel emotions he did not want to feel. Resigning himself to the fact that no matter how much he might want to do so, he was not going to be able to treat her with indifference, he stepped aside to let her enter. A romantic involvement was out of the question, but he couldn't prevent himself from caring what happened to her. She looked a little pale. "How are you?" he asked awkwardly.

"I'm fine. And you?" she queried, entering the office but remaining on her feet. Tyler closed the door behind her.

"Fine. Would you like me to ring for a pot of tea?"

"No, thank you."

They stood, watching each other warily for several moments, neither quite sure how to bring up the subject both knew she was here to discuss. It was Sarah who finally broached the matter.

"I read Mr. Sneed's journal," she stated.

He nodded.

"I can understand why you might be deceived into believing it is true," she continued.

Tyler opened his mouth to refute her claim that the journal was false, then clamped it closed again.

"Why don't you have a seat?" She indicated his desk chair with her hand. The way he was shifting from foot to foot, she feared he would bolt out the door before she had a chance to properly state her case.

"I prefer to stand," he informed her.

She should have realized he wasn't going to make this easy for her. She reminded herself she had not exactly made life easy for him these past months, and if she had, there would be no question he would believe her over the infamous Mr. Sneed. Sarah took a deep breath. "Tyler, I love you," she began, "and we belong together. I want to marry you."

His expression hardened. "We have already discussed this."

"I know we have, but my return took you by surprise and we both became too upset to think clearly. I took your love for granted, and I shouldn't have. When you rejected me, I thought all sorts of awful things about you but when I calmed, I realized they couldn't be true. I was hoping you might have come to a similar realization about me."

"I have not. Perhaps my admission the other day that I still loved you was misleading. I apologize. What I feel for you might more correctly be termed 'concern for a fellow creature.' I do not wish you ill, but neither do I wish to play the dolt."

His terse reply was a blow, but one her hope had not prevented her from expecting.

"The journal is convincing," she acknowledged. "Mr. Sneed included so much truth, it makes the fiction more difficult to refute. But I was there, and I know what I did and did not do. I am guilty of allowing Carlos to kiss me. Because I wish to be scrupulously honest, I will also admit that after you left, I considered taking him as a lover to help ease my loneliness. But I couldn't bring myself to do it.

408

My heart still belonged to you. The other men Mr. Sneed mentioned were nothing more than casual acquaintances or made up out of whole cloth."

"It is your word against his." Tyler informed her stiffly.

"Yes, I realized that, and I went to see him yesterday, but he is out of town on a case. When he returns, I intend to confront him and force him to tell you the truth."

"His absence is convenient for you, is it not?" he opined.

"No, it is not." The pitch of Sarah's voice began to rise, but she forcefully reminded herself she must be calm. "If I could bring him here, you would have no reason to doubt the child I carry is yours."

"What if he maintains he has already told the truth?"

"I am hoping he will find it harder to lie when he is faced with the victim of his slanderous lies. But just in case he cannot be convinced to tell the truth, I have sent a letter to Carlos's family. He will confirm that I am telling the truth if Mr. Sneed will not."

"And you expect me to accept the word of an outlaw?"

"It's the best I can do. What I would prefer is that you believe me. I love you. You once loved me. We have created a child together. Those things should count for something."

"The truth is what counts. When I found out you had made an appointment with me, I had a good idea why. I knew you would try again to convince me to marry you." He began to stroke his mustache and pace. "Though I was reluctant to do so before, I went to see Sneed. When I found him gone, I turned to Thaddeus. We had a long talk, and he helped me approach our situation logically, to weigh the evidence as a jury would. Mr. Sneed is a reliable and honest man. He had absolutely nothing to gain by lying. You do. I saw you kissing Carlos. You admit yourself the reason you came back to me is because you are pregnant. All the evidence points to only one conclusion: you are the one who is lying. I do not believe you love me or that the child you carry is mine."

"Then I will have to find a way to make you believe me."

She reached for his arm to stay his pacing, but he skittered out of reach. To let her touch him would be folly of the worst kind. Even now, as they stood calmly discussing her infidelity, he could feel the sexual energy arcing between them. He retreated behind a wall of detached professionalism, arguing his case as if he were representing a client and not himself.

"Listen, Sarah, I know you need a man to give his name to your child. I even sympathize with your plight. We shared a few laughs and some grand adventures. In deference to those memories, I will not throw you out on the streets. I can offer you friendship, and I will do what I can to help you, but to ask me to marry you is to ask too much."

Sarah faced him squarely, adopting the same logical approach he had when he presented the evidence against her. "I do not need your name. I can easily move to a new city and amend the date of my husband's death to give our child legitimacy. I am rich enough I can support our child without your help. What I cannot provide for our baby is a father's love. Only you can do that."

"The child you carry is blameless, and no matter who fathered him, I could provide him with love," he confirmed. "But you are asking me to do more than love an innocent child. You are asking me to marry you. I might have been able to forgive you the other men if you had come back to me offering honesty, but all you have offered me is deceit. I will not marry a woman I can't trust, and I don't trust you."

"What would you have me do to earn that trust?"

"You might start by telling the truth."

"But I am telling the truth."

"Sarah," he warned.

She sighed. "So I am to confess and you will forgive me?"

"To be honest, I don't know if I can forgive you, but I still care about you enough that I am willing to try." The moment he said the words, he regretted them. He knew they gave her too much power. He also knew they were the truth, and he made no attempt to revoke them.

Enough to try to forgive but not enough to believe without hard evidence to support her claim, Sarah silently summed up the situation. It was a painful reality to accept. The temptation to tell him what he wanted to hear was no temptation at all. Lies were the crux of their problems—her pretense that she desired freedom above him, Mr. Sneed's spurious journal. The truth might be the slower, harder road to tread, but it was the one she was determined to follow.

"I believe you when you say the truth is important to you, so much so that I am not willing to lie to you even though it might be to my short-term benefit. You should not have to spend your life wondering if our child is truly yours or the product of some sordid affair. I should not have to bear the title whore in your mind." She paused, her gaze capturing his before she continued, "Once a long time ago, you asked me to marry you, and all I was willing to offer was friendship. Now, it appears we have reversed our positions. My love for you is strong enough to sustain me until I am able to provide evidence of my innocence. I accept your offer of friendship, but I will not be content until I have coaxed friendship back to fervent and enduring love."

Chapter 23

Friends. It was a start. There were enough of the old feelings left in Tyler that he wasn't going to make this impossible, just extremely difficult.

Sarah toyed with the hair at the back of her neck as she walked back to the Grand Hotel. Mr. Sneed might return tomorrow or next week or next month. She couldn't afford to depend on him to undo what he had done. Carlos's letter, if he wrote one, might or might not be believed.

If a woman wanted a man to marry her, how did she set about it? Her mother's approach was businesslike. Sarah discarded such a method. It was too cold, and she didn't think it would work with Tyler in any case. She could publicly proclaim him the father of her child and hope society's censure would bring him to task. She could play upon his sympathy. She could walk naked through the streets. She chided herself for the nature of her thoughts.

If she wanted Tyler to marry her, the thing to do was love him with all her heart. The strength of her love would eventually break through the shell he had built around his heart. She had truth on her side. All she need do was be patient.

But how patient could she be? Already her figure had started to expand, and she feared it would not be long before she was unable to disguise her condition. She cared not a whit what the world thought of her, but what they thought of her child was a different matter. She could not allow her baby to be saddled with the title of bastard.

Sarah put herself in Tyler's place, trying to see the situation through his eyes, to feel what he must feel, and she could honestly sympathize. She felt hurt that he refused to believe her, but his feelings were the ones that really mattered at this point. He had put her emotional needs above his own many a time. Now it was her turn to prove the magnitude of her love.

She wanted marriage, but she didn't want it without love. Having never tried to woo a man, Sarah had no idea how to go about it. Perhaps one just strove to be as lovable as possible.

She still had a key to Tyler's house. She decided to surprise him with a sumptuous meal. Surely there must be some truth to the adage that the way to a man's heart was through his stomach. Detouring to the California Street Market, she purchased the necessary ammunition for the first foray of this battle of hearts.

Tyler put his key in the door and was disturbed

to find it unlocked. He frowned. He never forgot to lock up before he left. As he cautiously opened the door, his nostrils twitched. Delicious aromas were emanating from his kitchen.

He strode purposefully toward the back of the house. Sarah was dressed in an apron and standing at his kitchen counter.

"What do you think you're doing?" he demanded.

She jumped at the sound of his voice and turned to face him. "Heavens! You startled me. I'm cooking your dinner," she answered as she walked across the room and helped him out of his coat. She folded it neatly and laid it over her arm.

Tyler followed her as she walked out of the kitchen into the dining room. A bottle of brandy and a glass waited on the table, and she poured him a drink. "Why don't you retire to the parlor, put your feet up, and relax while I finish up our meal," she suggested.

He stared at her. After she had left his office, he had buried himself in his work to blot her out of his thoughts. If he had not been wholly successful, at least he had gained some relief. Now, here she was under his nose again—in his own home. "Why don't you tell me what you're up to," he rejoined.

"I told you." She gifted him with her most winsome smile. "I'm cooking dinner for you."

"Why?"

"Because I thought it would be the *friendly* thing to do."

"How did you get in here?"

"I used the key you gave me when we used to share this house."

"I'd like it back." He held out his hand.

"All right," she agreed without an outward show of emotion. "I'll give it to you before I leave."

"When will that be?"

"After dinner. Unless you invite me to stay longer."

"Why would I do that?"

"So we can get reacquainted. I would like to hear what you've been doing while I was away, and I was hoping you might be interested in what I thought of my father. Anyway, you can think about what you want while I finish cooking. I'll call you when it's ready." She left him standing alone in the dining room before he could reply. She had suspected he would be uncomfortable when he found her in his home, and she was right. Until he had a little time to get used to the idea of her being here, she preferred not to give him the opportunity to throw her out.

Tyler swirled his brandy as he gazed into the amber liquid. There were warning bells pealing in his head, telling him to get this woman out of his house before she had a chance to worm her way into his heart again. Instead of following their prudent advice, he tossed down the brandy he held in his hand and poured himself another.

He had said he would be her friend. Perhaps he should use this evening as a test to see if he really could carry on a platonic relationship with her or if he was going to have to rescind his offer of friendship. Besides, he was curious as to what she would do and say. He decided as long as she made no marital demands on him, he would play along.

Shortly after seven, Sarah served a dinner of roast beef, mashed potatoes, and peas . . . good, basic, home-style cooking. Apple pie was her dessert of choice.

Having fortified herself with a variety of current topics from the local papers, she kept up a running conversation throughout the meal. Tyler was not particularly cooperative, but neither was he contrary. It made her nervous the way he watched her, as if he were waiting for her to make a false move so he could pounce upon her, but she pretended she did not notice.

After dinner he did not hand her her coat and gloves, nor did he protest when she carried a pot of tea into the parlor. Sarah took this for an invitation to stay.

"Now, tell me about your father," he began, when they had both settled themselves into comfortable chairs.

An hour later Sarah rose to her feet and thanked him for his fine company. Their conversation had been a pleasant one and during short intervals, she had even been able to forget this was not just like many other quiet evenings she had spent with Tyler Bennet. She wondered if he had ever forgotten too.

She had previously arranged for a hack to pick her up at nine, and the clock on the mantel was chiming the hour.

"Thank you for letting me visit you," she said as he walked her to the door.

"Thank you for an excellent meal," he replied perfunctorily.

When he had gained his privacy, Tyler let the polite mask he wore fall from his face. The evening had been both heaven and hell. Heaven because even subdued, as she was tonight, Sarah filled his big, empty house in some intangible way that made it feel like a home. Hell because the lies that kept them apart still stood like an impassable mountain range between them.

He could not have both Sarah and his self-respect, and a man without self-respect was no man at all.

Then why couldn't he quench this desire to take her in his arms and make love to her while he promised her the world? Why had he lain awake each night since her return, praying lies would become truth and truth would become lies?

He was finding it far more difficult to cope with her presence than he had with her absence, but short of banishing her from his sight—something he could not bring himself to do—he could see no solution to his dilemma.

Sarah did not relinquish her key to Tyler's home.

Her failure to do so had been an honest oversight, but having realized her mistake, she made no effort to remedy the situation. Neither did Tyler.

She continued to come and go at will, preparing his dinners, mending shirts, straightening his desk, doing her best to insinuate herself back into his life. She watched him watch her, waiting for the distrust she saw in his eyes to be replaced with the light of love. Sometimes she thought she caught a glimpse of the tender emotion she craved, but she was never quite sure if it was really there or if it was merely the product of wishful thinking.

Tyler worked long hours at the office. She sensed he did so to avoid her, and she never bothered him there. Every day was a balancing act as she struggled both to respect his privacy and to win his heart.

Their relationship remained platonic, something Sarah found increasingly difficult. Even if he did not love her as he once had, she needed to lie in Tyler's arms, to feel the ecstasy of his physical touch. However, she feared if she asked him to take her to his bed, he would see it as further evidence she was wanton, just as Mr. Sneed's journal proclaimed.

The wall of distrust remained. She could see it in his looks, hear it in his curt tone, feel it in his refusal to touch her. Every night she prayed for guidance to reach his heart, but Providence ignored her pleas.

Twice a day she checked with the man she had

hired to watch Mr. Sneed's office. There was not a trace of the detective, and she hired a second man to set out in search of the missing miscreant. She arranged with Agnes to be informed if a letter from Carlos Rameriz was delivered to the office. Thus far, it had not been.

Sarah told herself she must be patient but as days turned into weeks, she began to fear her baby would be born long before outside help was forthcoming.

She continued to do little things for Tyler in the hopes of softening his heart, taking care she did not do too much lest she anger him. He neither encouraged or discouraged her, but she couldn't remember the last time she had seen him smile. He never took her out, and not once had he come to the hotel to see her.

Sarah did not bring up the subject of marriage again until the day she spent the morning at the seamstress having several dresses altered to accommodate her expanding figure. She tried to feel optimistic about the outcome, but such blatant self-delusion was beyond her capabilities.

That night she let herself into his house and cooked Tyler his favorite meal. After dinner, she broached the subject. "Tyler, if you were defending a client who you knew to be innocent, but all the evidence pointed to his guilt, what would you do?"

"I would find more evidence."

"What if you couldn't?" she pressed.

"I suppose I would have to rely on character

witnesses and hope for the best."

"Oh." She began to clear the dishes to give her hands something to do. "What if there weren't any character witnesses?"

His expression and tone never lost their chary edge, but now the testimony to his continued suspicion became more overt. "I get the feeling you are coming to some sort of point."

"Yes. I had to go to a seamstress today to have my dresses let out." She waited for him to say something. When he did not, she continued, "I have been doing my best to be the model of domesticity, but I'm worried we will not resolve our problems before our baby is born."

"I am not looking for a domestic servant, and it is not *our* baby. It is *yours*," he replied tersely.

Sarah sighed, but kept her tone carefully modulated. "How can you say that with such certainty? Even if the lies Mr. Sneed wrote about me were true, and they are not, logic demands you accept the possibility that this baby could be yours."

It was a possibility he did not like to think about, and his expression darkened. The reason Sarah had not produced one shred of evidence to refute Mr. Sneed's journal was because there was none. They both knew that. His anger at her continued deceit served him well when the old feelings of affection threatened his resolve to remain romantically detached from her, but the baby was a different matter. He hated the lies, not the baby. Sarah's lies were what were keeping them apart. But what if he was rejecting his own child along with Sarah? His hand raised to his mustache and began to stroke it as he stared at her.

At least the motives for her behavior are comprehensible, he chided himself. Your behavior is inscrutable. You have let this woman back into your life, let her set herself up as some sort of domestic slave, knowing full well the purpose behind her solicitous care is to procure a father for her child. You torture yourself with her physical presence, pretending dispassionate friendship when your true desire is to bury your head in her breasts and make love until you are too exhausted to think at all. You won't give her your heart, and you won't send her away.

"Tyler?" Sarah interrupted his thoughts. "Aren't you going to say anything?"

"The baby could be mine," he admitted.

"And that doesn't mean anything to you?"

"It complicates matters. It would be easier to demand you leave me be if I weren't faced with the possibility."

"Is that what you really want? You want me to go away?"

"Hell, I don't know what I want! I want the impossible. I want you to be a trustworthy woman. I want the last few months never to have happened." He stared at her, for the first time letting her glimpse the full measure of the pain he struggled so hard to hide. "What I have is a woman I can neither love nor hate, a baby of questionable par-

422

ntage, and a splitting headache."

"Tyler, I am sorry."

"But not sorry enough to consider telling me the truth."

"I have told the truth. What I haven't done is prove it," Sarah argued, but her argument fell on deaf ears.

Though she had been zealously avoiding the man, Sarah decided a confrontation with Thaddeus Johnson was long overdue. She didn't really think he could help, but he was the one who had hired the detective. Perhaps he unknowingly held some clue that could help her unravel the mystery of Mr. Sneed's deceit. In any case, she could not afford to overlook any avenue of help, no matter how unpromising. Sarah made an appointment with Agnes and arrived at the appointed hour.

"Good morning, Mrs. Williams. I trust you are well," Thaddeus Johnson greeted stiffly as he ushered her into his office and closed the door.

Sarah's nostrils twitched at the scent of alcohol on his breath so early in the morning, but she responded politely, "I'm fine, thank you. And you?"

After amenities were exchanged, she accepted the offer of a chair, and Johnson retreated to the chair behind his desk. "What can I do for you?"

"I would like you to tell me everything you know about Mr. Sneed."

Johnson cleared his throat. He had been up half

the night worrying over what he would say during this interview. He had even considered telling the truth. However, he had quickly disposed of the notion. The price was too high. The moment he had taken that first step on the road of deceit, there had been no turning back. Even if the widow Williams was not guilty of cuckolding his partner, he still believed her to be unsuitable to be Tyler's wife. He was not a bad man, he reassured himself. Any man who was in his position would do what he was about to do. He cleared his throat again. "You are still claiming the journal is false?"

"Yes, I am. I know it to be false. I just haven't been able to figure out a way to prove it so as yet."

"I don't know how you think I can help you."

"You can help me find Mr. Sneed so I can confront him," Sarah informed him.

"What makes you think I know where he is?" he protested angrily. "I gave Agnes his address when you requested it. There is nothing else I can do. I am not the man's keeper."

Sarah remained calm. "If you can't tell me where he is, then perhaps you can help me prove his journal false without his presence. Since you hired the man, I assume you know him well."

"I do know him well." He pulled at his beard and lowered his gaze to his desk; then he forced himself to raise his head and look her directly in the eye. "To save us both a lot of time, let me be blunt, Mrs. Williams. We both know Mr. Sneed's journal to be accurate. There is nothing you can do to prove otherwise. I understand your dilemma, but my loyalty lies with my partner. Because I am a Christian man and because I wish to spare Tyler the pain of your presence, I am willing to offer you a monetary settlement if you will leave San Francisco and never come back. That is the only thing I can do for you."

Sarah listened to his speech without interrupting, but the moment his lips stilled she protested, "But the journal is false."

"I can understand why you would want him to believe that. It is even possible you want it to be false so badly that you have managed to convince yourself you did not do what you did. But wishful thinking doesn't change the facts. We must all live with the consequences of our actions, Mrs. Williams. You had your chance to marry my partner, and you refused it. Now I would ask you to do the decent thing and leave the man alone."

His tone was terse and businesslike, and Sarah did not like it one bit. His offer of money was doubly insulting, since she knew he knew she was far from destitute. She laced her fingers tightly together on her lap and sat a little taller. If Mr. Johnson desired bluntness, he would have it. She did not like to bring the matter up, but desperate times called for desperate means. "And your wish for me to leave has nothing to do with your hopes for Agnes?"

His expression startled, he demanded, "What has Agnes to do with this?"

"I can think of no reason you would have hired a detective to follow me in the first place, except to find evidence to discredit me so Tyler would discard me and look to your daughter for a wife."

He was frightened she had deduced the truth of the matter, and he knew he must firmly deny it — but in a way that would not rouse suspicion. "You are astute, but not precisely accurate in your conclusions. Whether I had a daughter or not I would have hired Mr. Sneed. Tyler is like a son to me, and I felt strongly and still do that you are not the kind of woman who will bring him happiness. In light of the revelations contained in Sneed's journal, I feel my opinion is more than justified."

Sarah rose to her feet. It was readily apparent that Mr. Johnson believed every word of the libelous journal, and nothing she could say would change his mind. If Tyler, who had once loved her, believed them, it logically followed that his elder partner, who had never held a crumb of affection for her, would embrace them without question. The frustration evoked by not being believed caused her to choose her words less than wisely. "If you do hear from Mr. Sneed, will you at least have the decency to let me know so I might speak to him?"

"You are the last one who should question a person's decency; however, if I hear from Sneed, I have no objection to letting you know his whereabouts," he informed her. He stood, his face as rigid as his posture. "I can see you are determined to drag out this unfortunate affair interminably. You are a selfish woman, Mrs. Williams, a very selfish woman. I have never been a man to beg but I do so now. If you ever harbored even a whit of affection for my partner, I beg you to consider the damage you do to him and his reputation. I beg you to leave the poor man alone."

Chapter 24

Over the next few weeks, Thaddeus Johnson's words haunted Sarah. Each day her belly seemed to grow by inches, and it was becoming impossible to disguise her condition. She knew Tyler was watching her expanding girth as anxiously as she.

Since her return, they had not gone out in public together, but they both knew when her pregnancy became obvious, tongues would start to wag. There was nothing society praised so much as the pursuit of success and nothing it took greater delight in deriding than the man or woman who had achieved it. Tyler was successful enough to cause envy. The San Francisco press, ever hungry to sell more papers, would not be able to resist catering to the public's taste for scandal.

Though her concern for his professional standing was acute, her concern for his emotional well-being was even more intense. Nothing had changed between them. He still did not believe her. Each day she saw him turn more and more like Henry — cold, aloof, critical. He buried himself in his professional life. It was the only thing he seemed to care about.

She worried about him continually.

The final blow arrived when the Western Union boy lay a telegram in her hand. Mr. Sneed had been found—*dead*. Now she had no proof of her innocence, no logical explanation to give for the lies, and no hope she would ever have either.

Without proof, she had only herself to offer Tyler. She had already done everything she could think of to win back his heart. All her efforts met with resistance. When she spoke of her love for him, his face became a blank mask. If she tried to touch him, he pulled away. He made it abundantly clear that her presence was tolerated, not welcomed.

After staring at the telegram for the better part of several hours, Sarah accepted that the end had come. Whoever had said that Love conquered all was a starry-eyed optimist. If she continued to fight, she risked destroying everything she loved about Tyler. She cradled her belly. "I know I promised you a father, sweetheart, but we have to go away. I'm sorry. I want what's best for you, but I can't put you above your daddy. My love is killing him by inches."

Agnes Johnson could stand no more. Nobody was talking to her, but she had gleaned enough through observation and overheard snatches of conversation to have a fair idea what was going on around her. Sarah was in love with Tyler; she was pregnant; and she wanted to marry him. Tyler was in love with Sarah; he distrusted her; and he no longer wanted to marry her. They were making each other miserable.

The whole situation was so complicated and confusing that she had no idea where to place her loyalty, but she did know that if Sarah had married Tyler when he first asked her, none of this would be happening. She was not going to make a similar mistake.

After packing her valise with a few personal items, she composed a letter to her father and left it with a messenger service with strict instruction that it not be delivered until nightfall. She then ordered the driver of the hack she had hired to take her to the home of Clayton Bevington.

When the driver let her out at her destination, she strode purposefully to the door and knocked. Clayton answered. He took in her traveling clothes and valise in a sweeping gaze.

"Clayton Bevington, do you love me?" Agnes demanded.

"You know I do."

"And I love you."

"I'm glad to hear it," he replied, bemused by her uncharacteristically assertive stance. "Agnes, is something amiss? You're not acting your usual self."

"That's right; I'm not," she confirmed, her voice tinged with excitement. "I've been doing a lot of thinking lately. Clayton Bevington, it is high time we eloped."

Clayton grinned from ear to ear as he enfolded her in his arms. "Agnes Johnson, that is the best idea I've heard all day."

Tyler winced at the tentative knock at his door. He knew what he would find when he opened it. Sarah would be standing there, her arms loaded with groceries, a smile pasted on her face. With cheery efficiency she would cook him yet another meal. They would talk, each carefully measuring the effects of their words before they let them pass their lips. These evenings together were becoming a ritual torture.

No matter what he said to her, Sarah could not seem to understand that trust was a prerequisite of love. She still kept insisting he was the only lover she had taken to her bed, as if by saying it enough times she could *make* him believe her. He didn't like the truth any more than she did, but at least he was willing to face it.

What he wasn't willing to face was telling Sarah he wanted her to go away. He knew he should, for both their sakes, but he could never quite push the words past his lips.

The knock came again, and he reluctantly rose to his feet.

"Good evening, Sarah," he greeted.

"Good evening. May I come in?"

"Yes." He stepped aside so she could enter. He noted the absence of groceries in her arms and

431

might have felt relief if not for the taut expression on her face. He glanced at her rounding belly and braced himself for another proposal of marriage.

Sarah stared at him. She knew what she must say, and she intended to do it without hysteria. She moistened her lips, took a deep breath, then moistened her lips again. "Tyler, I have come to the conclusion that I should leave San Francisco. I am here to say good-bye."

He tried to conceal his surprise, but knew he had not been successful. "Is this good-bye forever?" he asked without any additional display of emotion.

Her eyes met his. "Do you want it to be?"

He didn't answer her.

"When I came back to you, I thought it would be different. I meant to bring you happiness, but all I have brought you is pain. I promise you I will take good care of our child. When he is old enough to ask, I will tell him his father is a fine man and teach him to love you even though you are absent." She waited, hoping he would say there was no reason for her to go, that he had decided he could marry her after all, that he wanted to know their baby first-hand. He said none of these things.

"Where will you go?"

"Seattle."

"Why there?"

"Nobody knows me there, and I can take a ship the entire distance. You may not want this baby, but I want him very much. I am not going to do anything to jeopardize his health."

432

"Why don't you go back to your father's ranch? Didn't you tell me he said if you were ever in trouble you could call on him? I think your present situation qualifies."

They both continued to discuss her impending departure with unnatural calm.

"I did think about going there, but his house is already overcrowded. Besides, there is the possibility he might feel compelled to intervene on my behalf. You do not need an irate father wielding a shotgun showing up on your doorstep."

"I don't like the idea of you being all alone," he stated, but he avoided looking at her.

"I have to go. While Mr. Sneed was alive I had hope, but the man is dead."

The unexpected news jolted Tyler. "Sneed is dead?"

"Yes, the detective I hired to find him sent a wire this morning. Apparently he was killed some weeks ago by a stray bullet in a barroom brawl. So, the only man who could clear my name is gone, and with him, my hope for redemption."

He instinctively reached out to comfort her, but jerked his hand back before he actually touched her. "If I could trust you . . ."

"But you don't," Sarah interrupted. "And you never will," she continued stoically. "I could fall on my knees and give a teary confession, but it wouldn't help. You would suspect the only reason I did so was to get you to marry me, and you would be right."

433

"I am sorry, Sarah."

"I know you are. It would be easier if you weren't. I could name you feckless and shallow and feel angry I ever loved you at all. You would marry me if there were any way you could. I know that." She blinked back her tears and schooled her voice back to steadiness. She was determined to do this with dignity, and she knew the limits of her self-control. It was time to leave. "It's silly to prolong this farewell. We've both been tormented long enough." She turned and started for the door.

"You'll write and give me your new address when you get settled?" he asked as she stepped over the threshold.

Sarah refused to face him. "If you'd like."

"Perhaps I could act as uncle to the baby."

"Tyler, let it go. We are no good at being friends. We never will be. The best thing you can do is forget me."

He wanted to say something more, but she pushed the door closed between them. Ever since she had come back he had told himself he wanted her to go, and now that she was going, all he wanted to do was tell her to stay.

Why couldn't he stop loving her? He had done everything he could think of to purge her from his heart. She was like a sickness with him.

As he buried his head in his hands, he felt an unaccustomed moisture on his cheeks and his hands clenched into fists. A man didn't cry over a woman. But he did cry, and no amount of chiding could stop the tears.

Thaddeus Johnson finished reading the letter from his daughter and walked directly to his liquor cabinet. Selecting a bottle of whiskey, he decided to forgo the amenities of a glass and took a healthy draught. He cradled the bottle to his chest as he settled himself into his favorite chair. "You may be the only friend I have left in the world," he told the amber liquid, then poured some more of it down his throat.

Drowning his sorrows was the most constructive thing he could think to do. It was pointless to go after Agnes. He knew his daughter well enough to realize she was not the impetuous sort. If she had been seeing Bevington behind his back for months, as her letter claimed, she must truly love the man. Besides, as her letter so bluntly reminded, she was of age. He took another pull on his bottle.

Agnes would never wed Tyler. The realization struck him like a blow across the face. He had had such dreams for them. They were the two people he loved most in the world. Hell, he had been willing to ruin an innocent woman's life for those dreams. The guilt that had been slowly consuming him ever since Sarah Williams's return awoke like a ravenous dragon and swallowed him whole.

He had been playing God. He had been behaving like a madman. He had violated his own code of morality, and most horrible of all, he couldn't even justify his behavior to himself. Johnson continued to consume the whiskey at an unhealthy rate. He must have had good reasons for doing what he did, he told himself. Why couldn't he think of them? Why did every reason he put forth mock him for an old fool?

Chapter 25

Tyler Bennet rose at his usual hour and began preparing himself for a day at the office. He stared at the face in the mirror. He didn't look good. He felt even worse than he looked, but he was used to feeling like hell, so much so that he couldn't remember what it was like to feel any other way.

His thoughts turned from himself to Sarah. He wondered how she was handling this. He hoped better than he. She had been calm enough last night, almost businesslike when she had said farewell. His instincts told him her composure was a mask, but long ago he had lost faith in his instincts where Sarah was concerned. He was not going to torment himself trying to read her mind.

No matter what either of them was feeling now, in the long run, her going away was really better for them both. They were beating themselves against a brick wall. He winced as he cut his chin with his razor. All the logical arguments in the world were not going to make him happy she was leaving. If she changed her mind and stayed, he would be equally miserable.

Shrugging on his vest and coat, he set out for the office, hoping to find a few hours' solace in work.

Upon arriving at the office, he found it empty. It was not unusual for him to arrive before Thaddeus and Agnes, but when neither had shown up by ten o'clock, he became concerned. Checking both his calendar and Agnes's to be sure he would not be standing up any of his clients, he was relieved to find himself free. He locked up the office and hired a hack to take him to the Johnson residence.

The housekeeper's face flooded with relief when she opened the door. "Mr. Bennet, I'm so glad you've come. Mr. Johnson has drunk himself into a terrible state, and I don't know what to do with him."

"Where's Agnes?" Tyler asked as he stepped over the threshold and immediately took charge.

"I don't know, but her bed wasn't slept in last night."

The news startled him, but he didn't waste time speculating. "Is Thaddeus in his study?"

"Yes, sir."

Tyler knew the Johnson house as well as his own, and he strode directly to the study. He was worried. Agnes gone and Thaddeus drunk . . . he had noticed the smell of liquor on Thaddeus's breath more than once of late, but the drinking never interfered with his work and he had not ried. Had he been so wrapped up in his own ersonal drama that he had missed signs of a crisis rewing in the lives of his longtime friends?

"Thaddeus," his eyes took in the empty bottles ttering the room as he crossed to his friend, "what as happened, and how can I help?"

Johnson stared at him through bloodshot eyes nd said nothing.

"Come on, let's get you up on your feet and valk you around a bit. I can't help you if you on't tell me what's going on." Tyler put his arm round him and tried to help him to his feet, but ohnson pushed him away. Pulling his knees into is chair, the older man curled into a ball and overed his head as if he was trying to hide.

Tyler hid his frustration and attempted to cajole 1e facts out of his partner. "Has something happened to Agnes?" he prodded.

"She's run away," Johnson murmured.

"Why?"

" 'Cause she's in love with Bevington."

"Are you saying she's eloped?"

Johnson nodded.

Tyler instantly relaxed. "Listen, it's not all that ad. Certainly not worthy of this sort of reaction." Ie swept his hand around the disordered room nd ended the gesture at the drunken man. "Beington is a fine fellow."

"He isn't you," Johnson grumbled.

"Of course he's not me," Tyler replied patiently, ismissing his comment as the senseless mumbling

439

of a drunk. He continued to speak slowly, enunci
ating his words. "Thaddeus, I can't believe you di
this to yourself. Mrs. Stuart and I are going to tr
to sober you up before I ask any more questions.

"Don't want to be sober, and I don't want you
asking me questions. You might find out about th
widow," he slurred.

Tyler tensed. "Sarah?"

Johnson cowered further into the cushion of th
chair.

"What has Sarah got to do with this? Do you
think she helped them elope?"

A series of pitiful moans rose from the chair
"Wouldn't blame her if she did."

"I really don't think she is involved in any o
this," he stated, hoping to abort the subject.

"A helluva lot you know! She stole your heart
Then she goes away and comes back after I'v
already done the deed. Lie after lie, I'm drowning
in lies."

He could deal with a drunk, but not if he kep
insisting on jabbering about Sarah. The pain o
her departure was still too raw. Tyler's tone becam
terse. "I know Sarah has told me lies."

"I'm the liar!"

He stared at him. "What?"

"I'm the one who altered the journal; then I sen
Sneed away so I wouldn't be found out."

"Sneed is dead," Tyler said blankly as his min
slowly digested what his partner was saying.

"Dead? I didn't murder him! I swear to you,

440

did the other, but I wouldn't sink that low." He burst into tears, and the rest of what he said was garbled beyond comprehension.

Grasping Johnson's head between his hands, Tyler forced him to look at him. "Listen, I don't care how drunk you are. I want answers, and I want them now! Are you telling me Sarah has been telling the truth all along? That the baby is mine? That there was never any question that it was? That you put us both through three months of hell?"

"I confess! I confess!" Johnson screamed. "Once I started the lies, I didn't know how to stop them. I'm a good man. I'm an honest man. I just . . . I just . . . Tell the widow I'm sorry. Tell her . . ."

Tyler dropped Johnson's head, and it lolled to his chest. He had heard enough. "Mrs. Stuart, tie him to the chair if that's what it takes, but I want this man sober the next time I talk to him," he shouted to the housekeeper as he strode out of the study. "I'll be back."

"What about Miss Johnson?"

"Miss Johnson is in good hands. There's no need to worry about her."

The hack was gone and Tyler started down the street, covering the distance with long, rapid strides. Halfway down the hill he broke into a full run. He had to see Sarah. He needed to explain, needed to beg her forgiveness, needed to stop her before she left San Francisco.

He thought about what Thaddeus Johnson had

441

done. He was shocked and appalled, but he didn't have time to waste on hatred. He would deal with him later. Sarah was the only thing that was important. He loved her. She loved him. She hadn't lied to him. He repeated the last thought over and over like a psalm.

Tyler burst into the lobby of the Grand Hotel and took the stairs two at a time.

As he lifted his knuckles to knock, the door to Sarah's room opened and a maid stepped out, her arms full of linens.

"Where is Mrs. Williams?" he demanded.

"She checked out, sir."

"When?"

"About an hour ago."

Tyler spun on his heels and retraced his steps, his pace still breathless. Once on the street, he hailed a hack and commanded him to rush him to the steamer docks.

The coach ride gave him a few minutes to catch his breath.

The wheels of the carriage were still rolling when he leapt out, shouting to the driver that he had left his fare within. He knew the docks well enough and did not have to pause to ask directions.

Tyler whooped for joy when he saw that the northbound steamer was still in its berth. Pushing his way through the crowds, he reached the boat just as the crew started to raise the gangway. He jumped, scrambled up the planks, and crawled onto the ship deck.

"Ticket, sir." The boarding agent eyed him dubiously as he held out his hand.

"I didn't have time to buy a ticket," he panted.

"You can't be on this ship if you don't have a ticket," the man insisted.

"Here." Tyler emptied the contents of his wallet into the man's hand. "That should more than cover the cost of a ticket. Now, direct me to Mrs. Sarah Williams's cabin." His eyes scanned the deck for some sign of her as he spoke.

The agent's expression remained tight. "Does the lady expect you?"

"No."

"I think we should go talk to the captain first."

Tyler had been as accommodating as he could, but every minute this man kept him from seeing Sarah was another minute she must feel the pain of his unwarranted rejection. He didn't have time to explain. "I don't want to talk to the captain. I want to talk to Mrs. Williams. Take me to her before I start tearing this ship apart board by board!"

The agent drew his revolver from his belt and centered it on Tyler's chest. "I said we are going to talk to the captain, mate, and that is just what we are going to do. Now move it!"

Tyler had more sense than to argue with a gun. He did as he was told.

Sarah was both perplexed and annoyed when she

received the summons to the captain's quarters. She wanted nothing more than the solace of her own company.

She was so tired of trying to make things work out between her and Tyler it was almost a relief to stop trying, but she needed time before she was ready to face the world again. Unfortunately, the captain had requested her presence, and one did not ignore a captain.

After taking a moment to pinch some color into her cheeks, she stepped out onto the deck and followed the purser to the captain's quarters.

"Mrs. Williams," the captain greeted. "I am sorry to disturb you." He ushered her into his office.

Her gaze fell upon Tyler and she froze.

"Do you know this man?"

"Yes," she answered numbly as she tried unsuccessfully to comprehend why Tyler was there at all.

The captain looked relieved and nudged her further into the room and closed the door. "He claims he wants to marry you."

"What!" she squeaked. "No. You must have misunderstood him. Mr. Bennet has made it quite clear he doesn't want to marry me."

"Mr. Bennet is a fool." Tyler's eyes met hers. "I have come to beg your forgiveness and ask you to be my wife."

She was not going to allow him to marry her out of pity or guilt, and she could think of no other reason for his sudden change of heart. "Why?"

444

"Because I love you."

"You said love was impossible without trust," she reminded.

"It is. Mr. Sneed's journals were falsified. I know who did it, though I'm still not entirely clear about why." His tone lost its confidence as he continued, "Do you think you can find it in your heart to forgive me for doubting you?"

The captain cleared his throat. "Would you two like to retire to someplace private and talk this out?"

Sarah opened her mouth to accept his suggestion; then, a hearty kick from their baby changed her mind. The only thing she really cared about was that Tyler believed her. She could read implicit trust in his eyes. She could read love. There was time enough to talk about the journal. There was time enough to talk out the hurt. There was another more compelling matter to tend to just now. She smiled. "Tyler, do you realize this is the first time in our acquaintance that we have both wanted to marry at the same time?"

His eyes brightened. "Then you do forgive me?" he asked.

"As long as you don't think me overcautious if I insist you marry me before we leave the captain's quarters."

"Not in the least," he wholeheartedly seconded the notion. He closed the distance between them and reached for her hand. "Captain?"

"Is that your baby she's carrying?" the captain

445

queried.

"Yes, it is," Tyler proclaimed proudly.

"In that case, I'll begin the ceremony just as soon as we're far enough out to sea to make it legal."

Epilogue

Tyler and Sarah Bennet sat at their dining room table sipping coffee and discussing various items of interest in the morning paper. Their conversation was punctuated by frequent coos and gurgling coming from the direction of the floor.

"Elise seems to have an opinion on everything this morning," Sarah commented with a smile.

Tyler lifted his daughter to his lap and bounced her on his knee. She squealed in delight. "She's a very intelligent girl and pretty, too, just like her mother. Aren't you, baby?"

Elise responded with more excited babble and reached for the butter. Sarah caught her hand just before she grabbed a fistful. "You better leave for the office before we have to send another suit to the laundry," Sarah warned.

"Mommy's no fun at all, is she?" Tyler commiserated with his thwarted daughter, but he handed her over to Sarah and rose to his feet.

"Do you really think I'm turning dull?" Sarah queried.

Tyler filled the room with rumbling laughter. "This is a question from a woman who made the front page of the papers three times in one month?

"You're the one who advised me the press could be an invaluable ally in my fight to improve the living conditions of the poor," she reminded him with a grin.

"So I am, and I am extremely proud of you," he assured her. "A man couldn't ask for a better wife.

A look of pure bliss stole across Sarah's face. "And I couldn't ask for a better husband."

Husband and wife exchanged heated glances. Elise was temporarily banished back to the floor— where she clapped her hands in approval as her parents passionately embraced and kissed and whispered promises of undying love.